DANCING WITH DRAGONS

AWARDS: GOLD: Independent Publisher Book Award (IPPY) for Best Regional Fiction, Australia /New Zealand-Aotearoa/Pacific Rim (2024)
SILVER: Reader's Favorite Book Award for Literary Fiction (2024)

"Dancing with Dragons reminds us of the power of friendship and the healing potential the natural world offers us. Jenni Ogden takes us to the beaches and coral reefs of Australia to tell this life-affirming story that calls us to open our hearts, even—or especially—when it's hardest to do."—**Ann Hood,** New York Times best-selling author *of The Stolen Child*

"Ogden crafts an inventive and vivid narrative that is beautifully told [with] a lightly poetic writing style that particularly comes alive when describing Gaia's dancing and the wildlife of Western Australia. Gaia is an immensely appealing protagonist who begins her story as a skittish loner and displays clear development throughout the novel. Ogden effectively weaves together two primary plots: Gaia's return to life after tragedy, and her quest to save her family's land from developers. Both aspects are finely executed and equally intriguing without feeling disparate." —**The BookLife Prize**

"Escape into Gaia's luminous world in this beautifully told story, where you'll root for her through tragedy and danger, smile at the warmth and love of friends who become family, and be renewed by the healing magic of Gaia's unique home that connects her and us to her namesake, Mother Earth."—**Sally Cole-Misch**, author of *The Best Part of Us*, 2021 Canadian Book Club Award for Best Fiction of the Year.

"A compelling story—both unique and universal, exotic yet grounded in the environment we all share. From the joyful beauty of dance to the brutality of human behavior, to the glory of underwater life, this page-turner of a novel embraces love, among people and all living creatures. The reader will learn new things and remember old truths within this finely crafted tale." —**Romalyn Tilghman**, author of *To the Stars with Difficulty*, 2018 Kansas Notable Book of the Year.

"…Kept me reading late into the night. Set in stunning coastal Australia, this is the story of a young ballet dancer orphaned after a family tragedy. Determined to make a life for herself she adopts a young kangaroo, befriends helpful neighbors, and dances on a beach near where rare sea dragons live and breed. Her life-affirming adventures continue when she begins to reach out to others, and they reach back."—**J. A. Wright**, award-winning author of *Eat And Get Gas*.

A DROP IN THE OCEAN

AWARDS
GOLD: Nautilus Book Award for Best Fiction, Large Publisher (2016)
GOLD: Sarton Women's Book Award for Contemporary Fiction (2015–2016)
GOLD: Independent Publisher Book Award (IPPY) for Best Regional Fiction, Australia and New Zealand (2016)
SILVER: Reader's Favorite Book Award for Women's Fiction (2016)

"Reading *A Drop in the Ocean* was everything a reading experience should be, endearing and enduring, time spent with characters who seem to be people I already knew. —**Jacquelyn Mitchard,** #1 New York Times best-selling author of *The Deep End Of The Ocean*

"In *A Drop in the Ocean*, protagonist Anna Fergusson learns that love is about letting go. Jenni Ogden takes us on a sweeping journey, rich with unique characters and places, moving backward and forward in time, to reach this poignant and heartfelt lesson." —**Ann Hood,** New York Times best-selling author of *The Knitting Circle* & *The Book That Matters Most*

"Readers will enjoy this novel of second chances, not only at love but at life, reminiscent of Terry McMillan's *How Stella Got Her Groove Back*"—**Booklist**

"A complicated, deep and passionate love affair that transcends stereotypes. . . . Ogden brought the island to life with her words. . . But the book's real treasure is how island life changes Anna." —**Story Circle Book Reviews**

"Evocative and thought-provoking, *A Drop In The Ocean* is a story about belonging—and the ripples that can flow from the family we choose to the family that chooses us."—**Anita Heiss,** author of *Bila Yarrudhanggalangdhuray*, 2022 NSW Premier's Indigenous Writers' Prize.

THE MOON IS MISSING

"Jenni Ogden is a beautiful writer. In this tale of domestic suspense, she tells the story of a neurosurgeon bedeviled by her own sophisticated brain and the memories of a long-ago tragedy that still has the power to destroy her and her family. Pick up *The Moon is Missing*. You won't put it down."—**Jacquelyn Mitchard,** #1 New York Times best-selling author of *The Deep End of the Ocean* & *The Good Son*

"With gripping scenes set during Hurricane Katrina and on a remote New Zealand island, this tightly-woven family drama—fueled by long-buried secrets and a daughter's desperate need to answer the question, 'Who am I?' —is ripe for book club discussion." —**Barbara Claypole White,** bestselling author of *A Perfect Son* & *The Promise Between Us*

CALL MY NAME

"An emotionally piercing and absorbing account of turbulent female friendship over time, *Call My Name* is also a keen meditation on the powerful pull of connection and belonging—the places and people that shape and change us, forever calling us home."—**Paula McLain**, New York Times bestselling author of *The Paris Wife* & *When the Stars Go Dark*

"*Call My Name* reminds us that love calls us to be generous rather than possessive and that we can go on, even when terrible things happen, because we're profoundly connected. Layered, sometimes shocking, yet shining with goodness and hope, it's exactly the kind of story we need right now."
—**Barbara Linn Probst,** Award-winning author of *The Sound Between the Notes* & *The Color of Ice*

"This is a love story...of couples, of friends, of families. It doesn't shy away from the messiness of love, the inevitable complications of long-lasting love...Most contemporary in its inclusion of topics such as adoption, abortion, and surrogacy, it also looks back on the atrocities of war. A page turning saga that is fresh in its story, yet provides the warmth of an old-fashioned classic.—**Romalyn Tilghman**, Award-winning author of *To the Stars with Difficulties*, 2018 Kansas Notable Book of the Year.

ALSO BY JENNI OGDEN

FICTION

A Drop in the Ocean: A Novel

The Moon is Missing: A Novel

Call My Name

NONFICTION

Fractured Minds: A Case Study Approach to Clinical
Neuropsychology

Trouble In Mind: Stories from a Neuropsychologist's Casebook

DANCING WITH DRAGONS

DANCING WITH DRAGONS

JENNI OGDEN

Sea Dragon Press

A catalogue record for this book is available from the National Library of New Zealand.

First Edition: July, 2024

ISBN 978-1-0670026-0-2 (Softcover)

ISBN 978-1-0670026-1-9 (Hardcover)

ISBN 978-1-0670026-2-6 (E-Book)

Cover by Sea Dragon Press

Cover photograph of Weedy seadragon: Picture by Neil Richardson © The Examiner/ACM. Coral Sea background © Andreykuzmin, Dreamstime.

Published by Sea Dragon Press

www.jenniogden.com

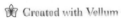 Created with Vellum

ACKNOWLEDGEMENT OF COUNTRY

I acknowledge that Aboriginal Australians are the Traditional Custodians and the first storytellers of the lands where this novel is set. I honor their continuous connection to Country, waters, skies and communities. I celebrate their stories, traditions and living cultures, and I pay my respects to Elders past and present.

DEDICATION

—For Josie and Belize, the ballet dancers in our family—

"Dance, when you're broken open. Dance, if you've torn the bandage off. Dance in the middle of the fighting. Dance in your blood. Dance when you're perfectly free."
  — *Rumi*

"Do we really care so little about the earth on which we live that we don't want to protect one of the world's greatest wonders from the consequences of our behavior?"
  — *Sir David Attenborough*, *Save Our Oceans*, 2016

PART I

"And hand in hand, on the edge of the sand,
They danced by the light of the moon."
— **Edward Lear,** *The Owl and the Pussycat*

CHAPTER 1

oshawk Gardens, Western Australia, January, 1977
Even with the massive doors that took up most of the front of the barn wide open, Gaia's skin was slick with sweat. Feet sliding like oil inside her pointe shoes, she focused on Bron's straight back in front of her. On the back wall of the barn the blue sky filled a large window, also open and letting in the teasing salt breeze.

Her mother's hand, somehow always cool, grasped her leg and eased it higher. "This leg is as dead as a stick," she said. "Can you feel it?"

"No," said Gaia, careful not to shake her head. "Not the way you mean anyway. It feels more like a burning bloody log about to burn off a burning bloody tree. Can't we stop now?"

Bron snorted, and with his right hand resting lightly on the barre he stretched his long, already straight back even taller, his arched foot at the end of his perfect alive leg pointing at her.

Gaia grinned and Margot's firm grip on her leg softened. "You'll never make a dancer if you let a little bit of sweat control you," she said. But she didn't sound too mad and Gaia let her poor leg flop back down and turned around, swiping at her forehead with her arm. Surely their mother would take pity on them. The temperature had been in the mid-thirties all week and even higher in here. All Gaia could think about was floating in the cool sea.

"It is a touch warm," Margot said, her ballet-teacher expression changing into her mother look. "Do your cool-down stretches, both of you, and get a drink and some fruit and then scarper. Only in the reef shallows though, Gaia. No going out into the deep without your father watching.

"Bron can watch," Gaia said.

"Bron has to look after himself. He can't look after you as well."

"Come on Mum," Bron said. "She's not a baby; she'll be fine."

"You know the rules. If you don't want to stick with them, by all means stay here and we'll spend another thirty minutes working."

GAIA LAY STILL ON THE SILKY SURFACE. IT WAS THE BEST feeling; the sun warm on her back while the cool water caressed her body, her arms, her legs, her feet; soothing her exhausted, taut muscles. If she turned her head to the side she could see the evening sun held like cups of gold in the dimples on the sea surface. It filtered through long strands of her hair, freed to float on the far side of the strap that held the mask over her eyes.

She returned her gaze to the gardens below. Most of the fish on the reef stayed in the same areas, around the same coral outcrops, whatever the season. But there were so many different species Gaia never tired of it. She loved seeing her old friends, the Squirrelfish, the Butterfly, the Moorish Idol, but with a flip of her feet she could be over another coral bommie and a fish she hadn't seen in weeks would scurry by.

She could hear her quiet breathing through her snorkel and wished she could throw it away and breathe like a fish. Discard her mask and flippers, even her swimsuit, and sink below the surface where the mermaids swam.

She could never quite decide which she loved best; swimming over the reef flats in the late afternoon light or in that perfect hour after dawn. Only possible when the tide was well on its way to full tide. Sometimes she and Bron, occasionally with one or both of their parents, took a reef walk when the tide was out, but more often they changed direction and swam in the amber waters of the freshwater lagoon she could see from her bedroom window. That was water to float on up the other way; eyes to the sky rather than to the underworld. From a tree bordering the lagoon, clouds of iridescent green budgerigars might take to the air, turn as one and, in a chorus of twittering, settle back in the same tree. Then, as if they had been waiting patiently off-stage waiting their turn, hundreds of pelicans would startle and fly up from the lagoon as one giant white cloud, perform their synchronized dance through the blue air and skid back on the water, rainbow showers shooting out behind them. A few times they'd landed all around her, leaving again with a rush of wind and spray when they realized she wasn't a floating log.

It was almost high tide now, the tops of the coral a meter below the surface. Swimming over to a large patch of sand between the coral outcrops, Gaia forced her flippered feet to the bottom and pushed off, catapulting high in the air, her face to the sky. Nothing dead about her legs now. She could see Bron further out past the row of small breakers that signaled the reef drop-off. He was swimming laps, his long arms and strong feet propelling him forward almost without a splash. As if he were in a pool, not floating above a wonderland of corals and myriads of tropical fish going about their business. Bron didn't share Gaia's obsession with the creatures that hung about in the coral. Scuba diving was more to his liking, prefer-ably around spooky shipwrecks.

For a second Gaia thought about swimming out to him, but her mother's voice rang in her head. She was a good swimmer but Bron could out-swim her without even trying. He could have been a competitive swimmer instead of a ballet dancer if he wanted. But he'd made his choice and in three weeks he was starting his new life at the Australian Ballet School in Melbourne—leaving Gaia here in the middle of nowhere for another two years until it was her turn to follow him. She'd go when she was sixteen, not wait until she was seventeen like Bron. She'd miss him. Her big bro.

Gaia flippered further out as the sun's rays slanted lower, her eyes scanning the coral bommies as they graded into white sand covered by patches of waving seagrass. She grinned around her snorkel mouthpiece as a Green turtle swam below her, focused on filling its belly with seagrass, entirely uninter-ested in the human form above. Perhaps she would nest on their beach? Some years there were a few nests; not many. One January they'd been on a camping holiday further north, up past Ningaloo, and Gaia had almost decided to give up ballet and work with turtles. Such an amazing creature; climbing up a beach, digging a pit, depositing a batch of eggs, covering them with sand, and dragging her heavy body back to the sea before the tide went out. All to continue her genes without the pleasure of meeting any of her offspring.

What if she did forget the whole ballet thing? Melbourne was so far away. Bron was only going to get to come home once a year, and the flights between Perth and Melbourne cost a fortune. It was bad enough driving to Perth; over four hours south from here in their old 4WD. And there'd be no turtles on the beaches in Melbourne. No coral reef. Just skyscrapers and too many people. And if she ever made it through the program and was accepted by one of the ballet companies her mother deemed good enough — preferably the American

Ballet Theatre in New York where Margot had danced—
she'd never be able to return to their patch. Gaia sighed into
her mask. Is this what she really wanted? Or was it her mother's dream, not hers?

Below her the seagrasses swayed in the gentle current and
she eyeballed a tiny blennie, only its head and eyes above the
sand. Now she was over a small bed of kelp, bigger fish swimming in and out—a Spangled Emperor, a Spotted Boxfish. A
different movement turned her head sideways and she blinked
behind her mask as some long strands of seaweed seemed to
pull away from the bottom and dance in a different direction
from the current. Entangled with the weed was something
else; red, yellow, blue. Then it clicked. She'd seen one years
ago but never since. A seadragon. Her heart pounded and she
held her breath, her hands flapping gently as she tried to keep
her body from moving. More than half the length of her arm,
the creature's long thin body had dark pinky-red paddle-
shaped seaweedy-like appendages rimmed neatly in black
sprouting from it, almost making it disappear. Gaia concentrated on the colors: a dark pinky-red body covered in yellow
spots, yellow on its ventral surface, a long purple neck circled
by a ring of vibrating yellow. As it moved away from the
seagrass she could see its head; like a seahorse head but with a
much longer red-spotted snout ending in a knob. Large red
dragon eyes looked up and down, and the pointed crown of its
head was capped with another frond of seaweed. A common
weedy seadragon. Not so common here at the southern edge
of the tropics, and even if they were present they were so well
camouflaged it was magical to see one.

Not one, two! She'd been so focused on trying to
remember the colors of this one she'd completely missed its
mate. It was a color match for the first seadragon, and as one
dragon turned on its side, swam in a circle, up, down, around,
the second one mirrored its movements. They were
performing their courtship dance.

Glued to their graceful display, Gaia almost leapt out of the water when something touched her side. Small white-tipped reef sharks were plentiful around here. They weren't dangerous but that didn't mean it was wise to swim into them.

"What are you looking at?" said Bron.

Gaia's heart slowed and she stuck her head up, her finger shushing him, then pointed down.

DARK CAME EARLY HERE, EVEN IN SUMMER IN MID-JANUARY. By the time they got home, not long after 7 pm, the house was in darkness. Off-grid, with no electricity, they relied on kerosene lamps and torches. A hopeless phone was their only nod to the modern world, and connected them to the outside by a copper wire that often failed to work when they needed it. Even that was a party line, shared with their only neighbors, Dave and Ros Mason.

Their parents were sitting on the twilit verandah with cold beers. "About time," Margot said. "What did you find this time?"

"You'll never guess. It was amazing," Gaia said. "Two sea-dragons mating. Well not quite mating yet, but doing an incredible courtship dance, on and on for ages. They were still going when we had to get out because it was too dark to see them."

"It was bloody spectacular," Bron said. "If I hadn't seen it with my own two peepers I wouldn't have believed it."

"On the reef flats?" asked Joe. "That's pretty special. I've always wanted to see that. Was it the weedy seadragon or the leafy one?"

"The weedy one. I'm sure it was. I've seen pictures and the leafy one has lots more leafy things hanging off it. But this pair was so amazingly colored. Both the same. I think they change colors and probably when they're dancing they change together. How do they do that?"

Joe shook his head. "Beats me. Bloody marvellous. Although I believe it's only the leafy seadragon that can change color. We'll go back at dawn tomorrow and see if your courting couple are still there. They can dance for days before they actually mate."

"I'll come too," Margot said. "This I can't miss. Do you think you'll be able to find the same spot again?"

"I reckon. We took careful note of the nearest bommies. What's the chance they'll stay in the same place?" Bron asked.

"We'll see," Joe answered. "They're about the slowest swimming fish on the reef, and I've read that they do their courting dance around the area they will actually mate; that's where the male will stay and incubate the eggs."

"What do you mean? How can a male incubate?" asked Margot.

"They're like seahorses. The male holds the eggs under his tail and the female disappears into the wide blue yonder, probably to knock up some other poor unsuspecting male." Joe winked at Gaia. "Way to go."

After dinner, Margot and Joe disappeared to have a few drinks with Dave and Ros. They owned a small farm about two kilometers from their place. Like Joe, they grew vegetables and fruit for the farmers' market in Jurien Bay, forty kilometers south of here, although their gardens were three times the size of Joe's.

As soon as they left, Bron disappeared too, and Gaia stuck on her head torch and plopped down on the screened verandah with her book. An hour later she reached the satisfactory conclusion and closed it with a sigh. She sniffed the air. Bron was smoking. In the basement probably. If Margot smelled it when she got home she'd be mad. Dancers don't smoke. Her torch shining her way, Gaia tiptoed down the stairs to the basement and threw open the door. "Ha. Caught in the act," she said, grinning as Bron turned around, his face lit by the kerosene lamp on the old metal table by his chair.

"Get a life," he retorted. "Little girls should be in bed."

"Geez, you stink. What on earth are you drinking?"

"Water."

"It's Dad's whisky, you toad. They'll both divorce you if they find out."

"They won't find out unless you tell them."

"Give me a puff and I'll keep my lips zipped." Gaia stuck her hand out.

"You'll hate it. Unless you've tried it before. Have you?" Bron's eyebrows went up.

"Nope. Where would I get fags from? Come on, let me try."

Bron passed her the smoke and she put it between her lips and breathed in…and spluttered it out again.

"Now you know," Bron said. "It's a nasty habit."

"So why are you doing it?"

"Bored. It goes with the whisky."

"You could try reading a book."

AGES LATER GAIA WAS STILL THERE. NOT SHARING THE WHISKY or the cigarettes but loving the chance to gossip with Bron, something he didn't do easily. The whisky had made him garrulous.

"I'm going to miss you so so much," she said. "You have to write and tell me what it's like. What if you hate it and decide you don't want to be a dancer after all?"

Bron shrugged. "I'll find another career I suppose. Go to

Melbourne Uni and do a degree. I'm not coming back here though, that's for sure."

"Why not? You love it here."

"Too bloody tense for me."

"What do you mean?"

"Mum and Dad. They've changed. Surely you've noticed?"

"That's because they've been married for ever. Look at Dave and Ros; they're always at each other's throats. All old couples are like that. That's why I'll never marry."

Bron looked at her as if he were about to say something. He poured himself another whisky, stubbed his cigarette butt out on the metal arm of his chair and fired it towards the ratty cane rubbish bin. Missed. Gaia rolled her eyes and stepped over to the butt, picking it up and examining it as if it might explode at any minute. They had been in drought for six weeks now. Satisfied it was out, she dropped it in the bin on top of the junk already in there. Old bits of metal, plastic bags, dried-up apple cores, screwed up paper. Margot never came down here and so the bin rarely got emptied out. Mostly Joe's rubbish. He had his tools down here and old bits of broken machinery, even the filthy generator and a petrol can. They should have been kept in the barn but that had been converted to the ballet studio, as empty and clean as this was cluttered and dirty.

"Mum and Dad will be home soon," Gaia said. "I'm going to bed. You should too or they'll catch you. They will anyway. This place pongs of smoke and booze."

"It'll be gone by morning if I leave the window open. Dad'll be too pissed to notice tonight. Close the door when you leave so the evidence doesn't creep out."

Gaia moved back to him, leaned over and kissed the top of his head, surprising herself as well as Bron. "Night bro. I really hope you love the ballet school. One day we'll dance together for the American Ballet Theatre. That's a promise."

~

SHE WOKE, SWEATING AND HEADACHY. VOICES. HER FATHER'S, shouting. He must be drunk. Poor Mum. She pulled the pillow around her ears. Then she heard another voice — a man, not her mother. It was the middle of the night. Who was here?

Getting out of bed she tiptoed towards the kitchen, her heart hitting her chest. The door was half open and she sidled up to it, her spine to the wall. Peering in, she could see her father's back and in front of him her mother's face lit by the flickering light of the kerosene lamp on the table. But Dad wasn't shouting at her; there was a man sitting next to her. Dave Mason. What was he doing here? Perhaps he drove them back from his place because Dad was too drunk?

"Get your filthy hands off her and get out of here," her dad roared.

"Back off, Joe. We need to talk this through. You need to calm down." Dave was shouting, standing up, her father was going towards him, grabbing him, Mum was trying to pull Dad off Dave, they were on the floor, chairs flying, the table screeching across the room, the kerosene lamp falling, Mum's clothes alight, screaming, Dad throwing himself over her mother. Screaming, screaming.

Dave yelling "Get the hose, get a bucket of water. Gaia, get the hose." Dave running water from the kitchen sink tap into a basin, throwing it over her parents, Dad on top of Mum, flames up the curtains, Dad standing, his arms around her burning mother, his hair on fire. Seeing her, shouting "Gaia, get out of here, get out, get Bron out, call 000, get out now."

Dad collapsing on the floor, Dave with the phone shouting into it, flames across the ceiling, running to get Bron, kicking shut the kitchen door, crashing open Bron's door, shaking him, screaming, "Wake up Bron, wake up."

Bron groaned and turned over.

"The house is on fire. Wake up, wake up. Bron, wake up." Gaia slapped him hard on the cheek.

"Lay off. Whadda matter?"

"Fire, the house is on fire. We have to get out. Bron, wake up…"

"Christ…" Bron flung his legs over the side of the bed, stood up and grabbed Gaia's arms. She could hear a roaring as he pulled her towards the closed bedroom door, Bron yelping as his hand touched the door handle. "I think the door is on fire. We can't open it. We'll have to get out the window." He pushed her towards it, wide open above his bed.

"It's too high. How will we get down?" She was screaming and sobbing above the roaring of the flames.

Bron shoved at the fly screen and it flew outwards, landing somewhere below. "Squat on the window-sill then jump as far out from the house as you can so you'll land on the grass. You'll be all right. Gaia, there's no other way. When you land get away from the house." He jerked as a window exploded below them and flames shot out into the night. "Hurry up, I'll be right behind you."

Gaia scrambled onto the window-sill, squatting in the big open frame. "It's too far down, I can't, Bron, I can't. You go first."

"Gaia, go. Jump outwards. Do it or I'll push you." She felt the heat as the door buckled and then she jumped, her scream echoing through the night. She fell through the flames shooting out the window below, the concrete rushing towards her…

CHAPTER 2

*S*he was floating, floating over the coral gardens, her body wrapped in water.

"Gaia, open your eyes, it's time to change your dressings."

She shook her head. *No, no don't wake me, leave me alone. I want to sleep.* She couldn't hear her voice, she wasn't talking out loud, it hurt her throat too much.

"Come on, there's a brave girl. We have to clean those burns. I'll be as gentle as I can."

Push them open. The smell of antiseptic, the two torturers looming over the bed, only their glasses showing between their caps and masks. Every bit of their bodies covered up as if she had the plague. Gaia moved her left hand to her throat. Tubes snaked from her arm. Her right arm was tied down so she couldn't move it, she knew that. Her left leg was in plaster and sometimes her skin under it where she couldn't scratch itched so badly she wanted to die. Almost as bad as the pain from the burns on her other leg.

She felt the edge of the horrible compression mask over her face. She'd seen her reflection in the TV screen suspended from the ceiling over her bed, and it made her look like she was about to hold up a bank. It had holes for her eyes, nose and mouth, and underneath it dressings covered half of her face.

The pain was boring back into her. That's why she wanted to sleep. She'd learned that. The only way out. "Can you pump up my morphine please?" Her voice hurt but she had to ask nicely.

"Hmm, better if you can hold out a little longer. How about it? Have a few sips of your water." The nurse held the glass near Gaia's chin and slipped the straw between her lips. The water was lukewarm but it felt good sliding down her raw throat. Ever since they'd pulled the tubes out of her nose, for some reason her throat burned like it had been scrubbed with sandpaper.

"Please give me a little shot of morphine. It hurts so much when you change my dressings. Tears pushed behind her eyes.

"What's your pain level?"

"Eight. Eight out of 10. Is that bad enough?"

"That's not good." The nurse fiddled with the slides on the tubes snaking from one of the bottles on the stand next to her bed. "There, that should make you more comfortable. I'll give it a few minutes and then we'll get this job done."

"Can I see?"

"Goodness, what sort of a question is that? All you need to know is that you're healing nicely."

"I want to see now. It's my face. I should be allowed to see it if I want."

"It'll only upset you, and we don't want that, do we?"

"I look like a monster, that's why. I can feel it. Half my face has been burnt off. It's not going to grow back, is it. So I may as well get it over with."

"Don't be silly. All your face is there. When the burns heal, the plastic surgeons will be able to make you look almost as good as new."

"Let me see then. If you don't, I won't believe you."

Her torturer sighed. "Nurse," she said, looking at the other masked person, "Can you go and get the mirror? Wash it in antiseptic first."

Gaia's heart felt as if she had run a marathon. Her back rose like some sort of spooky machine as the nurse pumped the top half of the bed up. Then she stuffed pillows around her to keep her from toppling sideways. They treated her like a wooden doll, as if she were paralyzed or something, not just the right half of her body burned and her left broken leg in plaster.

She'd caught glimpses of the mess on her chest and leg even though they'd tried to hide them from her while they were tweezering away, pulling off bits of dead skin and flesh, but when they were changing the dressings on her face and cleaning the burns, they even turned the blank TV screen away to stop her using it as a mirror. It didn't take an Einstein to work out what that meant. Her head injury might have dumbed her down a bit, but she hadn't completely lost her ability to think.

The other nurse was back. They swung the table with its implements of horror on it across her lap and started on her face. Gaia squeezed her eyes shut and tried to think of something nice, but it wasn't happening. The morphine helped; sort of made the pain float about somewhere else, as if it didn't belong to her.

"There. We have the bandages off. Are you sure you want to see before we put fresh ones on?"

"Yes. Yes please."

"The burns look much worse than they are, but that's because they're healing well. We're lucky that most of them are second-degree burns and only small areas are third-degree."

"That's bad though. I'll look like one of those fighter pilots in the war who had their faces burned, and everyone is scared of them forever more."

"You've been watching too many horror films. Your burns

are nothing like that. The doctors will decide later if you need a small skin graft on the worst burn areas on your face. Then all you'll have is a scar or two that you can cover with makeup if need be."

"What about my arm and leg? I know they're worse."

"Later they will need permanent skin grafts and lots of physiotherapy to stop the contraction of the scar tissue and help you get good movement back. So don't get yourself all upset. You just have to be patient. Now, do you want me to hold up the mirror? I think it would be better if you waited another few days."

"No. Show me."

∽

Two weeks later

She'd asked about Bron, over and over, but all they'd told her was that he'd been able to stay in hospital in Perth as his burns weren't anywhere near as bad as hers. Gaia had been flown to the specialist burns unit in Melbourne, thousands of kilometers away from Perth. Gaia had no memory of the flight or anything about what happened before or after it.

Miriam, the psychologist, came to see her every day, and at least that meant she had a sort of a visitor, even if Miriam had to put on a mask and a gown over her ordinary clothes. Otherwise, the only people she'd ever see would be nurses and doctors. Miriam was the one who told her their house had burned down, and she and Bron had got out but their parents hadn't. Gaia couldn't get her head around that, and sometimes forgot and had to be told again. Then she'd get given another pill or sometimes a jab in her backside, and that would calm her down.

Miriam was asking her again what she remembered. She kept checking in case bits and pieces started coming back. She'd explained that it was most likely that Gaia's head injury was the cause of her memory loss. "When you're unconscious your brain is offline so it can't consolidate or store properly any of the things that happened before being knocked out. And you were unconscious for two weeks because the doctors put you in an induced coma so they could treat you more easily. Some of your memory for the hours before the fire might come back as your brain recovers. We don't even know that for certain. You could be suffering from traumatic amnesia as well. That's how the brain protects you from reliving a traumatic event, like the fire. It blocks those memories out."

"Well, I still don't remember. Anything. I've tried and tried but it's just blank." Tears blocked her throat and she choked them down.

"Perhaps your brain is protecting you."

"It's a weird feeling, having blanks. What does that mean about my brain? How would you like to be brain damaged for the rest of your life?"

"Your brain is fine. I've seen the scans and talked to the neurologist. It just needs time to recover from having a big shake-up."

∼

THE POLICE CAME TO SEE HER AND ASKED HER WHAT SHE remembered.

"Nothing," Gaia said.

"What about earlier on the day of the fire? It was a Wednesday. Your mother… you and your brother, Oberon, you were home schooled, is that right?"

Gaia nodded. "Yes. We did school work for three hours after breakfast, and after lunch we did ballet for the rest of the afternoon. We'd usually go for a swim or a snorkel after that." She blinked hard. "It's not Oberon. That's his actual name.

After the ballet dude. 'A Midsummer Night's Dream.' But we never call him that. He's Bron."

"Oh. Yes, Bron is much better." He looked down at his notebook and scribbled something. "Is Gaia a ballet name too?"

Gaia shook her head. "No. Dad named me. It was his turn, I suppose. Bron was born in New York but they lived in Australia when I was born. We've got a small market garden. I suppose that's why Dad called me Gaia. The Earth Goddess." She felt a little snort squeezing out of her facemask.

"It's a very pretty name," said the woman cop. She cleared her throat. "On that day, the day before the fire, is that the last day you can remember? What did you do?"

"We went snorkeling. I do remember that. I saw a pair of sea-dragons dancing. Bron and I didn't get home until it was nearly dark. Mum and Dad went over to our neighbors' house after dinner. I read for a bit on the verandah and then Bron and I hung out. He's starting at ballet school in Melbourne in February and we had lots to talk about before he went." Gaia paused. "Well, he was meant to go, but he won't now. It's already February and if he'd started he would be in Melbourne and would have come to see me." She squeezed her eyes closed, feeling her eyelashes scrape against the holes on the mask. At least they hadn't burnt off.

"I'm sure he would have been here by your side if he could have," the woman cop said. "But he's still in Perth. Haven't you heard from him at all?"

Gaia shook her head. "He's not much good at writing letters, but he could have phoned."

"I'm sure he has a good reason. He's probably struggling with it all himself."

"He might remember what happened," Gaia said.

"Yes, the Perth police have sent us his statement."

"Why are you asking me then? What did he say?"

"It's important that we get independent statements if we're

to find out how the fire started. You said you were hanging out with Bron. Where were you?"

Gaia closed her eyes again, her head hurting, the smell of whisky and cigarette smoke flooding up her nose. "I can't remember. On the verandah I suppose. I went to bed before Mum and Dad got back. Bron probably did too."

"And you didn't hear your parents come home?"

"I've told you everything I remember. The next thing I remember is being in here and that was weeks after I got here. Can't you tell me anything? How did I get on fire and bash my head and break my leg?"

"No one has told you?" said the cop.

"I don't think so. I forget things easily though."

"According to your brother, you woke him up and probably saved his life. The only way you could get out was by jumping out the window."

"From Bron's bedroom? That's upstairs."

"The fire was right outside Bron's bedroom door so you did what you had to do. You landed on the concrete and hit your head, and your nightdress caught fire. Bron landed better, on the grass, and he must have been very quick thinking and managed to roll you on the grass and suffocate the flames before they did more damage. Your neighbor..." she looked at her notes—"Dave Mason, he was the first on the scene and called 000. Apparently he tried to rescue your parents but he was beaten back by the flames."

"Did Bron get badly hurt?" Gaia whispered. "You have to tell me the truth. Did he get bad burns too?"

"I believe he suffered some burns from when he was helping you, but I think he's on the mend now. Your neighbor too; he had some burns, but not as bad as yours."

～

THEY CAME BACK AGAIN TWO DAYS LATER AND GAIA TOLD them again she couldn't remember anything after going to bed before her parents came home.

"Never mind," said the woman cop. "But is it OK if we ask you a few more questions about the house? The Perth police are trying to put together a picture so they can work out how the fire might have started."

Gaia nodded, her heart thumping. She was glad she had the compression mask over her face; at least they wouldn't be able to read her expressions—if her face was even able to make them any more.

"Your house was off-grid so I believe your father had a generator. Do you know where that was kept?"

Gaia nodded. "In the basement. When he used it, he pushed it out the door onto the concrete."

"Where did he store the fuel for it?"

"Mostly in the garden shed. But I think he might have had one container in the basement. I don't really know; only Dad ever went into the basement."

"Was the generator going when you and your brother were hanging out when your parents were at your neighbors' place?"

"No. Dad only put it on when he needed it for some tools or something."

"So what did you use for light and your fridge and stove?"

"Same as everyone else off-grid. We used torches and kerosene lamps, and we had a gas fridge and a wood stove. The fridge was connected to a gas bottle outside, not in the house."

"Do you remember if you had a kerosene lamp on that night?"

"Only while we were having dinner. We used torches after that."

"What about the wood stove?"

"No. It was too hot to have the stove on. We had a salad

and cold sausages for dinner. I remember that because I don't like sausages."

"Can you think of anything else that might have started a fire? Did your parents smoke?"

Gaia shook her head. "No, Mum hated cigarettes. She was a dancer and you need good lungs to dance." She turned her head towards the window and tried to focus on the trees outside.

Miriam stood up from where she'd been sitting so quietly that Gaia had almost forgotten she was there. "That's enough of the questions. Gaia's exhausted."

"That's about it anyway. Thanks, Gaia, you've been very helpful," the cop said. "We'll let you know if we find out anything. You just concentrate on getting better."

FEBRUARY 20TH, 1977

Dear Gaia,

I'm sorry I haven't been able to get to Melbourne and see you but the police have told me you're doing good. My burns weren't too bad. My hands got burnt and my leg a bit, but they've healed now. Mum and Dad were cremated before I was even out of hospital. The ashes are in the Perth crematorium if you want to collect them when you come back to Perth. I can't face going there yet. It's not them, anyway.

I'm staying at the Perth YMCA and Mr Ludlow who was Dad's lawyer is really helpful and when you get back to Perth after you're better, he'll help you too. There's a copy of the property settlement in here for you. It just says you and I own Goshawk Gardens and Dad's bank account has been put in our joint names. It's only got about $4,000 in it but it'll keep you going for a while. Dad didn't have any insurance on the house, but he didn't have a mortgage either so that's a good thing. At least Mum and Dad left all their important papers and stuff with Mr Ludlow, their marriage certificate and our birth certificates and even all our passports. The house is gone but the barn is still there. Dave and Ros said they'd try and keep the gardens from going completely wild. I signed a form to say that you can do whatever you like with the money and sell the property if you want, without me having to sign anything. You have to go through Mr Ludlow to get money out until you're sixteen and then you can do what you want with it. I don't need any of it. I can earn my way.

The police haven't a clue how the fire started. They reckon it might have started in the basement because of the generator and Dad's petrol cans being stored there. I didn't tell them we were there and that I was smoking because you know what cops are like. They'd be knocking me around and making the fire my fault and I know bloody well I didn't leave any smoldering fag ends. I told the cops it was probably the pilot light flame at the back of the gas fridge. Mum was always saying that was dicey and we should get a new one. What's it matter anyway how the fire started? It's not going to bring them back or help you. The cops told me that you had no memory for anything that happened because of your head injury. I suppose that might be a relief. It must have been bloody terrifying. All I remember is being woken up by you. You saved my life. Mr Ludlow said you'll be looked after until you're sixteen and even longer if you stay at school. He said you would have to be in a rehab center for ages once they let you out of hospital, and then you'll probably live with a foster family. I know you think you'll hate it but you might not. Give it a chance. You can go to a real school and make friends. You'll be sixteen in less than two years and then you can do what you want. If I could I'd look after you but I don't think the social worker would be too happy about that.

The ballet school in Melbourne had started before I even got out of hospital but I don't care. A guy here at the Y gave me a heads-up about getting a deckhand job on a container ship. I'm going to give it a try. I've always wanted to do something like that and they pay quite well. I'll write to you when I get on a ship so you'll know where I am. I think you can even send letters to ships. I know you'll be mad at me, but I have to get away for a bit. I can't hack it here any more. I'll be back in Australia in a few months and you might even be well enough to come to Perth by then, or I'll come to Melbourne. I'm gutted about what happened to you. It's not fair that you got the bum end of all this. Love, Bron

"What about Mum and Dad?" Gaia whispered as she folded up the letter. "They got the bummest end."

CHAPTER 3

ecember, 1978

Gaia had insisted she be freed from the Perth Youth Home before Christmas. After all, she'd been sixteen for a month so they couldn't legally stop her. Mr Ludlow was nice. She'd never met him before but he'd been the family lawyer for ever. He asked her if she wanted her passport or birth certificate or any of the other papers he had in his safe.

"Why would I need them? I'm not going anywhere. Can you keep them please?"

"Yes, of course. You know where they are if you need them. Your brother took his passport and birth certificate. Both your passports are valid until 1983. They're important documents, especially given how much was lost in the fire."

"Mum was always organized about all that stuff. Always ready to fly back to the States if she got a chance. She took Bron and me there when I was 11 to see her mother. She died while we were there, that's why we went, to say goodbye."

"I wondered why you and Bron had US passports rather than Australian ones."

"Well, Bron was born in New York but I wasn't and Mum reckoned it was always possible the States would stop allowing kids like me, with an American mother but born in Australia, getting an American Passport. She had this idea we'd both go to the States to dance and she and Dad would move back there. She was always prepared." Gaia tried to laugh but it came out as a snort.

"Do you think Bron might have gone to America?"

"Why wouldn't he have written to me if that's where he is? He could be anywhere in the world. He was always on about seeing Africa and India and places like that."

"I'm sorry. It must be worrying for you not knowing."

Gaia shook her head, her long hair swishing in what felt like a who-gives-a-stuff manner. "He'll be all right. He'll show up one day. Perhaps he's making his fortune. Diving for lost treasure somewhere exotic. Probably got himself some other name by now. Neptune, likely." She tried to smile but knew it didn't reach her eyes.

"And now you want to go back to Goshawk Gardens? It could be very upsetting. There's not much left. What about waiting until we can find someone to go with you the first time? Perhaps your social worker? See how things are there."

"I'll be OK. I'd rather be by myself."

"You know the house was burnt to the ground. Where do you think you'll live?"

"The barn wasn't burnt. I'll stay there. It even has a shower and a sink. It's summer. It's easy to live there in summer. There'll be heaps to eat in Dad's gardens even if they are overgrown, and I do know how to fish. I did actually spend my whole life there."

"It's too remote. Where will you get basic food supplies? Isn't the nearest shop a long drive away?"

"Dave and Ros will help me. They live on the next farm. And Dave'll help me get Dad's 4WD going again. I knew how to drive by the time I was ten."

"Are you seriously contemplating living there perma-nently? What about a job? You could get one much more easily here in Perth. Even better, if you stayed at school for another two years the government would support you. Perhaps you could even get into university after that."

"I want to go home. I haven't been back since the fire. I need to see it." Gaia steeled herself against the tears that punished her whenever she thought of home. She had to show him, show her social worker, everyone, that she was tough.

"Well, you're within your rights I'm afraid. Perhaps you could stay with your neighbors? Have a holiday there, see how things are, and then decide?"

Gaia swallowed and made herself smile. "OK, if that makes you happy. I'll treat this as a reconnaissance mission." At least that slammed a smile on the lawyer's face.

"You're not lacking in brains, that's obvious." He sighed. "You still have most of your parents' savings as a backup, and you'll be eligible for a government benefit until you can get a job. You'll have to find a way to collect it. If there's a post office at Jurien Bay—that's the nearest town isn't it?—you would collect it there once a month."

"Can't they post it?" Gaia asked, the pulse in her throat throbbing so hard he could probably see it.

"Possibly. I'm not sure. That's one of the many things you'll have to sort out." The lawyer's face softened. "Call me any time and I'll do my best to help. No charge for phone calls!" He smiled. "You've got guts and I damn well hope it all works out for you. You're way overdue for some good luck."

THE BUS TOOK HER AS FAR AS JURIEN BAY. FIVE HOURS, stopping at every tiny wayside stop where one or two passengers would get off or on. From Jurien Bay it was forty kilometers to home. It was one o'clock in the afternoon so she had time to indulge herself. She sat on the beach and made a hole in the newspaper wrapping and pulled out crispy pieces of battered fish and every last salty chip before she paused to lick her fingers and think about the next step in her new life. It was hot and she rolled up the thin material of her trousers. There was no one within screaming distance to see the scars on her leg. Not that she cared about those too much.

Gaia knew where the post office was. She'd been there many times with her parents on their fortnightly trips to get supplies. Perhaps they'd remember her? She touched her face, the familiar feel of the raised scars reminding her to keep her head lowered. She'd practiced moving her head so that her hair covered some of them. The plastic surgeon had done his best, but making a silk purse out of a pig's ear and all that. She'd tried using thick stage makeup; it felt like she had that disgusting compression mask back on and she couldn't hack that. It was strange to think that if the fire hadn't happened she'd be about to start at the Ballet Academy and be plastering her face with makeup every time they had a performance. And Bron would have graduated and perhaps be dancing in a company somewhere exotic—she shook away those musings.

She didn't recognize the girl in the post office, who, like everyone else, widened her eyes when she saw Gaia and then glanced down. But with the help of her boss she managed to sort it out so Gaia's unemployment benefit got posted on the Rural Delivery. Gaia told her that there was a letterbox at the end of the road where the driveway to Dave's farm began. It had Goshawk Gardens written on it. She didn't mention her worry that it mightn't still be standing, but she'd put another one up if it wasn't. The girl gave her a look and said she'd need to collect the envelope with the benefit money in it quick smart on the first Wednesday every month, and put a padlock on the letterbox because of the lowlifes around there. They'd pinch it before she had time to collect it.

"What d'you mean, lowlifes?" Gaia asked. The girl jerked her head and looked past her out the Post Office window. Gaia turned and saw a bunch of Aboriginal kids larking about with a football. Stupid woman. Not once had they ever had anything stolen from their letterbox as far as she knew. "I'll stick a padlock on it," she said, pushing the form she'd signed in triplicate across the counter.

"You're from the place that burned down."

Gaia nodded.

"I'm sorry. That was terrible."

Gaia nodded again.

"Where's your brother now?"

"My brother? You know him?"

"He was nice. He came in here to get an envelope and a stamp ages ago. Perhaps a couple of months after the fire. Is he coming back too?"

Gaia looked down, closing her eyes for a moment. She looked up again, her hand covering her scarred cheek. "Perhaps later, when he's back in Australia. He's working on boats."

"He was lucky not to get burned. He's awfully good looking." The girl's pale face flushed pink.

"Did he say anything? Why he was back?" Gaia asked.

"Just that he needed to check the property. He posted a letter, that's all. I never saw him again."

The skin on her face stinging as if the grafts so painfully grown across her scars had been scraped off again, Gaia slunk into the small supermarket, grabbed a few necessities and paid, willing the kid at the counter not to ask her anything. He barely looked at her, his eyes flicking back to the comic he'd been reading when she interrupted him. She stuffed some of the groceries in her pack and the rest into two plastic carrier bags the boy gave her.

She started hitching, hoping her slim body and long golden hair would get her a ride, too late to drive off when they saw her face. But it was an hour before she was successful. Not because people were mean but because there was almost no traffic and what did come past—the occasional truck—

engulfed her in thick road dust before the driver likely even registered she was there. But an old 4WD finally screeched to a stop, meters in front of her. It was a woman, tough as shit, with long gray hair in a messy ponytail, a fag hanging out the side of her mouth.

"Christ, what happened to you?" she said, as soon as Gaia had closed the vehicle door.

Gaia told her. Not details, just the bare facts. If only everyone was as straight. It was the avoidance, the looking anywhere but at her, that was so hard to deal with. Unfortunately Thelma was on her way to a cattle station way past Ningaloo and Gaia's property. Likely Gaia'd never see her again. "I'm on the way home to my property; it's on a side road between here and Geraldton," she told Thelma. *My property.* That's how Gaia was making herself think of it. "It's a market garden. Let's hope we get some rain pretty damn soon."

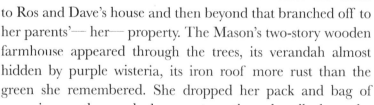

SHE TRUDGED DOWN THE OVERGROWN TRACK THAT LED FIRST to Ros and Dave's house and then beyond that branched off to her parents'— her— property. The Mason's two-story wooden farmhouse appeared through the trees, its verandah almost hidden by purple wisteria, its iron roof more rust than the green she remembered. She dropped her pack and bag of groceries on the cracked concrete path and walked up the worn steps. Paint was flaking off the once whitish walls and the front door looked very closed. Had it always been this uncared for? Perhaps she'd just never noticed before? She scrubbed the cobwebs and dirt from the window she knew looked into the front room and peered inside. Her eyes gradually accustomed themselves and her slightly panicky feeling calmed down a bit as she took in the same old furniture and the piano against the far wall. Tottering stacks of books and magazines on the floor rang a wrong note, but how often had she ever been in the Mason's living room?

"Hey there, you want somethin'?"

Gaia spun around, her brain clicking into the past before her eyes took in the tall skinny black woman standing at the bottom of the steps. "Mary? Oh Mary, it's you." She felt her whole face scrunching up as tears pushed through her tiredness, and stumbling down the steps she folded into the old woman's arms.

"Gaia? Gaia girl, you come back. I know you would some day. You all growed up now, look at you, jus' like your mummy."

"I can't believe I'm seeing you. I was thinking no one was here and I'm so tired and I didn't know if I would even be able to get into the barn and if I did it would be full of rats probably."

"Well, here I is and Eddie here somewhere 'bout too so he get the barn fixed good 'fore you go stayin' in it. Better you bunk down with us." Mary shoved Gaia out to arm's length and looked her up and down. "Crikey girl, you skinny as a frog. You need some good tucker. I got a rabbit stew fill you up a bit."

Gaia grinned and took the deepest breath she'd taken for a long time. "Where's Ros and Dave? This place looks as if they haven't been here for ages."

Mary shook her head. "Missus Ros left jus' after fire. Never come back. Mister Dave, he here sometime, and sometime he goes. Drinkin' likely in Jurien Bay or Perth even. Don't tell us when he show up. 'Spect us to look after him gardens for pretty much nothin'."

"That's awful. Why would Ros leave? I thought she liked it here?"

"Not after fire. Not before either I reckon. Fire give her reason to scarper. She gone when Dave get out of hospital."

"Oh no. He had burns too?"

"Some on arms and hands. Nothin' too bad. Not like yours."

Gaia felt Mary's fingers like feathers on her face. "I know. I look like a monster."

"Never seen a monster wi' gold hair and them sparkly eyes. I see you had bad burns but they don't look bad now. Just like the scars my mum had on her face so she be beautiful."

"Really?"

Mary nodded. "Lot of our mob still make scars to show they brave. You been brave girl but now you back home where you meant to be."

CHAPTER 4

"Your bro came not too long after fire. He and Eddie make sure barn was locked up good and no rats or snakes gettin' in," Mary said as she filled Gaia's plate with stew.

"Here? Did he say what ship he was going on?" Gaia held her breath.

"Didn't say nothin' much. Jus' that he was going off somewhere and he write a letter for you. I get it after. It with the key to barn door padlock. Bron put the padlock onit," Mary said.

"Was he OK? Did he have burns?"

"Nuh. Not like yours. His leg bit of a mess and his hands still, but nothin' worry him 'bout that. Him worry 'bout you though. Said you be back here when you better."

Gaia blinked hard and forked a tiny bit of stew into her mouth. "Could I see it now? His letter? Please?"

"Course you can. You eat that tucker an' I go get it." She grinned at Gaia and shuffled out of the room.

Eddie looked up from his plate, already almost empty. "It be good and dry in the barn. Not too hot neither if you leave the barn door open a bit. Me and Bron give it a sweep. You be right there. Good job it got water. I better look at that dunny. See what init. Might be rats."

"Thanks Eddie. It was always a bit dicey; sometimes mice nested there. Not rats anyway. Shit, I hope that couch hasn't been eaten by rats. I was counting on sleeping on it."

Mary was back with an envelope. She handed it to Gaia before ladling out another pile of stew onto Eddie's plate. Gaia's hands shook as she carefully prized the flap open. One page, torn from a notebook.

Dear Gaia, I knew you'd come back here when you could. I've done what I can to clean up the barn and bung up anywhere that might be big enough for rats but the bastards can get in anywhere. Get Eddie to check for snakes before you stay there. I thought there might be something left of the house but it's completely burnt out. I'm sorry Gaia. I know I'm letting you down going off like this. One day I'll come back. You'll be OK. You have more balls than I ever did. Love, Bron. xxx

The three kisses were the bit that choked her up.

GAIA STAYED AT MARY AND EDDIE'S THAT NIGHT, SLEEPING ON the narrow bed in the tiny second bedroom. She'd told them she'd be fine in the barn but it was almost dark by the time they'd eaten Mary's jam sponge, and Eddie said he'd take her in the morning when they could see what was what. She thought she wouldn't sleep a wink but she was wrong. As soon as she thought it, her eyes were open and light was coming through the window.

Mary as well as Eddie came with her, their rackety old truck loaded with four boxes of stuff: some crockery and old cutlery, tin cups, two battered saucepans and a frypan, matches, candles, and one of Eddie's two precious gas bottles. Even a pair of worn sheets and a pillow and an old blanket. One box was full of fresh veges and fruit out of their garden. Mary had filled the last box with bits and bobs from her cupboards; tomato sauce, salt and pepper, some tins of something, a loaf of bread, even a bag of flour and some milk powder. And a box of fresh eggs still with bits of straw stuck to them. On the top she'd placed a plastic ice-cream container filled with stew and a great hunk of sponge cake wrapped in greaseproof paper.

Squeezed into the cab of the truck between Eddie and Mary, Gaia's insides were quivering. How had she thought she'd even feed herself without all this? The two tins of smoked fish, bread rolls and butter she'd bought in Jurien Bay would have fed her for about two days. How the hell was she going to get supplies? Hitchhike into Jurien Bay and back whenever she ran out? She couldn't take Mary and Eddie's food again.

Her head ached with the whole craziness of it. Perhaps she could borrow an old fishing rod from Eddie or even Dave, if he ever came back? She shuddered. She'd fished when she was a kid, but by the time she'd got to twelve, she'd refused to have anything to do with it. Dragging those beautiful shimmering creatures out of the sea. With luck there'd at least be some greens gone wild in her dad's gardens, and perhaps some spuds. Lots of fruit, if the fruit trees hadn't been burnt. She might have to become a vegetarian.

"You gonna open that gate?" Mary said, nudging her. Stumbling from the truck, Gaia fumbled with the loop of wire that held the gate shut. Her hands felt like Melbourne in the winter, not the tropics in the summer. Then Eddie was beside her, lifting the wire free of the fencepost as if it were a piece of cotton and pushing the old wooden farm gate through the weeds.

Gaia started down the track, her eyes staring ahead, her heart shoving into her throat like a sledgehammer. She wanted to close her nostrils so the smell of burned wood, burned beds, burned bodies couldn't get into her head and start the dreams again. The psychologist at the rehabilitation center had told her that her nightmares about the fire meant she must have memories of it stored in her brain. All she had to do was find a way to haul them out into consciousness. Apparently this would be good for her. Then she could remember the fire when she was awake and dream about it when she was asleep. Well, she wouldn't have to. She could see it for herself now.

The truck was crawling along behind her, and then Mary was at her side. "They beyond the sun now," she said. Gaia turned her head and her eyes connected with the dark pools in Mary's wise old face. Her breath slowed and her eyes spilled over and trickled down her cheeks, and she felt them finding a new way through the scars that were all she had left of them. Mum, Dad. Beyond the sun.

PAST THE BLACKENED PILE OF TIMBERS, OVERGROWN BY WEEDS and softened by the canary yellow blossoms of slender acacia saplings growing defiantly through the carnage, was the lake. Somehow, Gaia had almost lost the lake. But here it was, blue and sparkling in the sun, pelicans sailing over it just as they always had, a hawk gliding on the hot currents, a cloud of pink and gray galahs screeching from their favorite tree. And there, pasted like a child's drawing onto a grove of silver and green, was the barn. High and wide, red rust roof, soft gray timber walls, massive double doors, the windows so perfectly placed on each side a memorial to her dad's loving restoration of the utilitarian barn. His labour of love to make a dance studio worthy of his wife's grace. Her ambitions for their children.

The padlock securing the big doors was crusted with salt, bringing back the scent of the sea on the other side of the trees. For a moment, the sting of burned dreams vanished as the seadragons flickered through Gaia's head.

Inside, her hope dipped. Mary pulled the faded curtains

back from the windows and Gaia took a deep breath. This was it. She looked around. Dust covered every surface and spider-webs almost obliterated the full-length mirrors behind the barre that stretched for six meters along the end wall. But the piano and long couch were covered with sheets. Bron must have done that. She walked over to the small kitchen tucked away behind a partition. The sink was bigger than she remembered, dwarfing the small gas stove beside it. She lifted her mum's old copper kettle off the hob. It was heavy with water. Did water go off? Could she boil it and make a pot of tea from the same water that made Mum's very last cup?

Gaia turned the big key in the normal-sized door next to the stove. It resisted, but only for a second. She pushed it open and walked out on the cracked concrete slab with its outside picnic table where they used to sit in the shade of the tall euca-lypts that overhung this side of the barn. The table was white with bird droppings and the concrete thick with dry leaves. She'd keep the leaves.

Eddie appeared from the overgrown track that led to the outside dunny. "Bog's good," he said. "Dried up."

"What about spiders? Redbacks on the toilet seat?" She supposed Eddie would know the song.

"Won't know 'til you sit down init," he said, his grin flashing white.

"The broom over there, old man," Mary said. "Get you lazy butt over to it an' start sweeping. Then y'can clean them filthy windows. Me and Gaia is gonna wash out them cupboards an' stash the tucker init."

THEY LEFT GAIA THERE, ALONE, JUST BEFORE DUSK. DIDN'T ask if she wanted to come back with them for the night. She'd told them this was where she was going to live and they didn't question it. Just took her word for it.

She sat on the couch and bounced a little. Dust motes climbed through the last rays of the sun coming in the windows. Good job she wasn't an asthmatic. She'd sleep on it tonight and if it was too terrible she'd get a mattress from somewhere and stick it on the floor. She was used to a hard bed. Margot had brought them up that way and every bed she'd slept on since might as well have been a floor. But she wasn't a dancer now and a soft bed could hardly matter. Broken springs though?

Eddie had hooked up the gas bottle and they'd already boiled the kettle and made tea twice using the tea still in the cupboard. Tea lasted forever if it was in a good tight tin. They'd used fresh water though, just to see if the pipe from the water tank was bunged up. The water came out dirty for a while then changed to amber. Mary had drunk some cold and said it was good. "If I get the squits you'll have to boil it," she said.

It would be dark soon so she'd better sort out some candles. She went over to the giant cupboard in the corner of the barn and cautiously pulled open the double doors, ready to leap out of the way if a rat or snake had made it a cozy retreat. Nothing. She realized her heart was pumping. What a wimp she'd become, afraid of a rat. If there was a snake in the bottom somewhere he'd likely stay put and slither out later, when she was asleep. But she grabbed the broom anyway and poked it into the dark corners. Still nothing moved. Her pulse returned to steady, she stood back and gazed at her past; the things that once symbolized her two passions, ballet and snorkeling. On the right was a wardrobe space hung with Bron's body suits, and a crush of tutus and long ballet gowns, some from her mother's glittering past, and plainer, smaller versions that belonged to Gaia. She touched the yellow netting on the skirt of a tiny tutu; Gaia's very first. She can't have been older than three. She could still sense the bubbling excitement she'd felt every time she'd put it on. Most of the tutus and leotards had been sent to the second-hand shop in Jurien Bay as she and Bron grew out of them, but her mother treasured that tiny first one. Two wetsuits, one black, one blue, were squashed in at the far end of the colorful array. On top of the wardrobe were two boxes, the first full of pairs of ballet shoes neatly circled together by their ribbons. Ballet flats, black for Bron, pink for Margot and Gaia, and pointe shoes. Only the last few pairs of those as they didn't last long with the hammering they received. But in the second box there were more, all new, waiting to be worn for the first time. Her mother ordered them by the dozen. On the right, the bottom shelf held snorkels, facemasks and flippers, hers and Bron's. They'd kept them here so they could go straight from ballet to the beach. Gaia closed her eyes, a sudden wave of relief almost bringing tears. The seadragon danced through her head. Thank god they hadn't kept their snorkeling gear in the house.

She flipped through the neatly folded clothes on the other shelves: leotards, knee warmers, sweaters, T-shirts, shorts, track pants. And on the top shelf, the tape deck and Margot's ballet tapes and her sheet music, and the candlesticks. The brass pair and the china pair, all still with candles in them. No candles stuck on saucers for Margot. There was a kerosene lamp behind them, but Gaia hated the smell of kerosene. Strange. She'd never realized how much. They'd always had kerosene lamps burning in the evenings in the farmhouse. She supposed she'd just put up with them because they'd always been there, like the rock-hard mattresses. At least in the farmhouse they'd had a flush loo and a bath with hot water from an actual hot water tank heated by the wetback in the wood-burner. There was an old clawfoot bathtub around the side of the barn though, the fire pit under it covered with sheets of iron to keep creatures and rain out. Sometimes in the winter they'd filled it with a hose connected to the hand-driven pump that sucked icy-cold water from a reservoir somewhere deep in the earth. Then they heated the bath water by lighting a fire in the pit. That's one thing she wouldn't be doing, lighting any fires. If she wanted hot water in the sink here she'd have to heat it on the stove. She'd use the cold shower that spouted from the side of the water tank. She and Bron had used it sometimes to swill the sweat off after dancing, before they went swimming. More to cool down than anything. Then they dived in the sea and got covered in salt.

Tomorrow she'd go to the beach. Somehow there hadn't been time today. Then she'd see what she could do with the gardens. Perhaps clean the spiderwebs off the mirrors behind the barre and cover them with the sheets she had taken off the couch and piano. She didn't need a mirror staring at her all day and reminding her of who she had become.

CHAPTER 5

*S*he had forgotten how idyllic the beach was. Remembering it and actually finally being here were poles apart. A bit like pain; recalling the horror of having her burns cleaned and the dressings changed was something she tried to avoid, but the memory was mild when compared to actually experiencing it. Gaia shuddered. So, nothing like burn pain other than the difference between memory and reality.

Bugger burns. Why did she even think about them any more? All that agony was over for good. She was home now. She stepped into the warm sparkling water, so clear that she could see the tiny pink markings on the pearl shells lying on the white sand beneath. Pure happiness. A feeling she thought was gone forever. No mere memory of how this sea felt on her skin had been able to give that back to her.

Gaia sat down in the sparkle, laughing as a river of tiny silver fish parted and curved around her, joining together again and swirling into the blue. She pulled on her flippers, a little tight but not uncomfortable, then spat into her mask, swilling it in the sea before she settled it in place over her eyes and nose. She closed her lips over the snorkel mouthpiece and finally she was home, floating over the corals, the seaweeds, the clams, the fish she knew as well as she knew the color plates in her favorite book, *The Little Mermaid.* Burned in the tomb of their home along with all their other books, their photos, their pictures, their old toys. At least she could replace the book. Hans Christian Anderson would never go out of print. She'd write to every second-hand bookshop in Australia until she found a copy of the same edition. It wouldn't be the treasure that had been passed down from her grandmother, to her mother, and to Gaia, but she'd rather have an old, well-read and well-loved copy with the illustrations she remembered than a shiny new version.

Clown fish, angel fish, a glittering coral trout with its pink and green face, seagrasses waving, but no seadragon. She knew she'd see one soon if she came every day. It was the same time of the year when she and Bron had watched the dancing lovers; the last day her family would ever be together. She had to see the dragons again. She needed to know some things precious hadn't been lost forever.

Gaia's days took on a shape, and the shape kept the loneliness in check. She woke every morning before dawn and went to bed when she was tired. All by the clock in her body. Her watch had stopped a few months after she had trudged down the track to Dave's empty farmhouse. She'd missed the feel of it around her wrist for a while but then realized she didn't need a watch to tell her when to wake up or eat or go to sleep.

Dave had come back a week or so after she'd arrived and had done his best to be courteous. Gaia supposed he felt embarrassed about looking at her. She had a couple of goes at thanking him for trying to save her parents, but he obviously didn't want to talk about it. It took her a while to get used to how different he seemed from before. She and Bron hadn't known him or Ros especially well, but he'd been basically normal, and nice enough to them. He was mostly silent around her now; even Eddie got only grunts when he asked him stuff. Gaia found him a bit creepy. His once short hair was now long and greasy and he had a straggly beard that was going gray.

Mary said it was the booze. The fire and Ros giving him the boot had turned him. He didn't do a stick of work round the place, she said, and if it weren't for her and Eddie, his market garden would be in a worse mess than Goshawk Gardens was when Gaia first got home.

THE BARN MADE A GOOD HOME AND MARY AND EDDIE KEPT AN eye out for her. They didn't intrude like some neighbors would but seemed to know when she might be grateful for something. Eddie would leave a skinned rabbit or a piece of fish or a few eggs, and one day after she'd been there only a few weeks he showed up with a second full gas bottle and an old gas fridge on the back of his truck. "Mister Dave don't want it so you may as well have it," he said.

Gaia wasn't keen on it at first; she still felt nervous around fire, even the pilot light at the back of the fridge. She wasn't sure what burned their house down but it could've been their gas fridge. At least with the gas stove she could turn it off when she'd finished cooking or boiling the kettle. But she felt safer when Eddie put the fridge on the concrete outside the door and rigged up a sort of lean-to roof over it with rusty sheets of iron.

Mary showed up with some old stainless steel bowls and a pyrex casserole dish. "Heap of stuff in Mister Dave kitchen," she said. "Mister Dave say get whatever you want. He never use it." Then came an iron camp cooking pot that was good for rabbit stew slow-simmered on the top of the stove, although Gaia was leaning more and more in the direction of eating only vegetables and fruit. When Eddie and Dave somehow managed to drag the old Aga wood-burning cooker out of the burned remains of the house and clean it up and get it going again, she appreciated it sitting there on the concrete slab looking comforting. At least she could make a fire in it and close the iron door so the flames couldn't escape. Winters here were mild, but the temperature dropped as low as nine degrees at night in July and August. On those evenings when dark came by six o'clock and rain pattered on the iron roof of her outdoor kitchen, it might feel less lonely sitting by a glowing stove with the smell of a rabbit stew giving her something to look forward to. Gradually, with a bit of help from Eddie, she built side walls from old bricks Eddie dragged over from a heap on Dave's farm, so that her outdoor kitchen was closed on three sides, only the side opposite the barn wall open to the bush.

She cleaned out the holes in the outside shower-head, and every time she stood under it, cold water cascading over her body, she remembered before, when she'd swill the sweat off after ballet. Usually those memories made her feel almost happy, but if a few tears squeezed out they got lost in the shower.

WITHIN A FEW WEEKS SHE'D GOT SOME OF HER DAD'S gardens to look tidier, so she had room to grow new seedlings. Some she rescued from the naturally seeded lettuces and tomatoes hidden everywhere in the gardens, and Mary gave her heaps more from their gardens. The fruit trees didn't need any help; they'd been there before she was born, some of them from the time her grandfather had started the gardens when her dad was little. She remembered her granddad. Perhaps it was better that he'd died before his son did. Mary said it wasn't right if kids died before their parents. All four of Gaia's grandparents had stuck to the rules and died young. Sometimes she wondered if it would have been different if she'd had at least one grandparent to look out for her.

A while after she got home, Eddie said she should box up all her fruit and come with him to the Saturday Farmers' Market in Jurien Bay. She needed to get some supplies anyway; flour and yeast for a start so she could make more bread. She couldn't rely on Mary's pantry for ever. They had barely enough for themselves. Her first unemployment benefit payment had arrived on the previous Wednesday and she'd managed to get the brown envelope out of the letterbox before it was pinched by one of the lowlife types the post office girl had warned her about. She'd never got around to getting a padlock and she expected she never would. The only lowlife around here was Dave.

It was good to get away from the small world she'd been confined to, looking out the truck window watching the trees and farms go past, then the sea stretching out forever. Perhaps Bron was on one of massive container ships on the horizon. One day he would be.

The houses became more frequent and then they were in Jurien Bay. She went into the shop with Eddie and they each filled their trolleys and stashed their boxes of supplies in the truck. No one took much notice of her. At the market they set up their stall, her fruit at one end and Eddie's vegetables and fruit at the other. A little girl came up and grabbed a peach from one of her boxes, her mother, engrossed in conversation with another woman, not noticing.

"Hullo," Gaia said. "Those peaches are yummy."

The child looked up at her. She screamed and dropped the peach, then turned and ran to her mother.

"What's the matter, what happened?" her mother said, her arms gathering the child to her.

"She's scary, I was just looking, I wasn't taking the peach," the girl cried, hiding her head in her mother's stomach.

"Of course you weren't. Let's get a whole bag of peaches." She looked over toward Gaia.

Her heart pounded as she watched the woman's expression transform from pleasant to horror and she pulled her daughter closer. "It's fine," Gaia managed. "She's welcome to the peach. I didn't mean to scare her." But the woman was already hurrying away, the little girl running to keep up.

"Can't let them whitefella upset you," Eddie muttered. "Plenty don' come near me anyway. You sell your peaches, don' worry."

But the disturbance was infectious and it seemed to Gaia that their stall had far fewer customers than the stalls on either side of them. She stuck it for another 45 minutes and sold only three bags of fruit before she slunk off to the truck and hid, leaving Eddie to sell her produce as well as his.

That was the last time she went to the markets. Eddie didn't seem to mind and from then on picked up her produce at 6.30 every Saturday morning and took it to the market to sell for her. Refused to take any of the proceeds for his trouble. He took her short list of essential supplies she needed as well and got those at the same time as he got his and Mary's.

ONE DAY, AS GAIA WAS DIGGING OVER A GARDEN BED READY for a second crop of beans, she heard Eddie's truck bumping along the track. Getting off her knees, she stretched her back, the familiar sensation of tired muscles spiking a fleeting regret as her body, so estranged now from ballet, remembered.

"Morning Eddie," she called. "What's up?"

Eddie put down the box he was carrying. "Mary think you might like company. Mister Dave shoot big roo this morning and joey already out of pouch. Him gonna leave her die but you can feed her if you want. I been into town and got special kangaroo milk it need. Wambaroo it called. Mary know about joeys; she had 'em before. They get sick wi' cow milk. Got you special bottle and teat. Her already eatin' grass so her be good."

"Is she in here?" Gaia said, leaning over and opening the box. The little face looked up at her, its huge dark eyes with its long lashes melting her heart. She gently scratched the soft gray fur between its quivering ears, murmuring softly. "Shh, shh, little one, shh, shh." It stretched up, its nose twitching.

"She like you. Keep her wrap in that towel so she think it pouch."

"It's a female?"

"Yeah. Male not so good when grow into buck. Better have a doe." Eddie set down a paper carrier bag and pulled out a bottle and two packets of Wambaroo.

Gaia lifted the quivering little creature out, keeping the towel tucked around her. "Oh, she's so pretty. Is she a Western gray?"

Eddie nodded. "They good pet. Once you give her bottle a bit she think you her mum. She probably gettin' hungry. You need any help, jus' ask Mary. "

"I always wanted a joey but Mum didn't even want a dog or cat around the place. Thank you. I love her."

"You OK to sort milk out? It tell you what to do on packet. I better get back to farm. Mister Dave wonderin' what's got me."

"I'll be fine. I'll take her inside now and make up a bottle for her. I have to decide what to call her."

"That the way. She need a good name. Mary say she come later and see how you two gettin' along."

⁓

RITA ROO SOON SETTLED IN AND BEFORE LONG WAS FOLLOWING Gaia everywhere, jumping along behind her, sometimes so close she almost tripped her up. At night Rita slept in a dog basket lined with a towel. The dog basket was another thing Mary scrounged from the piles of junk in the shed on Dave's farm.

The weeks went by and then the months and it got colder and lonelier. Even with Rita to talk to it could still feel lonely. Mary had given her a calendar from 1978, even though it was now 1979. Each month was illustrated with a photo of a tractor or harvester in a paddock somewhere in Australia. Gaia hung it on the wall by the sink and every evening after she brushed her teeth, she drew a diagonal line across the right day of the week on the nearest date to what it actually was this year. It was more important to know when Saturday was coming up and Eddie would collect her market boxes, as well as the first Wednesday in the month so she could rescue her benefit money from the letterbox before some mysterious lowlife pinched it.

By June it made her shiver to wash in cold water so she boiled it on the stove and poured it into the sink and washed in that. Every so often, when she was feeling extra lonely, she went to the trouble of bucketing hot water into the old bath outside, then lying in the amber liquid, the milky way stretched above her. Sometimes she imagined Bron somewhere in the Southern Oceans on his cargo ship looking at the same stars and thinking of her. She soon got cold though as the water was never more than forty centimeters deep.

CHAPTER 6

*E*very day except the very coldest winter days, Gaia swam, often twice. She swam in the lake when the tide was too low to swim over the reef, and she snorkeled over the reef flats whenever the water was deep enough. Every day she made a wish; that today she'd see the seadragons again. She was beginning to think she must have dreamed them. Perhaps they hid when they weren't mating? She might have to wait until November when the water became warm enough to start them dancing. But there were myriads of other fish and starfish and crabs and corals to watch. She began taking notes after every snorkel, listing and describing everything she could remember and sketching the color patterns of the trickiest fish with the color pencils she'd asked Eddie to get her. It almost brought tears when she thought of all of her dad's books on fish and plants that they'd used for identification. All burned. Then she'd remember everything else that was lost. The photos of Margot dancing Odette in *Swan Lake*, the albums of her parent's wedding in New York, Bron's baby pictures, her baby pictures. Would she forget what her family looked like as time went by?

Every evening she pasted a syrup made from honey and

water on the trunks of four eucalypt trees that stood no more than five meters from the open side of her outdoor kitchen. It took only a night for the first honey possum to find it, and within a week there were four or five of the cute little animals with their long twitchy noses running down the trunks so they could lap up the sweetness. The next arrival was another long-nosed visitor; a bandicoot about the size of a rabbit poking around the base of the trees, perhaps attracted by the drip of the honey syrup on the ground. Likely the roots and insects they preferred tasted better with a little honey. Sitting quietly at the picnic table with her mug of tea every moonlit evening and watching the show was better than the TV she'd sat dumbly in front of most nights in the Youth Home in Perth.

"IT A ZOO ROUN' HERE," MARY SAID, HER DEEP CHUCKLE, AS always, making Gaia laugh too.

"A kangaroo and two chickens? Hardly," Gaia said. Mary had given her two chickens a while ago and they were pretty much full grown now. She was getting two eggs most days; that's if she could find them.

"Them and that hawk. You wanna watch him or he take your chooks."

"He'd better not. I think the hens are almost too big for him now. Anyway there're plenty of mice and little creatures around to keep him happy."

Gaia had found the young Goshawk crouching under a bush. It was feathered but not flying yet, and she watched it from a distance to see if the parent returned to feed it. By nightfall it was still there and getting weaker and she put a towel over its head and picked it up. The first night she fed it some of the meat from the rabbit stew that was one of her staples, holding small portions out to it on the end of a fork. It grabbed the meat hungrily and she breathed a sigh of relief.

Force feeding would have been a difficult task; its beak already looked lethal. After that she fed it on mice she caught easily in a couple of traps she set each night in her outdoor kitchen, and on raw rabbit meat when Eddie dropped one off. It seemed right to have a Goshawk at Goshawk Gardens. She called him Gos. Somehow it didn't seem fitting to give him a human name. She didn't try to tame him, but he was unafraid of her, and sometimes came inside the barn and perched on the back of a chair or on the ballet barre. She took down the sheets that covered the mirror and the hawk shuffled along the barre, his yellow eyes staring ferociously at his twin. Sometimes he flapped his wings and even did a little jig. Gaia wondered what he was thinking. Perhaps he saw the jigs and wing flapping of his new friend—or foe—as separate from his own efforts. Gaia knew only too well how easy it was to see the person in the mirror as someone else; someone you would never want to be.

One morning Gos flew away and didn't come back. Gaia missed him, but knew it was best. He needed to be wild. But a week later he flew through the open barn door as if he owned the place. After that she never knew when he might show up, but she kept some raw rabbit meat cubes in the freezer just in case he decided to drop by for dinner.

She didn't have to wait for long; whether he came back for the mice she caught for him or to make sure his twin in the mirror was still there, she didn't know, but whenever he showed up her heart sang. One day when Gaia was laughing at Gos's antics with his reflected friend, she felt the smooth wood of the barre warm beneath her hands. Shifting her gaze away from Gos and his twin, she saw a girl in blue denim shorts and a gray singlet, her body moving through a barre sequence Gaia had once found second nature: pliés, battements tendus, battement glissés, ronds de jambes, fondus, frappés, petits battements, developpés, ronds de jambes en l'air, grands battements. Then Gos screeched and twisted on the barre, his wing hitting Gaia's face as he took off and disappeared out the barn door. The mist that was shielding Gaia's gaze from the truth lifted, and the girl in the mirror covered her face with her hands and sunk to the floor. Rolling herself into a ball, Gaia shivered, every muscle in her body aching, the scars on her leg and arm throbbing and stinging as they returned to the contracted ugliness they preferred.

Rita Roo found her there when she bounced in, looking for company.

AFTER A NIGHT OF DREAMS THAT WOKE HER IN A SWEAT, HER feet in first or fifth position, she made a decision. She would begin her physiotherapy exercises again. If she'd stayed lazy, if she remained in denial, she would end up as the physiotherapist had warned, with her left leg, the one that had been fractured, becoming increasingly stiffer and prone to rheumatism as she got older. And if she didn't stretch her burned limbs the scars would continue to contract. She would start making herself a good supply of aloe vera gel from the giant plants she had growing in Goshawk Gardens, and massage her scars as they used to do in the Rehabilitation Unit. They'd always be ugly, but if they were more supple they wouldn't sting and itch as much when she stretched her body.

The next nights, after her evening workout, sleep came quickly, and her dreams didn't linger when she woke at dawn. So she rose and did her barre warmup and then walked to the beach and began to dance.

CHAPTER 7

oshawk Gardens, January, 1981

The boy stood still, the tendons stretched tight along one side of his skinny neck. He listened. Music, coming and going like waves licking a shore, whispering, soaring, dancing. He'd never heard music like this before. Not like the loud beat of the insistent songs the other kids at the children's home danced to; not like the hypnotic dirge of the didgeridoo Hannah sometimes let him and the other kids listen to on the special new CD player in the common room. Jarrah swayed side to side, his ears picking out the warm wind sighing high above him in the tops of the tall gum trees, the rustles of the tiny feet of lizards and insects in the dry leaves around his bare feet, the whistles and screeches and melodious calls of the birds darting like jewels through the bushes, the lull and swish of waves on a beach somewhere in front of him. The music wove in and out of all the familiar sounds, making his small body throb with a desire to dance.

He knew he couldn't dance. "You've got two left feet," Hannah had said, as he'd tried to follow the other kids and their snake-like gyrations. They didn't bother to laugh at him any more; not the kids who'd been there forever. And he knew

Hannah was making a joke—his right leg worked OK; it was only his left leg that tripped him up. The doctor had tried to get him to wear boots to help him walk like everyone else; the left boot had a bottom as thick as a python. Jarrah hated it. His feet worked better bare.

He placed his wide right foot with its long toes on the ground in front of him and lifted his stubby left foot with its five nubs over beside it. Then again and again. He needed to be silent as he limped over the parched red ground with its covering of leaves left dry and brittle since falling last September. He didn't want to frighten the music away. When Hannah took the kids on walks in the park, he was always the one who made no sound. The others with their two good legs and two good feet scared off everything—birds, lizards, insects, snakes, kangaroos.

The lull and swish of waves grew louder, the music swelling and fading with it. Jarrah stopped and narrowed his dark eyes, sending his sight through the trees and out the far side. When Hannah took the kids stargazing, she always asked him to point out the stars—the Emu in the Sky, the Canoe, the Seven Sisters—she said he could run rings around all the other kids when it came to seeing and hearing. Jarrah knew she didn't really mean he could run rings around the others. It was just her way of saying that his eyes and ears were sharper than anyone else's. When he'd told Auntie that, she had explained that whitefellas didn't need to see and hear very well because they mainly lived inside where everything was close by.

Apart from him there were only four other kids like him in the children's home. Two of them were little and the other two lots older than him. He was eleven and stuck in the middle with only white kids. Well, some of them were brown, but that was because the sun liked them, not because they were meant to be dark. Hannah shouted *slip slop slap* at them before they went outside, to remind them to put sunscreen on. All he had to do was put on his hat with the wide brim Auntie had given him. It used to be his dad's hat before he went away when Jarrah was little. It was still a bit big, but not much, and he liked wearing it.

The blue sea was glinting through the trees now and he breathed in a great gulp of air. In it he could taste salt and smell seaweed and coral and fish and rock oysters and dolphins and crabs and sharks and whales. His smell ran rings around the other kids too. He could smell even a piddle of water in a dry river bed way before he saw it. Sea was easy; it was so huge even whitefellas could sniff it out. Not the things that lived in it though.

Jarrah limped closer and closer to the music—now he could see a wide stretch of rough white sand, low green plants with white flowers thick on it. Out of the shade of the trees the sun was already hot and he forgot to be silent and pulled his lazy leg faster and faster through the scratchy plants from one clear sand patch to the next, towards a strip of low trees nearer the sea. Panting, he stopped beneath the first tree he reached, its needles white with bird droppings and its branches loaded with messy nests and birds squawking and chattering and taking no notice of him. Concentrating on blocking their noise out so he could hear the music better, he limped from one tree shadow to the next, nearer and nearer to the heavenly sounds.

And then he saw her. He froze, his breath caught in his chest, his eyes following her dancing shape. Her skin was like the inside of the nautilus shell that Auntie let him hold sometimes, and her hair tumbled down her back, glowing as gold as the flowers of the wattle trees that grew around Auntie's hut. Jarrah knew elves and fairies weren't real, just made up for the stories Hannah told the little kids. But perhaps there were fairies? What would a whitefella like Hannah know? Fairies were tiny enough to sit on flowers, but the dancer might be a fairy in a human body.

He watched, enchanted, as she twirled and leapt and spun

and glided back and forth across the sand where the low tide had left it hard and damp. She hovered and stopped, her bare right leg long and straight, its foot arched above her tippy toes, her back and left leg a curved new moon, balanced like a bowl in the blue, her left foot pointed and as high as her head. One arm was a swan's neck reaching for the sky, the other a swan's wing. But most beautiful of all was her face, eyes closed, worshipping the sun.

Jarrah watched until the music died and the fairy dancer walked, as light as a winged gum seed, towards him, her body shining in her sleek blue swimsuit. His body tingled and he hugged his arms close as she reached the edge of the bush, only meters from him. He heard a click and she picked up a black box and, like a firefly, disappeared into the shadows.

The sea, bereft of the music, swished and cried on the sand, and Jarrah's heart leapt with a love so immense he could see it shimmering in the air she'd left behind.

CHAPTER 8

*J*arrah returned every morning for the next four days and hid in the shadow of the Casuarina tree before the fairy dancer came through the bushes, no more than thirty steps from where he stood. When he heard the sweet crackle of her feet through the dry leaves, his heart would boom as loud as the sea echoing in a cave at high tide; so loud he shrunk back so she wouldn't frighten and disappear like the will-o-the-wisp in the picture book he'd loved as a little kid. The one about the boy who tried to follow the glowing spirit girl across the marsh but could never catch her.

The black box was a tape recorder like the one at the children's home, but the music coming from it was like the wind and the sea and the wings of thousands of birds flying towards the moon through the summer stars, or diving through black storm clouds. Sometimes all plaited together, stars and storm. He wanted to close his eyes and listen better, but he didn't because then he would miss her leap through the air, or her body twirling so fast her hair flew in front of her face.

He was worried. His holiday time would be over in less than four weeks, and then Uncle Eddie would drive him to

Jurien Bay to catch the bus to Perth. Perhaps he'd never come back? This was his first time here since he was six when he came with his dad—only a month before Auntie and Uncle visited him at the children's home and told him his dad had died on his motorbike. His Auntie and Uncle were nice but they were very old, much older than anyone he knew. What if they died before his next long school holiday? He knew Auntie Mary was the sister of his dad's mum. She would have been his nanna, but she died a long time ago, a long time before Jarrah was even born.

ON THE FIFTH DAY, THE DANCER DIDN'T VANISH WHEN THE music stopped. Jarrah watched as she stooped and picked up a cloth bag on the sand beside the tape recorder. She pulled out a pair of flippers and he saw the sun glint off a facemask as she wandered down to the edge of the sea. Today it sparkled like a mirror across the reef flats. Jarrah knew that there was coral underneath; on most mornings bits had been sticking out, but not this morning. The dancer sat on the edge of the water and pulled on the flippers, then walked backwards into the sea. Jarrah held his breath as she donned her mask and spread her body on the surface, her golden hair floating all around her. She flippered along, stopping and starting, and then suddenly disappeared, her flippers twitching before they too vanished. Jarrah knew that underneath the sea there were hundreds of colorful fish and coral gardens and turtles. He'd seen them on TV, but when Hannah sometimes took him and three of the other boys to the beach in Perth for a special treat, they played in the surf, but there was only sand underneath. Hannah said they had to drive hours and hours up north to the Coral Coast before they could see coral gardens. And now he was here.

He eyed the kangaroo resting in the shade near the

dancer's tape recorder. It was the same one he saw often. Sometimes the dancer even scratched the big doe between her ears. Jarrah wasn't surprised. Why would the roo be afraid? She knew the dancer was part of the wild, like her. He wondered if the doe would let him scratch her head. Perhaps she was like a dog; she would like Jarrah if the dancer liked him. He'd walk along the beach a bit and perhaps the dancer would smile at him if he was right there on the sand when she came out of the sea.

He made his way through the trees so he wouldn't come out on the beach right in front of her and frighten her off. Then he limped down to the water and swished through it at the edge where it frothed a little on the white sand. It didn't feel like the sea in Perth. It folded over his feet like something gentle and warm. Lapping at his toes, but not like a cat with its raspy tongue. Perhaps a little baby's kiss. Not that he had ever been even close up to a little baby, but he thought it would be nice, like this. He went very slowly, his head down but peeking up quickly every few seconds to check where the dancer was. When he saw her turning toward the beach he limped along a little faster, and as she stood up and began to wade backwards the last little way to the sand, he was only a few steps from her. When she stopped and turned around his pounding heart almost leapt out his ears. Then she smiled and Jarrah paused, quivering, the warm sea around his feet. He looked at her wet hair, darker now, the sun making it glow and showering its heat over him as well. His face felt stretched wide by his smile. He couldn't stop it even if he wanted to. It felt like her smile was sending magic across to his smile.

She was there so close he could reach out and touch her to see if she was real. But he held his hands tight at his sides. Leaning down she pulled her flippers off and stepped onto the sand. "Hullo," she said. "Where did you come from?"

Jarrah didn't know what to say. Did she mean what mob

did he come from? Did she mean did he come from Perth, or from Auntie's place?

"I haven't seen you around before," she said. "Do you live near here?"

"Um, I live in Perth but I staying with my Auntie and Uncle that way." He pointed to the trees and through them to Mister Dave's farm.

"Oh. Are Mary and Eddie your Auntie and Uncle?"

Jarrah nodded.

"I know. You must be that little boy I met years and years ago when you were staying there with them, you and your dad. Is that who you are?"

Jarrah nodded again. "Dad got killed on his motorbike and I live in Perth at a children's home," he managed. "I never came back here 'cos kids aren't allowed on the long bus by themselves 'til they're twelve."

"Wow! So you're twelve?"

Jarrah nodded, then shook his head, his eyes looking down. "I'm eleven actually but Auntie told them I was twelve when she got my tickets."

"Good on her." She didn't say anything for a bit and Jarrah sneaked a look up at her. She looked sad and he wished he hadn't told her his Auntie lied.

"I'm sorry about your dad. I didn't know he'd died. How long ago was that?"

"'Bout five years," Jarrah said, his heart slowing down. "I had a mum but she had to give me to the children's home when I was little 'cos I couldn't walk and she had no job and couldn't look after me. My dad told me about her. She was pretty and a whitefella like you. Dad never even saw her from when I was a little kid. He said she probably died 'cos she had to live rough. That's why she never came to see me."

"My dad and mum died too so I know it's terrible. But more for you because I was fourteen and you were much younger."

"It's all right. Auntie and Uncle are nice and Hannah in Perth is nice too. "

The dancer's eyes sparkled. "This is the best beach. Have you been swimming yet?"

Jarrah shook his head. "The sea feels nice. Did you see any turtles?"

"Yes, I did. Just one. Probably a male. We don't get too many turtles here. They nest further north and that's what they're doing now."

"Oh, I'd like to see a turtle."

"Can you swim? Even if you can float, and you'll easily be able to float, you can learn to snorkel. Eddie could take you in. You can borrow my mask and snorkel if you like. They'll fit you."

"Really? I don' know if Uncle Eddie swims much. He goes out fishing in his boat."

The dancer giggled.

Jarrah thought about Maisie at the children's home. She was one of the bigger girls and he liked her. She was always giggling.

"Well if Eddie can't show you how, I will if you like," the dancer said, her eyes still giggling.

"When? I have to go back on the bus soon."

"Oh, no. Perhaps you could hide until the bus has left?" She giggled again.

"It isn't yet. Three weeks an— he counted on his fingers— five days left."

"That's heaps of time. Hey, we haven't even introduced ourselves. I'm Gaia." She held out her hand like adults do, and he took it and they shook their hands up and down. Her hand was cool from the sea.

"I'm Jarrah," he said.

"Like the tree. What a wonderful name. My name means Earth. Earth and tree. That means we're already friends. Friends from the beginning of time."

GAIA GRINNED AS GOS CAUGHT THE FRESHLY DEAD MOUSE SHE threw to him, dropping it from his hooked beak to the floor so he could steady it with his sharp talons while he ripped it to pieces. "Jarrah will love you," she said, and the hawk looked up, cocking his head to one side, his yellow eyes glaring at her. She knew he wasn't glaring; he had no alternative, rather like her with her frightening face.

It was strange how she'd forgotten her appearance when she met Jarrah. She hadn't given it a single thought. In reflection she decided that it was because the boy hadn't even flinched when he saw her. Perhaps Mary had warned him? Unlikely. Mary and Eddie were so used to her they never seemed to notice. It was something to do with their values. So different from the values of white Australians with their obsessions with superficial appearance and owning stuff. Whitefellas. Sometimes now days she had a hard time thinking of herself as one of that mob.

Jarrah. He was lovely. His whole face smiled. Gaia remembered the little boy—he must have been about four—visiting Mary with his dad. Poor little kid could only walk with horrible braces on his legs. He was much happier sliding around on his bottom. Her dad had got on well with Jarrah's dad—Billy, that was his name—not very old himself. Mary and Eddie were like Billy's family because his mum, Mary's sister, died when he was a kid and he never had a father; well not one that stayed around.

Gaia's parents were mad about what happened to Billy. He was only nineteen, working in a garage in Perth, when Jarrah was born. The mother apparently was a drug addict and living on the streets and Jarrah had been taken off her by Social Services when he was a toddler. Neither Billy nor Mary and Eddie were allowed to look after him because he became a Ward of the State and ended up stuck in a kid's home so he could get his club foot fixed. The poor mother disappeared god knows where, and Billy was only allowed to see his son for a few hours on weekends and would sometimes bring him back to see Mary and Eddie.

And now he was eleven. Still had a limp but he seemed to get along pretty fast. So at least he must have had operations on his leg and foot so he could walk without the braces, even if he never got to live with his family.

Gaia took in a gulp of the sweet salt air. No parents, his only home an institution—no doubt racist as hell— and a limp to make life even more difficult. And she thought she'd had it tough.

GAIA. FOR A WHILE JARRAH STRUGGLED TO THINK OF HER BY her name. Earth. That was strange. She was more like the air to him. He told Auntie about meeting her on the beach. He had to, really, because he wanted to learn to snorkel and see a turtle swimming underwater, and he knew Auntie would guess if he came back all salty.

"She nice girl," Auntie said. "You help her in her garden sometime."

"Is that why her name is Gaia?" Jarrah asked. "It means earth, an' she grows things like you and Uncle Eddie."

"Could be if it was her dad called her that. He an earth man. Her mum not, though. She a dancer."

"Gaia's a dancer too," Jarrah said, his eyes skittering about.

"Use t' be. When she a kid like you. Her big bro was too. Their mum teach them to dance every day, then the fire burned Gaia's face an' that stop dancing."

Jarrah shook his head. "She does dance. I've seen her. Every day real early she dances on the beach. So her face doesn't stop her dancing. Why would it? She doesn't dance with her face."

"Yeah? She dance? Dinna know that. That good though. She need more 'n diggin' garden and being 'shamed 'bout her face."

Jarrah looked down as his feet. "Like my stupid stubby foot. Some kids say mean things and it stops me doin' stuff sometimes. Hannah says to forget 'bout them; they're not worth a sparrow fart."

Auntie grinned. "That right. More like a dirty big cow fart. Gaia shell too soft still. She come right when she ready. See them scars as brave." She reached over and put her hand on Jarrah's cheek. "Eddie and me, we watched them dance. Christmas jus' a bit 'fore that fire. They did a show jus' for Mister Dave and Missus Roz, an' us got seein' them too. Their mum, she big dancer in America, an' Bron, him Gaia's bro, he sure could jump. Higher than a roo. Gaia, that girl prettiest of all, like a bird flying on the wind. I like to see her dance again.
"

"I think she's like a fairy." Jarrah felt his face all hot. "I know she's not a fairy but she sort of floats through the air sometimes."

"Don' you go gettin' in her way then. You jus' bitty kid," Auntie said, giving his arm a little poke with her fist.

"She likes me. She said she'd show me how to snorkel."

"'Course she like you. You good kid. But she got other stuff t'do so don' go bein' roun' heaps."

Jarrah shook his head. "I won't. Can I go and see if she's goin' snorkeling though?"

"You know where she live?" Auntie said.

Jarrah shook his head again.

"She live in big barn 'jus down that track an' through gate. She work in garden mostly." Auntie went over to the food cupboard and pulled out a cake tin. "I give you some jam roll to take. She like that."

GAIA GAVE HIM HER MASK AND TOLD HIM SHE COULD USE HER brother's; it fitted her fine now she was older than Bron had been when he last wore it.

"How old are you?" Jarrah asked.

"Eighteen. And two months. Pretty old do you think?"

Jarrah shrugged. "I s'pose. It's better to be grown up than a kid."

"Well, we have no say in the matter. By the time you're eighteen you'll be swimming like a dolphin.

Jarrah didn't mind the mask and snorkel but his lame foot fell out of the flipper, even when Gaia gave him a thick sock to wear under it.

"You could wear just one flipper on your right foot and then you would go round and round in circles," she said. "That might be fun."

Jarrah didn't know if she meant it or was teasing. He sneaked a look at her face and saw her grinning. "I can float without flippers. It's easy."

"OK. Let's go." She spat in her mask and swilled it out, then pulled it on. So Jarrah did the same with his mask, stuck the snorkel in his mouth, and put his face under the surface of the water. He looked at the white sand below. No fish but a bright blue starfish sat on it. He ducked down and picked it up and suddenly his nose and mouth were full of water and he was spluttering and choking. He stuck his feet down and his head up and pulled his mask off and the snorkel out of his mouth.

"Whoops," Gaia said. "Lesson number one; keep the end of the snorkel above water. Let's leave the diving until you've learned to float."

"It's too big for me," he said, banging the mask down on top of the water.

"No it's not. I'll fix the strap so it's tighter. You'll soon get the hang of it."

"There's only sand to see anyway." Jarrah knew he was

sulking, but it was always like this. He could never do things like other kids.

"Just you wait. Look out there a bit. See the dark shapes in the water? That's coral, and where there is coral there is fish. Heaps of fish. Perhaps even a turtle."

"P'raps I'll jus' wade out a bit and put my head under and see. It doesn't look very deep."

"It's not, but you can't walk around on the coral. It'll cut your feet and it kills the coral as well. Anyway it's deeper than it looks. Here, I've adjusted the mask for you. Let's try again."

Jarrah sighed. She was tougher than she looked. He took the mask and began to pull it on but she shook her head and held her own mask like a plate and spat into it and then swilled her spit out with seawater. He copied her again. It did make the plastic window clearer. This time, once he had the snorkel in his mouth he lay very carefully on the surface, his face only just in the water. He breathed the smallest breath in, waiting for the sea to flood into his mouth. It stayed out and he breathed again. It was easy. Just like breathing in the air. Well it was the air, he knew that. He relaxed, seeing Gaia's legs standing next to his floating body. He looked down at the white sand again and saw the blue starfish upside down with its white suckers showing. He stopped himself ducking under to turn it up the right way.

Gaia nudged him. She was floating beside him now. She'd left her flippers off so they could be the same. She pointed out to sea and then started moving away from him, kicking her feet very gently. He kicked his feet, half expecting to go around in a circle, but his body went forwards and followed hers. He was floating, as good as a kid with two good legs and two whole feet.

CHAPTER 9

*J*arrah didn't ever want to stop floating and snorkeling that first day. The water was warm but even so, after a while, he was shivering, and Gaia said she was getting out so he needed to as well.

"Your Auntie wouldn't like you snorkeling without me with you," she said. "When you've done it a few times it will be different. I wasn't allowed to snorkel way out there over the reef edge without my dad with me even when I was fourteen. It used to make me mad. Especially as my brother was allowed."

"That's 'cos boys are stronger than girls," Jarrah said.

"Bullshit," said Gaia.

Gaia wasn't like the girls at the children's home. 'Bullshit' was what the boys said when Hannah wasn't around. "Well, I mean boys are better swimmers than girls. Girls are better at different things," Jarrah said. He didn't want to piss her off.

"Like cleaning the floor and cooking, you mean," Gaia said.

"I suppose," Jarrah said, getting a funny feeling this was going all wrong. "They're good at reading and stuff too. Dancing. They're real good at dancing."

Gaia grinned at him and he felt his heart wiggle back in place. "My bro was the best dancer," she said. "And I can swim as well as most boys. Perhaps almost as well as Bron could swim back then."

"You're the best dancer in the whole world," Jarrah said, his face and whole body getting so hot when he heard himself saying it that it dried up the sea on his skin.

"How do you know? I'm terrible, anyway. I used to be OK; good actually, but that was before I broke my leg and now it's too stiff."

"I watched you one day when you danced on the beach." He thought it best not to say he watched her every day, and he'd watched her this morning even.

"How come I didn't see you? Did you hide?" Her face was all pink.

Jarrah looked down, misery creeping up through him. "I'm sorry. I didn't mean to see you but it was so...so like a fairy that I couldn't stop. I didn't let you see me because I was scared I'd frighten you away." He heard the little sounds of the sea swishing on the sand where they were standing, and the screech of a parrot somewhere in the trees. Why didn't she say something? She was mad at him and she'd never snorkel with him again. He looked up, ready to look down again.

"It's OK," she said.

Jarrah caught the sadness in her voice and tears shot into his eyes. He blinked them away. "I won't watch you again," he said, his voice hardly bigger than a whisper.

"Hey, it's no big deal," she said, the sad in her voice gone. "Tomorrow I bet we'll see a turtle. Perhaps even a dragon."

"Dragons aren't real. Not actual dragons."

"I've seen dragons," Gaia said.

"I used to think Frilled Lizards were dragons, but they're not, and they don't live in the sea anyway," Jarrah said. She was teasing him again.

"Well, these are special dragons, called seadragons. Have you heard of them?"

Jarrah shook his head. Was she for real? "So what do they look like? If they breathed fire the sea would put it out."

"Smarty pants. No, these seadragons are only about the length of this snorkel tube and as skinny, but they have a dragon head and a dragon tail and they have seaweedy fronds attached all over their bodies. They are lots of beautiful colors and they dance. Before they mate the male and female dance together. It's the most beautiful thing I've ever seen."

Jarrah didn't know what to do when Gaia looked so sad. So he took a little step nearer her and put his arms around her waist, feeling little quivers coming through her wet bathing suit. Then he felt her arms come around him and hold him tight like Auntie had when he got off the bus in Jurien Bay, but no one else ever did, not even Hannah, although she cuddled the little kids when they hurt themselves.

JARRAH HELPED GAIA IN THE GARDEN, AND WHEN UNCLE Eddie went to the Farmers' Market each Saturday, Jarrah stood at one end of the stall and did all the selling of Gaia's produce. His uncle pretended to be cross because everyone bought Jarrah's stuff first. He said it was because they all liked a cute kid with a big grin better than a grumpy ole Blackfella. Jarrah guessed he was likely right but it felt good 'cos behind the stall no one could see he had a stub for a foot. Also while he was waiting for Uncle to sell all his stuff, he bought himself a hot dog and some chips and then an ice-cream. Gaia had told him that he could only sell her stuff if he took some of the money for himself. He asked her why she didn't come to the market with them, but she just said she preferred staying at home. It didn't make much sense to Jarrah. She was home enough anyway.

He was good at snorkeling now and could even clear his snorkel after he dove down. Every day when they came out of the water they went back to Gaia's barn and drew pictures of any new fish so they could remember the colors and patterns. Gaia told him about the fish books her dad had that all got burned in the fire. Jarrah had an idea to ask Hannah to help him find a fish book he could buy for Gaia. That's what he was saving his market money for.

Every day they looked out for seadragons. Jarrah wanted to find one for Gaia, but he wasn't quite sure what he was looking for. She'd drawn him a picture so he knew it was sort of like a big seahorse but much harder to see because of how it looked like seaweed. Gaia had seen a pair last summer and the summer before and she thought it was the very same pair who came back to mate in the same spot every year. She thought they might even be the same pair she and her brother had seen when she was fourteen because they could live for six or even ten years. Jarrah knew she was worried that something had happened to them and somehow that would be worse even than if something happened to Rita Roo or Gos, because of seeing them first with her brother and him going away and never coming home. Jarrah wished he could make up for her losing her brother but he knew he couldn't. Bron, he was called. He wasn't like most brothers because he danced, and Auntie had told him that when Bron and Gaia danced together even Uncle Eddie clapped because they were so beautiful.

Jarrah hated his short leg with the ugly stub on the end of it. He would never be able to dance like Bron.

～

ONLY TWO WEEKS AND FIVE DAYS BEFORE HE HAD TO GO BACK to Perth. Jarrah thought about it when he went to bed and sometimes he felt like he never went to sleep at all and was still thinking about it in the morning. He'd asked Auntie if he could stay here with them and help Uncle Eddie in the gardens, but she said he wasn't old enough to leave school yet and he needed to stay there as long as he could and get an education so he could be something better than his dad or his uncle. He liked school but he wished there was a school near Auntie's place. Gaia had told him that if he worked hard at school he could go to university and learn to be a marine scientist and then he could snorkel and dive properly with a tank every day. He could study turtles if he wanted. Jarrah liked that plan but thought he'd study seadragons as well as turtles. It was years and years away though and by the time he had got through school and university, Gaia would be lots older and probably married and living somewhere else.

THEY'D BEEN EATING THEIR TEA, JARRAH STARVING AFTER snorkeling and Uncle Eddie ready for it after digging the garden all day, when they heard a crash and then a man's voice swearing and a dog barking.

"Sound like Mister Dave back," said Uncle Eddie.

"Drunk again." Auntie pulled herself out of her chair and grabbed Jarrah's empty plate. She looked cross, so he didn't ask if he could have some more. There was a bang on the door and it flew open. A man in a dirty check shirt and khaki trousers stuffed into his socks, his boots red with dust, clumped into the room without being asked. Had to bend his neck to get through the door he was so tall. He didn't even take his hat off.

"Bloody truck's stuck in the ditch by the gate," he growled. He twisted around and stuck his head back out the door. "Shut the fuck up, ya mongrel." His yelling made Jarrah jump, but the dog's barking stopped. The booze on the man's breath made Jarrah's nose twitch, even though he was sitting on the other side of the table.

"Fucking ditch shouldn't be there. Fill the bastard in tomorrow and get the tractor and pull my bloody wheels out. I'm done in. Get ya truck and gimme a ride to the house."

Uncle Eddie was already up, his second helping of bangers and mash not even started. "Jus' git me boots on," he said.

The man's eyes landed on Jarrah and he looked down.

"Where'd the kid come from?" the man asked.

"That Jarrah," Auntie said. "He me sister's grandson. He live in Perth. Goin' back soon."

"You cleaned my house?" he said.

"Yeah. It cleaned day after you go 'way."

"Christ. That's weeks ago. It'll be running with cockroaches again by now."

"I give it a do over agin in mornin'."

The man nodded. "And make me a decent feed."

Jarrah heard his uncle's truck start and the man walked backwards through the door, bashing the back of his head on the top of the door frame, his hat tipping over his eyes. "Shit. Hang on, ole man. I gotta have a piss."

The sound of his pee hitting the side of the house made Auntie's eyes roll, and she grabbed Uncle Eddie's plate of tucker and shoved it back in the oven.

GAIA KNEW THAT HE WATCHED HER DANCE EVERY MORNING, but she said she didn't mind. Rita Roo had given him away, leaping over to see him however carefully he hid. This morning the tide had been way out so they couldn't snorkel after Gaia finished dancing. Instead he had to go and help Uncle who was fixing fences and needed a hand. He could hardly wait until later in the afternoon when the tide was high enough to snorkel. But when he stopped at the barn to see if

Gaia was finished her jobs, he heard a man's voice and shrunk back. It was Mister Dave. Jarrah recognized his rough voice from last night.

Jarrah didn't want to see Mister Dave again so he limped back to Auntie's house. He waited a while, picked a ripe peach and ate it sitting in the shade behind the house. No one was home. Auntie was cleaning Mister Dave's house again and Uncle Eddie had to sort out a leaking pipe. Jarrah wondered how long he needed to wait before going back to the barn. He didn't like Mister Dave being at Gaia's place. Probably he was OK when he wasn't drunk. He knew he'd given Gaia the fridge and other stuff, so he probably liked her.

After a bit he heard Mister Dave's dog barking and figured that meant he was back at his own house. Grabbing another peach, he limped down the track to the barn. Outside the door he stopped and listened, but there was no sound. He knocked his rat-a-tat-tat like he always did but Gaia didn't call out, 'Come in,' almost singing it, like she aways did. He checked around the back gardens to see if she was there. Nope. Perhaps she'd gone snorkeling without him? He pushed the door a little open and peered in.

She was lying on the couch, her face to the wall, Rita Roo lying on the floor beside her. She must be asleep. He stood looking at her for a while wondering if he should nudge her a little. She wouldn't want to miss snorkeling. Rita Roo got up and he scratched her between her ears, and she made her little clicking noise. Gaia turned over and sat up and put her fingers on her forehead and rubbed it. "Jarrah. What are you doing here?" she said.

"I thought we could go for a snorkel. The tide's up now."

"Oh, sorry. I've got a stinker of a headache. Too much sun probably. We'll have to put it off for today. Sorry."

"You don't look too good. Will I make you a cuppa tea?" Jarrah asked. He could see her scars glowing white on her face and the whites around her blue eyes red as if she'd been crying.

"That's sweet of you, but I think I'll stick to water. I'll be OK tomorrow. I just need a good sleep."

"I can stay and look after you if you like."

"Thank you Jarrah, but I'll be better by myself. Why don't you come over tomorrow afternoon and we'll go snorkeling then?"

Jarrah nodded, his disappointment like a football in his chest.

CHAPTER 10

*O*utside the barn he looked longingly at the masks and snorkels hanging on the big hooks by the outside shower. Then he had an idea. He'd go and look for the sea-dragons. The other night he'd dreamed about finding them. Sometimes dreams showed things. Gaia had told him that once they found where the seadragons were, they would stay in the same place for days and days, dancing. If he found them he'd be able to take her to them tomorrow. Jarrah's whole body tingled. He lifted the smaller mask and snorkel off the hook and limped fast down the track to the beach. He was a star snorkeler now, that's what Gaia said, so it would be OK for him to go in without her there. She'd be so happy when he found the seadragons she wouldn't be cross, and Auntie didn't need to know. He wasn't going over the reef edge anyway. He'd been twice with Gaia and it might be a bit scary without her.

He planned his snorkel carefully. He wouldn't just swim about all over the place, following whatever fish he saw as he usually did. He'd start at one end of the coral gardens and go back and forwards, back and forwards, getting closer and closer to the other end of the coral, like cops did when they were searching for clues in the bush. He spat in his mask, pulled it on, stuck the snorkel in his mouth and began.

~

THE SUN STILL HAD SOME WARMTH IN IT WHEN HE KICKED BACK to the beach, ripping off his mask and snorkel so fast the strap of the mask got tangled in his hair. He had to get to the barn quick, before it got too dark to snorkel. The seadragons might be gone tomorrow and Gaia would think he was making it up. He almost thought that perhaps he was; all those days when they had looked and looked and seen nothing, and today, the very first time he snorkeled by himself, there they were, just as Gaia had drawn them; like dancing seaweedy seahorses.

Now he was running, his short leg trying to catch up with his good leg, the seawater drying salty on his skin. What if she was asleep? Perhaps she would be cross if he woke her up when she was so tired? But he had to tell her. If she saw the seadragons it would make her smile again.

He pushed open the barn door, forgetting to knock, and she was standing at the barre. He saw her face in the mirror before she turned around and made her lips smile at him.

"Jarrah, what's up? Why are you back?"

"I found them, the seadragons. They're there, dancing. You need to come and see them before they go away again."

"You've been snorkeling by yourself?"

Jarrah nodded. "I was careful. I only stayed where it's shallow and I wanted to find them for you."

"You really saw them? Are you sure?"

Jarrah nodded and grabbed her hand. "You have to come quickly before it gets too dark."

"Go then; I'll get my swimsuit on and catch you up in two secs."

~

HIS THROAT PULSING SO HARD HE COULD HARDLY BREATHE through his snorkel, he led Gaia through the glowing sea, past the big brain coral, around the hard coral bommie where the pink and blue and green parrot fish chomped noisily at the algae stuck to it, past the clumps of orange anemones where the clown fish darted out, trying to frighten him off, over the heart-shaped white sandy oasis decorated by a single blue starfish, just like the very first one he'd seen before he could even float, and over a garden of seagrass. A turtle swam past and Jarrah didn't veer from his path. In two seconds more he saw the patch of browny-red seaweeds waving him over. Please let them still be there.

His eyes aching with looking he saw the bright yellow circle first, vibrating like a live thing, the seadragon's haughty head with its long nose sticking out of it. He twisted his head back towards Gaia, his hand fluttering the sign to stop in the water, then his finger pointing down. She was beside him, hanging in the dapples where the sun kissed the sea, her hair floating against his cheek, her hand finding his and gripping it so hard it made him want to cry and laugh and sing. And then there were two, circling and bowing and dancing together, their seaweedy fronds waving in time to the music that was playing in his head.

"PLEASE COULD YOU TEACH ME TO DANCE?" JARRAH SAID. HE was standing with Rita Roo by the tape recorder as Gaia tripped across the sand, her body slick with sweat, her smile like the sun and the moon and the stars. When he'd left her yesterday, the sun almost gone, she was smiling like that, and all through her dancing this morning she glowed. Somehow it had given him courage. If he could find the seadragons for her, perhaps he could learn to dance.

But as soon as he heard the words come out of his mouth

he wanted to disappear. He could never dance, not even if Gaia taught him, not even if he gave up ever again being able to snorkel with her if only he could dance with her. She wouldn't laugh at him, he knew that. She wouldn't even tease him. But she couldn't make miracles.

He looked at her lips moving and looked down, fighting away the tears. "I didn't mean it," he mumbled. "It was just a silly joke."

She had taken his hands, warm around his. He heard her voice and blinked hard and looked up.

"I would be honored," she said.

"What?" said Jarrah.

"I would love to teach you to dance. I thought you would never ask."

CHAPTER 11

$\mathcal{T}$he only good thing about catching the bus back to Perth was that Gaia came with them in the truck. They couldn't all fit in the cab so Jarrah and Gaia sat in the back, with the wind blowing their hair around and the sun on their faces. Auntie sat in the cab with Uncle. When they got to Jurien Bay, there was a bit of time before the bus left so they got ice-creams and sat on the beach. Jarrah tried not to think about the long bus ride and whether he would ever come back. What if he never saw Gaia and Rita Roo and Gos ever again? Auntie might come and see him in Perth one day but Gaia didn't like going anywhere outside Goshawk Gardens. He'd nearly fell over when she said she was coming to Jurien Bay with them so she could hug him goodbye.

Gaia knew he was sad. She could feel it like he could feel her sad. Now she was telling Auntie what a good dancer he was getting to be. "He's a natural," she said. "It's as if the music is being made inside him and it's finding its way out."

Auntie stuck her arm around Jarrah and pulled him into her. "I like t'see that," she said. "Your nanna dance good too."

"Next time you come," Gaia said, "we'll have a special performance for your Auntie and Uncle. So you need to practice every day. Find some place you can hold onto, like a barre, and ask Hannah if you can play the tape I gave you so you can do your floor exercises. And you need to do your free dancing every day as well. Promise?"

"But I won't have you to dance with."

"I know, and I'll miss you too. But you don't need me there to do your exercises. Perhaps some of the other kids might want to dance as well, once they see how much fun you're having."

Jarrah shook his head, the sad pushing behind his eyes. "They laugh when I try an' dance."

"They used to laugh, and that wasn't very nice, but they won't now, I bet. What about Maisie? You like her. Ask her if she'd like to dance with you."

Jarrah sighed. "She's older than me."

"And I'm not? "

Jarrah looked up at her through his eyelashes. She was grinning at him.

"Come on, be brave. You won't know until you ask. You don't have to dance holding hands, just at the same time to the same music," she said. "And I want to get a letter every week telling me how it's going, and about school and Hannah. All of it. I never get any letters so I'm counting on you."

"I never get any letters either."

"Get ready then. Because you're going to get one every week from me. Tell that to any of those kids who think they're cooler than you."

Jarrah grabbed Auntie's arm. "Why can't I stay here with you, Auntie? I can do my school work and everythin'. Gaia would help me."

"You have t' go t' school. That the law. You come back next holiday, "Auntie said.

"Really? You won't forget?"

"Forget? Silly boy. How we forget?"

"But the bus costs too much. P'rhaps I can get a job after school diggin' gardens or somethin'."

"That good idea. You good at diggin'. But Uncle and me save up anyhow."

"I tell you what," Gaia said. "I'll put aside some of my market garden money every week towards the bus fare. When you come back you can help me again in the gardens and selling it at the market, so that would be fair."

"Really? You'd do that?"

"Really. I would." Gaia pulled him into a hug. He felt tears sneaking out, and screwed his eyes tight and breathed in her special smell of sea and sun and a bit of Rita Roo.

Uncle got up off the sand where they were sitting. "We gotta get bus now. You be all right, Jarrah."

~

From Jarrah Nangala,
St. Matthews Children's Home,
Perth,
Western Australia,
Australia,
Southern Hemisphere,
Planet Earth,
The Universe
Wensday 4th of Febrary

Dear Gaia,

The bus ride was ok and Hanna was waiting for me when I got there. Maisie made a banana cake for tea cos she said everyone missed me. I told her about floating over the coral and dancing a bit, but that I wasint much good cos of my leg. I didint tell her about the seadragons yet cos nobody wood bileve how they dance. I went back to skool on monday and it was ok but not the sums. I did my dance on monday after skool. I used the back of a chair to hold on to for the bar. I dont know how good I was with no mirrer. Hanna put the tape on and watched me do my floor exercises and when I did my free dancing some of the other kids came and watched. They didint laugh! they clapped. Jane is nice and in my class at skool to and she danced to and it was fun like you said. How is rita roo and gos? I miss them. I hope the seadragons are still there and are they still dancing or have they had there eggs yet??

    Love from Jarrah. xxxooxx

GOSHAWK GARDENS,
    Coral Coast,
    Western Australia,
    Wednesday 4th February.

DEAR JARRAH,

    I was very sad when you left. You and your Auntie and Uncle are my best friends. But I know you will soon feel happy at the children's home again with Hannah and Maisie and some of the other kids. It is so important to go to school and learn as much as you can so that when you're older you can become a marine biologist if you still want to do that, or anything else you want to be.

    I have been dancing on the beach in the mornings and doing my barre and floor exercises like I know you will be doing. I pretend you are there beside me doing yours at the same time. This morning one of those beautiful blue wrens, they are called Splendid Fairy Wrens, came and kept me company while I was weeding the garden. I think they are my favorite bird, although Gos would screech at me if he heard me say that! (So perhaps they are my second most favorite bird.) Rita Roo misses you too. I think it might be time for her to leave home and find herself a mate. Perhaps next time you are here she will have a joey! I hope I will get my first letter from you soon. It will be very exciting! Say hi to Hannah and Maisie from me.

    I have left the best until last. The seadragons are still dancing but I think they are getting closer to mating. Then the male will collect up all the eggs under his tail and hide in that hole below their dancing spot until they hatch. You would think it would be hard for the mother seadragon to swim away and never see them. Perhaps you could do a school project on them? Can you see if they have a book in the school library about reef fish and corals and look up seadragons? Let me know what you find out.

Love and hugs,

Gaia, your friend and dance and snorkeling partner.

xxxx

CHAPTER 12

*J*arrah closed his eyes as he danced to the music soaring out of Gaia's tape. He could hear the others behind him, their bare feet making little pops and sliding noises on the floor boards as they tried to follow him, the air puffing out of them when he twirled around and they twirled too. Behind his eyelids he was following Gaia. She was dancing in front of him like a see-through moth. He wished as hard as he could that the sounds Hannah and the kids were making was the sea whispering onto the sand and if he opened his eyes Gaia would be real and he'd dance up to her and they would hold hands and the kids and Hannah would disappear like clouds when the sun shines through.

Not that he didn't like Hannah and the other kids dancing with him. He didn't feel outside them any more now they wanted to learn to dance as good as him. Even the little ones could do all the main ballet positions although they were funny to watch and the other kids watching them got the giggles sometimes. But they all liked the free dancing best. That's what Gaia called it, free dancing. Listening to the music and letting their bodies turn into notes going up and down without their heads thinking.

Jarrah opened his eyes because he had started thinking and he could feel his moves getting stiff. He looked down at his red track pants hiding his skinny legs, and his bare feet shuffling about, and tried to turn his mind off again. But he'd lost the feeling of the music. So he spun around on his good foot to face everyone and pushed his arms high into the air. They all followed him and then collapsed on the floor, breathing hard or giggling, one of the little kids jumping on top of Maisie.

"What a load of eejits; is this what you call dancing?"

Jarrah grinned at Seamus. He looked like a pirate with his hands on his hips, his dark eyes twinkling below his thatch of black hair.

"Well, you could at least pull me up," Hannah said, and Seamus swept his hand towards her and hauled her to her feet.

"Fancy steps there, Jarrah," Seamus said. "Has our Hannah been teaching you the kaylee then?"

Jarrah liked his voice; he sounded like Hannah. He was her cousin so they both had the same sing-song laughing way of talking.

"What's the kaylee?" Maisie asked. "Jarrah's teaching us ballet, not kaylee." She twirled around.

"It's the Irish jig, that's what it is." Seamus's feet suddenly started to dance while his arms stayed glued to his sides. He stuck his head on one side and gave Hannah a look. "Come on woman, get some real music on and let's show these scoundrels how to dance."

"Oh you," she said and went over to the stereogram and stopped the ballet music and stuck in another tape and the room filled with the jumping, happy music she sometimes put on for them all to leap around to on a rainy Sunday afternoon when it was too miserable to go outside. Then she hitched up her skirt and her bare feet started to go in and out so fast it made Jarrah dizzy. Now she was beside Seamus and their feet were going like pistons, Seamus's trainers slapping on the floor like a drum. Some of the kids were jigging up and down too and Jarrah's whole body was pumping from the inside but he knew he'd trip himself up if he tried to do those moves with his feet. He couldn't even play soccer without looking silly. So he backed out of the way a bit and jigged inside his head. He wished Gaia was here. She'd be able to do it as good as Hannah. Perhaps she could teach him some of the steps so he wouldn't trip. Like she taught him with ballet.

The tape finished and Hannah stopped, her face pink and happy and her hair flying out of her ponytail.

"Kaylee's so cool," Maisie said. "Hey Jarrah, you should try. It's so fun."

"Why's it called kaylee?" Jarrah asked, hoping Maisie would shut up.

"It just is. Like ballet is ballet I suppose," Seamus said. But I bet you can't guess how it's spelled."

"K-a-y-l-e-e is how," shouted Jackson, who was always the smart fart in school.

"Nope. It's c-e-i-l-i, that's how. It's a Gaelic word, that's what we wicked Irish speak."

"That's stupid,' Jackson muttered. "It's stupid dancing without your arms moving."

"Well, you can move your arms if you want. Some Irish dancers do, but Hannah and I were taught the old-fashioned way, and now we're stuck with it. You can call it a step dance if you like. The Irish step dance because we step without using our arms." Seamus shoved his arms out straight in front of him and moved them up and down like a robot. Jarrah giggled.

"Right everyone, calm down, hands washed, hair brushed, and be back here in ten minutes for tea," Hannah said, shooing them all towards the door.

Seamus stayed back. "Hey Jarrah, when did you learn to dance? I've never seen you do that before."

Jarrah's face got hot. "When I was at Auntie's I learned. I'm not very good yet."

"You looked pretty damn good to me, and you must be if you can get this lot doing it. Ballet's too hard for me," Seamus said. "It must be cool to have an auntie who does ballet."

Jarrah grinned. "Auntie doesn't dance ballet. Gaia taught me. She's a ballet dancer and she taught me to snorkel too. She knows everything about the reef and the coral. And she has a pet kangaroo and a hawk. And chickens."

"Dude, why did you come back? Sounds like heaven."

"Seamus," said Hannah. She'd turned back and was frowning at him and shaking her head a little bit. "Jarrah has school. He'll see Gaia again when he next visits his auntie and uncle."

"School, eh. Well, that's true enough. Even I had to go to school. Might even go back one day." Seamus winked at Jarrah, and Hannah's mouth turned up. She had a laughie face and could never frown for long.

"You're too old to go to school," Jarrah said.

"Not me. I'm still a lad. Once I've had enough of traveling 'round Oz, and getting a job when I need to so I can top up the coffers, I might go to university. My mam says I have to grow up some time and get a real job."

Hannah smacked him on the arm. "Twenty-two isn't a lad. It's high time you started acting your age. You could be a doctor instead of an orderly if you put your mind to it."

"Nah, not clever enough for that, and anyway, being a hospital orderly would put anyone off being a doctor. They have do all sorts of gross things and they work their arses off."

Hannah did a little frown at him.

"Oops, language. Take no notice of me, Jarrah." Seamus smiled his big smile at Hannah. "Sorry, I forgot meself. I think I'll do a degree in social work or something like that. So I can work with canny kids like this one here. Like you do, Hannah." He winked at Jarrah again and Jarrah winked back.

Hannah pushed through the door but Seamus held back with Jarrah. "Your Gaia sounds like someone out of a fairy tale."

"I thought she was a fairy when I first used to watch her dancing on the beach," Jarrah said, looking down, his face hot again. "I know fairies aren't real, but she's so pretty and I never saw anyone dance like her before."

"Of course fairies are real. 'Specially bonnie ones. In the Emerald Isle we all have 'em living at the bottom of our gardens. Does your fairy live near your auntie's place?"

Jarrah nodded. "She lives in her barn all by herself just near the beach."

"And here's me thinking Gaia might be about your age, but I guess not if she lives by herself."

"She's eighteen and four-and-a-half months. But she doesn't have any friends 'cept for me and Auntie and Uncle Eddie. I went with Uncle Eddie to the Farmers' Market at Jurien Bay every Saturday and sold Gaia's veges and fruit for her. She didn't like going anywhere away from her place. But she came to the bus when I came back here, and gave me a hug."

"She definitely sounds like a keeper. Where did she learn to dance?"

"Her mum taught her but she died and now she just practices by herself."

"She's obviously bloody good at teaching as well. I'd like to meet her if she ever comes to Perth to visit you."

"Gaia won't come here," Jarrah said. "She doesn't like going anywhere and she hasn't got much money for the bus anyway."

"It's great that you're keeping up the ballet though, and teaching the other kids. Good for your gammy leg I reckon.

Perhaps you'll be able to get back there next school holidays? Where there's a will my man, there's always a way."

∽

JARRAH COULDN'T THINK OF A WAY THOUGH. HE ASKED Hannah if he could help with the vacuuming and pulling weeds out of the garden but he didn't ask her if she could pay him but she did anyway so he started to save up but he didn't think he would have enough for the bus by Easter holidays. He didn't feel like eating anything much most days and even doing his ballet wasn't fun any more and his leg hurt. He'd run out of different things to teach the others and they'd got sick of it anyway. They'd sooner dance about doing the silly Irish jig with the silly name. He'd rather get some peace and quiet in the bunk room where he could read the big book he'd got out of the school library on coral reefs and fishes. But today he was too tired to read it so he just lay on his stomach on his bed and tried not to think about Gaia and why he hadn't got her letter today. She'd forgotten about him. He was only a silly kid and she was grown up and had better things to do than write letters to him.

He almost jumped off the bed when something touched his back.

"Sorry buddy, didn't mean to push you off. Were you snoozing?"

Jarrah turned over and scrubbed at his eyes. Seamus sat himself on the edge of the bed. He wasn't smiling like he usually was. "Hannah's worried about you. She said that you've given up on the dancing."

Jarrah shrugged. The stupid tears were going to leak out if he said anything.

"I was wondering if you'd be keen to come up north with me at Easter? I'm taking good ole Trusty up the coast for a few days camping. I could do with some company. I could drop you off at your auntie's and then I'd carry on further north and pick you up at the end of the hols on my way back and get you back here before school starts again. Or if you like you can come all the way with me and we'll have the whole holiday together. You can teach me how to snorkel. Your choice, man. Stay at your auntie's or come camping with ole Trusty and me."

"Why do you call it ole Trusty?" Jarrah asked, because he needed to say something ordinary while his tears slid back inside his head instead of coming out his eyes.

"She, not it. My trusty green van. She's been with me the whole year I've been driving around Australia and she's never let me down."

"But you've been here for ages. Is that why you're going north now so you can get round the rest of Australia?"

"Yes and no. I am feeling a tad itchy-footed. I stopped in Perth because I was running out of cash and needed to work for a while. Also my dear ole cousin Hannah was here, and to be honest I was feeling a bit homesick for the Irish blarney and the occasional hug from a good woman. But the Easter jaunt is just a holiday. I haven't made enough dough yet to give up working and anyway I'm actually really enjoying my job at the hospital, pushing patients around on their beds."

"I thought you were an orderly?"

"I am. That's what orderlies do. And I get to take you kids out in the weekends on jolly trips to the beach and stuff. I've missed you coming with us."

"Sorry. I haven't been in the mood and sometimes I can't keep up and the others get sick of me."

"Bollocks. But never mind that. What about this trip at Easter? Are you a starter?"

CHAPTER 13

*J*arrah's insides were jumping worse than Rita Roo by the time they bumped through the farm gate to Auntie and Uncle Eddie's small house. P'rhaps Gaia would be there, even though he hadn't said anything about them coming in his last letter so she'd get a big surprise. But he'd sent a letter to Auntie telling her he and Seamus were coming today so she might have told Gaia. It was already getting dark so Auntie probably wouldn't let him go to Gaia's tonight.

Seamus pulled up outside Auntie's house and Jarrah had the car door open before Seamus even came to a full stop. Auntie and Uncle were standing outside by the door, looking like they'd been waiting. Gaia wasn't there. Jarrah wished he'd told her after all.

"You back boy," Auntie said, and Jarrah's insides stopped jumping about as she hugged him tight and her special smell almost sort of made him want to cry but he didn't because now his insides were making hungry noises as the smell of her Sunday rabbit stew puffed out the door."'Bout time you here boy," she said. She looked over at the car as Uncle thumped Jarrah on the back. Seamus slid out of his seat and stuck out

DANCING WITH DRAGONS | 91

his hand. Jarrah grinned. But Auntie shook his hand up and down.

"I'm Seamus," he said. "Kelly. Seamus Kelly. It's good to meet you both. Jarrah's missed you."

"He good boy. Thanks for drivin' him. Now come on in. Got some nice rabbit stew for tea."

"But it's not Sunday, Auntie," Jarrah said. "It's Thursday." Perhaps she'd got her days mixed up. It was hard to remember sometimes out here where it didn't matter much except for knowing when to have rabbit stew.

"It special day though, innit. You back," Auntie said, giving his ear a little pinch.

Jarrah heard another rumbling noise. It was coming from Seamus's insides. Seamus winked at him and he winked back.

They ate every last spoonful of gravy in the bottom of the big iron pot after they finished all the stew, and then Uncle took Seamus out the back of the house to find a place where he could stick his tent. Jarrah wiped dry all the dishes Auntie washed and hung the tea towel nicely over the rail next to the stove. "Auntie," he said, looking at her with his biggest eyes, "Can I please go and see Gaia?"

"It too late. She'll still be there in mornin'."

"But she'll be 'specting me," Jarrah said, making his eyes even bigger.

"She don't know you here," said Auntie.

"Why didn't you tell her?"

"She get good surprise. That better init? An' don' you go hangin' round all day long. She got other jobs to do. You here long time. Can see her mos' day."

"Gaia wants to see me. She writes to me every Tuesday."

Auntie grinned at him. "She good girl. You good boy. It be alright, you see."

So Jarrah went out the back and helped Seamus pitch his tent in a clearing in the eucalypts not far from the house. It didn't help his mood much.

～

"*Hoo hoo*" Jarrah called. The edge of the sky had only just begun to lighten but he could see Seamus behind the tent swilling his face in the cold water in the bucket. Jarrah had nearly gone to see Gaia dance without telling Seamus, but that would be mean as Seamus was leaving this morning and he really wanted to meet Gaia and see her dance. She'd be on the beach already probably while the air was still a tiny bit chilly before the sun heated it up. "*Hoo hoo*" he called again. He sounded like an owl all right, but he'd told Seamus last night that he'd *hoo hoo* and even did it for him. He told him they had to be silent as they walked to the beach to hide in the shadows of the trees and wait until Gaia appeared and began to dance.

"I'll need to tell her 'bout you first 'cos she'll be scared if I don't," he'd told Seamus.

Seamus was quite good at not being noisy as they tip-toed through the dry leaves. Probably because of that jig he could dance. When he danced he mostly made thumping noises with his feet but sometimes the dance wanted him to make only the quietest swishing. Like a leprechaun, he was, Hannah had said.

The sky and sea and sand were all glowing pink by the time Jarrah had got them hidden in the best spot under his favorite tree. The birds had almost stopped making their early morning racket and Jarrah and Seamus looked up at the sky at the hundreds of dark shapes as they flew out to sea. And then Jarrah heard it, Gaia's music, the orchestra swelling through the still air, vibrating through his body. Seamus grabbed his arm. Then she was there, as if she was part of the air, tripping across the soft sand, standing still, her back to them as she gazed out to sea, then rising on her toes, her arms floating at her sides, her body slim as a sprite in her blue swim suit, her hair glowing gold in the sunlight that was now turning the sand white and the sea blue.

Jarrah's heart raced, his breath caught between in and out, his soul soaring with the music and the flying dancer. He felt Seamus's hand as it gripped his, and heard his breathing, sighing almost. Then he saw Rita Roo over by the log where Gaia always put her tape recorder. "Rita Roo is over there," he whispered. "She'll smell me and Gaia will know we're here. I'll go and surprise her now before she sees you and gets frightened. Don't move."

"I won't," Seamus whispered, back. "But can't we watch her dance a bit longer first?"

But Rita Roo had her head up and was looking across at them. Jarrah slipped away from Seamus and tip-toed towards her. She stood taller and then leapt, once, twice, and was beside him, almost nuzzling him. Tears pressed hot behind his eyes he put his arms around her warm neck.

Gaia still hadn't seen Jarrah, her leaps taking her away from him to the other end of the beach, along the hard sand at the edge of the sea. But as she twirled and danced back, Jarrah left the kangaroo, and, forgetting his limp, ran down the sand towards her. Rita Roo didn't follow him. She knew he wouldn't hurt Gaia.

Gaia's smile burst all over her face like the sun in the sky and he knew she had seen him. They came together and their hands joined and she didn't say anything and he didn't either and they began to dance together as if the long long weeks without each other had never happened.

The music ended, and he and Gaia stopped and then they were hugging tight.

"Oh, Jarrah, I have missed you like... I don't know, like not having Auntie's Lilly Pilly pies for ever." She tossed her golden hair back and her special singing laugh sang through the air. Jarrah's grin became a laugh and he swung her around as if he was as tall and straight as she was. He pushed away what he had to tell her, just for a minute or two. He suddenly didn't want to share her with Seamus, even for a little while.

But he had to because he had sort of promised and he couldn't leave Seamus hiding under the tree. It would be all right. Seamus was gentle and Gaia wouldn't be scared of him. He took a deep breath as they both came to a stop, hands still holding, eyes still shining.

A sound behind him. A throat-clearing sound. Jarrah spun around, Gaia too, her long hair whipping in front of her face and then flying away. Seamus was standing so close Jarrah could have touched him if he stretched out his arm. He turned his head to tell Gaia it was all right but her expression struck him like a slap. Fear. He could smell it. Her eyes wide, her mouth open, her body tense, one side of her face suddenly slashed across with purply-white scars shining tight in the sunlight, hiding her other perfect side of her face. Jarrah had only ever noticed her scars once before, when he'd found her curled up on her bed after Mister Dave had frightened her.

Then she turned and ran, back towards the trees, disappearing as Jarrah limped after her, his voice croaking, his heart breaking, as he called "Gaia, stop. It's only Seamus. He's my friend. Don't be scared. Please Gaia…wait for me…"

Behind him he heard Seamus groan and looked back. He was sinking down onto the sand, his arms pushing down his head like a weight. But Jarrah didn't stop and turn back even though he felt Seamus's guilt and stupidness steaming through the air. He needed to catch up with Gaia first. He should never ever have let Seamus come with him before he'd told Gaia. It was his fault too. What if she never trusted him again?

Jarrah's breath rasped through his throat as he stumbled after Gaia, his stupid leg tripping him up again and again. She had disappeared along the track too fast for him. He could see the barn now and he limped between the tall eucalypts and across the rough paving stones, past the scarred wooden table and the old stove and the pots full of Gaia's herbs and flowers with their special Gaia smells. He batted away a butterfly and his hand hit his sweaty face. The door was closed tight. His stomach churned as he did his special tap on the door. What if she didn't want him to go in? "Gaia, it's me," he called out, his voice sounding all wrong. "I'm by myself. Please can I come in?"

The door opened and he crept in. Gaia was already on the other side of the big space, sitting down on her bed.

"I'm sorry, Gaia. I told him not to come over 'til I'd asked you if it was all right. I wish I had never told him 'bout your dancing. I'm sorry. I'll tell him to go away and you'll never have to talk to him." He was standing in front of her now, and her face looked the right color again, not all white and showing those scars.

"Who is he?" Gaia said, her voice cross like he'd never heard it before.

"Seamus. He's Hannah's cousin and he drove me here from Perth in his van 'cos he's going camping and he said he'd drop me off and pick me up after the holidays finish. He likes dancing too and he watched me dancing and asked me where I learned, that's all. I didn't mean to frighten you. Seamus isn't scary. He's quite nice, but I'll tell him to get going as soon as I get back to Auntie's".

Gaia did an enormous sigh. "It's OK. How was I to know he was with you when he creeps up on us like that when we were dancing? He could have been some horrible man."

"I'm sorry. I'll never bring anyone to watch you again."

"Well, not without asking me first." She reached out her hand and touched his arm and he blinked hard. "I over-reacted, Jarrah. It's not your fault." She stood up and her arms come around him and he put his arms around her and hugged her tight back.

Jarrah felt like skipping as he got near Auntie's. The tent behind the house wasn't up any more and then he saw Seamus shoving it into the tent bag. Jarrah made a rustle as he came up behind him.

Seamus turned his head. "Jarrah, I'm so sorry," he said. "Is Gaia OK? Are you?"

Jarrah nodded. "You should've waited. I told you she'd be frightened. I needed to tell her you were my friend and you wouldn't hurt her and you didn't give me 'nuff time."

"I know. I'm a bloody eejit. I saw you talking to her and I thought you'd told her. I feel like such an arsehole."

Jarrah frowned. "She needs lots of time for me to tell her."

"Yes. I see that now. What can I do to make it up? I think I should get going, go off on my camping trip and leave you to tell Gaia I've gone and she doesn't need to be frightened that I'll appear. I'll come back and get you like we planned in two weeks, but I won't stop, just collect you and take you back to Perth."

"You can stay a bit longer. Gaia knows you're my friend now. She's shy but she's OK. I told her you're Hannah's cuzzie and you're nice and you can dance the jig."

"Thank you. But I don't want to upset her again. I think I'd better go."

"No. Then she'll think you don't like her."

"Well, I would love to meet her and tell her I'm sorry at least."

"Come on then. She's at her barn."

They followed a track through the trees, Seamus trailing after Jarrah.

"Jarrah?"

"What?"

"Gaia's scars. They look like burn scars. Do you know what happened there?"

Jarrah nodded. "Her house burned down ages ago. That's why she lives in the barn because the house is gone."

"That's terrible. How long ago? Does she have any family around?"

Jarrah shook his head. "Her bro works on boats and she hasn't even seen him since the fire and her mum and dad burned in the fire and died and she was in Melbourne in the hospital for ages. She was 14 in the fire but she came back here all by herself when she was 16 and Auntie said she was extra brave."

"Oh, Jarrah. I'm so sorry."

"You don't need to be sorry. It's not your fault."

"No, but it is such a tragedy. How brave she is to live here by herself and to keep dancing like that. Where did she learn to dance?"

"Her mum taught her and her bro. She dances all the time now because it keeps her happy. And she likes snorkeling and that makes her happy as well, 'specially when she sees the sea-dragons." Jarrah walked faster. "She's happy when she's dancing with me too."

"I could see that. You danced together like...like..." — Seamus caught up with him—"like the wind in a tree."

CHAPTER 14

*S*he wasn't in the barn and Jarrah went back out to where Seamus was standing, right at the very edge of the patio, under the eucalypts. "Gaia's out in her gardens," he told him. "Come on."

She was leaning over one of the raised gardens, and she wasn't in her bathing suit any more but in her shorts and tank top and bare feet. She always had bare feet, just like him. He called out to her. He didn't usually, but he didn't want to surprise her again. She stood and turned towards him and her smile stopped and she grasped her long hair, pulling it across her cheek. Jarrah had seen her do that sometimes when she was tired or something. She didn't like people seeing her scars. That's what she'd told him once and he told her back that he liked her scars and he couldn't even see them anyway. It was because she'd seen Seamus. Perhaps he should have told Seamus to go camping. But he wouldn't be mean about her scars. Jarrah could tell he thought Gaia was beautiful. He heard Seamus behind him, so it was too late now.

"Hullo Gaia," Seamus said. "I'm so sorry I startled you before. I hope you'll forgive me."

"This is Seamus," Jarrah said.

"Yes, sorry, I should have introduced myself. I'm Seamus Kelly."

His voice sounded really Irish. Perhaps Gaia would like that. It was sort of sing-song a bit and usually sounded like he was happy. He was still talking and Gaia was looking at him as if she might like him. Everyone else seemed to. Maisie said he was as handsome as a wicked pirate. Girls. He heard his own name and listened again.

"I feel I already know you a little because of Jarrah and knowing how much you've helped him... teaching him to dance... and now he's teaching all the other kids. It's pretty bloody amazing."

Jarrah saw Gaia's face go soft again and she smiled at Seamus and let her hair go and stuck out her hand. Seamus grabbed it and shook it quickly. Jarrah felt Gaia's arm around his shoulders and he grew taller and couldn't stop grinning.

"Thank you for driving Jarrah all that way from Perth," Gaia said. "I've missed him so much."

Her arm squeezed him tighter. She smelled so good, like sun and flowers and herbs.

"Sorry I ran away. I'm not used to visitors," she said, sounding a bit quiet.

Jarrah felt a whisper of a wind and looked over to the little tree Gos liked. "Hey, Gos," he said. "I'm back." Gaia's arm dropped and he crooked his arm and held it in front of him. Gos glared at him like he always did, but jumped from the branch to Jarrah's arm anyway, his wings barely needing to flap. Jarrah tickled him under his chin and he cocked his head to one side and gave a little shiver. That's what he did when he wanted Jarrah to keep tickling him. Gaia said it was like a cat purring.

"Those skinny arms of Jarrah's are as tough as ironbark," Gaia said. "I've given up telling him to use a glove when he's tussling with Gos."

"They must be. Don't think I'd like those talons gripping my arm."

Jarrah looked sideways at Seamus. He was smiling his big smile at Gaia and she was smiling back.

Then Rita Roo appeared from nowhere and bunny-hopped over to Gaia, pushing against her leg. She scratched the top of her head. "And this girl is jealous of Gos. The pair of them are worse than spoilt brats." She grabbed one of the kangaroo's forelegs and shook it. "Come on, Rita Roo, be friendly. Say g'day to Seamus." Rita Roo's long eyelashes fluttered, and as soon as Gaia dropped her leg she hopped a few yards away from them and lowered her head to graze the scruffy grass poking between the stones lining the path. Gos gave Jarrah one of his looks and flew off, flapping above the tallest eucalypts then soaring up into the blue sky and around in a circle before vanishing.

"Do you want to see the gardens?" Jarrah said, happiness bubbling inside him.

"You bet. They smell incredible. I had no idea they would be so expansive."

"Gaia's gardens are almost as big as the ones on the farm that Auntie and Uncle look after," Jarrah said. "Gaia is a born gardener."

Gaia laughed. "Where did you get that from? Doesn't sound like something Auntie would come out with."

"I read it in a book. Not about gardening though; about a girl who was a born scientist."

"Ah. Well, thank you. And you're a born flatterer."

"What's that?"

"Homework for you when you're back at school. You can look it up," Gaia said.

"Meanie. Anyway that's ages away. I'm here almost two weeks!"

Gaia looked at Seamus, her whole face showing. "Are you staying that long too?"

"I wish. But I'm off tomorrow on a camping trip north. I'll pick Jarrah up on my way back and deliver him safely to Perth."

"You could stay," Jarrah said. "You could learn about gardening and we could show you the seadragons."

"I'd be in the way. You're here for a holiday with your Auntie and Uncle, and to spend time with Gaia and learn some new dances. You see too much of me already, back in Perth."

"No, I don't. Anyway, it's different here than in Perth and you can show Gaia how to do the jig."

"I'm too shy to do that after seeing her dance."

Gaia laughed. "Hey, it's only fair. You watched me so I get to watch you. I love the Irish jig."

"Of course, you can do it already. Don't need me to show you at all."

"I can't at all. My mother was strictly classical ballet. But I watched the Irish dancers when we went to competitions in Perth sometimes. They were fantastic."

"So that's that," said Jarrah. "You'll have to stay for a bit and then we can take you snorkeling as well."

Gaia stuck her thumbs up at him and grinned at Seamus. "Sounds like a fair bargain to me," she said. "But it's not all good fun here you know." She spread out her hands and looked at them. "You'll have to get your hands nice and dirty with me and Jarrah."

～

JARRAH GLOWED HE WAS SO HAPPY. TWO WHOLE WEEKS. His stupid limp even almost went away and he ate so much of Auntie's good tucker that sometimes his stomach stuck out a bit. But if he kept working in the gardens this much it would turn into muscle. Seamus worked even harder than he and Gaia did. He hummed and whistled and sang while he worked and sometimes he did a few little jig steps. Rita Roo liked him and she was always bumping him with her nose so Seamus would scratch her between her ears.

Jarrah and Gaia couldn't help giggling when Gos finally landed on Seamus's arm and glared at him, his yellow eyes piercing, his savage beak plucking the small dead mouse dangling from Seamus's fingers. His talons left red marks on his arm and Gaia told him he should wear the leather gardening gloves she'd said he could use. "Nope," Seamus said, putting his arms in the air like a boxer and showing his muscles. "You two don't wear gloves so why should I?"

"I'm covered with scratches from the garden anyway," Gaia said. "What's a few more?" She held up her right arm and looked at the burn scars. When the sun shone on them like that, Jarrah could see how they cut through her tanned skin. He hated thinking about how they'd got there.

And the dancing. The beach at dawn and in the late afternoon, Gaia's slim body in her blue bathing suit flying over the sand, twirling Jarrah around, Seamus making them laugh as he tried to copy them. The second evening they were back in the barn ready for a giant glass of water after their efforts and Seamus started to do his jig steps, better than when he was just fooling around in between weeding. Gaia clapped and then her feet were following his, her arms clamped by her sides and getting her feet a bit mixed up sometimes but then getting them matching Seamus's steps again. Jarrah thought she was almost as good as Hannah. All he could do was sit on the bed and thump his feet on the floor, trying to keep in time. The next day Seamus pulled a tape out of his shorts pocket and put it in Gaia's tape recorder. Jarrah knew what it was; they'd played lots of Irish music and jigs on the drive up from Perth. Gaia's eyes sparkled so bright Jarrah almost had to blink. Then she opened her cupboard and got out some ballet slippers and put them on, winding the ribbons around her ankles. "Ye-oop" she hollered, putting one arm in the air and

the other on her hip as she tripped around and around
Seamus whose feet were going like a duck's paddles, slap, slap,
slap.

Even more precious was that time of the day when the tide
was high. Spreadeagled face down on the warm water with
Gaia on one side and Seamus on the other, Jarrah's eyes ached
with looking for all his favorites, pointing out to Seamus two
cheeky orange and white clown fish darting in and out of their
poisonous sea anenome home and a yellow, pink and green
Lined Dottyback, with its dotty front end and lined back end.
He knew it was the wrong time of year to find seadragons
dancing and mating—but he was certain they would find at
least a solitary one. But not on this snorkel. "We have to," he
said when they were back on the sand after their first snorkel.
"We damn well have to." He saw Gaia and Seamus grinning.
"What?" he said. "What's so funny?"

"Not a damn thing," Seamus said, and Jarrah stuck his
tongue out at him.

Two snorkels later and it was Jarrah who spotted it first. A
lone male probably... although without eggs glued beneath its
tail it was impossible to tell.

"Wow," Seamus said when they finally forced themselves
back into the shallows where they could stand on the white
sand. The light had almost gone. "You could have blown me
clean out of the water when I finally realized what you were
pointing at."

"They're our favorite," Jarrah said. Wait 'til you see two
together dancing."

"Not until spring though," Gaia said. "That's when their
long mating dance begins." She'd pushed her mask up on top
of her head like Maisie's headband, and her wet hair was so
long it stuck in bits on her shoulders and down her arms. She
looked like a mermaid now and not a fairy. A mermaid who
swam out of the sea and her tail turned into dancing legs.
Then she became a fairy. He could tell by the funny look on

Seamus's face that he thought so too. "But I suppose you'll be gone by then," Gaia said.

"Gone where?" Seamus asked.

"Around the rest of Australia or back to Ireland?"

"Is that what you want then?"

"No, I didn't mean that. But it's only April, and I thought that was your plan."

"My plan is to be where I want to be and go where I want to go. And I want to see those seadragons dancing. If that's OK with you two."

Jarrah nodded and Gaia sort of laughed. "You can come back whenever you want as long as you bring this rascal with you," she said, slapping her hands down on the water and splashing Jarrah's face.

"Well, thank you." Seamus slapped his hands down on the water and then they were all doing it. When they finally got out and wrapped themselves up in their towels and walked in the nearly dark back to the barn, Seamus told them how he'd watched seadragons gliding about in the Perth Aquarium, and he'd thought they were the most beautiful and mysterious living things he had ever seen. But he never in a million years thought he would see one swimming and quivering in the wild, with even more amazing colors than the aquarium ones.

Like Gaia, Jarrah thought. A wild thing dancing on the beach and swimming under the blue water. He didn't want anyone to ever capture her and put her in an aquarium or a place like Perth where there were roads and cars and too many houses and planes flying over making a noise all the time. She would shrivel up like a seadragon if it got taken out of the sea if that happened. He felt like that sometimes at the home and at school but he was used to it, not like Gaia.

～

ON SATURDAY IT WAS JURIEN BAY MARKET DAY AND SEAMUS sat in the cab of the old truck with Auntie and Uncle, and Jarrah sat in the back with the boxes of produce from the two gardens. He'd begged Gaia to come, and Seamus had asked her too, but she still shook her head like she always did. The day was fun anyway; Seamus helped them sell stuff and talked the blarney to everyone (that's what he said he was doing), but Jarrah could work out the right change faster than Seamus could. Seamus said it was because he was used to Irish money and he never had much Aussie money for long so it was still strange to him. But by late afternoon when they were packing up their stall, Jarrah just wanted to go home to where it was quiet and see Gaia. So he felt mad when Uncle turned into Jurien township and pulled up at Binda's place where as usual there was a mob of kids and three dogs playing under the sprinkler that was going round and round on the brown grass at the front.

"This is Binda's place," Auntie told Seamus when they piled out of the truck. "We stopping for tucker." Jarrah figured he may as well make the most of it and raced under the sprinkler. They would never get back home before late now and it would be a whole day without seeing Gaia.

So the next Saturday he tried to get out of it when Gaia said she wasn't coming, but Auntie wasn't having any. Sometimes she could be real tough. But when Seamus asked her if she'd mind if he didn't join them because he had a few overdue letters to write and later he was keen to try a spot of fishing in the lake, Auntie didn't tell him he had to go.

"I'll stay with you," said Jarrah, as quick as a slippery eel. "I can show you how to fish."

"Hey, thanks, but no. I really need to get some letters written. You need to go and help Uncle, anyway."

"Yeah, you do," said Auntie. "I goin' to Binda's for the day 'cos you here to help Uncle."

Jarrah's mouth turned down but he knew she wouldn't budge. He'd have to go and Seamus got to stay.

CHAPTER 15

*a*fter four hours in her gardens Gaia was hanging out for a swim. The tide was low so she pulled on her swimsuit and her shorts and singlet over it, stuffed an apple and a bottle of water in her beach bag, grabbed her fishing rod and headed for the lake. Rita Roo wasn't about to be left behind and Gaia was happy for the company. She'd been feeling sort of sad all day without Jarrah and Seamus. They were leaving tomorrow and she would be all alone again. What was the matter with her? She'd never needed company, not for years. She and Jarrah would write to each other and he'd be back again perhaps even in the next school holidays; he'd be twelve soon and officially allowed to ride on the bus by himself. She'd keep as much of her market money as she could; it wouldn't take long to save enough for his return bus fare.

Her feet did a few Irish jig steps and she dropped the fishing rod and beach bag and closed her eyes and danced faster, imagining dancing in perfect step with Seamus. She could sense his warmth beside her, his wicked laugh, his joy to be alive. Her feet stopped dancing and Seamus's spirit vanished. After tomorrow she might never see him again. He

said he'd come back to see the seadragons dancing, but
spring was five months away and she knew he'd be gone by
then. An Irish rover. She'd never had feelings like this
before…was she falling in love? Was this what it felt like? Is
this what she had missed out on, hiding herself away all
these years? She shook her head, tried to shake away her
sadness. Sadness because she now knew what she had missed
out on and sadness because she had no way of changing it.
It's not as if young men dropped in every other week, or
even every other year. She'd end up a withered, crazy old
hag with only wild animals to talk to. Even Jarrah wouldn't
be devoted for ever. He'd get his own life, his own girlfriends,
one day his own children. It was pitiful the way she so
desperately clung to an eleven-year-old boy for company.
Bloody pitiful.

She bent down and picked up a stick and fired it along the
track in front of her. What did she expect, Rita Roo to leap
after it and bring it back to her like a dog? Is this what her life
had become? Now Rita Roo had disappeared goodness knows
where. Deserted even by a kangaroo. She wandered on,
making for her favorite little curve of the lake where she liked
to swim. There was a hidden sandy beach there with some tall
rushes that gave some shade. Seamus hadn't even seen it, and
unless they came here tomorrow he never would. The two
weeks had gone so fast and all she did was garden, garden,
garden, when that's all she ever did. Why hadn't she taken a
break sometimes and shown Seamus the lake and gone on
more hikes through the bush? Poor man, all he'd got to do on
his holiday was pull out weeds and do a bit of snorkeling.
Jarrah too. They could have done heaps of things. And now it
was too late.

She heard some rustling up ahead; sounded like Rita Roo.
At least she was waiting for her. She'd be settling down for a
sleep on the little beach, taking the best shady spot as usual.
Gaia pushed through the scrub onto the hidden side track that

led down to the beach. She saw Rita Roo's long tail first and then her back and then…

He was asleep, cocooned in a sandy hollow, shaded by a thick brush of reeds, the shallows of the lake lapping only a meter from his body. As she stood, frozen, he swiped at his face, his eyes still closed. Then his eyes jerked open as Rita Roo's soft nose nuzzled his cheek, her long lashes fluttering as she nudged his cheek again. He sat up, pushing her away a little. She gave him a sideways look and then sat down, her long tail sticking into the reeds behind her.

"What are you doing here," Seamus said, reaching over and scratching the soft fur between her ears.

"She's with me," Gaia said. She moved closer and looked down at him, his brown eyes still sleepy as he looked up at her. Gaia felt her face flushing hot and she hoped her big straw hat hid her embarrassment. She jammed her hands into her scruffy old denim shorts, too small and too short for her now. She only wore them when she knew no one would see her, which usually was pretty much all the time except for the last two weeks when she'd worn some newer shorts that weren't so skimpy. She swallowed. "I thought you'd all gone to the markets today. Are you back early?"

Seamus scrambled to his feet. He looked different without Jarrah beside him. More adult. "No, I didn't go. I had some letters to write and thought I'd try a spot of lake fishing. Otherwise I'd have brought my fishing gear all this way and never used it."

"Did you catch anything?" His fishing rod was lying on the sand but she didn't see any signs of fish.

Seamus shook his head. "Haven't even thrown it in yet. I lay down for a few minutes and must have fallen asleep. What's the time? I could've been sleeping for hours."

Gaia looked up at the sky. "I'd say about three? Sunset in another four hours. Do you want me to leave you alone so you can sleep some more?"

"No, god no. It's lovely to see you. What are you doing here?" He made a fist and hit himself on his forehead. "Christ, that sounded wrong. It's your lake."

"Don't be silly, it's not anyone's lake. The ducks' lake. The fishes' lake. Rita Roo's lake." She laughed, and inside her heart pounded and danced and the happiness she'd felt when they had danced the céilí together filled her up again.

Seamus ruffled the hair on the top of his head, and bits of dead leaves and reeds fell out.

"I came for a walk," Gaia said. "Thought I might have a swim and perhaps see if I could catch a fish for tea." She laughed again. "Looks like we both had the same idea."

Seamus stooped down and grabbed his hat and the towel he'd been sleeping on, slinging it around his neck. Shoving his feet into his sandals he smiled at her. "I'll leave you in peace then. I'm sure Jarrah will be over to see you tomorrow, and if it's OK I'll come by too, to say goodbye? We'll be leaving early the following day."

"Oh," Gaia said.

"I've loved every minute of being here. I'll miss it when I go."

Seamus's voice sounded so sad Gaia wanted to wrap her arms around him and hug him tight, like she hugged Jarrah when he had to leave. But instead she looked down, one foot nudging at a stone. "Me too. Miss you. Miss you and Jarrah being here. I've got so much done in the gardens with you two helping."

"And teaching me how to dance," said Seamus. "I loved that."

"Me too. You teaching me the céilí." She looked up. "Will you keep dancing do you think?"

Seamus nodded. "But it will be strange dancing alone. I'd sooner dance with you."

"What about your girlfriends? Girls love men who are good dancers."

"I haven't got a girlfriend. I'll be dancing with Hannah and the kids, if they'll let me."

"But you'll get a girlfriend. There must be lots of girls dying to go out with you. All that Irish blarney, and ..." she pushed on —"so good looking..." —she turned her head to the side, then stretched over and patted Rita Roo's back —"and so lovely."

Seamus looked at her as she turned her head back to face him. She thought she could see right into his dark eyes, deep into his soul. She blinked hard.

"Oh, Gaia," Seamus said, "beautiful girl." His hand was on her cheek, stroking it gently, sending tingles and pulses through her that became so intense she needed to clamp her legs together and stop herself from pushing herself against him. The throbbing got stronger as his fingers whispered over the edge of her scars. "You're the one who is so lovely. I couldn't bear it if I never saw you again. Can I come back soon?"

Her hand covered his, still on her cheek. "Yes please," she whispered. And then they were so close she could feel his breath on her face and their lips were together, so soft, so fragrant, so very right.

THEY DID SWIM; SWAM AND DOVE DEEP THROUGH THE WAVING weeds on the lake bottom, then floated on their backs and watched the pelicans as they flew in their hundreds above them before landing further up the lake as an island of white. Sitting on a sandy knoll, their bodies drying quickly in the still-warm sun, they threw in their fishing lines and talked. Really talked. Before, Jarrah had always been with them.

"Tell me about Ireland," Gaia said. "Your family."

"I've got two sisters, one older and one younger than me, and me mam has raised the lot of us on the smell of an oily rag."

"Oh. Is you dad around at all?"

Seamus shook his head. "Died when I was nine."

"Gosh, that's hard. Was it scary living in Belfast?"

Seamus shrugged. "Never known anything else. Feckin' eejits the lot of 'em."

"Is that how your dad died? Was he in the IRA... or the other side... my knowledge of all that is pretty terrible."

"It's a bloody mess. I can hardly work it all out meself and I live there. We're Presbyterians—well Mam is—so definitely not the IRA. No. Da killed himself on a motorbike."

"That's terrible. Jarrah's dad died in a motorbike crash too."

"Yeah, Hannah told me. Poor kid. I sort of feel the two of us have something in common there."

"You're great with him. He thinks the world of you."

"Dunno about that but he's a spunky kid. I like being around him. Just looking at his bright face makes me smile and feel like doing a bit of a jig."

"That's lovely. I'm sorry about your dad. Your mother must miss you being so far away."

"She does but she wants us kids to do better than her family. They've always had it hard. She thinks me being a hospital orderly is a step up." He grinned. "If only she knew."

"My mum's whole life was about ballet and wanting me and my brother to become as good as her." Gaia ignored the sting behind her eyes and instead grimaced.

Seamus put his hand over hers. "She loved you though. She wanted the best for you. What she believed would make you happy."

"I know she did. And we did love ballet. But we loved all this too, just as much." Gaia gestured to the lake with her free hand. "Dad gave us our passion for all this. I think it's more important to me now than ballet ever was." Her smile wobbled. "Luckily."

They sat in silence for a while, their fishing lines floating, fishless, in the water.

"Da killing himself wasn't the worst," Seamus said after a while. "He was speeding, drunk, after a night in the pub, and crashed into another car almost outside our house. He was on the wrong side of the road. He killed the young couple in the car. They lived in the next street over from us. They'd left their baby at home with his grandma. She never spoke to Mam again and they'd been close friends and in the same church an' all. Me mam gave up on the church after that. Me an' me sisters weren't too popular either. The Irish never forget."

Gaia felt the air cold on her hand as Seamus released it. He sat, his elbows resting on his raised knees, and stared out over the lake. Gaia waited.

"Poor little family wiped out by a no-good drunk. That baby growing up never knowing his parents. We didn't blame anyone for hating us. But it was hard on Mam. Still is."

"How could it be your fault? You were only a child." Inside Gaia was crying for him. For her too. Both of them.

"Bloody wars. Civil, between countries, it doesn't matter. They're all so pointless, so cruel. I joined the Peace Movement in Belfast a few years ago but so far we've been as useful as a sparrow fart."

"Oh, Seamus, come here," Gaia said, drawing him to her. She kissed his head as he burrowed like a child into her chest, and she felt him shaking. After a while he raised his head, and she kissed his forehead, his damp cheeks, his sad lips. Then he was kissing her back.

Finally Seamus pulled back. "Was that too much? I got swept away." He outlined her lips with a gentle finger. "Your lips are so soft."

"It was nice. I wanted it never to stop."

"Truly? You don't think I'm a bit old for you?"

Gaia shook her head. "Too old? Twenty-two? Four years older than me. Perfect, given girls are years ahead of boys in pretty much everything. Perhaps we shouldn't get *too* carried away though." She looked at him through her eyelashes, then laughed. "I'm no good at flirting. I was going to say that if we stop now, you'll be sure to come back. And perhaps you won't find another girlfriend when you're back in Perth."

"Never. Are you my girlfriend?"

"Am I?"

Seamus smiled and kissed the tip of her nose. "Do you want to be?"

"Yes please." Her heart was leaping around in her chest. "I've never had a boyfriend before but I'm a fast learner. But let's not tell anyone. Especially not Jarrah. Not yet."

"Poor Jarrah. He'd be devastated. He's in love with you."

"I love him too. I don't want to hurt him."

"No. We mustn't. Our secret for a while. I shall try and steer him towards a cute girl back in Perth. One his own age."

As they strolled back towards Seamus's camp so when Jarrah, Mary and Eddie got back Seamus could look like he'd been there all day, writing letters, Gaia asked him when he planned to return to Ireland. Better to know.

"Not sure. Not until next year at the earliest. May as well make the most of my working holiday visa. But I am going to New Zealand in three weeks. Booked the flights already. I've got a school pal on a student working visa there and we're going to hitchhike around a bit. It seemed a good idea to go while I'm on this side of the world." His arm tightened around her. "Now I wish I wasn't going."

"Don't be silly. You must. I'd love to go to New Zealand."

"Come with me then."

"I can't. There's Rita Roo and the gardens, and I haven't got anywhere near enough money for a flight to New Zealand. How long will you be away?"

"Four weeks. Then I'll be back."

"Will you come and see me again before you go? Please?"

"I promise. And as soon as I get back to Australia, I'll be

here. Perhaps sometimes I can come without Jarrah. Camp secretly in the bush. So we can be together without worrying about Jarrah finding us."

"Oh."

"Hey, I didn't mean anything by that. All I want is for us to be together and keep getting to know each other. Be able to talk alone like this sometimes."

Gaia reached up and kissed him, as soft as a moth, on his lips. "I'll dream about you while you're gone."

"Me too. I've been practicing already."

Gaia's eyebrows shot up. "Practicing?"

"Dreaming about you. I'm already a champion."

CHAPTER 16

$\mathcal{J}$arrah tried not to be miserable on Sunday, but it was hard. Yet he didn't want to miss a single second of being happy with Gaia. Last night as he'd tossed and turned in the tiny room in Auntie's house, he'd decided that he'd work his fingers to the bone when he got back to Perth, and earn enough to pay for a return bus fare so he could come back again in July in his next school holidays. He'd be twelve by then and definitely allowed to travel on the bus alone. Perhaps Hannah would pay him if he cleaned the dunny and bathroom every morning and did the washing for her on Saturdays. His leg was much stronger now and he reckoned he could probably push the lawn mower around the grass as well. It might take the rest of his Saturday after he finished the laundry, but he didn't care. He could even practice some of his dance steps using the handle of the mower as a barre.

Probably Seamus wouldn't come back again. He liked seeing new places. It had been fun having him here but it would be even better without him. Gaia wouldn't have to waste time explaining stuff to him then and she would be much happier if there was just the two of them. Jarrah and

Gaia were two of a kind. That's what Gaia had told him. Both orphans, both dancers, and both winners who didn't let silly physical problems with their bodies hold them back. Seamus didn't have a single thing wrong with his body and his dancing was OK but not ballet. Jarrah wondered for a moment whether someone as old as Seamus would have parents. Probably. But it didn't matter much anyway once you were grown up. Parents were for kids.

Auntie invited Gaia back for a farewell meal Sunday evening. She had a hard time swallowing her favorite rabbit stew because it was the last night and she didn't know when she'd see Jarrah or Seamus again. Seamus said he'd come back before he went to New Zealand but what if he couldn't get time off from his orderly job or he forgot how nice it was for them to be together? As soon as they'd finished eating and Jarrah had started washing up the dishes with Seamus drying, Gaia told them she was tired and needed an early night. Both Jarrah and Seamus wanted to walk her home but she said no. Instead she hugged Jarrah for a long time, and then hugged Seamus so quickly that she barely had time to feel his body against hers. Then she brushed her lips against his cheek, and turned and almost ran out the door.

Waking before dawn she pulled on her shorts and tee-shirt. A fitful sleep had left her exhausted and ugly. She needed to smell the ocean. By the time she stepped onto the beach the stars were dimming as a flicker of light crept over the horizon. She looked through her little box of tapes. The same ones she and Bron had danced to so long ago. Something gentle. A waltz. She didn't have it in her to spin and leap. She pulled out Tchaikovsky's *Sleeping Beauty Waltz* and slid it into the tape recorder. Standing tall and still for moments, she let the music fill her up and take her with it, over the sand and over the sea.

She began to dance, ghosts of her mother, of Bron, of herself as she used to be, waltzing, freestyle, apart and together, lessons over for the day, their worlds only the joy of the music and the movement of their perfect bodies. Her eyes closed, her face lifted to the first rays of the sun, the sand flying away from her feet, she waltzed. Then he was there, a mirage, black hair messy, eyes sparking in his tanned face…like the sun firing the ocean awake. With a whisper of a sigh she was in his arms and they were waltzing together, timeless, his heartbeat on hers. Their lips touched and tasted and she was trembling and opening, a butterfly's wings, her body touching his from their lips to their bare legs, bare feet sliding and gliding across the wet sand, the cool sea lapping their toes and drawing back, his body the only body that had touched her so completely since she was a child in her daddy's lap, a young girl enfolded into her mother's rare spontaneous embrace, a big bro big hug from Bron when they finally earned their mother's applause for their *Sleeping Beauty* pas de deux.

The cry that fractured Tchaikovsky's soaring song separated them like a gunshot straight through her heart and into his. Spinning around, already knowing, she heard him, their lad who never made a sound, however many dried leaves covered the ground, heard the tearing and crushing as he stumbled and crashed through the bushes, away from them, away from their terrible deception of him, the precious boy who had brought them together.

JARRAH HUNCHED OVER BY THE CAR WINDOW AS FAR AWAY FROM Seamus as he could get, his face smashed against the glass. Seamus twiddled with the car radio until he found some music. At least it filled the silence and stopped Seamus talking at him, going on about how he and Gaia felt terrible about upsetting him.

Jarrah hated himself. Stupid kid was all he was, thinking Gaia loved him best. Stupid to bring Seamus here and let him watch Gaia dancing. He gazed out the dirty window at a row of peeling houses with their rusty Holden cars dumped on the ugly dried-up grass at the front. He hated houses and junk and no sea and no sand and no trees and no barn and no Rita Roo and no Gos. And no Gaia. He'd never be able to go back now and he wouldn't see Auntie and Uncle again either and he'd be stuck forever at that stupid kid's home in stupid Perth. Now they were slowing down in an ugly little town with its silly little shops and kids and dogs riding their rusty bikes up and down. The van pulled up by the store with its ugly big signs with bread and ice creams on them. Jarrah hated all those signs.

"I'm going to get an ice cream. Do you fancy one?" Seamus said.

Jarrah didn't move.

"OK. Stay put in the car. I'll be just a tick."

Jarrah didn't move when Seamus came back. Then he poked Jarrah on his shoulder. "You'll have to turn around if you want this ice cream. Chocolate with chocolate chips dipped in chocolate. Bloody good."

Jarrah squirmed around and put his hand out without looking at Seamus. Seamus shoved the cone into his hand. They licked in silence. Ice cream dripped off Jarrah's chin and his other hand came up and swiped it away. Seamus pulled a tissue out of the box on the dashboard and handed it to him.

"Here's the thing, Jarrah," he said. "I'm not willing to drive for four hours with this wall of tension between us. We've got to have it out sometime. You can bottle it up, but I need to get it off my chest. So I'm going to say my piece and then it's up to you."

Jarrah shoved the last bit of the ice cream cone in his mouth and turned his face back into the window.

Seamus put the car into gear and drove back onto the road. He turned the radio off. "I know you're mad at me and probably mad at Gaia, and you're upset, and feel we've let you down, and I understand that. I've been there when I was about your age when the girl I was in love with married my cousin. Hannah's big bro he was. I didn't understand that it was different when you're grown up. But it is. Gaia loves you, but she's eighteen and you're eleven, so the way she loves you is different from the way she might one day love a man of her own age. It'll be like that for you when you grow up. Then you'll fall in love with a girl your own age in a different way from the way you love Gaia."

Jarrah blinked his stupid tears away.

"In case it cheers you up, Gaia does not love me like that either. We're only just getting to know each other. It takes ages for two people, adult people, to find out whether they love each other. Kissing each other is part of it, that's all. Mostly it never becomes anything else. Gaia will probably have lots of boyfriends—grown-up boyfriends— before she falls in love."

Jarrah shuffled a little and turned around a bit.

"So does that make any sense? When you're say sixteen, you'll start feeling different around girls. Perhaps even when you're fourteen. It's the best fun, once you start fancying girls."

"Gaia's only seven years older than me. An' I'll be fourteen in not even three years." He saw Seamus grinning and wanted to bop him on his silly nose.

"You will, so not long to wait. But when you're fourteen, Gaia will be twenty-one."

"So how old are you then?" Jarrah asked.

"Twenty-two. An old man, already."

"So you're way too old for Gaia. That's four years older than her."

"Perhaps I am too old for her. But it's different when two people are both adults. They could be ten years apart or even twenty, once they're adults. It's all about the maturation of our bodies and our hormones and how our emotions change."

"Sez you. You can't know everything about me. I might be an early adult."

Seamus grinned again. He was always grinning.

"I reckon you are pretty early but you still have a few years to go. Tell you what, see if there are any girls at school you fancy, and get some practice in at chatting them up, then by the time you're an adult, if Gaia still hasn't got a boyfriend, who knows? After all, you'll both be adults then."

"She'll have a boyfriend. She's beautiful. She won't want me. I'll never be able to even dance properly." Jarrah thumped his fist down on his stupid leg.

"Hey, falling in love when you're an adult isn't about stuff like that. Just like loving people in your family or loving your friends hasn't got anything to do with how you look or what you can do. It comes from inside, from how you treat each other, and whether your personalities click. That's why you and Gaia love each other as the closest most friends, because you fit together from the inside and because you think and feel the same way; sort of like the way you can dance together. Love is like an inside dance I suppose. A dance of two souls."

"It's not fair. Gaia will love you more than me because you're an adult and I'm not."

"It's not fair when you think of it like that. But on the plus side, love between friends like you two who are true soul mates usually lasts forever. Even grown-ups who fall in love and probably get married and have kids and buy a house and all that sometimes end up not loving each other. Not even liking each other."

"Why?"

"I don't know. I suppose because there's so much pressure on that sort of adult relationship, whereas the love between friends is more forgiving. Perhaps it's because friends don't live together all the time and can get away from each other for a break."

"Some parents don't love each other even at the start,"

Jarrah said. "My dad and my mum didn't love each other at all. They just got pregnant because they had sex and they didn't know what to do with me, and my mum wasn't allowed to even look after me and probably died and then my dad killed himself on a motorbike."

"That's a terrible story, and it's very very sad, and you must never let it decide who you will become. You're you, not anyone else, and already Gaia and me, and your auntie and uncle, and Hannah and Maisie and all your friends at the children's home can see that you are strong and loving and far too bright and sensible to get yourself into trouble like that."

"What if my mum's not dead? Nobody actually knows what happened to her or where she is. She might find me one day."

"She might. When you're older perhaps you can look for her."

"She was only a kid when she had me. That's what Auntie said. Dad was only a kid too."

"That's sad. But I guess that was sort of what I was trying to say. It's important to grow up gradually and learn about love as you go. So when you are really grown up you know how to deal with love. You've sort of learnt about it on the way by having girlfriends of your own age right through."

"I suppose. But I don't see how I can find a girlfriend I love as much as Gaia."

"No. That's a tough one. But you will, I'm sure of it."

"Are you going to be Gaia's boyfriend then?"

"I'd like to be, but that's up to her. It will take time and I'll have to go slow." Seamus sighed.

"Well, if I can't be her boyfriend, I'd rather it was you and not some other horrible man like Mister Dave."

"Who's that?"

"The farmer Auntie and Uncle work for. He sometimes goes to her barn and makes Gaia cry. Well, once he did."

Seamus's face went funny. "How do you know?" he asked.

"I went there and heard him in the barn and when I went back later after he'd gone back home, Gaia said she didn't feel good and her eyes were all red. That's when I went snorkeling by myself and found the seadragons dancing and went and told her and she came and saw them too and that made her happy again."

Seamus bashed his fist on the steering wheel and said something mad-sounding in Irish. So Jarrah said "Mason's a feckin' creep." They didn't say much for ages after that and Jarrah still felt pissed off but not as much. He felt they'd reached an understanding.

CHAPTER 17

*I*t took Gaia many attempts to compose a letter to Jarrah, but when she raised the stick with the faded red cloth tied to it on the side of the Goshawk Gardens rural letter box—the sign to the rural postman that there was a letter for him to take—and opened the swollen old front to place her letter inside, she discovered the postie had already been and gone. Had left a letter for her. The heaviness in her heart jumped a bit and she stood motionless for a second or two, perhaps not wanting to know if it was good news or bad.

It was only Thursday, three days after they'd left. Jarrah would have had to write it and post it the day after they got back to Perth. She pulled it out and saw the writing on the front. Not the round, careful letters made by Jarrah. A black scrawly, almost indecipherable writing. It was a wonder it had got to the right address at all. She knew, of course, it must be from Seamus. She'd never seen his writing. She turned the envelope over and drew a finger across his name. Seamus Kelly.

It changed him, somehow, his writing. An orderly in a city hospital with city friends. Another side of the guy who gardened and swam and lay in the reeds and marveled at pelicans in flight, a boy-man who wanted to hold her and kiss her. Finding a fallen log in the shade of an island of scruffy bushes, she checked for hidden snakes or the types of spiders best not disturbed, and sat down. She peeled back the envelope flap, careful not to tear it. This might be the only writing of Seamus's name by Seamus she would ever possess. Her heart didn't know where to go, down or up. He was breaking off their fledgling relationship, she was too young, Jarrah was too hurt, Seamus was too busy.

'My sweet Gaia' she read, and her heart flipped over. Her eyes ate up his words, her lips curving, laughing at the bit about Jarrah telling him that Seamus was too old to be Gaia's boyfriend. Sad for Jarrah's hurt. Jarrah, her dearest friend. For a second she imagined him at twenty, her at twenty-seven. He was right, it wasn't impossible. Not because of their ages anyway. But they'd met too soon. Her love for him was for a little brother, and it always would be, she knew that. It could never become something else. Perhaps that's what she needed to try and explain to him. She looked at her letter to Jarrah, still not posted. She'd rewrite it now she knew about Seamus's man-to-man with him.

Tears slipped down her cheeks as she read again the part about Jarrah's parents, his lost mother. His belief that his parents didn't love each other. He was probably right, but how terrible that he understood that so young. How lucky she and Bron had been. Then she screwed her eyes shut as she heard Bron's voice. It had been a long time since he had been so clear in her head. *"Too tense for me here… haven't you noticed how Mum and Dad have changed?"*

Had she? Noticed? Gaia tried to take herself back. Dad had always been the one to show his feelings. It was different for their mother. She lived by discipline. She had to, to be a dancer. Real feelings weren't permitted, not in everyday life. Feelings were channeled into dance, expressed in dance. Gaia rubbed her forehead. She'd never thought such thoughts before. Simply accepted that that is how it was. But earlier, before she was born, before even Bron was born, it was different for her parents. That had been her favorite bedtime story, how they had met. It was Dad who told the story, but Margot used to laugh when he told it, laugh in a happy way, and Dad would grab her and swing her around. Margot. Although she and Bron called her Mum, Gaia often thought of her as Margot. That was the dancer thing too. Dad was always Dad, not Joe.

She stretched her legs out and wiggled her toes. Her dad's voice now murmured in her head—his Australian drawl, slow and easy, always with a laugh in it. So different from Margot's American accent, a New York accent apparently. Not that Gaia would know.

But she knew now, a little bit, how her dad had felt when he first fell in love with Margot. She smiled through her tears, new ones, for Dad, so gentle, so there for them always. She tried to bring back his face but it was wavy and out of focus. She had no photos of him, none of either of them. None even of Bron. They had all been destroyed in the fire. She could almost visualize Margot by thinking of the formal ballet photos they had showcased on the walls of their house. Static photos of her as Odette in *Swan Lake* and, Gaia's favorite, as Blanche in the ballet of *A Street Car Named Desire*. Her first role as Principal Dancer. But she couldn't retrieve an image of her as Mum at Goshawk Gardens. What did she even look like without her stage makeup? Dad used to tell Gaia that she looked more like her mum every birthday. Is that what Margot had looked like; like her—if her face hadn't been burned? They'd never had many photos of Dad. Some in an old photo album, two or three packets of family photos taken at birthdays and Christmases. All gone forever. And she didn't think Dad looked like Bron, so even if Bron ever came home that wouldn't help.

Did her mother fall in love with her dad the first time she

saw him? Gaia closed her eyes and saw Seamus, his face relaxed and soft as he lay asleep in the reeds by the lake, Rita Roo nuzzling his cheek. His eyes when he kissed her. Did he feel the same about her? Could he? She looked at her scarred leg, her fingers worrying the raised edge of the worst scar on her face. Then her eyes read again his letter. *My sweet Gaia* —she skimmed over the first part about his man-to-man with Jarrah and whispered his last paragraph.

I am ashamed of myself for being so thoughtless on our last morning. I should have known that if I had to sneak away and hope to see you on the beach one last time, Jarrah would too. I should have known and made sure we were alone and could not be seen before we danced together, before I kissed you. It was selfish of me and I can only hope Jarrah will forgive me and won't blame you. But I can't feel sorry that we did dance and we did kiss, because for me it was the most beautiful moment of my life. I understand that for you this isn't so important. You are just starting out on your adult life, and I am about the only man you've so far had the chance to meet. All I hope for is that we can be friends, and see where it might lead. Please write to me, Gaia, at least once, so I know how you are feeling about us, and if you can forgive me for hurting Jarrah and for kissing you. Yours, Seamus.

Gaia had already tried to write to Seamus, but failed miserably to say what she wanted to say or even what she thought she should say. This afternoon she would try again. Perhaps she would tell him the story of how Dad met Margot and fell in love.

～

DEAR SEAMUS,

Thank you for writing so quickly. Your letter made me sad and happy. I'm not sure I could have said those things to Jarrah, but I think what you said was just right. It's horrible not being told the truth when you're a kid. Thankfully I got your letter before I posted the letter I had already written to him. So I have written him a new letter and in my own way tried to say the same sorts of things that you did. As long as he knows I will always love him as much as I love Bron, and that's about as big as it is possible to love anyone.

What you said about how it takes ages for adults to find out if they are in love, and Jarrah saying his parents never loved each other, made me think about my parents. My dad used to tell us a bedtime story. He was a country boy and had lived at Goshawk Gardens with his parents all his life. When he left school his father thought he should go to college, so he did an agricultural diploma in Perth, and turned out to be quite good at it. He got a taste for seeing more of the world than Western Australia and was accepted on a horticulture exchange scheme which involved working on crop farms and in food processing plants in New York State. Every second month he went to New York City for classes, and stayed with some other exchange students in an apartment in Brooklyn. One of the other guys was dating a dancer in the Corps de Ballet of the American Ballet Theatre and he convinced Dad—Joe—to come with him to a performance of 'Giselle'. Joe went only because he wanted to see the Metropolitan Opera House and that's where the ballet was being staged. He knew nothing about ballet. (Mum would always pipe in at that point and say he still didn't). After it was over they met up at a jazz club with his friend's girl and some other dancers in the Corps. Margot was one of them. Dad would say how he'd picked her out in the Corps on stage and fallen instantly in love with her and Mum would roll her eyes and say that the whole point of the Corps is that they all looked and danced exactly the same. "Where was I?" she'd ask, and Dad would wink at us. "Third from the left in the back row" he'd say. "Wrong," Mum would say. "I was second from the right in the front row. The one you fell in love with was Mary-Lou." "Shit," Dad would say. "But never mind, you're all the same."

They had an on-off relationship for a few years (Dad would say he never even looked at another woman the whole time) and after Dad's two-year exchange scheme program finished he had to save up and return to New York as a tourist every year. Margot got to be Principal Dancer by the time she was 25, and Dad still waited. Then just before she turned 30, she began to have bad problems with her ankle. The company made her retire from dancing and offered her a job as a Ballet Master. But that's not what she wanted, and she finally decided to marry Joe. She got pregnant almost immediately (Dad always winked at us then) and baby Oberon was born. Dad still couldn't get US residency so they moved to Australia and I was born three years later.

I miss them both so much, but I miss Dad the most. I'm more like him inside than I was ever like Mum. If he was here I would tell him I'm beginning to understand what he felt when he first met his Margot.

Still your new best friend, Gaia.

CHAPTER 18

*G*aia stood up, arched her aching back and swiped her hand through her sweaty hair. Rita Roo lifted her head and then hopped over to the side of the barn, disappearing in the shade.

"Surprise!"

Gaia started as Seamus came into the sun. "Shit. You gave me a fright. What are you doing here? Is it Jarrah?"

Seamus shook his head and walked towards her. "No. Jarrah's fine. Everything's fine. I had a few days off and thought I'd come and see you. Camp somewhere. I've got four days. Is it OK?"

"Oh. Goodness. I look a mess."

"You look beautiful. I've missed you."

"Truly?"

"Truly."

"Is Jarrah back at Auntie Mary's?"

"No, he's stuck at school. It's just me. Sorry."

"Poor Jarrah. I bet he wanted to skip school and come with you." Gaia grinned.

"Well, actually he doesn't know I'm here. Nor do Mary and Eddie."

"Oh. So where's your camp, or are you on your way further north? You never did get up there last time."

"I was hoping I could camp somewhere on your land. Out of your sight."

Gaia's hand came up and touched Seamus's cheek. "But not out of my mind," she said.

THAT DAY AND THE NEXT WENT BY AND IT FELT TO GAIA THAT someone had put a spell on them, a spell she never wanted to break. They got closer and closer, tentative kisses, Seamus watching her dancing at dawn and sometimes dancing with her, the spell of snorkeling over the reef and searching, unsuccessfully, for weedy seadragons. On Sunday morning the tide was too low to snorkel and they took a picnic to the lake, soaking up the still-warm sun, racing each other across the lake, the water already feeling colder as autumn crept nearer. They could have been on an uninhabited island; seeing no one, not even Mary and Eddie. Seamus had stayed hidden in his tent on Saturday morning when Eddie came by to collect Gaia's produce to take to market. Gaia had felt bad about sort of lying to him; as if he or Mary would ever had said a word or thought anything bad. She would tell them after Seamus went back to Perth. They probably knew he was here anyway. There wasn't much they didn't see.

Over their evening meals she and Seamus talked. Once they began it seemed nothing could stop them. It was as if neither of them had opened their past to anyone before. For Gaia it felt more intimate than even their kisses. Seamus's stories of his childhood immersed her in him: growing up in a poor area of Belfast, Black Friday when he was eleven and the IRA bombed the shite out of Belfast and all the shite that followed that, and then his dad killing himself only two months later. And Gaia talked about Bron, the brother she adored, looked up to, the only family she had left. Her crazy hopes that one day he would return and surprise her and take away her fear that he had died somewhere alone.

She could see the anger boiling away inside Seamus as she talked. Why couldn't she feel like that? Perhaps then she could let go of her dream that one day Bron would come home and he'd have a good explanation about why he'd never even written to her. She read Seamus the letter Bron had left at Mary and Eddie's for her to read when she finally returned to Goshawk Gardens, and, of course, ended up crying. "He must be dead," she said. "If he was alive he would have come home, or at least sent me another letter."

"Don't think that. There's no reason to think he's not living his life somewhere, trying to be happy," Seamus said. "He's got to feel feckin' guilty for staying away so long, for bloody leaving you in the first place. Perhaps he blames himself for the fire, for not saving you."

Gaia nodded, her tears still falling. "He did save me. I would have burned to death if it hadn't been for him. I don't think the fire started in the basement. I remember checking that his cigarette was properly out. We were always so careful about anything that might start a fire. It was something else, I can feel it. Something to do with Mum and Dad."

"Well, probably the reason will stay a secret. The important thing is that you are here with me, and the loveliest girl I have ever known."

"Don't be silly." Gaia laughed through her tears, then touched his lips with hers.

～

SHE COULD SEE SEAMUS HAD SOMETHING ON HIS MIND ON Sunday. He even said he didn't want eggs.

"What's the matter? Are you sick?"

Seamus shook his head. "Sad because it's my last day."

"Don't let's talk about that. I want it to be the best day so I can remember it while you're away."

Seamus smiled and leaned across the table, kissing her as he liked to do right on the tip of her nose. "But it's something else. I'm not sure I should even say it, it's none of my business."

"Well, you have to now. Go for it. I can take it." She hesitated as a horrible thought came to her. "Unless this is it and you're not ever coming back." Her throat was so tight she had to swallow before she could get the next words out. "You're going back to Ireland."

"No, no. It's nothing like that."

"So, what is it then?" she asked.

Seamus closed his eyes for a moment. "I quite often work on the Burns Ward at the hospital. The patients there need lots of pushing about to treatment rooms and sometimes I have to help lift them and things like that. I sometimes play cards with this guy Derek after I finish work. He showed me the photos of him before he'd had much plastic surgery, years ago, and he's getting more plastic surgery on the scars now. They are already massively improved. All sorts of new techniques have been developed since he was burned."

"Poor man. He's brave going through it all again," Gaia shuddered. "Are you telling me this so I know you understand what I went through?"

"I don't know, no, that's not why. I can't bear to think about what you went through. It's hard enough even working in the ward as an orderly. I wanted to tell you about this plastic surgeon there. Murray Belfer. I've actually sat at the same table in the cafeteria with him a couple of times, he's not the least stuck up like some of them. Just wanted to talk to me about my travels and Ireland. His dad came from Londonderry and he's been there a couple of times."

Gaia stayed silent. What did he really want to say?

"Gaia, I've watched him with his patients; they really like

him. He sits down and chats with them about the book they're reading and what music they like and asks them about their family. Derek told me Belfer is the absolute top burns plastic surgeon in Australia, and compared to the treatments Derek had in the past, this time it's way easier."

"You're telling me I should get my scars fixed? Is that what you think?" Gaia yanked her hair across the scars on her face.

"No, no, no. Don't do that Gaia, not with me. I don't care about your scars. Christ, I don't even see them. I should never have brought this up." He got up and walked back and forth, back and forth across the paving stones, disturbing Rita Roo from her spot under the table. She bunny-hopped crossly over to the edge of the patio and started grazing.

"Sit down, for heaven's sake. Sorry I bit your head off." Gaia didn't know whether to scream or cry or giggle as he paced away.

Seamus sat back down. "So, do you want me to tell you why I even brought it up at all?" Now he sounded grumpy.

"Go on. I'm all ears."

"I was just wondering if having your scars made even less obvious might help you feel confident enough to go back to dancing. Perhaps train for some sort of career in dancing?"

Gaia's head throbbed.

"What do you think? Perhaps you could see him, Murray Belfer? See what he says? When I get back from New Zealand I could come up here and drive you to Perth and back home again if you did want to see him. As a bonus, you could see Jarrah and meet his friends and Hannah."

Gaia looked down. "There's no point. I hated being in hospital and away from here. I'm used to who I am now. "

"Is it because your plastic surgery was so hard?" Seamus asked.

She nodded but couldn't raise her head. "That's part of it, I suppose. And plastic surgery takes forever. Who would look after Rita Roo and my gardens?"

"Mary and Eddie would, you know that. And I'd be with you in Perth, Jarrah too, if you decided to go ahead. All you would need first is an assessment, that's all. It wouldn't mean you would have to have anything done, even if it turned out to be possible."

She looked up, her eyes swimming as he returned her gaze. "Would it matter a lot to you if I didn't have these on my face and everywhere?" She crossed her arms across her chest. He hadn't seen her worst scars. He didn't know she hardly had a right breast. Try fixing that with easy-peasy plastic surgery.

"Oh, Gaia, how can you think that? I care about you; you must know that. I don't even notice your scars. I just want you to be able to feel free to do whatever you want; perhaps even go to dance school."

"Even if my scars completely vanished, no dance school would ever take me on now. I'm way too old."

"You're only eighteen. I bet there are great ballet dancers who didn't even start until then. And if there aren't you can be the first."

That made her smile. "Perhaps I can train as a marine biologist and then I can stay right here and study seadragons with Jarrah."

"That would be bliss. Or we could set up as an Irish jig duo. But think about it; having the assessment. I'm sure you would like Murray Belfer or I would never in a trillion years even suggest it."

"OK. I'll write and let you know if I do decide." She turned and put an arm around Rita Roo who had sidled up to her. "But Seamus, don't get your hopes up. I'm truly fine as I am."

"All I hope is for you to be happy. If you did want to have a career in dance, no one would give a toss about your scars."

CHAPTER 19

hey were going to see Gaia again. Him and Seamus. He wished he could go alone but it didn't cost the bus fare to go with Seamus. They were getting on good again anyway. And when they got back Seamus was going to New Zealand for ages and there was a school holiday while he was away and he'd have enough for the bus fare by then. It would be just him and Gaia like it used to be. Jarrah wrapped his arms around himself and hugged himself tight. He felt bigger than he used to be. Shooting up, Hannah said. Soon he would be almost as tall as Gaia.

They left Perth at seven on Saturday morning, and had to drive back on Sunday afternoon. Hardly any time. Seamus had brought a box full of food for everyone.

"What's in it?" Jarrah asked, itching to look. They didn't get many chocolates and things at the kid's home.

"Hmm, well for your Auntie and Uncle there are some big fat juicy steaks, and some olives, and some cheeses, and a giant box of chocolates."

"They'll like that. They probably get sick of rabbit and fish."

"Hope so. But wait 'til you see what I've got for our picnic lunch we can have when we arrive. You, Gaia and me."

"What?"

"You'll have to wait and see."

"What about chocolate?"

"Like I said me little snooper, wait and see."

"Auntie will give me some of their chocolates."

"You'll be too full to eat any by the time we've eaten all the picnic."

~

GAIA TRIED TO STOP THINKING ABOUT TOMORROW AFTERNOON and the next day and the next day and on and on for weeks without seeing Seamus again and enjoy now. They were sitting on a rug under a shady tree with the white sand and turquoise sea of the bay looking like a postcard. The three of them chomping on crusty-bread sandwiches, stuffed with ham and some type of soft cheese, and a fancy delicatessen salad, and a chocolate cake with a filling of cream and cherries about an inch thick. Jarrah wasn't so keen on the fancy sandwich fillings but he managed two enormous slices of the cake, along with two bottles of teeth-rotting coke. Seamus and Gaia stuck to the iced tea with lemon, somewhat reluctantly keeping the bottle of Savignon Blanc to share with Mary and Eddie at dinner that evening.

When they had licked the last crumbs of chocolate cake from their fingers, Seamus dipped his hand into his backpack and pulled out a small parcel wrapped in silver paper. "A thank-you gift, " he said, handing it to Gaia.

"Thank you for what?" Gaia said, her face hot under her tattered straw hat.

"For letting me show up like this and camp on your land, and for teaching me how to dance, and snorkel. And for being you," he said.

"Open it," Jarrah said, bouncing on his backside.

Gaia scratched at the sellotape, but it was stuck fast.

"Give it to me," Jarrah said. "I'll do it." He grabbed it out of Gaia's hands and within a second he'd neatly pulled the sellotape free. "Here, you can open it now." He gave it back to Gaia.

She unwrapped the pretty paper and lifted out the small gray case. She looked up at Seamus, her eyebrows arched into her hair.

"Unzip it," he said, grinning. "It won't bite."

Gaia did as she was told and pulled out a camera. She turned it over and turned it back as Jarrah's hand hovered over it.

"It's nothing fancy, " Seamus said. "I thought you could take photos of the beach, and the lake, and Rita Roo. Anything you like." He pulled out a brown paper bag from his backpack. "I've got you four films and there's already one in the camera. The films are dead easy to load, just follow the instructions. Gaia opened the tiny manual that had fallen out when she'd opened the camera case. "When you finish a film —there are 24 photos on each—you put it in one of these envelopes and stick it in your post box. They're all prepaid; the postage and the film developing. You'll get back the negatives and two copies of each of the prints once the chemist in Perth where I got them develops them. Probably take about a week I suppose. I thought if you had two copies of each you could keep one set for yourself and you'd be able to give Jarrah, or me, or Mary and Eddie, photos you think we might like.

"You can take photos of us," Jarrah said, his hands hovering over the camera. "I can take photos of you, and you can send me them and I can stick them on the wall by my bed."

Gaia grinned at him and gave him the camera. "I think you'd be better at this than me," she said. "You could take photos of Hannah and all your friends."

Seamus frowned at her. "It's for you, Gaia. To make memories of everything you love here. The sunrises, the sunsets, your gardens, us too of course if you like." He put his arm around Jarrah's shoulders. I have an old camera just the same, and you can have it. I'll give it to you when we get back to Perth and you both can send me photos when I'm away and that will stop me feeling homesick for the wicked pair of you."

"Really?" Jarrah said, his dark eyes sparkling. "A camera for me to actually keep?"

"Yep. And some films as well to start you off. After you've used them up you'll have to save up for more though, so you'll need to be choosy about what photos you take."

Jarrah handed the camera back to Gaia and she took it and carefully zipped it back into its case. "Thank you," she said. She wanted to kiss Seamus right then but instead grinned at Jarrah.

Late that afternoon Gaia tried out her camera. She took photos of Jarrah and Seamus and Roo with the sunset behind them, and then let Jarrah take a photo of her and Seamus, although she took some persuading. "Only our top halves and my left side," she said. Then Seamus admitted he had his own camera with him. "There won't be time to get your photos developed and sent to me before I leave for New Zealand, so can I take a couple of photos of you and Jarrah to take with me?"

Gaia nodded, surprising herself. Sitting here in the sun with Seamus and Jarrah she felt almost pretty.

Then they swam because the tide was perfect, but didn't snorkel as they had forgotten to bring their snorkels and face-masks and were too lazy to go back to the barn and get them. The seadragons wouldn't be there anyway. It was late after-noon before they wandered back to the barn, salt on their skin, sun in their hearts.

Back at the barn, they had turns in Gaia's outdoor shower and then wandered over to Auntie's and more food. Gaia still felt too full to eat, but perhaps dinner would be late tonight. Seamus had offered to barbecue the steaks over a campfire. Auntie seemed to like that idea. Gaia took a deep breath. She'd been putting off talking about her scars. But she had to get it out of the way before Seamus left. She'd been waiting until she and Seamus were alone but Jarrah wasn't about to let that happen. Anyway, he could hear what she had to say. It was no big deal. She took another deep breath. "Seamus, I've thought about what you said about my scars. I don't think I can do it. The very thought gives me the shits. I hate hospitals. I never ever want to be stuck in one again. And I don't want to go to Perth."

"Fair enough. But it could be a really quick visit. We could drive there one day and I would have you back here the next," Seamus said. "You could even see Murray Belfer in his private rooms. You wouldn't have to go near the hospital."

"Who's Murray Belfer?" Jarrah asked.

"He's a doctor at the hospital. He fixes people's scars so they can hardly be seen," Seamus said.

"Gaia would hate all the cars and people and stuff in Perth."

Seamus took Gaia's hand and squeezed it. "I know she would. But it would be nice if she could see where you live and meet Hannah and your friends there, wouldn't it?"

Jarrah glared at him. "She doesn't want to go." He grabbed Gaia's other hand.

"It's OK Jarrah," Gaia said, grinning at him. "Seamus is only trying to help. One day I'll come and meet Hannah and Maisie and all the others, but no doctors if I can help it. I've had enough of them to last a lifetime."

THEY HAD THEIR BARBECUE UNDER THE STARS AND ATE HALF the chocolates and drank the wine and it was almost midnight by the time Gaia stumbled sleepily to her feet. "Bedtime for me," she said. "It's been the perfect day." Feeling suddenly weepy, she turned away and pulled on her jacket. Seamus leapt up, saying he'd walk back with her, as he had to go past her barn on the way to his tent.

"I'll come too," said Jarrah, as quick as a weasel.

"Hadn't you better get yourself to bed?" Seamus said. "It's been a long day."

Gaia glanced at Mary, hoping she'd back Seamus up, but she seemed oblivious to the need for an eleven-year-old to get to bed before midnight. "Don' you make noise when y'come back then," is all she said.

For all Gaia knew Jarrah never even went to bed because when she got up next morning there he was, outside the barn with Rita Roo. On guard. She looked around, hoping Seamus might appear. It was their only chance to dance with the dawn. "He'll be down there waiting," said Jarrah, reading her mind. So they danced together, all three of them, her family.

It wasn't until they left Goshawk Gardens on Sunday afternoon that Seamus finally got to kiss her. In front of Jarrah of course. But he kissed her on the mouth anyway, quickly, then pulled back and captured her eyes. "I'll write from New Zealand," he said. He pushed a large envelope into her hand. "There are some aerogrammes in here with Jimmy's address on them. They include the right postage. We'll be based at his flat in Queenstown."

Gaia kissed him again, another simply-sweet kiss, nothing Jarrah could be hurt by. "OK," she mouthed. Then a whisper. "Four weeks seems a long time."

She hugged Jarrah last. Tight. Like Bron hugged her. Had sometimes hugged her long ago. When she let Jarrah go he looked into her eyes, this boy who once only looked at the ground. "Don't be sad, Gaia," he said. "I'll be back as soon as soon, I promise."

~

RITA ROO DISAPPEARED A FEW DAYS AFTER JARRAH AND
Seamus drove off into the sunset. Gaia wasn't too worried at
first; the roo often went walkabout for a few days, but never for
longer than a week. But the week passed, then another, and
she still hadn't returned. Mary and Eddie thought she might
have a joey in her pouch. "'Bout time init. She ready. P'raps
she come back with joey soon."

But Gaia wasn't convinced. What if Dave had shot her for
dog tucker? She'd be easy to shoot, she was so tame. It was
lonely without her. Lonely knowing Jarrah was stuck in Perth.
Lonely wondering what Seamus was doing, whether he was
meeting lots of pretty girls who weren't afraid of cities and
people. Dancing on the beach at dawn became too hard. She
was so tired and the air so early in the morning was too chilly.
The days were nice; they didn't get a real autumn here, but
even working in her gardens didn't help her mood much.
Some days she forced herself to do some barre work later in
the day, but she hated seeing her face in the big mirrors, her
scars screaming back at her. What was the point, anyway? She
was never going to dance anywhere but on the beach all by
herself. No one to watch her; not even Rita Roo. No one to
dance with, no one to care.

She wrote to Jarrah every week and he wrote to her. If his
letter didn't arrive every Wednesday her whole world turned
even grayer. The only bright spot was when she got back the
photos they'd taken on the camera Seamus had given her. She
carefully pinned the best ones above the old kitchen bench:
Jarrah, Seamus and Rita Roo; Seamus with his arm around
Gaia, their faces glowing in the evening light, and even one of
her dancing on the beach. The second copy of each of them
she sent to Jarrah. She wrote to Seamus every Sunday, but the
space on an aerogramme didn't give much room. Not that she
had anything to say that was different. He had left her four

aerogrammes so she couldn't write more often even if she wanted to. She had no idea how long a letter would even take to get to New Zealand, so she sent the first one on the Sunday that he flew out of Australia. By the time she posted the second letter, she still hadn't got even a postcard from him.

Every hour was endless, every day the same; she could see her life stretching forever as she got older and older, and uglier and uglier, and clumsier and clumsier. Lonelier and lonelier. Sometimes she would catch herself talking to herself and answering back like a crazy woman. She knew she needed to see someone, anyone. Just so she could remember how to have a conversation. Mary was her only friend, and they didn't have much conversation. She'd ask Eddie if she could go with him to the market on Saturday. Surely she could manage that?

❧

IT WAS OK. THE MARKET. SHE COPED AND EVEN MANAGED TO say a few words other than "That'll be a dollar, thanks." But she seemed to be the only one in the whole bustling market who knew no one. Even Eddie had folk hanging around his stall, yakking on while he sold stuff, and he usually wasn't much of a talker.

Seven days after he left Australia, Seamus's first letter arrived—well, not a letter, but a postcard of a lake and mountains, with a message *"Sweet Gaia, In Queenstown, off on a 4-day hike in the mountains tomorrow. Will write properly when I get back. Miss you SO MUCH. Love, Seamus xx."*

Then to make her day even more miserable, Mary and Eddie told her they were going up Country for a bit to hang out with Mary's mob. Would likely be back in about a month.

"My cuz come and do garden and fences and farm stuff, but him won't clean no house. How 'bout you do Mister Dave cleaning?" Mary said. "Mister Dave say if we don' get some fella to clean him house and wash him clothes we might find no job here when we get back. You get some cash for it. Not much but better 'n nothin'."

"How often? What would I have to do?" Gaia asked.

"Jus' sweep the floor 'bout once a week and do him shitty dishes p'raps two or three days in week. Throw out them whisky bottles and beer cans an' wash him sheets an' clothes sometime, else they stink the place out. An' you better set them rat traps in kitchen." Mary grinned. "Take out the dead ones first 'fore the maggots eat 'em."

Gaia shuddered. "It sounds gross. Especially if Dave's hanging around."

"He never there much. Jus' stay outta him way when him drunk."

"If I don't do it will you lose your job?"

"Might do, if boss get some other girl."

"I suppose I haven't got anything else to occupy me," Gaia said. "I'll come with you and see what you do."

"You good girl. Make sure boss give you your money. Him forget when he drunk."

CHAPTER 20

*I*t *was* gross. She shouldn't have waited a week after Mary and Eddie left before going to the house. She considered writing a note for Dave telling him she wasn't going to clean for him after all, but then she thought about Mary. What if he wouldn't give her the job back? Thankfully Dave's truck and his dog were gone and with luck he wouldn't come back for a week or more and next time she came she wouldn't have to spend over four hours trying to clean up his disgusting mess. It was impossible to even remember the Dave that had been her parents' friend. He'd been quite nice looking, and as far as she knew he wasn't a big drinker back then. A few beers on a Friday and Saturday, that's about all. And now look at him. Was it just because his wife had left him? Is that what happened to people who lived alone with no family or friends?

She got used to cleaning; it wasn't so bad. Dave never went into most of the rooms. The bathroom and kitchen were the worst. He never washed up any dishes, so there were stacks of plates on the table and kitchen bench, mostly with dried baked beans stuck on them and even disgusting sheep bones, already fly-blown. Beer bottles by the dozen. At least two empty whisky bottles a week.

On her second week cleaning he showed up, surprising her as he stomped through the back door and into the kitchen. He seemed as surprised as she was. "Gaia, g'day. Sorry about all the dishes. I never seem to have time to do them, what with old Eddie away. And that cousin of theirs is as useless as a rat without an arse."

Gaia dried her hands on the tattered tea towel. Was he sober? Seemed like it. "That's OK," she said. "It's my job. Thanks for the pay last week."

"You're a bloody sight better than Mary. She's as lazy as all that lot are."

Gaia stared at him but kept her lips buttoned.

"How about a nice cuppa? I could do with a bit of company. I bet you get lonely too, eh?"

Gaia shook her head. "No, not really. I've got too much to do in my gardens, on top of cleaning your place."

"Well, put the kettle on and we can have a natter. Catch up on things. We've been through a lot together; the fire and all."

Gaia filled the kettle and stuck it on the gas burner. "I'll make you some tea, but not for me, thanks. As soon as I finish these I have to get going." She turned towards him and jumped back. Dave had been standing right behind her.

"Don't be like that. I'll pay you extra if you keep me company for a bit."

Gaia shook her head and tried to sidestep him.

"Think you're too good to talk to me, is that it? Your mother didn't think like that."

Gaia shook his hand off her arm. "If you don't let me past I won't be cleaning your house any more." She stared him down, her heart pounding through her body.

"There's plenty of sheilas who would leap at the chance of such a cushy job, so you go and that'll be no work for Mary when they get back. Eddie can get lost as well. Huh, see if they can find another job and house." He shoved his face closer to hers, his foul breath making her gag. "No blighter 'round here will give them a job. There's no work even for whites, anyway."

Gaia shoved past him and grabbed the last of the dishes draining next to the sink. "I'm finished here. I'll clean your house but not if you're here in my way."

"For Christ's sake, lighten up. Anyone would think you hadn't known me since you were a baby. You and your brother would probably be dead if I hadn't saved you from the fire. No thanks for that. And for all the bloody burns I had to suffer."

"How did you know there was a fire? Were you there when it started?"

"I saw the bloody flames from here. Your parents had just left our place a while before and I was outside having a fag. I called the fire brigade and got in the truck and drove to your place like a maniac. Fucking terrible it was. Too late for Margot and Joe. You on fire on the ground and Bron in a fucking state. I managed to stop you burning to bloody death by the time the fire brigade arrived."

"I thought Bron smothered the flames?"

"He was in a panic. Christ, his hands were burning too, and he wasn't much more than a kid himself. He probably believed he helped, but he was useless. I thought it was best to let him think he'd acted the hero."

Gaia squeezed her eyes shut, Bron's face swimming in her head. Then she felt Dave's arm come around her as he pulled her against him.

"Get off me," she hissed, shoving him away.

He stepped back, his palms in the air. "Christ, keep your shirt on. I was only trying to comfort you."

"I don't need comforting. Thank you for what you did in the fire, but it's years ago now and it's over. I don't want to talk about it."

"All right, all right." The kettle was screaming and Dave

leaned over and turned the gas off. "Go and sit down and I'll make a cuppa."

"No thank you. I'm off now," Gaia said, her heart still pounding. She walked out the door, shutting it behind her, and then started to run, her legs shaking so much she tripped on a rough patch of dusty ground and fell heavily, grazing both knees as well as her hands.

She made sure Dave wasn't there after that whenever she went to clean, and got through her jobs in double-quick time, her ears always primed for the sound of his truck. But he never showed again when she was there, and every week her pay would be on the kitchen table, half again what Mary had been paid for the same job. Gaia figured it was bribe money; the creep knew he'd gone too far. If only Mary and Eddie would come back.

She missed Rita Roo. She missed Jarrah. She missed Seamus. Even Gos had all but deserted her. He showed up every couple of weeks but didn't hang around. He loved her only for the easy tucker she provided.

Then one morning as she was kneeling, weeding her garden, a soft nose poked between her arm and her body. "Rita Roo, oh Rita Roo, where have you been?" She turned and hugged her, tears streaming down her cheeks. And then she saw her pouch, more obvious than before. She would ask Mary, but she already knew. Rita Roo had a tiny joey growing in her pouch.

Seamus's first real letter arrived ten days after he'd left Australia. They'd had a great time on their hike, staying in huts and meeting all types of interesting characters. But mostly it was about Gaia and how he missed her. His words should have made her heart sing but instead she felt a new emotion. Jealousy? Gaia screwed up her face. He cared about her and he hadn't even mentioned any female characters in the huts. She didn't own him. She needed to get a life.

So she forced herself to get up at dawn, pushed herself

along the track to the beach, made herself dance. Terrible at first but she didn't give up. Rita Roo, with her joey snuggled deep in her warm pouch, watched her every morning and she almost believed that if she stopped they would disappear again. She began snorkeling again too, wearing a wetsuit now as the sea wasn't as warm as in the summer. She kept writing to Jarrah and Seamus, and she collected two more funny and silly letters from Seamus. She felt she almost knew Jimmy, his crazy friend. Would she ever be able to do something like that? Travel to exciting places?

Mary and Eddie showed up two days before Seamus was due to fly back to Australia. Gaia couldn't stop grinning that night; she hadn't realized quite what a toll cleaning Dave's house had been. Not the cleaning, but the hypervigilance that was ever necessary when she was in his house. She made sure Mary knew that the pay had gone up and left Dave a note, thanking him for the work and that Mary was pleased that the pay for the job had increased.

A week later Jarrah's letter gave her even more to grin about.

"Seamus told me he'd have to work flat out for ages when he gets back if he wants to keep his job at the hospital. So I'm coming to see you by myself next Saturday! I'm catching the bus and Hannah said cos I'll be 12 soon we can pretend that I'm already 12 so I'm allowed by the bus driver. Then I have to get the bus back again on Monday."

CHAPTER 21

"*C*oo-ee? Anyone home?"

Gaia returned to first position and frowned at herself in the mirror. Who on earth? She never got visitors. She walked over to the barn door, blinking as the bright afternoon sun hit her eyes. A man and a woman stood there, both dressed city casual, the woman carrying a briefcase. Light-colored trousers and nicely ironed white shirts with the sleeves rolled up. The woman's getup was a more feminine version of the man's. Gaia looked down at her stained tee-shirt and torn denim shorts. The scars on her right leg shone white against her healthy brown skin. Without thinking, she pulled her hair across her right cheek.

"Good afternoon," said the woman, in the voice that had coo-eed. "You must be Gaia Christie." She held out a slim hand and Gaia wiped her left hand on her shorts before taking it. It was more of a clasp and drop than a shake.

Gaia nodded, still holding her hair over her cheek. "Yes. Is there something wrong? Are you lost?"

The man grinned at her. "No, we're here to talk to you about something very exciting. I'm Colin Pritchard, and this is Suzanne Henderson. We're with Morton and McMillan,"

Gaia's heart stopped. "Is it Bron? Are you lawyers? Have you found him?"

"Bron? No, sorry. Who's Bron?"

"My brother. I haven't heard from him for years. I thought..." Gaia's voice petered out as a tide of disappointment surged through her.

"We're so sorry," said the woman. "Is Bron short for Oberon?"

"Yes. How did you know his name?"

"It was on the title deeds to this property. Your name and Oberon Christie."

"Who are you then? How do you know that?"

"It's public information. Look, can we sit down? Perhaps out here at your table? We've got some drawings to show you," said the man. "We're from a Perth company that develops beautiful holiday resorts."

"This property isn't for sale if that's what you're after," Gaia said.

"Look, we've been negotiating with your neighbor, Dave Mason. He can see what a fantastic opportunity this is. Just give us half an hour to explain before you make a snap decision."

Pushing down the fury boiling in her gut Gaia sat down, no longer bothering to cover her scarred face. "What's Dave negotiating?" she asked, fear replacing her fury.

The man, Colin—she'd always disliked that name—was already spreading a large map on the table between them. "Look, here's Mr Mason's property inside the red line. He's got 200 acres, mostly farmland, but it includes the south half of this lake and the south beach front—a shoreline about two kilometers—and all this bush between the lake and the beach. Your property has the blue line around it. It's much smaller of course—forty acres—but it's mostly wilderness and includes the north end of the lake and the north stretch of the beach front. Our proposal is to build a small settlement around the lake and in the trees fringing the beach; about 50 cabins, with walking paths through the bush and an administration building with a upmarket restaurant and perhaps a gymnasium between the lake and the beach. Very tasteful. The buildings will all be in natural timbers. Half will be individually owned by people who use them as holiday homes or retirees who use it as their permanent residence. The others will be holiday rentals, administered by Morton and McMillan. There'll be staff cabins around the admin building for a manager and the restaurant and cleaning staff."

Gaia stared at him. Was he for real?

The woman—Suzanne—reached a hand across the table and patted Gaia's arm. "It's a lot to digest," she said. "The best thing is that we could plan it so you retain this patch of land with your lovely gardens, and we could build you a beautiful home here. You could even keep this quaint barn; perhaps we could turn it into a double garage. In fact, if you wanted to, you could still keep your market garden business. Goodness, think how much you could sell to the restaurant and to the holiday renters and residents. Not that you'd need the money. Wait until you see what our company is offering for the land." She beamed.

Gaia shook her head. "No way. This is a wilderness area. What would happen to all the birds and animals if you did this?"

"They'd be part of it. That's the point. City people love coming for holidays in places like this. Wilderness experiences are the thing nowadays."

"No."

"Look," said Colin, "give it some time. Talk to your neighbor about it. He's on the verge of signing. We're thinking of repurposing his farmhouse for the admin building; moving it to the lake edge and restoring and extending it. We could have a small museum section in the information bay showing the history of the place. How your family started the market gardens here."

"Yes, and perhaps a display about your mother," said Suzanne. "That would be lovely; a tribute to a great American ballet dancer and how she fell in love with an Aussie gardener and gave up her career for love."

"How do you know all this?" Gaia asked, her head feeling as if it was being slowly squeezed in a giant clamp.

Colin tapped the side of his nose. "Ah, we could tell you but then we'd have to kill you."

"Stop it, Colin," Suzanne said, slapping the top of his hand. "Ignore him, that's his idea of a joke. We need to make absolutely sure our developments are going to work before we approach landowners, so we do extensive research first. It would be terrible to get landowners all excited and then not be able to carry through."

"I suppose it would, but it seems like a crazy waste of time and money, all that planning, if the landowners haven't even put their land on the market."

"You'd be surprised how many have never even thought of selling up until we show them what their land could become. They have no idea," Suzanne said, taking out some more sheets of paper. "Look at these artist's sketches. Aren't they extraordinary?"

Gaia looked. Cabins tucked between tall eucalypts and scattered artfully along the edge of the beach. No untidy Casuarina trees with their carpets of needles littering the sand. Where were they? Beach umbrellas and loungers here and there on the sand where she danced. Families in the water, masks and snorkels at the ready, eager to find a pair of sea-dragons. She had a sudden image of herself throwing up all over the glossy bullshit. She felt nauseous enough.

"We can leave copies of the maps and sketches for you to look at. We have floor plans for the different cabins as well. Of course, yours could be one of the larger ones; perhaps the

'Traveller's Rest' plan. That's my favorite. Although I think that's the one your Mr Mason was keen on for his residence, so perhaps you'd want a different one." She pulled more paper from her bottomless brief case. "'Lake Idyll' is lovely too. Let me show you that plan."

"He's not my Mr Mason. I hardly know him."

"I thought he'd saved your lives in that terrible fire. Your brother and you?" Suzanne said, her eyes wide.

"My brother saved my life, not Dave Mason. Are you telling me that he is going along with this... this development?"

"He's very excited about it," Colin said. "There are just a few details to work through before it's finalized."

"Like how much money he can get for it, you mean," Gaia said.

"Well that's always a big part of it, of course. That and making sure he's happy with our ecological values. Like you, he cares about the wilderness. But he can see this is going to enhance the whole area; save the wilderness for future generations to enjoy."

"So how much are you offering him?" Gaia said.

"Well, that's confidential, of course, but as well as keeping a patch for himself with a beautiful home built for him, we're talking six figures for his 200 acres. A great deal more than he could ever get if he sold it as a farm."

"And if I won't sell you my bit? Will that mean you can't go ahead?" Gaia asked, her fingers crossed beneath the table.

"We'd negotiate that bridge if we ever came to it," Colin said, his smirk replaced by a serious mask. "Obviously, the integrity of the concept would be rather fractured if parts of the lake and beach weren't included."

"What we'd love to do is bring you to Perth where our architects and planners can talk you through all the possibilities. We can show you one of our resorts on the coast just south of Perth, then take you for dinner in their amazing restaurant. Put you up in one of their 5-star cabins for the night. You'll adore it. It's a stunning beach; a different style to your beach of course, massive surf and wild as," Suzanne said, her arms flailing about as she presumably tried to demonstrate the magnificence of her offer, the resort, and the surf.

"I'm afraid I couldn't get to Perth. I don't drive," Gaia said.

"Good heavens, we wouldn't expect you to! We'd take you there in our car and bring you back the next day. Or you could have two days at the resort, so you could see how wonderfully it all worked." She laughed. "Just think, you too could have all this right here, and a wonderful new home *and* a truckload of cash!"

For a split second Gaia almost said yes to the Perth trip. She'd never cave in and sell her gardens and the seadragons, but it would be something different. Why not get a free holiday out of them? How hard could it be? She'd know no one there so it wouldn't matter how she looked. She shook her head. "No, thank you. I'll never sell, whatever you offer. Never."

WHEN SHE WOKE ON SATURDAY, IT TOOK HER A FEW SECONDS to work out why she felt lighter. The air had felt ominous since the sales duo had left, leaving their plans and maps and still trying to convince her to change her mind, telling her that she really should have a chat with Dave. Since they'd disappeared down the track, every unexpected noise—the snap of a twig, a sudden gust of wind, a shadow thrown across her path as a cloud passed over the sun—had quivered through her like an electric current as she waited for him to appear. But he didn't.

But this afternoon, Jarrah would arrive. After his market day was finished, Eddie was going to pick him up from the bus in Jurien Bay. Tonight she was going to eat with them all, and tomorrow she and Jarrah would dance on the beach at dawn. She'd been too scared to dance since her visit from the hateful duo with their perfect clothes and white teeth. Bugger them. Bugger Dave. Why the hell should she let him rule her emotions. Drunk slob. Even if he did show up she could probably down him with one strong ballet kick in his balls. She'd make Jarrah's favorite herb bread and then go for a swim in the lake. Her lake.

Feeling cool and relaxed after her swim, the smell of her bread filling the barn, Gaia sat down at the old piano. She'd taken up playing pretty much daily over the past few weeks, even attempting singing along. She and Bron had both had piano lessons from Margot as an adjunct to their ballet, and Gaia could still sight-read. Her latest venture was trying to play Scott Joplin's 'Maple Leaf Rag'; the sheet music was in the pile in the cupboard and she'd heard it on the radio the other day. It had taken her back to the times when she was little and her dad and mum had danced to it. Danced together. Her dad would throw Margot around like a rag doll, and she'd be laughing and he'd be glowing and sometimes he'd spin Margot free so she could dance with Bron, and her dad would dance with her. When did that all stop? Was she about ten? Twelve even?

Gaia stuck her piano-practice tape in the tape recorder and pushed the record button. She was nothing if not determined. Play it through, listen to her pitiful attempts, play it again and again. Tomorrow she'd play it for Jarrah. They could invent a dance to go with it. Dance to her recording. It was the perfect style for Jarrah; much less exacting than ballet for his uneven gait. She could incorporate a sort of lopsided step into the music.

"Catchy music. Didn't know that old piano could still make a noise."

Gaia's hands froze above the keys. She took a breath and

twisted around on the piano stool. "What are you doing here? You gave me a bloody fright sneaking up on me like that."

"Not my fault you didn't hear me knock. Just making a neighborly visit." Dave sneered, his whisky-and-onion breath bringing her hand up to block off her nose. "Thought it was time we had a chat about this fancy real estate plan. If we teamed up I reckon we could get them to cough up a lot more."

"I'm not selling my property and you shouldn't either."

"Too late. I've already given them my word that I'll sell once the price is right. And I never break my promises."

"How can you? They'll destroy it."

"What's to destroy? Bloody vegetables that are more fucking trouble than they're worth. I don't even make enough to pay your precious mates. Good for nothin' Abos. Pocket most of what they get for themselves, I reckon."

"How dare you say that. Eddie and Mary both work their butts off for you and you treat them like shit. I don't know why they stay."

"Well, they don't most of the time, do they. Always on one of their convenient walk-abouts. Spending my cash."

Gaia stood up, her hands clenched. "Get out of here. And don't come back."

Dave was in her face, his big filthy hands digging into her bare arms, his greasy hair hitting her across her cheek as he shook her.

"Take your hands off me," she hissed, and brought her knee up to smash into his balls. But all she hit was his thigh, and then she was shoved back against the piano.

"Quite the little wild cat. Just like your mother. She was a tigress when she wanted something bad enough."

"What did you do to her?"

"Wouldn't you like to know. Well, I'll bloody well tell you. I gave her the best fuckings she'd ever had. Old Joe was no fun at all, that's what she said. Bloody growing flowers was all he could do. Bored Margot silly. You lot all bored her silly."

"Shut-up, you creep. How dare you lie about her. How dare you."

"You were just a silly little kid prancing about with that pansy brother of yours. You didn't have a clue. She was leaving you and we were pissing off away from you lot. You'd never see her again."

With all the force she had in her, Gaia pushed her arms out to the sides and Dave's right hand slammed into the piano.

"Shit, you fucking little wild cat." Gaia's face whipped to one side as Dave's left hand crashed into her cheek. Dazed, she tried to push him away. He stepped suddenly backwards, toppling her off balance and catapulting her into his chest. Vomit filled her mouth as the stink of stale sweat and onions and whisky pushed up her nose as he clamped his arms around her. Dragging her away from the piano he shoved her hard down on the floor and sat on her, one hand on her throat. She heard her own strangled yelp, and forced her legs to kick. Then she was choking, unable to breathe, as his hand pressed down on her neck.

"Lie still, bitch." He grabbed the neck of her shirt and yanked it so hard the buttons ripped off and she felt the air on her bare skin.

"Christ, what the fuck?" His hand came off her neck and she saw him staring at her chest, his face ugly with disgust. Behind him the late afternoon sun was blasting through the open door, turning him into a monstrous silhouette. Then caught in a shard of light she saw a figure in the doorway, his arms raised, and then she heard a sickening thud before she was squashed under Dave's dead-weight body.

CHAPTER 22

"Gaia," Jarrah screamed, squatting down beside her and pushing and shoving at Dave's body. "Has he hurt you?"

Gaia tried to raise her body to help him and felt Mason's weight lift as he rolled off her, turning over so he was flat on his back beside her. She rolled the other way and grabbed Jarrah's hands as he pulled her up. "What did he do to you, he was going to kill you," Jarrah's words tumbled over each other as he stared past Gaia at the man on the floor.

"Quick, we've got to tie him up before he comes around," Gaia said, blood pumping so hard through her that she thought she might have a heart attack. She saw the spade on the floor and at the same time realized her shirt was hanging open. Grabbing the two ripped sides she pulled them together, but Jarrah hadn't even seemed to notice.

"Is he dead?" he said. "Did I kill him?"

"Shit, I hope not. Get that rope. It's outside where the snorkeling gear is. You know, it's hanging on a hook there."

"But he might attack you again. I'll sit on him while you get the rope."

Gaia was on her knees, her ear close to Mason's mouth.

"Thank god, he's breathing. He's just knocked out. Hurry up and get the rope before he comes around."

Jarrah ran and Gaia swallowed bile as she stared at the creep. He would have raped her if he hadn't seen her chest. If Jarrah hadn't cracked him over the head with the spade. He was back now and they rolled Mason over and tied his hands tight behind his back.

"His feet too, look, the rope's long enough. That will stop him from getting up," Jarrah said. He was already wrapping the end of the rope around Dave's filthy ankles.

"Right. He's not going to get out of that. Let's roll him on his side. We don't want him to choke to death."

"Why not? Serves him right." Jarrah sounded like he might cry now.

"I know, and you saved my life. But it would get messy if he died because we might get blamed or something." Gaia pushed Mason onto his side but his weight turned him back onto his face. She had to stop herself from standing up and stamping on his head.

"Grab those chairs. We'll get him on his side again and stick the chairs by him so he can't roll onto his face again."

That done, they looked at each other. The expression on Jarrah's face seemed almost triumphant, but then a bit wobbly. Pretty much the way she was feeling. Gaia grabbed Jarrah's hand and moved away from Mason to the barn door, her finger over her lips. "Don't want him to hear us if he wakes up," she whispered, once they were outside. "Can you run and get Uncle Eddie? Ask him to bring the truck. We have to get the creep away from here. Probably take him to the Jurien Bay hospital, but Jarrah, we can't let anyone know you hit him with the spade."

"Why not? He would've hurt you if I hadn't. I wouldn't care if I did kill him."

"I know. And thank god you arrived like Superman. I didn't think you'd be getting here until later. But Jarrah, we don't want to have to spend days at the police station and even have to go to court to prove he was going to hurt me. What if they don't believe us? I think we should say we found him on the concrete by his house. He could have fallen off the bedroom deck. He stinks of booze so that would be easy enough to believe."

"But he'll tell them what happened when he wakes up," Jarrah said, his face scrunched up.

"He might, or he might be too scared to. He'd know I would accuse him of attacking me first if he did. Perhaps he won't even remember. When people get knocked out they often lose their memory, especially if they are already drunk."

"I suppose. What will I tell Uncle Eddie?"

"Just tell him to come fast. I'll tell him what happened. You don't need to. Don't say anything ever to anyone about the spade. I'll shove it back in the garden."

"OK. I'll be as quick as I can." He took a big breath and then ran, his lurching gait almost bringing Gaia to tears.

Back in the barn she pulled off her ripped shirt and stuffed it in the cupboard before putting a tee-shirt on. Feeling less vulnerable without her chest scars on display, she grabbed the spade and for a second held it above Mason's head. Would she bash him again if he showed any sign of coming around? Thank heavens he was still out cold. She peered at the floor around him. No signs of blood, and none in his hair as far as she could see. That was probably good.

By the time she had washed the spade and the handle and taken it out the back of the garden and stuck it in the soil as if she'd just left it there, Eddie's truck was pulling up as close as it could get to the barn. Mary and Jarrah were both with him.

"Is he still knocked out?" Jarrah asked as he slid from the back of the truck.

Gaia nodded.

"Wha' this about girl? Wha' happen to Boss?" Mary sounded scared.

"He attacked me, and I shoved him off me and he hit his head on the floor and got knocked out."

"Tha' not wha' Jarrah say."

Gaia looked at Jarrah.

"Sorry, but Auntie made me tell her," he said.

"Hey, it's all right," Gaia said. "But we need to get him away from here quick."

Eddie had disappeared into the barn without saying a word and was already back, opening the truck's tailgate. "Git an ole blanket or somethin' and we put him on that. Need all of us to lift him in."

It was a mission, but they finally had him on the truck, padded with blankets and all of Gaia's pillows. He stayed dead to the world.

"Jarrah, you get in the front with Auntie and Uncle and I'll get on the back to stop Mason rolling over," Gaia said. She waited until Jarrah was out of earshot and then spoke quietly. "He's been unconscious for too long. I think we need to come up with a story for the hospital and police. If they even suspect Jarrah had anything to do with it, it could destroy his life. You know how the cops treat kids like him. I'm going to tell them Mason must have fallen off his bedroom deck and knocked himself out on the concrete. I'll say I found him there when I went to feed his cat. I'll throw a whisky bottle from the deck to make it look like he was drinking. He stinks of whisky so that won't be a stretch. And we need to hide Jarrah if the cops come here; get him on the bus back to Perth as soon as possible tomorrow."

Mary nodded, her face almost pale. "You right. P'raps you stay here with Jarrah and 'tell him. Him listen better to you. Me and Eddie take Boss to hospital and say he fall and you find him."

Eddie patted Gaia on her back. "You all right? Did Boss hurt you?"

"He was about to but Jarrah arrived just in time and

cracked him over the head with my spade." She felt the tears coming and closed her eyes for a moment.

"Jarrah love you. We do too. We fool them dumb cops, you see," Mary said.

Eddie was getting in the truck.

"Thank you Mary," Gaia whispered. "Drop Jarrah and me at Mason's house and when you get back from the hospital I'll make sure we have our story sorted. We'll find a place for Jarrah to hide just in case the cops come here today. If you have to tell them what happened say I found Mason lying on his back and came and got you."

"BUT I DON'T WANT TO GO BACK TOMORROW," JARRAH SAID. "I only just got here." They were standing on the concrete at the back of Mason's house, the broken whisky bottle scattered convincingly below the railing of the small deck high above them. It would look as if Mason had been sitting on the railing drinking, and fallen backwards. Gaia had found an empty whisky bottle in the kitchen; in fact there was a choice of five whisky bottles, so she selected the one still on the kitchen table, handling it with a dirty tea towel.

"I don't want you to go back either, but this is the only way, trust me. Jarrah, this is hard to say, but the cops might decide you were to blame even though you only did it to save me."

"Because I'm black you mean."

Gaia nodded. "It stinks, I know, but we can't risk giving them any reason to find a way to blame you. So you need to pretend you're a secret agent or something and never tell a single soul you were ever here."

"But Hannah knows I'm here."

"If we can get you back on the bus tomorrow, tell her that Mary and Eddie had to go and see one of their mob who was sick."

"But I could have stayed with you then."

"Stop finding problems with everything. This is serious. What if Mason dies?"

"I don't care."

"Well, don't ever say that to anyone. And remember you don't know anything about the accident. Don't even tell Hannah. In fact, tell Hannah that when Auntie and Uncle met you at the bus they were already at Bindi's house because she was sick and you stayed there the night and Auntie made you get back on the bus next morning. So you never came here at all."

"But how did Uncle and Auntie take Boss to the hospital?"

"Christ, Jarrah. They did that first and didn't tell you because they didn't want to upset you. OK?"

Jarrah frowned. "OK. But if I was a cop I would see right through that."

"Well, you're not a cop, you're a secret agent. And anyway, if they never find out you were here they won't go asking Hannah, will they?"

Jarrah shrugged.

"And they'll think Mason fell on the concrete, drunk, and it'll all be an accident and we can get on with our lives."

"As long as Boss doesn't tell."

"He definitely never saw you. And what's he going to say? He tried to ra..— he attacked me in my own house and I defended myself? I'll just deny it and it'll be his word against mine. A drunk's word against mine?" Gaia cupped her palms beneath her chin and fluttered her eyelashes. "Who do you think they'd believe, eh?" She poked Jarrah in the stomach and he finally grinned.

GAIA WAS BESIDE HERSELF BY THE TIME MARY AND EDDIE'S truck clattered to a stop outside their house. She and Jarrah had long since attempted to eat the pancakes she had made in the hope of cheering them both up, and the extra batter she'd kept aside for the late-comers had separated out into an unappetizing gray gloop.

"What happened to you?" Jarrah almost shouted as Auntie slid down from the cab.

In the light from the doorway Mary's dear face looked as gray as the pancake batter, and Gaia's heart twisted in her chest. What had she put them through? "Jarrah," she said. "Give Auntie some time to rest a bit, eh? Stick the kettle on and we'll have a cuppa first."

Mary collapsed in her old rocking chair, giving Gaia a little nod as she did so. Eddie almost stumbled through the door, looking twenty years older than he had when he'd driven off with Mason's unconscious body in the back of the truck. Mason must have died. Nothing else could have done this to them. Gaia's hand was shaking as she poured four large mugs of strong tea, stirring two spoons of sugar into each mug. If they'd had any brandy or whisky in the house she would have added that too. "Have you had anything to eat?" she asked. "I could make you some eggs or perhaps cheese on toast?"

Mary shook her head and Eddie seemed too exhausted to even do that. But they were both drinking their tea.

"What happened to Boss?" Jarrah said. "Is he dead?" Gaia started to frown at him, but seeing his terrified expression, stopped herself. Poor kid knew what that might mean, for all his bravado earlier and telling Gaia he didn't care if Mason did die.

Mary shook her head, and Gaia's heart started beating again. "Thank goodness," is all she managed to get out.

"Him in hospital all right," Mary said. "Still alive then. We been at cop station. Them think Eddie done it."

"Shit Eddie, that's horrible. It's all my fault. I should've come with you and told them what happened," Gaia said.

"But then they would put me in jail," Jarrah shouted. "I don't want to be in jail."

"It all right boy. Them don' know you even here. Me and Eddie both tell them Gaia found Boss on concrete." Mary reached out her hand and pulled Jarrah to her chair. "You never tell anyone, ya' hear me? If ya tell, we liars and we all in jail."

"I won't. I promise. But what about Uncle Eddie? That's not fair."

"We'll make them understand, Jarrah," Gaia said. "I'll go and see them tomorrow and make them understand that it was me who found Mason. No way are they going to blame Eddie for this."

"Them cops coming here tomorrow," Eddie said, his voice sounding so weary Gaia was frightened. He was an old man. She should never have put them in this position. It had worn him out.

"Tha' right," Mary said. "Jarrah, we have to git you to bus quick first light. We take you to Bindi's and she put you on bus later when it come. Bindi not tell. Cops can't know you here. Them talk to Gaia and see where Boss fell. Then Eddie OK and not go to jail."

WHEN THE COPS STILL HADN'T SHOWN UP AT GOSHAWK Gardens by midday on Sunday, Gaia almost began to relax. Had they decided they didn't need to question her? If Mason wasn't very badly hurt perhaps they didn't have to investigate further. Could it possibly be that easy?

Eddie had been back for hours after driving a glum Jarrah into Jurien Bay before it was even light, parking him at Mary's cousin's place. Bindi was going to put him on the bus on Monday, the same bus he would have got anyway. That way Hannah mightn't even suspect anything was wrong.

Mary had told her last night that after questioning her and Eddie separately for hours, giving them nothing but a glass of water the whole time, they read them what they said were their statements and asked them to sign them.

"What did the statements say? Did they believe you?"

"We never said nothin' but Boss fell on concrete an' you found him. Like yo' said. That what we signed."

"Did they hurt you?"

Mary shook her head."Jus' push Eddie back in chair when him stan' up an tell them him didn't ever hit boss an' boss was drunk and mean an' never did nothin' aroun' place."

"Good on him. Perhaps they believed him. The hospital must have seen Mason was drunk. He stunk of whisky." Thank goodness.

But it wasn't quite that easy. Two cops, who looked not much older than Gaia, showed up just after 2pm. They seemed more interested in looking at her garden and asking her about the beach and whether it was good fishing than grilling her about what had happened. They walked with her from the barn where they'd parked their cop car to Mason's house and she showed them where she'd found him and they took a few photos and put gloves on before shoving the bits of broken whisky bottle in a plastic bag. Then she took them upstairs to Mason's bedroom and out onto the deck. They looked over the edge and seemed satisfied it all made sense. Gaia thought she'd got off lightly until they had the cheek to say that Eddie could easily have shoved Mason off the deck and lied to Gaia. She lost it then, told them Eddie would never lie. Told them Mason was a drunk and nasty and aggressive, and Eddie never drank and was as gentle as a lamb. She didn't know if they believed her but they acted like they were sick of the whole thing and just wanted to get back to Jurien Bay. She had to go with them so she could make a statement and sign it.

The youngest-looking cop drove her back to Goshawk Gardens and got quite chatty. Told her Mason had been helicoptered to Perth Hospital within an hour of Eddie and Mary dropping him off at Jurien Bay Hospital and while Gaia was signing her statement they'd had an update. Mason had a traumatic brain injury and had had to have surgery to remove a blood clot, and he was conscious now and not critical.

"So Eddie saved his life," Gaia said.

"I reckon. Mason has been held overnight in our station plenty of times on drunk and disorderly charges. I wouldn't blame old Eddie if he did give him one."

"So why question him and Mary for so long yesterday? They were exhausted."

"Not me. I'm just the new boy. They have to look like they're doing everything by the book. He's a nice old bloke, your Eddie. Not like some of them, always drunk."

"Like Mason, you mean?" Gaia said.

The cop glanced at her and grinned. "None of the Abos are a patch on Mason when it comes to drunk and mean."

When he drew up at the barn and she got out, he got out as well. "Have you got good locks on your door?"

Gaia nodded, the sick feeling that had stayed lurking inside her even after the cop had told her Mason's condition wasn't critical, returning with a vengeance.

"Good. Make sure you lock it when Mason gets back. If you're worried, you let us know, OK?"

THREE DAYS LATER MARY AND EDDIE SHOWED UP AT THE BARN. Gaia knew by their faces she wasn't going to like what they were about to tell her.

"Gaia, we goin' 'way for a bit," Mary said. "It time we go Bunuba Country, see our mob."

Gaia's breath shuddered deep into her. So far away. Up near Fitzroy Crossing. She wanted to beg them not to leave; not to leave her alone. But she had no right.

"We sorry Gaia. You come wi' us if you want."

"Oh Mary. Thank you. I wish I could but I can't leave here. How would I get back again? I need to be here for Jarrah when he has his holidays."

"You good girl. You tell Jarrah in next letter we probably be back before his next holidays or him come up Country. It time my mob saw him again. Them not see him since little kid." She opened her arms and Gaia fell into them, tears stinging behind her closed eyelids. Eddie patted her on the back. It was like losing her parents all over again.

"We be back, don' you worry," Mary said.

So now she would be completely alone when Mason returned.

CHAPTER 23

The days went by and Gaia forced herself to eat and sleep and keep her garden weeded. It was Autumn and the lettuces and tomatoes were well over, and mostly she ate spuds, onions and cabbage. She still had half a sack of cereal, but being colder her hens had almost stopped laying so she had to ration the few eggs she got. She couldn't be bothered to make bread so she made damper; she'd run out of butter but she had bottles of blackberry jam and apple jelly from last summer when she and Mary had their jam-making frenzy. Mary had lots of bottled fruit in her cupboards and she wouldn't mind if Gaia scoffed the lot. She only had fruit twice a week as something to look forward to. But she needed some protein. Fishing helped and sometimes she took her rod to the spot Eddie fished from and usually managed to catch a snapper. She hated fishing up reef fish and if she hooked a coral trout put it back. One medium-sized snapper fed her for three days, including making stock with the fish frame and making cabbage, spud and onion soup with bits of fish swimming in it to give it some flavor. Sometimes she had a feed of cockles. No rabbit stew though. Eddie hadn't left his rifle and anyway she wouldn't know how to use it. It gave her the shits even thinking about shooting anything.

She was outside washing her sheets in the bath when the same young cop who had driven her back to Goshawk Gardens after she'd signed her statement showed up. He hadn't seen her yet, around the side of the house. Her first thought was to run into the bush. She didn't of course. Running wouldn't help if they'd found out. Perhaps Mason had got his memory back and had told them he'd been whacked over the head. She'd always known they'd find out and she had her story ready. She'd tell them he tried to rape her and she'd managed to shove him off and he'd fallen and cracked his head on the corner of the table. It was three weeks ago so they wouldn't be able to find anything to prove it one way or the other. Mason never saw Jarrah, so as long as they didn't know he'd been here, she could handle it. She'd say she hadn't told them the truth before because she didn't want to end up in court having to defend herself and everyone knowing. Which was true.

"Gaia, there you are. Well hidden," the cop said.

What was his name? Graeme? Grant?

"Greg," he said. He'd read her mind. "Greg Grant. I drove you back here after that accident with Dave Mason."

"Hi," Gaia said. "I wasn't hiding but I don't get many visitors."

"Just teasing. How've you been?"

"Good. How are you?" Gaia wiped her hands dry on the towel dumped on the ground beside her.

"Bonzer. Nice to be away from the police station though." He looked around. "Great spot you've got here. I'm jealous."

Why didn't he just get on with it and stop pretending he was her friend?

"Look Gaia, I have some bad news. Shall we sit down?"

Gaia nodded. Here it comes. "OK. Do you want a drink or something? Cup of tea?"

"Wouldn't mind. But let's get the bad news over first and then have tea. I'm finished for the day after this so I wouldn't mind having a look around. Have a walk on your beach if you were OK with that?"

What the hell is he on about? Telling me I'm in the shit and then having a stroll on the beach? Gaia sat down opposite him.

"It's about Dave Mason. We thought we should warn you, just in case he shows up here."

"Is he out of hospital?" The queasiness churning in her stomach shot into her throat.

"We got a call from the Perth police this morning. Mason discharged himself from hospital last night, against medical advice. They couldn't hold him but he's been aggressive on the ward so the police are keeping an eye out for him. Apparently his head injury and the brain damage from the blood clot they had to remove has likely made him worse—more aggressive and unpredictable—than he was before. He's after booze of course. But just in case he decides to come back here, we thought you should be warned."

Gaia sat there in the sun, frozen to the seat.

"You don't look too good. I'll grab you a glass of water. Can I go inside?"

Gaia managed to nod and closed her eyes while she waited. She needed to leave. She couldn't stay here alone. Where could she go?

"Here you are. Get that down you."

Gaia emptied the glass. "Thanks. What did Mason say about the accident? Did he remember falling off the deck?"

Greg shook his head. "Doesn't remember anything. Too drunk the doctors reckon as well as his head injury on top of that. If it weren't for you finding him and your friends getting him to the hospital he'd be a dead man. But you can count on it, he won't be bringing you thank-you chocolates."

"He hasn't got his truck though so how would he get back here?"

"He probably won't so don't worry too much. He's got a one-track mind and that's getting drunk. But if he did decide to come back he wouldn't think twice about borrowing a vehicle without the owner's permission. He could be half-way back here before the owner even discovered his wheels had vanished."

"What should I do?"

"Keep an eye out, and let us know if he comes back. We'll pay him a little visit. And keep your place locked at night or whenever you're inside." He bent down and scratched Rita Roo between her ears."Pity you don't have a big dog. Not sure this kangaroo will chase anyone off."

"I don't have a phone so how can I let you know?"

"Crikey, you should get one all the way out here by yourself. What if you had a fire or something?"

Gaia stared at him.

"What about your friends? Eddie and Mary? Do they have a phone?"

"No. And they're away for a while. And the phone in Mason's house has been cut off for months."

"Perhaps you should go and bunk with friends for a spell until we find Mason and make sure he's not going to be a nuisance. You got any family near here you can stay with?"

"No, all my family died when our house here burned to the ground," Gaia said. Why am I being so mean? He's only trying to help.

"God, I completely forgot. I right stuck my stupid big foot in it. I wasn't here then but Graeme told me—Graeme's the police sergeant I was with when we came to talk to you after Mason's accident."

"It's OK. I know you were only being helpful. I don't expect everyone to remember a fire that happened in the back of beyond four years ago."

～

JARRAH WAS LYING ON HIS BED, HIS FACE TO THE WALL. He
could hear the other kids laughing and shouting all the way
from the common room, having fun.

He heard the door open, but didn't move.

"Hey, Jarrah, I'm back."

Jarrah turned over. "Oh, Seamus, I didn't know you were
coming tonight." Suddenly he jerked upright. "Is something
the matter with Gaia? Is she all right? What's wrong?"

"Hey, no, Gaia's fine. This is the first spare hour I've had
to come and see you since I got back from New Zealand on
Wednesday. I haven't even seen Gaia yet."

"Well, how do you know she's all right then?" His heart
was jumping into his throat.

The mattress sunk as Seamus sat down on the bed. "Why
wouldn't she be?" he asked. "Was she sick when you were
there the other weekend?"

Jarrah shook his head. "No, no. She was all right. I just
thought..."

"Didn't you get a letter from her this week? Is that it?"

Jarrah shook his head. "No. Yes, I did get a letter from her
but it wasn't very long."

"Probably because she'd just seen you. Nothing much has
happened I guess."

"When are you going to see her?" The room was nearly
too dark to see Seamus properly.

"Next Thursday night I'm driving up there as soon as I
finish my shift at the hospital. I have to drive back to Perth on
Sunday night. Wanna come? Hannah and I thought we'd ask
the school if you could have Friday off."

Jarrah pulled his legs up onto the bed and hugged them
tight, his head buried in his knees. "Nope."

"Sorry, I didn't get that. Say again?"

"No. Thank you. I don't want to miss school again. I'll get behind everyone else."

"Is that the problem? You're worried about school?" Seamus leaned over and switched on the lamp between Jarrah's bed and the bed next to him.

"A bit. I'm dumb."

"That's definitely not true. Are some of the kids saying that?"

"Nope."

"Perhaps I can help with some of your homework?"

"It's OK. I don't care. It don't matter anyhow."

"It do matter anyhow if it's worrying you. Once you get behind in some subjects it seems impossible to catch up. Like in arithmetic."

Jarrah shrugged. "You can help if you like. But I don' wanna go an' see Gaia. Anyway I can't 'cos Auntie and Uncle have gone."

"Gone? What d'you mean? Where have they gone?"

"Up north. They might never come back."

"Why didn't you tell me in your last letter? Gaia never said anything either."

"They jus' went. They don't like it there any more."

"But that means Gaia will be all alone. Was Mason around when you were there?"

Snakes writhed in Jarrah's belly. "Yep. But he's gone too now."

"Jarrah, look at me."

Jarrah didn't move.

"Look at me, Jarrah. Tell me what's going on."

Jarrah finally took his head out of his knees and looked at him, tears balanced in his eyes. "Nothing. Nothing's going on. Auntie and Uncle don't like Boss and Gaia doesn't either. He's always drunk and mean, that's all. He's hardly ever there anyway. Auntie and Uncle jus' miss their mob an' get sick of

Boss shouting at them. Gaia's glad he's gone. I hope he never comes back again."

"Did he do something to Gaia?"

Jarrah dropped his head again. "Nope. Didn't do nothing but get drunk and yell. She cleaned his scummy house when Auntie and Uncle were away and he was horrible to them when they came back so they went away again so I can't go there any more."

"Of course you can. You can come with me and we can camp together. Or I bet you could stay with Gaia in the barn and I could camp."

Jarrah shook his head. "You go. Gaia missed you. She won't want me there, gettin' in the way."

GAIA LIT THE KEROSENE LAMP AGAINST THE CREEPING DARK. Curled up on the old couch with Rita Roo asleep on the floor beside her, she tried to stop thinking. She'd hoped Seamus and Jarrah might come today but they hadn't. The short letter from Seamus that had arrived yesterday had said he'd try and get here this weekend and bring Jarrah. He'd said that Hannah was worried about Jarrah; thought he might be depressed. Missing his Auntie and Uncle and Gaia.

It seemed forever since she'd seen Seamus. He'd met some other girl in New Zealand and didn't want to tell her. He'd been back in Perth two weeks. If he really cared about her he would have been here the second he got off the plane. She didn't believe his story that he had to do some shifts at the hospital or they would sack him. So what. She didn't need him. He wasn't going to be in Perth for long anyway; he'd be off again soon, seeing the rest of Australia. Then he'd be gone, back to Ireland and his real life. But she needed to see Jarrah. She couldn't bear to think of him upset and miserable and having to keep their secret. If they didn't come tomorrow she had enough money for his bus fare. She'd send the money to Hannah and ask her to put him on the bus. She'd hitch-hike to Jurien Bay to meet him and they could hitch-hike back together. It would be fun. They didn't need Seamus.

But she missed Mary and Eddie. What if they never came back? She sometimes hadn't seen them for days but she'd known they were there if she needed some company. Covering her face with her hands, she tried to close out the terror that never went away. Even asleep it haunted her and she woke over and over in the nights, shaken awake by some noise outside, a possum snuffling and grunting, looking for scraps for food, an owl screeching as it swooped on a defenceless mouse far below. She used to love the night sounds, they were her lullaby, but now her head couldn't get rid of the fear of Mason coming back and coming to get her, punishing her for almost killing him. And she was so alone here now, no one would even know. He could strangle her and bury her and no one would know.

The knock on the door jerked her upright, her heart pounding. The door was bolted top and bottom and the table was shoved across it, but Mason wouldn't let that stop him. Sliding off the bed she crept over to the table, eyeing the hammer and sharp fish-gutting knife on it's top, ready. Her axe and the spade were propped against the table legs. The knock came again and then a voice.

"Gaia, are you there? It's me."

Her legs almost giving way she dragged the table from the door and fumbled with the bolts. "Seamus? Oh, Seamus."

The door pushed inwards the second the bolts were open, almost knocking her over. As the dark shape came towards her, for a terrified moment she thought it was Mason.

"Gaia, it's me." His smell, his lovely Irish lilt, his arms around her. It really was him.

"Hey, what's the matter?" Seamus had pulled back and was looking at her. "You're crying. What's happened?"

She rubbed her eyes with the heels of her hands, her whole body shaking. "I didn't know it was you. I thought you'd be here earlier. You frightened me, that's all."

"You were terrified. Who did you think it was?"

Gaia's hands were covering her eyes again and she shook her head.

"Mason," Seamus said.

Gaia dropped her hands and stared at him. She'd never heard Seamus angry. Now he'd picked up the knife, glinting in the light of the kerosene lamp. "Has the bastard hurt you, Gaia? Christ, I'll remove his feckin' head if he has."

"No. No, he isn't even here I don't think. I thought he might have come back, that's all."

"And you have to barricade yourself in here every night with a knife and a hammer? And an axe? You must have some reason."

Gaia couldn't seem to stop trembling and she tried to take some deep breaths, but that seemed to make it worse.

"You're shaking like a leaf. Macushla, come here." Then his arms were around her holding her tight, and she buried her face in his chest, her tears hiccuping out as he rubbed her back, stroked her hair, murmuring Irish she couldn't under-stand. And slowly, slowly her body quietened and her tears stopped and he was almost carrying her to her chair and sitting her in it, bringing her water, then hot tea, and the smell of toast as he browned it over the gas ring on the little stove by the sink made her realize how very hungry she was.

"I'm sorry," she said a while later as they finished up the vegetable soup she'd prepared this morning, hoping he and Jarrah would arrive for lunch or tea. So long ago, it seemed now.

"It's me who's sorry for letting you down; not getting here earlier in the daylight. I was trying to convince Jarrah to change his mind and come, but he's a stubborn kid when he wants to be. But it meant I didn't get away until one, and then ole Trusty decided to stop half-way between nowhere and nowhere. She was right out of petrol and like an eejit my spare can was as empty as my head on one of my better days. I had to flag down a truck and catch a ride ten kilometers up the road to a garage, and it took me ages to get a ride back. I was almost back at the van by the time I got picked up."

"I missed you," Gaia said. "Not just today, all the time you were gone."

His eyes darkened as he reached across the table and took her hand. "Can I kiss you?" he said. "Please?"

Gaia nodded. He stood and stepped around the table and she rose to meet him, her hand pulling her hair across her cheek. He put his hand on hers and together their hands stroked her hair back behind her ear. He brought her fingers to his lips and kissed them, and then he kissed her cheek, and her nose, and her other cheek, and then hovered close to her parted lips, so she was breathing in his breath, Seamus breathing her into him. Her eyes closed as he kissed her, and when she opened them again his face was blurred through her tears.

"Don't cry, Machusla. I'm back now, and I have three days before I have to go back to Perth."

"I've, I've missed you so much." Her voice wobbled.

"I'm here now. I'm here and I'm never going away again for so long unless you come with me. I couldn't stand it."

Gaia buried her head in her hands. Why was she being such a wimp? Get a grip. She took in a deep breath and dropped her hands. "Why wouldn't Jarrah come? Is he all right?"

"He's rather glum and missing you, but he didn't think he should take another day off school, or so he said. He told me that Mason had been causing trouble, and chased Mary and Eddie away. I think he's worried he won't be able to come here, even when he has holidays, if his Auntie isn't here."

"He knows he can stay with me, and I think Mary and

Eddie will come back when they're ready. All their stuff is still in the house."

"Well, to be honest, I'm just a tiny bit glad that I'm here without Jarrah." He leaned towards her to kiss her again, and she turned her head away. All she wanted was to see Jarrah, make sure he was OK. Not kissing and carrying on as if nothing had happened.

"Sorry," Seamus said. "That was a stupid thing to say."

Gaia shrugged. "I'm tired, that's all. Who's Macushla, anyway?"

"You, silly. It's an Irish word. My darling, my sweetheart. Is it OK? It just sort of came out. I don't think I've ever used it before."

Gaia's face got warm and when she shyly looked at Seamus she saw his face was pinker than usual too. "It's nice. Sorry I'm being so grumpy."

"You, grumpy? Never. I've kept you up way too long." Seamus looked at his watch. "Jeez, it's past midnight. I'll kip in the van tonight. If it's OK to stay a couple of nights I'll pitch my tent tomorrow."

"You can sleep at Mary and Eddie's place. I've got a key. They wouldn't mind at all," Gaia said.

CHAPTER 24

*G*aia was sitting at the outside table, trying to calm herself before Seamus appeared, when a Landrover drove up and parked at the end of her drive. She squinted at the slogan on the side of the door. *Pommel and Wright, Surveyors* it shouted. What the hell? They must be something to do with that horrible real estate lot. How dare they come here. She slid along the bench and stood up, back as straight as her mother's at the height of her career, legs planted like a bridge that no man would dare pass under, and arms crossed, barring any man who would even think about it. Two of them, leather Akubra hats dipped low over their leather faces, got out of the vehicle and came over.

"Gaia Christie?" the short man said, sticking out his hairy hand. Gaia nodded, but held her stance.

"Hey, sorry to disturb your morning, but we've got a job to do. Thought it would be polite to introduce ourselves. Charlie Dickson's the name, and this beanstalk is Brian Hill."

"What sort of a job?" Gaia narrowed her eyes.

"We've been contracted by Morton and McMillan to survey Dave Mason's property boundaries. He's selling it to them so they can build a resort here."

"Mason's not here, didn't they tell you? He had an accident and probably won't be back for ages. As far as I know, he hasn't agreed to sell."

"Yep, Suzanne Henderson told us that but she wants us to go ahead so that when Mr Mason has recovered they can get onto the project without more delays." Shortie crossed his arms and gave her a look.

The beanstalk grinned at her. "Nice bit of land you have here. We're going to camp a couple of nights on the beach while we're doing the job. Do a bit of diving. Perhaps try our hand at fishing. You might be able to show us some good spots?"

"I'd appreciate it if you didn't camp on the beach," Gaia said, her eyes slits.

"No worries. We'll be camping on Mason's end of the beach. We'll only need to step onto your land briefly when we're hammering in our boundary pegs."

"I don't want you camping anywhere on the beach."

The short one raised his eyebrows. "As far as I know, no one owns the sea or the beach up to mean high-tide mark."

"There are plenty of spots in the bush near Dave Mason's house. And please try not to disturb the wildlife." Her face was frozen in a scowl.

Beanstalk dipped his head. "Got it," he said. "No shooting birds for our supper. We'll bring you some nice fish though for your tea if we catch any. Come on Charlie, let's get out of the lady's hair." With a thumbs up he headed for the door, his mate close behind. Then he turned back. "Oh yeah, and Suzanne Henderson said to tell you that she's arranged for an agricultural student to stay in Mason's house and look after the place and the stock until Mason gets back."

As soon as the men drove off, Gaia collapsed on the bench, her head in her hands. She jumped as something touched her shoulder.

"Gaia, what is it? What was that Landrover doing here?"

Seamus sat down opposite her. "You're upset. Was it Mason? Jeez, if he's been hassling you I'll drop him."

"No, not Mason. Just about as bad though. But I need some breakfast first. Then I'll tell you. Do you want some?" she said, pushing herself up.

∽

GAIA TOOK A DEEP BREATH. TELL A LIE AND IT NEVER ENDS. Start with the easy stuff. She took a few swallows of her water. "Those guys in the Landrover are surveyors. Apparently that company who came asking me if I would sell Goshawk Gardens—I told you about them in a letter—they've contracted them to survey Mason's boundaries. I didn't even know he'd agreed to sell yet, in fact I'm almost sure he hasn't. I wouldn't put it past them to try and trick him into signing when he shows up again. Make out he'd already agreed or something and that he couldn't remember because of his head injury."

"What head injury? Feckin' hell, Gaia, what's been going on?"

Gaia picked up a slice of toast, already going cold on the plate between them. She looked at it and put it down again. "Mason was drunk and fell from a deck off the top floor bedroom in his house. Knocked himself out on the concrete. I found him and Eddie and Mary took him into Jurien Bay Hospital. That's why he's not here."

"When was this?"

"It was the Saturday Jarrah arrived. So four weeks ago. Eddie picked him up from the bus at Jurien Bay and they'd only just got back. I hadn't even seen Jarrah when I found Mason. I went over to his house to make sure he'd fed the cat —poor thing is always starving—and found Mason, his head smashed on the concrete. He was out to it." Gaia forced herself not to avoid Seamus's eyes as she lied to him. "I checked he was breathing and he was. There was a broken whisky bottle by him. He must have been leaning against the deck railing, drunk as usual, and fallen backwards. Or perhaps he passed out and fell backwards. God knows how long he'd been lying there."

Seamus put his hand over hers and waited. Then he moved around the table so he was sitting beside her, and pulled her into a hug. "Sounds as if he was lucky you found him."

"I ran and got Eddie and Mary and we got him into the back of Eddie's truck and they took him into Jurien Bay hospital. I should have gone with them, but I was too shaken up and I wanted to talk to Jarrah." The words were spilling out of her now, and Seamus kept his arm close around her. "We had to protect Jarrah from getting implicated. You know how the cops treat Aboriginals. Eddie and Mary agreed. We didn't want them questioning him. I made him promise not to tell a soul about Mason's accident, not even Hannah. So Eddie took Jarrah into Jurien Bay to stay with Bindi first thing Sunday morning before the cops came here to question me. Bindi put him on the bus on Monday as if he'd been staying here having a good time."

"Jeez. What a drama," Seamus said. "No wonder Jarrah was a bit cagey."

Gaia sighed. "Poor Jarrah. Not much of a welcome. He'd been so excited about coming here on the bus by himself. I was afraid that if the police had any excuse to blame Eddie or Mary, or even Jarrah, they would. They would have thrown Eddie into jail and probably stuck Jarrah in a borstal."

Seamus's fist hit the table. "Christ, this country's worse than the idiot eejits in Ireland."

"It was a nightmare. Eddie and Mary didn't get back until really late on Saturday. Jarrah and I were worried sick. After they'd got Mason to the hospital the police questioned them for hours without even giving them a cup of tea. Tried to blame Eddie for pushing him off the deck. Anyway, in the end the police believed them and they were fine with me of course. I'm white."

Seamus leaned across the table. "Sounds like you saved the creep's life. Surely he'll be grateful?"

"I don't suppose he'll even remember. Anyway, I might find out soon. One of the cops showed up last week and told me Mason had discharged himself and I should lock my doors at night in case he comes back. Apparently his head injury has made him even more aggressive."

"Feckin' hell. You shouldn't be here alone at all. Come to Perth with me until Mary and Eddie get back."

THE SURVEYORS WERE CLUMPING BACKWARDS OUT OF THE water when, later that morning, Gaia and Seamus went to the beach to clear their heads.

"Hey guys, look what we caught," the tall one yelled.

"Shit," Gaia muttered. "How dare they. Walking all over the coral I bet, stealing shells for their kids without a thought for the animals inside."

The men were opening a bag and hauling stuff out; seaweed, bits of coral, a sea urchin, shells…

"It's illegal to rip off the reef like that," Gaia said, stooping down to pick up a shining red and white cowry shell. 'These have live animals inside. If you have to take shells, find an empty one on the beach."

"Oops. This one is so pretty. My little girl would love it. Surely taking one won't hurt; there are dozens in the sea."

"If everyone thinks like that, there soon won't be. And think what bad behaviors you're teaching your daughter."

"Well, we'll go easy. I'll just take this one and get any other shells from the beach. How's that?"

"What about this though," the short man interrupted. He

had a handful of seaweed. "It was just sort of floating in the seaweed. Real easy to grab." He held something up and Seamus peered at it.

"Is it a seahorse?" he said.

"Christ, be careful," Gaia said, her hands shaking as she reached over and cupped her hands gently under the seaweed. "That's one of the rarest creatures around here. Give it to me."

The man looked startled and did as he was told.

"Oh no, my beautiful seadragon. Seamus, we have to put him back quickly or he'll die. Look, he's already losing all his colors. I need to take him out to where we usually see him." She began walking towards the sea, holding the seadragon hidden in its seaweed as gently as she would hold a spiderweb in her hands.

"Let me take him back," Seamus said. "The water will be cold and you haven't got your wetsuit on."

"Nor have you. We haven't time to go back and get wetsuits. He'll die if we don't get him back right away. It's probably already too late." Tears were choking her. "I need to take him. I know where he likes to hide."

"Hey, sorry. I'll take him back for you," the tall man said, holding his hands out.

Gaia didn't even glance at him but handed the precious seaweed to Seamus. Kicking off her sandals, she pulled off her jeans and the light sweater she was wearing and gently took the delicate handful back. She walked into the sea and almost immediately was floating, her legs scissoring as she propelled herself as smoothly as she could out over the coral until she was over the seadragon's favorite spot. Diving down she opened her hands and the seaweed sunk a little then settled into the seagrass. She hovered on the surface, praying, praying that he was unharmed, that he'd not swim away somewhere else where he could never be found again. He didn't appear. Should she dive down and part the seaweed and see if he was still there, still vibrating his delicate fins? Oh, how she wanted to, but she mustn't. He needed his space. He'd been violated and it would take time for him to find his courage again, his trust of his special world. Only then could he go back to being strong and independent and fully alive. Only when he was sure he wouldn't be disturbed would he be free to dance again over his patch of white sand.

DRY AND WARMER, AT LEAST ON THE OUTSIDE, GAIA PICKED AT the lunch smorgasbord of cheeses and olives and cracker biscuits Seamus had brought with him.

"Come on, Gaia, you'll feel better with something in your stomach. You deserve it after saving your seadragon and putting...Brian and Charlie?... in their place. I'm betting they'll stay out of the sea for the rest of their stay."

"But that won't stop them banging in their horrid pegs everywhere. If Mason has already signed away his land, do you realize that everyone who stays in their horrible resort will be able to use the whole beach and swim everywhere they like? Who could even stop them putting buildings right near my boundary? When they were here trying to get me to sell my land, the real estate woman told me that part of Mason's deal was that they'd build him a fancy house wherever he likes on the property. What if he builds right next to the beach? He could watch me swim from his window. I could never ever..." her voice wobbled..."never ever dance there again."

Seamus was up, pacing. "So, we simply have to find a way to stop it. Surely there must be some sort of environmental restrictions on building a resort in a place like this?"

"I've been wondering if Mr Ludlow could do anything," Gaia said, nibbling the corner of a biscuit. "He's my lawyer. He was nice to me when I wanted to come here as soon as I turned 16. He told me to get in touch if I ever needed his help with anything, and he set up a bank account for me with the money Dad and Mum left us. He even sends me a Christmas card every year."

"Worth a try. Would you like me to go and see him on your behalf? You could write a note to him explaining it all, and I'll go and see him. Face to face is always more effective."

"How are you going to find time to do all this for me?" Gaia took in a long shaky breath.

"I've got bags of time. And I want to do it. It's criminal to think this could all be turned into some tourist playground."

Gaia was standing up now. Her head felt as if it had steam coming out of it. "OK. I'll come back to Perth with you tomorrow. I need to see Jarrah, and see Mr Ludlow and those real estate agents and do something. I cannot let them destroy all this. I cannot."

"Atta girl. Jarrah will be so happy."

"I hope so. I feel terrible about making him keep all that stuff that happened with Mason secret."

"Well, it's a silver lining for me at least. I wasn't feeling too good about leaving you here alone, without even Mary and Eddie. And I can show you Perth. You can bunk in with me" —he caught her look— "or if you're not into that I'm sure you can stay with my friend, Sally. She's in the same apartment block as me and her flatmate just left. You'll like her."

Gaia managed a smile. "Sounds good. I mightn't stay too long though. I did live in Perth after I got out of rehab, and it's a city. A nice city, but I don't think I'm much of a city person."

"I know. But it will be different with me and Jarrah there to entertain you. You can meet Hannah, and Jarrah's friends. Perhaps you can help with Jarrah's dance lessons; get him back into it. Would that be a plan?"

Gaia nodded. "And I wouldn't be here when Mason came back." She shivered. "What if Mary and Eddie don't come home? I can't stay away for ever. This is where I'm happy." Gaia head seemed full of tears and her thoughts choked out of her. "Why should he force me out of my home? How is that fair? What if Rita Roo needs me?"

"It isn't fair." Seamus was looking at her strangely. Gaia took in another shaky breath. She must sound like a mad woman. He was talking again. "Gaia, Jarrah told me that when he first came here, when you first taught him to dance, he heard Mason in your barn and he sounded angry. He said that after Mason had gone, he went into the barn and you were crying. What happened? Did Mason touch you?"

Gaia shook her head so hard her hair whipped across her cheek. She was shouting, she couldn't seem to stop. "Do you think I'd let that bastard get anywhere near me? He was drunk and he scared me. But no way would he have got anywhere near me without me kicking him so hard in his balls he wouldn't be able to get out of a crouch for a week. Creep. Trying to chat me up and talk about Mum and Dad and how he heroically saved my life and Bron's too when we had the fire." She clamped her hands to the sides of her head, her face squeezed so tight she could feel her worst burns back again. Breathe, breathe. She wiped her hands across her cheeks, smoothing away the fear and fury.

Grabbing the glass of water Seamus shoved towards her, she drank the lot. "I don't know why I got so upset when Mason left; adrenaline and anger I suppose. And that's when Jarrah walked in and found me. But later he found the seadragons, thank goodness. They calmed us both down. How dare those surveyors touch them. What if the seadragon dies? If his mucous covering got rubbed off he could get an infection. Then when his mate arrives she'll have no one to dance with and they'll have no offspring and they'll be lost from here forever."

"Shall we go and look for him? Make sure he's good?"

Gaia nodded. "Yes, we must. I can't leave here until I know he is still alive and seems OK. What if that dim-witted surveyor grabs him again when I'm not here?"

"I think they got the message loud and clear. And anyway, they said they'd be gone tomorrow. Come to Perth for a spell. Rita Roo can look after herself, you know that. She'll miss you but I bet as soon as you get back, she'll know and she'll be here."

At midday next day they floated over the reef, Gaia's eyes and mind focused on finding the seadragon. And as if he knew she cared, as soon as she flippered to his favorite spot he was there, glowing and vibrating his fins at 70 flickers per second. Not that she could even see his translucent fins but she knew that was how he stayed upright, giving him the control to swim so gracefully, so slowly, so perfectly in harmony with his surroundings. Her fingers touched her throat, feeling its pulse, the tears that were filling it, and she knew. The seadragon was her spirit animal, her truth, her happiness. To be here, living, dancing—in tune with her environment, peaceful and fulfilled. That's what she needed to fight for, to do whatever she had to even if it meant leaving here for a while. To save this place, this seadragon, this home.

PART II

"What you do makes a difference, and you have to decide
what kind of difference you want to make."
—*Jane Goodall*

"The greatest threat to our planet is the belief that someone
else will save it."
—*Robert Swan*

CHAPTER 25

Perth, June, 1981
Gaia knocked on the door of the Children's Home, her heart going like the céilí. Was she nervous about seeing Jarrah? An eleven-year-old? Apprehensive. Guilty. That was what she was feeling. How could she have asked so much of him? Lying to Hannah, keeping silent. Now he was so sad and upset and scared that he'd stopped dancing.

The door opened and a tall woman, her long dark hair caught in a messy bun on top of her head, smiled at Gaia. "Hullo."

"Hi. Sorry to show up here without even phoning first," Gaia said. "I'm a friend of Jarrah's and I wondered if I could see him?"

"Oh, you're Gaia! How lovely. I recognize you from the photo Jarrah has above his bed. He'll be so happy to see you. Come in, come in. I'm Hannah, by the way."

"Thank you. Sorry it's so late."

"It's perfect. We'll be having dinner in about half an hour, so you can join us. Jarrah will be too excited to eat. They all will. You're their star."

"Me? Why?"

"Because you're a famous ballet dancer and they're all besotted by dancing." Her voice lilted. So like Seamus.

"I'm not a famous anything," Gaia said. "And definitely not a famous ballet dancer. Is that what Jarrah told you?"

"Not really. But you're a star in his eyes and so you're a star for us all. Especially now we've seen photos of you dancing on the beach."

Gaia's hand went to her hot cheek, and she drew her hair across her scars. "How embarrassing. They'll be disappointed when they see me."

"I doubt that very much." She hesitated, her smile disappearing. "Jarrah's been rather unhappy since he got back from his visit to you. Three weeks ago? Seamus thinks… we both think… he might be missing you, of course, but it's more than that. He's stopped dancing and he spends too much time lying on his bed. Even Maisie, the girl here who is his special friend, can't get him to start teaching them all his dances again."

"Seamus told me. That's why I'm here. He drove up to see me and I came back to Perth with him. We just got here and I asked him to drop me off. He'll collect me later. But I didn't think. I should have waited until tomorrow and not turned up right on your dinner time."

"Don't be silly. We love having people stay for dinner. It doesn't happen very often. Most of the kids here have no family and even if they do, they almost never visit."

"Oh. That's sad. I know what that's like, having no family." Gaia let go of her hair.

Hannah touched her arm. "I know you do and I'm so sorry. What I do know is that you've become Jarrah's family. In his heart, anyway."

"He's very special to me, too. I hope he wants to see me."

"Tell you what, I'll take you to the dorm where his bed is. He's probably there alone. He wasn't in the den with the others when I was in there earlier."

"The den?"

"That's what we call the common room where most things happen; they do their homework there, play games, bang the piano, dance. Well, they did when Jarrah was teaching them. After dinner, sometimes they're allowed to watch a video or something suitable—like a wildlife doco—on the telly. The TV is about as old as me and pretty grainy, but they glue themselves to it anyway."

"It will be so good to meet them. Jarrah has talked about Maisie. She sounds lovely."

"She's quite a character. A couple of years older than Jarrah but she's taken him under her wing. Come on, let's find Jarrah." Hannah led her along a narrow hallway with doors along both sides and stopped at the end door. "This is Jarrah's dorm. He shares it with seven other boys." Opening the door, she peered in, turned, and gestured to Gaia. "He's over there on his bed. Reading one of his books. Go and surprise him. Ask him to show you around and he can bring you to the dining room when the bell goes."

Her heart squeezed so tightly it hurt, Gaia tip-toed down the long room, four narrow beds along each side, each neatly covered with a gray blanket. Some had a teddy or a toy truck propped against the pillow and most had a picture or two pinned on the wall behind the bed. If it hadn't been for those touches it would have been a scene out of Dickens. Three small windows along one side and another in the wall at the end of the room let in enough of the late afternoon light to show her that only one bed was occupied, the one at the end. The still body on it lay with his back to her, a large book in his hands.

He would know she was there. Jarrah could hear every little sound, however soft. But he wouldn't know it was her. She stood behind him, tears already pressing to escape. Jarrah's back quivered. Did he sense it was her?

"Jarrah," she said. "It's me. I've come to visit you."

The book fell with a bang to the floor and Gaia jumped.

Jarrah slowly turned onto his back, the whites of his eyes startling in his dark face. "Gaia?" he said, his voice a squeak.

Gaia nodded and sat on the bed. Her hand went to his crazy curls. She felt them springing under her palm and blinked hard. "I've missed you so much. I had to come. I've been worried about you."

Jarrah rubbed at the tears spilling out between his long lashes and Gaia fumbled in her pocket for her hankie. "I don't know who needs this more, me or you," she said, smiling at him. She pushed it into his hand and he jabbed it across his eyes.

"You should have told me. I thought you didn't like leaving home?"

"I don't, but then again, home is where the heart is, and you're here."

"What's that mean?"

"It means I care about you. Lots and lots. It wasn't fair to ask you to not say anything and bottle it all up."

"I don't ever want to say anything. You can't either. You haven't, have you?"

Gaia shook her head. "No. It's OK; I'm not going to either. I told Seamus that I found Dave out cold and we stuck him on the back of the truck and Eddie took him to hospital."

"Are they home yet?"

"Mary and Eddie? No, not yet. I thought I might stay in Perth a while until they get back."

"But if they come back the cops might put them in jail."

"They won't," Gaia said firmly. "They've signed their statements and I did too, and the cops know it wasn't anything to do with us and they don't even know you were there. No one does, other than us and Seamus, so stop worrying about it. Perhaps Dave will never come back."

"What if he dies? He might already be dead."

"The cops told me he was doing all right so he definitely isn't dead and he's not going to die. Not from that bump on the head, anyway. They knew him already because he was always getting thrown in a cell overnight from being drunk and getting into fights."

"Are you sure?"

"I am one hundred and fifty percent sure," Gaia said.

"You can't have one hundred and fifty percent. It stops at one hundred per cent."

"Smarty pants." She went over to the other side of his bed and picked up his book. "What are you reading, smarty pants? Einstein's Theory of Relativity?"

"I know who Einstein is. It's much better than him. I got it out of the library."

"Wow. *The Coral Reefs of Australia.* Are there photos of…" She got no further.

"Yes, on page 102 and all the way to 106."

Gaia flipped through the heavy book and there they were in bursting color. Their seadragons.

JARRAH TOOK HER INTO A BIG ROOM WITH TWO LONG TABLES and a kitchen at one end.

"This is Gaia," he said to the cook, a white apron straining around her ample middle.

"The mystery Gaia," she said, her red cheeks bulging as she smiled. "Never thought we'd see you here. Thought you never left that beach Jarrah is always talking about."

"I don't usually, but I wanted to check on Jarrah. Make sure he was behaving himself."

The two girls, also wrapped in long aprons, giggled. "He's not," said the shorter girl, her red curls dancing. "He won't dance any more and we're hopeless without him showing us." She shook her head at Jarrah and he shuffled his feet and lowered his eyes. "Boys," she said. "They've got no manners. I'm Maisie. And this is Janet, and that's Mrs Jacobs."

"Lovely to meet you all." Gaia's stomach rumbled. "Something smells delicious. Do you two girls always help with the cooking?"

"No. All the girls take turns. Me and Janet do Sundays. It's roast mutton."

"It's always roast mutton on Sundays," said Mrs Jacobs. "The best meal of the week. Plenty if you want to stay."

"Thank you, I'd love to. I'm starving, actually. We drove from Jurien Bay area this afternoon and all we had was a sandwich hours ago."

Jarrah showed her where he sat and pulled out the chair next to him for Gaia to sit on. Hannah sat on her other side and introduced her to three other staff. The roast, which, it turned out, was four large meat-falling-off-the-bone legs of mutton, mountains of golden spuds, carrots and spinach, and four enormous jugs of seriously yummy gravy, fed 25 kids, four staff and Gaia. Once that lot was demolished, Mrs Jacobs and Janet dished out generous helpings of trifle sloshed over with custard. Gaia detested trifle, and custard was even more disgusting, but she thought she'd better get it down somehow. It seemed rude not to.

Throughout the meal, Maisie, who was sitting opposite them, barely stopped talking, but somehow managed to consume a fair pile of food at the same time. Gaia was so engaged with Maisie's commentary on every kid in the room that the trifle disappeared down her throat without her even thinking about gagging.

"So you'll dance for us tonight after we clean up," Maisie said. It wasn't a question.

"She can't," Jarrah said. It was about the only thing he'd uttered throughout the entire meal, although Gaia noticed he'd managed to eat every last morsel of his dinner.

"Don't be dumb. Of course she can," Maisie told him.

"She doesn't dance in places like this. She needs ballet shoes and stuff." Jarrah looked daggers at her.

"We all dance in bare feet. And anyway she's probably got some ballet shoes in her bag." Maisie's tone made it clear that that was the end of the matter.

Gaia grinned. "Do I get a say in this?"

Maisie shook her head. "We need you to dance. We've tried without Jarrah but we're hopeless." She broke into song. "We need some…" —she flung her arms in the air— "inspiration!"

Gaia hid her smile. "Well, I can't argue with that. I'm a bit full though. Perhaps we can dance tomorrow after you all get home from school and before everyone has stuffed themselves."

"Nope. Tonight we must begin. Just don't do any leaps and twirls. Do the floaty sort of dance."

"OK. But only if you kids who usually dance with Jarrah join me."

"Deal," said Maisie, raising her palm. Gaia put hers up quickly and Maisie slapped her so hard her hand stung.

Dinner over, cleaning up occupied four of the other girls in the kitchen on dishes, and four of the boys wiping down the tables and sweeping and mopping the already clean floorboards. Gaia's offer to help was firmly refused and she allowed herself to be pulled to an armchair in the den next door where she was surrounded by a crowd of little kids showing her their treasures. On her lap was the smallest of them, one of the few Aboriginal children. This little fellow, as cute as a button with his Jarrah hair and Jarrah smile, informed her he was free. Not two, free. When the big Jarrah appeared after finishing his sweeping duties, Seamus was with him.

Gaia smiled at him over the heads of the kids and he smiled back, his eyes soft. Heat crept up her neck. Seamus looked down at Jarrah and put his arm around his thin shoulders and left it there. Gaia swallowed. The small boy on her lap patted her cheek and without thinking she enclosed his little hand in hers and kissed his palm. "OK troops," she said, lifting the child in her arms and standing up, "Are we going to dance or what?" At least her voice sounded steady. "Come on Jarrah, it's you and me on this. Seamus too, seeing as he's here."

"Then Seamus and Hannah can dance the céilí for us," Jarrah said, and Gaia saw in his dark eyes the sparkle she feared he had lost.

CHAPTER 26

$\mathcal{N}$ext morning, when Gaia opened her eyes, she saw above her a low, whitish, slightly stained ceiling, and hard beside the narrow bed was a wall of old-fashioned rose-trellis wallpaper interrupted by a small window with the merest puddle of light coming through its murky glass. For minutes she lay there, stiff and unmoving, her heart missing desperately the bright morning light pouring in through the windows on one side of her barn, bouncing off the big mirrors on the opposite side and dancing like water on the high half-round corrugated iron barn roof. Here, in the small staff bedroom of the Children's Home, there was no sound of the sea, no wind rustling in the tall eucalyptus trees, no tiny grunts from a kangaroo lying asleep by the side of her bed. Only cars revving as they pushed faster up the small incline on the road outside, trucks breaking as they slowed down before they rounded the next corner, the bark of a dog in the distance.

She looked up at the window, too high to see out of from her prone position on the bed. It was open no more than a smidgeon at the bottom, the orange curtains blowing a little. She took in a deep breath. Fresh air — but where was its scent? Where was the salty air mixed with the dry, earthy, alive green air of home? Her arm flopped over the side of the bed. Nothing there, no soft warm fur to scratch between a sweet Roo's ears.

Pushing herself into a sitting position she threw off the checked blanket and twisted around so she was sitting on the edge of the bed. Her dear, dark blue, scruffy backpack in the corner was the only familiar thing left in her world.

"Hey Bazza, catch," came a shout through the window.

"Over here. Chuck it to me." A different voice.

Boys. Perhaps Jarrah was out there. He was so happy last night, like a different kid. When Hannah said Gaia could sleep in the empty staff bedroom, Jarrah had lit up. From there it had all been arranged. They were short staffed so Gaia was going to stay and help out with the cleaning, but mostly getting the neglected garden into shape. Their some-time gardener had left weeks ago and now only the lawn got mowed, mainly by Seamus, but while he'd been away, by the kids in the weekends.

"Gaia is the best gardener," Jarrah had informed everyone. "She can make a rock grow."

"Who eats rocks, dummy?" Bazza said back.

"It means she can grow anything, dummy yourself," said Jarrah. "It's a metaphor. Gaia will be able to grow all our veges and stuff so Mrs Jacobs won't have to buy them any more and she can buy more chocolate instead."

Gaia's heart lightened as the kids playing outside got rowdier. She wasn't going to be here for long and making Jarrah happy made her happy. She owed him that for his promise not to tell anyone about Mason. And at least here she didn't have to worry about the creep showing up. She'd been nervous about having to meet Seamus's friend and become her flatmate. So much better to sleep here. Here, it felt easy. It would be fun to work out what she could do with the garden. She could start with some winter plantings that would provide some of the Home's veges. See if any of the kids were interested; they could make some cloches and get some seedlings started that the kids could plant out in early spring, when she was back at Goshawk Gardens.

After breakfast she'd phone Mr Ludlow and make a time to see him. There must be some law that protected wilderness areas and the wildlife.

~

It was strange being back in the lawyer's office. He hadn't changed a bit; in fact he still had the same blue-checked shirt on with a navy tie. It seemed forever since she'd been here last; much longer than two-and-a-half years. Did she look different? She felt different. So much had happened even though probably from the outside it would seem nothing had changed. Just gardening and dancing and Rita-Roo and Gos and Mary and Eddie. And Jarrah and Seamus. Those were the good things. She didn't want to think about the bad things.

Mr Ludlow asked his secretary to bring them in tea and biscuits and listened without interrupting as Gaia told him about Morton and McMillan's bid to buy up Mason's land and build a resort. Then she told him about the seadragons. And last, she told him about Mason's accident, and how she'd found him unconscious on the concrete and how she was scared to stay there alone now in case he came back.

"So first things first," Mr Ludlow said. "I'll phone the police here in Perth and get an update on Mason. Then we'll make a plan to save your beautiful wilderness and those precious seadragons."

Gaia thought she might be hallucinating. Could it really be so easy? Mr Ludlow seemed entirely confident.

"I don't suppose it will be easy to stop the development but you know better than anyone that persistence and passion is what it takes to do what's right and what truly matters. To tell you the truth, I'm a frustrated environmental activist. If there was a branch of law that would allow me to fight causes like this, I'd retrain. So this will be free, pro bono; it will be like an apprenticeship for me."

"Really?"

"Really. We'll work together on it and we'll win."

He called in Stephanie, his junior, and asked her to phone the Central Perth Police Station and find out who he should speak to about the current whereabouts of Dave Mason. "Tell them I'm acting for Gaia Christie, Mason's neighbor, and I'm concerned for her safety if Mason should return to his property before he has been thoroughly assessed and found to be low risk." Ten minutes later his phone rang and he picked it up and put it on speaker. Gaia listened as a man introduced himself as Constable Riley and said that Mason had been found four days previously in a back street gutter, unconscious and beaten to a pulp. He was now back in Perth Hospital in the same ward he'd discharged himself from. His blood alcohol had again been high and he had sustained another head injury, this time mild, and broken ribs.

"So what will happen if he discharges himself again?" Mr Ludlow asked.

"He has a Drunk and Disorderly charge against him; his fifth in three years. If he wants to discharge himself the hospital has to notify us. According to his doctor the most likely scenario is that he'll be transferred to a drug and alcohol rehabilitation unit once he no longer requires specialist medical care. A discharge of his Drunk and Disorderly charge will be reliant on him being assessed as of low risk. There is also a note on his file that Miss Gaia Christie, your client, must be notified if he is discharged from supervised care."

"Excellent. Miss Christie is currently here in Perth, so please notify me of any change to Mason's status, and I'll pass on the message."

Mr Ludlow put the phone down and grinned at her. "I wasn't sure the police would give me any information. It always helps to get a constable. They're much more likely to spill the beans when a pompous lawyer questions them."

Gaia sat on her trembling hands. "Thank you. I've been a bit nervous. Terrified actually. Now I'll be able to go home."

"Well, before you do, what about a quick bite of lunch? We can talk while we're eating. I need to get all the information I can about Mason's land, the ownership conditions and so on. Does he have any family that you know of?"

"I know he and Ros—that's his wife but she left him after the fire—haven't owned their land as long as my dad's family have owned our land. I think he and Ros purchased that block around the time Dad brought Mum and baby Bron back home to take over from my granddad. So that was around 1960."

"Right. I'll leave a note for Stephanie asking her to see what she can find out when she gets back from her lunch break."

To Gaia's surprise Seamus was waiting for her when she came out of Mr Ludlow's office, and a shimmer of pleasure zipped through her when he bent and kissed her cheek. A young woman walking past smiled at them. Gaia smiled back. It felt good to be standing here in this big city with a man that other women found attractive. A man who seemed to like her in spite of her scars and shyness and strange ways.

"So, spill," Seamus said, as they drove back to the Children's Home.

"Mason is back in hospital with another head injury. The police have promised to let Mr Ludlow know when he is discharged."

"Jaysis. What a loser that man is. Does that mean you'll be going home?"

Gaia sighed. "I'd love to but now I need to track down

Ros, Dave's wife. Mr Ludlow has found out that the Mason land is jointly owned by Dave and Ros, and there are no divorce records for them. He phoned the developers right while I was sitting in his office and talked to Suzanne Henderson, the woman who came to see me. He told her he was the lawyer representing my interests, and that he was interested to know if Ros and Dave had both signed the sales contract, as an extensive search had found no record of any divorce. He had her on a speaker so I could hear everything she said. She was huffing and puffing and finally told him that Mason had assured them that when he and Ros split up Ros had said she didn't want the land and he could have it, and then she disappeared. He'd tried to track her down but she'd vanished. So the land was his."

"Some developer. As if she could get away with not even checking the facts," Seamus said.

"Well, she wasn't quite as silly as she sounded. She admitted that they had been trying to find Ros, and were still looking. She sounded really pissed off. Then she said that when they did find her, she would bet her commission on Ros leaping at the chance to sell, given the payout she would get for her half."

"She could be right about that, I suppose," Seamus said. "Still, it buys you some time. You just have to find Ros first and persuade her not to sell."

"That's what Mr Ludlow said. And he said he'd talk to a friend of his at the university who is passionate about saving the reef, and has already been involved in the university buying up land that would otherwise be developed. It's being used as a field station for researchers and students go there on field trips."

"That would be mighty, wouldn't it just. Get Mason off the property as well."

Gaia nodded. "I'm trying not to get my hopes up, but I can't help it."

"Get 'em up, I say. We'll find Ros somehow, and then if the university doesn't come to the party, we'll find a way to set up a fund or something to raise enough money to buy Mason and Ros out."

∽

HOPE SHRUNK AS DAY AFTER DAY WENT BY AND ROS STAYED lost. Mr Ludlow had put a private detective on the case, all at his own expense. Gaia kept busy, gardening and teaching the kids dancing and pushing away her homesickness. Then Hannah had an idea. Gaia was buzzing with it when Seamus dropped by that evening for dinner; according to Hannah he seemed to be dropping by quite a lot these days.

"How about we have a picnic at the beach in the weekend," Seamus said. "I've got the day off. We could take Jarrah and Maisie too… unless you'd rather it was just the two of us." He contorted his face into what Gaia guessed was his attempt at a leer. Just made him look more like a leprechaun.

"Sounds fabulous but no can do. Not this weekend. We've decided to turn the den into a real dance school for this whole weekend. So no beaches for me. Not for Jarrah or Maisie either. We're going to begin work on a proper ballet for the concert the school is having in September to raise money for a new swimming pool. It was Hannah's idea."

"Of course it was," said Seamus. "She has some good ideas, that woman. Usually involving a lot of hard work for everyone else."

"Not fair. She puts as much effort into everything herself. More. She's dedicated to those kids."

"It isn't. She does. She is. I stand corrected. So, what is the ballet? *The Nut Cracker? The Firebird?*"

"Well, smarty, don't you know your ballets. Nope. I don't think we're quite up to that standard yet and we only have fifteen minutes for the whole dance. We're going to choreograph our own. Jarrah thinks we should all be seadragons. Or perhaps a seadragon corps de ballet and a whaleshark principal dancer."

"A whaleshark? Hardly a ballerina-type figure."

"Tell that to Jarrah. Whalesharks are his latest thing. I'm trying to gently talk him out of it. He was thinking that about four of the kids could be one whaleshark, sort of like those shows where there is a horse with one person as the head and the other as the tail."

"Creative kid. That could work. At least it would be a way to include the kids who can't dance for peanuts."

"They can all dance. Well, by the time the weekend is over, they'll be able to."

Seamus grinned. "I'll look forward to it. I don't suppose I can come and watch you practicing?"

"Nope."

"What about if I join in and do a bit of the jig?"

"Nope."

THE NEXT TIME GAIA WENT TO MR LUDLOW'S ROOMS TO discuss what they could do next, he invited her and Seamus to dinner at his house. Sitting around the table in their comfortable home with plates of roast chicken and crispy roast potatoes in front of them made Gaia homesick for Mary and Eddie's Sunday rabbit stew. It was the first time Gaia had met Yvonne, Mr Ludlow's wife, and their teenage son. Their twin daughters had already fledged, as Yvonne called it, and were hitch-hiking around the UK and Europe. By the end of the evening Gaia was feeling so relaxed she even managed to call Mr Ludlow by his first name, James, as he asked her to do, although it felt rather strange.

"Imagine growing up with parents like Mr and Mrs Ludlow," Gaia said. She and Seamus were having one last cup of tea at the Children's Home before he was dispatched to his apartment.

"From what you've told me," Seamus said gently, "your dad was every bit as lovely as James, and your mum could hardly have been more dedicated to her family and you. Look what she gave up for you all."

"You're right. I was lucky. That's if they hadn't died and if Bron hadn't deserted me. It's hard to remember the luck now. I barely even remember what they looked like any more."

"That's sad. Aren't there photos of your mum dancing somewhere? Perhaps that American dance company has some in their archives?"

Gaia shrugged. "I suppose. One day I might see what I can find; write to them or something, but those sorts of photos aren't really Mum; they're whoever she was dancing. All that stage makeup. Anyway, I do sort of remember her like that. What I miss is how she and Dad and Bron looked when they were just being themselves."

That night, as sleep remained elusive, Gaia's better self berated her. How selfish and self-centered she'd become. She'd had fourteen years of happy family times, so much more than most of the kids in the Home. So much more than Jarrah. And both Jarrah and Seamus had lost their dads when they were kids. Perhaps it was easier for them because they weren't there when their parents died. They weren't to blame. If she'd made absolutely sure Bron's cigarette butts were out, run them under a tap, would she be in Melbourne now, a senior student at the Australian Ballet School, her mum and dad so proud when they came to see her dancing at the gala at the end of the year? Would Bron be dancing in a world-class ballet company, on course towards their mother's dream for him—to dance the part of Oberon, King of the Fairies?

CHAPTER 27

*I*n July, Seamus invited Gaia back to his place for a meal; he wanted to talk to her about an idea he had to mark Jarrah's twelfth birthday in two weeks. When he opened the door to his apartment, Gaia swooned at the smells that wafted from his small kitchen. "You've been cooking," she said. "It smells incredible."

"Well, of course. I did ask you to dinner. Did you expect beans on toast?"

"No, but perhaps takeaways! I know you don't have time to cook. I didn't even know you could cook fancy stuff."

"Ah, there you go then. Heaps of things you still have to find out about me."

The dinner was even better than it smelled. Fresh crayfish from the fish market slathered with cheese sauce.

"Crayfish Mornay, doncha know. A dinkum Irish dish."

"Yum! This is better than any restaurant."

Seamus's wicked smile shone in the candle-light. "Now, to birthday surprises for our lad. I've managed to get a week off, with Jarrah's birthday slap in the middle. What do you think about driving to Exmouth and taking Jarrah out on the reef to see manta rays and orcas, and hopefully even swim with whalesharks?"

"How? Is that even possible? Seeing whalesharks, just like that? Jarrah would be in heaven."

"It is. I know a man who knows man…" Seamus grinned. "There's a nurse I've got to know a bit—Chrissie Johnson. Her dad's a fisherman in Exmouth. The whalesharks are out there in large numbers right now, feeding on plankton, and Chrissie has swum with them lots of times. She said it never stops being awe-inspiring. The biggest fish in the sea. The season on the Ningaloo Reef is from April to August, so next week would be perfect. We can go out for the day on Chrissie's dad's fishing boat. Take two days to drive there and two days back. Long days driving but we could sing our way through it. Then we'd have three days at Ningaloo and hopefully one of them would be good and calm for going out and swimming around and hopefully spot some amazing wildlife. Chrissie said we can stay at their place."

"Oh yes, that would be incredible. This Chrissie must like you a lot!"

Seamus wiggled his eyebrows. "I reckon."

"Will she be there?"

"I reckon not. She has better things to do with her fancy doctor boyfriend."

"Oh, that's a shame."

Jarrah couldn't keep still as Ray's fishing boat rumbled over the flat calm sea. Already they had been snorkeling over the best parts of the coral in the lagoon, then had scoffed sandwiches and cake before they bounced over the surf breaking at the edge of the lagoon where the reef dropped away, and snorkeled in the deepest sea Jarrah had ever swum in. He'd been scared at first but then Gaia had taken his hand and he'd been good after that. Before they even went in she'd told him how it felt scarier in the deep ocean but in fact it was exactly the same as in the shallow water if you were floating on top. He had even done some duck dives and then shot the water out of his snorkel without his mouth filling with salt. It wasn't even cold, although he had a wetsuit on so he could stay in for hours in case the whalesharks took a while to pass by.

He almost wouldn't mind if they didn't see one because they'd already seen a family of Orcas frolicking like puppies only fifty meters from their boat, and when they were snorkeling, some ordinary little reef sharks and giant shoals of fish that looked like one big fish until they got to you and split in two to get past. And they saw turtles, and dolphins, and most amazing of all, a giant manta ray. It was so giant that when Gaia pulled him down in a dive and pointed up, he could see its great wings silhouetted by the sun. It was hard to think a whaleshark could be better than that. But now Ray was on the search. He knew some of the best places they hung out, where there were heaps of the plankton they liked to suck through their giant filter mouth.

The boat was stopping and Ray and Seamus were dropping the anchor. Were they here? Jarrah's heart was pounding so loudly he thought the boat engine was still going.

"Ready?" Ray said. "I reckon if you three jump in here and hang around, sooner or later you'll see a whaleshark swimming by. Remember what I told you; stay on the surface and at least three meters away from it or it'll get frightened and dive deep and that will be that. As soon as you see one, swim like the clappers beside it. They seem to glide slowly but they can be a bugger to keep up with. If you disappear over the horizon I'll bring the boat to you so you don't need to swim back."

So the three of them put on their flippers and masks and snorkels and held hands and jumped in off the backboard, all together. Jarrah sank and then started to come up again past his own bubbles, ready to blow his snorkel clear, and right in front of them coming directly at them was the most enormous creature he had ever seen in his life, its giant curved mouth in its blue-gray white-spotted head split in the biggest smile in the world. Then its mouth opened like a cave so huge that Jarrah flippered full speed upwards. His head broke the water and he shot his snorkel clear so fast he could taste water still slopping in the bottom of it but there wasn't time to clear it and his head was back under, Gaia and Seamus's hands holding each of his so tight, and there was its enormous body gliding past, its massive half-moon flat head with tiny eyes, its long, long body, like an Aboriginal painting with all its pretty white spots, its pale whitish underside, its big shark dorsal fin then the littler fin then its giant tail sailing past them, and he shook free both his hands and flippered as fast as he could beside it, so fast he was ahead of Gaia and Seamus, and his legs were going like pistons, both of them, and he felt like he was a fish, a baby whaleshark swimming after his mother.

THAT NIGHT, SEAMUS TOOK THEM TO THE POSHEST restaurant in town. There wasn't in fact a lot of competition in Exmouth, a small strange town of hot spaces and red dusty sand and not much to do or see until you drove along Cape Range National Park and took one of the side roads to the coast where the white beaches and blue sea of Ningaloo Reef took off. Where beneath the blue swam whalesharks.

So they didn't care that it was only pizzas and they were pretty good and cooked outside in a big coal oven with a mouth like a whaleshark's, and their table was on the grass with a red and white checked tablecloth and candles and trop-ical leaves and flowers all around them smelling as good as Gaia so they couldn't even see the people at other tables. They ate two giant pizzas and chips and salad and Gaia and Seamus drank Guinness and Jarrah drank a special cocktail which had no alcohol but lots of mango juice and a coconut taste as well and a toothpick with a cherry stuck on it, and then Gaia and Seamus had one chocolate mousse between them and Jarrah had an enormous ice-cream sundae with nuts and chocolate all to himself. Then Seamus asked the waitress to bring them three glasses of port. One for Jarrah too because Seamus said he had to start sometime and twelve seemed a good age and it was a special occasion. It was yummy, not like beer which he had actually tasted once before and didn't like.

Gaia and Seamus clinked their glasses together and sang Happy Birthday to him and Gaia looked like she was going to cry and he felt a bit like crying himself. He'd had birthdays before at the kid's home and everyone sang happy birthday but not as good as Gaia and Seamus. It was actually the best day of his entire life.

DRIVING BACK FROM EXMOUTH, THE REEF IN HER HEAD, GAIA started worrying. What if those surveyors had found the sea-dragon again? She needed to be home with Rita Roo and Gos. Perhaps Seamus could drop her off at Goshawk Gardens and she could catch the bus back to Perth in a few days? While Mason was still in hospital. Perhaps Mary and Eddie were back? Oh please be back. Of course she couldn't desert the kids for long when they'd been working so hard on their sea-dragon dance. She'd just stay a few days and be back by the following weekend.

Seamus of course had no problem with her plan and even Jarrah didn't seem to mind too much when she asked him to make sure everyone practiced their dances daily. Gazing out the window as home got closer and closer she let Jarrah and Seamus's chatter waft over her head. In Perth, however busy she kept herself, she felt as if she were losing her colors. She needed to be home alone to center herself. Once she was in her gardens and floating over the reef and poised at the barre she'd feel them there, see them there with her—Dad with his hands deep in the soil, Bron's arm brushing hers as they watched the seadragons dance, Mum beside her at the barre, the dancers in the big mirror performing twin grand battements, front, side and back. If she stayed away any longer she knew they would vanish forever.

Insisting that they drop her off at the gate—they were already going to be late home and Jarrah had school tomorrow—she opened her letterbox and took out the envelope stamped by Social Security on the back. She laughed out loud as she remembered the girl at the Jurien Bay post office telling her she'd better put a padlock on the letterbox to stop the lowlifes pinching her benefit check before she had time to collect it. How long ago that seemed. She danced along the track to Mary and Eddie's house, her heart singing with the freedom of knowing Mason was imprisoned in hospital 250 kilometres away. When she saw Eddie and Mary's dear old truck outside their house she let out a cowboy holler that had Mary almost falling out the door.

"You back girl, makin' noise as usual. Thought you a cow dropping her calf."

Gaia flung herself at her, almost knocking her flying. "You're back, oh, thank you, thank you, thank you."

'That plenty thank yous. You good? How you get here?"

"I danced all the way from Exmouth. I'm good. Good, good, good now I'm home and you're here." Then Eddie was there given her a pat on her arm and grinning his biggest whitest grin.

Passing by Mason's house she saw the young farmer student outside. He smiled at her and told her he'd done a bit of weeding in her gardens.

"That's nice of you," Gaia said, taken aback by his kindness.

"No bother," he said. "I stole a couple of your hen eggs so it was well worth it. And there's not much else to do around here at this time of the year. There's even a kangaroo that keeps me company. Totally bizarre. She almost seems tame. Has a very cute joey too."

And there she was, waiting in her favorite spot by the outside table when Gaia opened the barn door the next morning. She hopped over and nuzzled Gaia's chest. Her joey was big enough to peer over the lip of the pouch, and Gaia lifted him out gently, looking all the while into Rita Roo's soulful eyes as she did so. Rita Roo batted her eyelashes and nuzzled Gaia again. She cuddled the warm little creature close, her tears dropping on his soft head as she kissed it. "Hullo, little fella," she whispered. "Jarrah is going to love you. He can find you the perfect name."

With the joey back in his mother's pouch, together she and Rita Roo went down to the beach and Gaia danced again on the sand, so different from the hardwood floor of the den. After breakfast she explored her gardens; they were in their winter plumage and not too overgrown, thanks to the young farmer, so she didn't feel too guilty about delaying the weeding until tomorrow. Best of all Gos flew laconically onto his favorite branch and then onto her arm when she held it out. He glared at her and she glared back. "I've got no fresh mice for you, so you'll have to wait until I catch one tonight," she said, scratching his favorite spot low on the side of his head.

"We're trying to find out what happened to Ros Mason," Gaia told Mary, later that day. "My lawyer discovered that she and Dave never got divorced. We were hoping to find her before the developers do, and try and convince her not to sell the farm. Both she and Dave still own it."

"She might be same place she go when she find her man," Mary said.

"What do you mean? Do you know where she is?"

Mary shrugged. "Long time init. She wi' bloke las' time I sees her. Came here t'git stuff. Mister Dave not here. Ros seem happy. Told me not to tell Mister Dave or no one."

"Did she tell you where she was going?"

Mary nodded. "Write it down in case. Her won't mind if you know but don tell Mister Dave."

"I won't. Of course I won't." Gaia shuddered. "Do you still have it?"

"Yeah. You get her to stop Mister Dave selling. P'raps she come back and Mister Dave stay gone."

CHAPTER 28

*J*arrah scuffed along beside Gaia. They were walking on Cottesloe Beach in the pink and gold sunset. It wasn't as pretty as the beach at Gaia's gardens, but it was heaps better than being stuck at the kids' home all Saturday. Seamus had driven them here in his van first thing this morning and they'd had a picnic at lunchtime to celebrate Gaia being back. When Seamus stopped swimming they had even more surprise food in a box to have for a picnic dinner. He and Gaia had got out ages ago because it was too cold for them. Seamus was tougher because he was used to freezing Irish sea.

Tomorrow after the kids got back from Sunday School they were having a whole day rehearsing their dance. Jarrah didn't really like Sunday School because it was all about a whitefella god and jesus and a holy ghost, but they had to go at least once a month. That was the rule, Hannah said, even if most of the kids, even the whities, thought it was boring. Even Hannah had to go and she said at least it wasn't Catholic because if it was she would put her foot down.

Jarrah giggled inside as he thought about how surprised Gaia was going to be when they showed her the new dance part they'd been practicing. The sun was half in and half out of the water now, its light getting redder as it disappeared into the depths of the sea. Would there be seadragons down there, dancing in its glow? Somewhere there would be. He looked sideways at Gaia. She was gliding along, her head raised to the sky, her eyes actually closed but he knew she wasn't sleeping, just soaking in the warm salty air. Her face was glowing like the surface of the sea and there was a streak of shining red down her cheek. Like she had been painted with an artist's brush. It was her white scar catching the last rays of the sun. He thought it looked beautiful. She looked beautiful. He wished he had his camera with him but it was in his backpack over with their towels and stuff. Anyway she wouldn't want him to take a photo. She still hid her scars whenever she thought about it. Pulled her hair over her face.

"Gaia," he said.

"What?" Gaia walked a bit slower and opened her eyes and turned her head to smile at him. The sun left her face and the pretty red brush stroke glowed whitish-silver against her tan.

"You know how you're scared to have that doctor Seamus knows have a look at your scars, so he can see if he can make them disappear more," Jarrah said, his heart thumping a bit faster. What if he upset her and their lovely day got spoilt?

"I'm not scared. What made you think that?"

She didn't sound upset. Jarrah's heart skipped a little and slowed back down. "Well, why won't you then?"

"Because I don't care about my scars. Why should I? What difference would it make even if they could be made less obvious?"

She sounded a bit cross. He should have kept his mouth shut. Too late now. "I don't mind them. I don't even notice them," he said. They kept walking, Gaia looking straight ahead now. "But, Gaia, what if they can be fixed and you can be a real dancer and not just do dances with us kids?"

"I'm too old to take up dancing seriously. It's nothing to do with the scars. And going to dance school would cost a fortune and I don't have a fortune." Gaia walked a bit faster and Jarrah had to speed up.

"You could be a dance teacher. You're the best dance teacher."

"Then that's fine isn't it? I don't need any dance school for that. Why would I go through all those horrible surgeries just to do something I can already do?"

"You could be a proper ballet teacher at a ballet school if you got trained. That's different than just teaching us kids. I don't blame you being scared. I'd be scared too to have that surgery stuff." He shuddered.

"Well, shut-up about it then. And I'm not scared, I'm just realistic." Gaia walked even faster and Jarrah had to drag his leg behind him like a cripple.

"Stop going so fast. You're being mean." The words flew out of Jarrah's mouth before he could shut it. Gaia stopped so quickly he banged into her. "Sorry," he said. "You're not mean. You're never ever mean. You're kind."

Gaia swung around and he stumbled back before he got his dumb feet to balance again. He wanted to look down at the sand but his eyes felt glued in place, staring up into her eyes, her face around them sort of flattened, as if she'd crashed into a door. He was going to throw up. How could he say such a horrible thing to her? And now he felt like he was going to blubber like a stupid little kid. He forced his eyes shut and looked down. "I… I… I'm sorry, Gaia. I didn't mean it. I truly don't think you're mean. I'd never think that." He couldn't look up. He couldn't look at her. She touched his arm and he went stiff. Then her arms were around him and his face was in her T-shirt and her special smell was going up his nose and he was making her T-shirt wet.

"It's OK. It's OK." She was squatting down and he was too and then he was sitting on the sand, his skinny right leg and his stubby left leg stretched out in front of him next to her long legs, the one with the scars touching his dumb shrunken leg all the way along. "Tell me why you're so upset," she said, putting her arm around his shoulders. Her voice sounding like she felt like crying too.

"I'm not. I don't care if you never have that scar surgery but I don't want you to be unhappy because you can only dance with us kids." He touched her leg where the shiny white scar showed. "I like your scars."

"Thank you. I know they don't matter to you. That's why you're my best friend, because you love me, whatever I look like."

"You look beautiful," Jarrah said, risking a glance into her face. It wasn't flat any more, but smooth and tanned and rosy.

"I know, because you're beautiful to me too. She drew her hand along his stubby leg, and her smile made his own mouth smile back. "That's why we're friends for life, whatever happens and even when sometimes we get mad at each other. I think we're more than friends really. I feel like you're my family."

"Really?" Jarrah looked into her eyes like the sea.

"Really, truly."

"Me too. That's how I feel."

"And that means you can say anything to me and we will still always be family."

They sat for a while, their different legs still touching and not minding what they looked like to anyone else.

"I love what we're all doing together, dancing our sea-dragon dance. Nothing could be better than that," Gaia said, her voice sort of sad.

"Maisie thought you might want to be a ballet dancer in a ballet company like your mum was and the ballet masters mightn't choose you because of having scars even though you're the best."

"Oh. Well, I did once want to be a professional dancer but

it's not going to happen. Even if all these ugly scars vanished. It's a crazy idea."

Jarrah looked at her again. Her blue eyes were sad. "I don't think it's a crazy idea, but it's not fair if you have to have horrible surgery done to you if you don't want to and it makes you scared when you could just stay the same and dance with us and dance on the beach at Goshawk Gardens."

~

ON SUNDAY EVERYONE WAS THERE IN THE DEN, BREAKFAST finished, ready to show Gaia what they had been practicing all week while she'd been away. Seamus walked in while they were all still jumping about and doing their stretches.

"Good grief," Gaia said. "What are you doing here? I thought after yesterday we wouldn't see you again for at least a couple of days."

"Well, my friend, it's your lucky day," Seamus said. "I thought I'd better check out this dance. Apparently it's becoming quite the major event."

Gaia saw Seamus wink at Jarrah. "What's going on here? You two have been up to something. I can't even go away for a few days without the pair of you getting into trouble." She looked around as Jarrah did a little laugh-snort and saw all the other kids grinning and Hannah too with a smile as bright as a Christmas tree. "So who's going to tell me?" She tried to sound bossy but her voice came out too bubbly for it to work.

"The school wants us to be the main event at the concert. We are going to have a whole half hour instead of just fifteen minutes. The entire time after the intermission." Jarrah gave a little hop-jump.

"The intermission is it. That's a fancy word for a break in the middle of a little school concert." Gaia put her finger on the end of her nose and pushed it upwards.

"Wait until you see what we've choreographed now," Jarrah said.

"Choreographed? Another fancy word. Crikey, I was only away five days and this has become Covent Garden?"

"It's not a garden. It's a dance company. The Flying Gos Dance Company." Gaia saw Seamus's eyebrows hit his hair.

"So, who thought that name up? As if I couldn't guess," Gaia said.

"I did, right this minute," Jarrah said, doing another little hop. "The Flying Gos Dance Company performs *The Dance of the Seadragons* starring Whelan the Whaleshark."

"Whelan? Where does that come from?"

"It's an Irish name and it means joyful, so it's perfect for our whaleshark," Jarrah said.

Gaia frowned at Seamus. "I see you all over this," she said.

"Me? Not me. Blame Hannah," Seamus said.

"Are there even any whalesharks in Ireland? I thought they liked warm waters?" Gaia said. "Not melted ice like in Ireland."

"Ah, it be clear you've never been to the Emerald Isle. The whalesharks there are as common as leprechauns doncha know."

"So, *The Dance of the Seadragons* has been relocated to Ireland while I've been gone? Even though there are definitely no seadragons in Ireland or anywhere else in the entire universe other than in the bottom half of Australia."

"Says the marine biologist. But, my sweet Gaia, your co-choreographer"— Seamus bowed towards Jarrah —"understands that this is a mythological story, not a science thesis, and an Irish whaleshark called Whelan can swim through the seagrasses of Goshawk Gardens Beach and dance along the sand wi' the fairies and leprechauns and clown fish and whatever takes his fancy."

"Do you want to see?" Jarrah said. "You'll understand when you see it."

Gaia shot her arms in the air. "Yes, Mr Jarrah, show me what you have."

"Right," said Hannah. "We whalesharks will go and get into our costume, and Maisie, you get the music ready. We'll do the Whelan the Whaleshark entry."

Gaia let herself be pulled onto one of the front chairs, the other kids crowding around her. Maisie stood with her finger at the ready to push the button and start the tape rolling. Hannah, Jarrah, Bella and Seamus had disappeared. What was going on? Bella was one of the best dancers in the Children's Home but her love was tap dancing. And Seamus?

"*Da*, da, *da*, da" shouted Maisie, and pushed the button. A rollicking Irish jig filled the den and through the side door came a lumpy gray vision, its vast bulk covered with white spots. From its underside protruded four sets of black legs, the front and back pair shorter and ending in ballet pumps and the two pairs in the middle longer and ending in Irish jig shoes, the hard kind. Gaia felt her mouth open and stay that way as the slightly lopsided front legs led the other legs across the floor. "They're on the sand" whispered Maisie who was now sitting beside her. Then the middle two pairs started to dance, their feet flashing in and out, back and forth, banging on the floor in perfect synchrony, while the front and end pairs each flashed rather more slowly, stamped first one leg and then the other in time to the music. By the end of the dance the rest of the kids—the entire Flying Gos Dance Company—were up and jigging along with them, some better than others for sure but all of them with leprechaun grins.

My work here is done, Gaia heard in her head, as clear and beautiful as the song of a gray Shrike-Thrush.

CHAPTER 29

"*G*aia, I have great news," Seamus said, surprising her as she was weeding the vegetable garden at the Home. It was late afternoon on Wednesday, and she hadn't seen him since Sunday when she'd been charmed into Jarrah's new additions to their ballet. Not a ballet so much now as a multiformat modern dance—classical ballet comprised of Gaia on pointe as the sad male seadragon and Maisie as her seadragon partner (on tippy toes rather than pointe), their dance sad because their reef was being destroyed by a nasty developer (bad boy Bazza in a character role); contemporary ballet featuring the clown fish, the octopus, the gobies with their big eyes on top of their heads, peering out of the sand on the sea bottom, Rita Roo with her long tail and Gos with his swooping cries as he slammed his wicked beak into the nasty developer's head, his claws dragging him away to somewhere off stage, and of course the Irish jig finale where joyful Whelan led the whole troupe in a dance of frenzied triumph.

"I have single-handedly got rid of the wicked Mr Mason," Seamus said, pulling her up from her kneeling position. "Listen up. This morning I had to fill in on the neurology ward because their usual orderly was off sick. And the first job I got was wheeling that very fellow, that nasty glob of shite, down to the ambulance bay. I couldn't believe my luck getting to see him off. I'd never have recognized him from Jarrah's description; he's lost his greasy long hair and straggly beard and he doesn't even stink of smoke and booze. His face had as many whiskers as a baby's bottom, and his hair was really short, and not a whiff of smoke, more disinfectant. But of course I had to take all his notes as well so I had a quick look at the summary. Part of my job doncha know, making sure he was the right patient for the right ambulance."

"Stop it. Where did they take him? Was he being let loose?" Gaia's mouth was so dry she could hardly get the words out.

"Nope. That's the beautiful thing. He was being transferred to an Alcohol and Drug Rehabilitation Institution in South Perth. In his summary it said he required rehabilitation for his head injuries as well as his alcohol addiction, and that he'd need help with memory and planning strategies and daily living activities. He still has a Drunk and Disorderly charge on his head, and can't be discharged without the police being informed."

Gaia closed her eyes as something heavy churned through her and vaporized into the gloriously warm air. She stretched herself up and out and flexed her neck and shoulders back and opened her eyes on Seamus's smile. "I can't believe it. He could be in there for months. Perhaps he'll even stop drinking and then he mightn't be so creepy." She slapped her hands over her face. "Oh-my-god."

"Yep. Oh-my-god is right."

"And now we've got more time to find Ros before the developer lot get to her first. I told James yesterday what Mary told me, and he's going to check out that address. He phones Suzanne Henderson pretty regularly and he's convinced her that finding Ros is to both their advantages, as nothing can happen until they do."

"You mean he's charmed her," Seamus said.

"Probably. I hope we find Ros soon because I can't stay here forever. What if Rita Roo needs me? She'll be wondering why I've deserted her again. I've only just come back here and already I want to be home on my beach. As soon as the school concert is over I can go."

"You can. What about the university? Has James heard anything from them about buying the land?"

Gaia nodded. "His university friend is going to put in an application to their granting body and he wants James and me to write supporting letters and if we get through to the interview stage, we both might have to go and put our case in person."

"That's fantastic. How could they turn you down?"

"I don't think it works quite like that. It's all about money and how much value they can get out of it for their students and researchers."

"I have a good feeling about this, Gaia." Seamus tipped her chin up and gave her a quick sweet kiss on her lips. "It's all going to work out and make your having to hang out in Perth worth it in the end."

"It's worth it anyway because of our seadragon dance. I'm sorry I get gloomy."

"Hey, what about a quick trip home next weekend? Could you swing it or do you think you need to stay here to rehearse?"

"Oh please, yes. Just a night even. Can we take Jarrah? Mary and Eddie will be missing him."

∼

THEY WERE GATHERING FIREWOOD FOR THEIR LAST EVENING cook-up and Jarrah was still shivering from flapping over the reef seeking out their seadragon. Gaia wasn't too worried when they couldn't find him. "As soon as the water warms up they'll both be back and stay right through summer," she said. "Like me."

They needed a good fire in the old coal range. Gaia wasn't too keen on fires. But given Seamus and Jarrah had frozen themselves for her she said she was willing to trust them. Rita Roo was grazing nearby, Joey Jandamarra safe in his mother's pouch but with his head and front feet sticking out so he could graze at the same time as his mum. Jarrah had given the joey his name. He'd had a dream and the joey was in it and was called Jandamarra. Auntie had told him stories about Jandamarra. He was a leader of the Bunuba mob up in the Kimberleys where Auntie and Jarrah's grandmother came from. He could disappear and become a bird and had spiritual powers. Joey Jandamarra would always spirit Gaia back home to Goshawk Gardens. Even Gos had flown in yesterday when they'd arrived. Seamus said he found it slightly spooky how these wild things knew when Gaia was back and Jarrah tried to help him understand. "Gaia was born here," he said. "Rita Roo might be her spirit animal. Or Gos—he might be her birth totem, because of her dancing. It's like flying."

Gaia overheard them. "No, the seadragon is my birth totem," she said. "Perhaps Gos is your totem, Jarrah."

Jarrah looked up at Gos sitting on his favorite branch. He put out his arm and called the special call he kept for his friend. Gos cocked his head on one side, and fluffed up his feathers. Then he swooped low over Jarrah's head, up into the evening sky and round again and down to land gently, without any digging in of his sharp yellow talons, on Jarrah's skinny arm. He glared at Jarrah with his orange-red eyes and fluffed up his feathers. Jarrah's heart soared. His totem. Eyes that see clearly, ears that hear the smallest sound, wings that fly silently, a heart that beats strongly. A soul that stays faithful to one partner.

After they'd eaten every last morsel of their feast, with Rita Roo—her joey poking his little head out—sitting right by the table as if they were the main guests, Gaia took their empty plates inside. When she came out, Jarrah could see she had something to say.

"Seamus, I want to have your Doctor Belfer assess my scars. If he thinks there is any chance they can be made less obvious, like *really* less obvious, perhaps I might get something done. It won't hurt me to at least find out."

Seamus stayed sitting at the table as if he hadn't heard. Jarrah stared at him, and then looked up at Gaia, standing like a warrior woman, bits of her lit by the flickering light of the flames through the open door in the coal range.

GAIA TOOK SOME DEEP BREATHS AS SHE WATCHED DR. BELFER warm his fingers on one of the gurgling heaters that punctuated the walls of his clinic. It was too warm in here already for Gaia but it was too cold outside. It seemed impossible to get room temperatures just right in a city chilled by winter sun and shadowed by high, close buildings. Back at her barn, she could be sitting at her outside table with only her T-shirt and shorts on, the air fresh with dry leaves and salt.

She tried not to tense as the doctor's long thin warm fingers moved her head to one side and stroked down her scars. In her peripheral vision she watched his expression, but couldn't read anything into it. He had a strong crease between his eyebrows but perhaps that was permanent.

Next he examined the scars on her arm and leg, warming his fingers again before he touched her. He measured the scars, pressed them and watched them spring back, compared their color with a chart of squares of mottled colors she knew were photos of other peoples' burns. He measured the thickness of the scar edges with a pair of calipers, pressing the sharp sides of them into her skin. He took out a camera and snapped her face, the scars on her face, her arm and leg and their scars, and both her arms held out together, both her legs standing together. She was grateful he wasn't one of those doctors who tried to relax his patients by chatting inanely about the weather and how their day had been so far.

"Excellent," he finally said. "The plastic surgeon who treated you did a fine job. But I think I can make a significant improvement on his work with our updated techniques." His face turned from serious to gentle when he smiled. "But you need to look after your feet. I see they have been well danced on. Have you had your pointe shoes measured specifically for you lately?"

Gaia blushed and shook her head. "I've been using my mother's shoes. She had boxes of new ones. They seem to fit me pretty well, although I do get bloody feet sometimes. But I use pointe pouches and tape my toes and separate them with lamb's wool."

"That's important. I know you'll take no notice if I tell you that the tips of your toes were not designed to be balanced on. But why not have the pointe shoes you've been wearing assessed by a professional while you're in Perth? There are better shoes being developed all the time. Expensive, I know, but necessary I'm afraid if you want to make ballet a career."

"I don't think that's going to happen—a ballet career, I mean—but I will get fitted properly." She shook out her right leg and then her left, and flexed and pointed each foot. "I didn't know plastic surgeons treated ballet feet."

"We don't. But I have a daughter who has just begun on points, so I'm up-to-date. In fact it's my turn to take her to her ballet class after I finish up here today. Her ballet school is her second home." He smiled. "You'd know all about that."

"I never went to ballet school. My mother taught us—me and my brother—at home."

"I'm sorry, I didn't think."

"That's OK. It's way in the past now. But it must be fun to be in a class with lots of others."

"Are you thinking of taking some classes while you're in Perth?"

"I haven't really thought about it. I won't be here for long."

"Imogen's ballet school has casual classes for all ages. I know because my wife takes a few as well. It's not too far from here if you want to drop in and see what they offer. I'll give you the address before you leave, just in case." He looked at Gaia over his glasses. "And I'll add the address of the dance-wear shop she gets her pointe shoes from while I'm at it."

"I'll go there at least, I promise. Even if I give the ballet school a miss."

"Good. I'll give you some tubs of 'second skin' squares that you can use to prevent or soothe any blisters you get on those hard-working feet of yours. You might have used the same sort of thing when your burns were beginning to heal."

"Wow, thank you. That's a bonus!"

"No problem." He pushed his glasses back into place on the bridge of his nose. "Now, I need to have a look at your chest scars. I'll give you five minutes to take off your top and bra; you can leave your underpants on. Slip on the gown with the opening at the front and lie on the table. There's a blanket to cover yourself with. I'll ask the nurse to pop in while I examine you."

He vanished out the door, and Gaia did as he'd bid, and lay shivering under the blue cotton blanket in the hot room. Why had she ever agreed to this? Could she leave now? Say she'd changed her mind?

But then the nurse was there with her cheerful smile, and strangely, a cup of strong tea and a glass of orange juice.

"Sit up Gaia, and have a few mouthfuls of one of these; tea or orange. Both if you like."

"Oh, thank you. The tea looks good."

"Do you want me to load it with even more sugar? It has a

fair bit in it already." She picked up a couple of sugar sachets and wiggled them.

Gaia shook her head. "No thanks. This is perfect."

"Nothing like it for bolstering us for unpleasantnesses."

"Will it hurt?"

"Do your scars usually hurt when you press them?"

Gaia shook her head. "No, they get a bit itchy and tight sometimes, that's all."

"That's normal for old scars. No, I was thinking of the psychological unpleasantness of being laid out like this while a doctor examines you. You must have a fair few bad memories from the past."

Gaia nodded again, tears pressing behind her eyes.

"It will be over soon, and Dr. Belfer is as gentle as a lamb. I'll be right here with you holding your hand. You have the choice of shutting your eyes tight, or looking at me."

Gaia forced a smile. "I'll see what works best." She took the tissue the nurse held out and wiped her eyes. "Thank you," she said, her voice trembling the tiniest bit.

Back in the waiting room, fully dressed, and with a second cup of strong tea, Gaia filled in the forms about her scars— soreness, itchiness, tightness, color changes. She felt shakily jubilant. Perhaps she'd take up sweet black tea drinking and save her home-made herbal teas for bedtimes. It was over and it hadn't been too terrible. Perhaps she could go through with it if Dr. Belfer thought he could make her scars vanish? Well, almost vanish.

She'd even had the courage to ask him about her chest burns. "Absolutely they can be improved," he'd said. "I could perform the surgery here, but I'm wondering whether you would like to consider getting involved in a research study on improving well-established burns scars? It's in Boston, at one of the top burns scars clinics in the world. Their results are on another level to what we can achieve here. The head researcher is a woman called Esta Matthews, and giving burns victims complete new breasts is one of her specialties. I think your case would have a good chance of being accepted. I know Dr. Matthews well and I think she'd welcome the opportunity of improving all your scars even further with her pioneering techniques."

Gaia's head was exploding.

"It's major surgery of course, and you'd be given counseling to help you decide how far you want to go. But all your costs would be covered, even the air fares. However, if that's not what you want I can put you on the wait-list for surgery here; we'd start with your facial and arm scars. Once they're healed we can work on your leg scars. We have to make sure we have lots of nice healthy skin for grafts so we can't do them all at the same time. The public health service is the only option for this sort of plastic surgery. I'd think you might get a spot by about late November. Repairing the scars and continuing to use a bra with a pad in it is a perfectly good option if you don't want a breast reconstruction. But there's plenty of time to think about that. First things first."

A new breast. Could that really happen? Would she be able to wear a tutu with spaghetti straps? A bikini? She had found her mother's old bikini in the barn cupboard with all her leotards, and sometimes when she knew there was nobody around, not Jarrah or Seamus, she wore it when she went snorkeling, just to feel the sun and sea on more of her skin. Would she be able to let Seamus see her? Perhaps he already realized she wore padding in her bra and her swim suit where her breast should be? She closed her eyes against the memory of Seamus's shocked look when he first saw her face. Then as Mason's disgusted expression when he ripped open her shirt flashed in her head, nausea surged into her throat, almost choking her. He was creepy, but how could any man ever want to make love to her like this? However much she was loved, no man would be able to control his repulsion. Could she really go to Boston for months of lonely

234 | JENNI OGDEN

horrible surgery and come out the other side with two breasts?

She pushed through the hospital doors onto the busy main road. At the end of the street she could see her bus already at the stop, its door closing, about to drive off. Waving at the driver, she ran towards it, and it slowed to let her in. As the bus rumbled through the busy Perth streets stopping and starting at the lights, people getting on and off at the end of their working day, her mind wandered from Dr. Belfer and his twelve-year-old dancing daughter, to what she would tell Seamus when, dying to know how the assessment had gone, he came around tonight as soon as he'd finished his hospital shift. Then Jarrah's dear face filled her head. Would there be time to squeeze in a short dance session before dinner?

Jarrah had the courage to dance on his stubby foot. She would at least think about having Dr. Belfer work on her face scars. Boston felt way too scary.

CHAPTER 30

*J*ames Ludlow's private detective took ten days to track down Ros. Fortunately she had written down for Mary her partner's name—Tony Cox—as well as the small country town south of Perth they were living in. They were no longer living there, but on a small dairy farm a few miles inland from Bunbury. So on the Saturday after they got her address, Gaia and Seamus drove down there. Gaia was afraid Ros wouldn't want to see her if she phoned first so they decided just to show up. They arrived around 11.30am, with offerings of cheese, pastries and wine. To their relief, Ros was home, and when she came to the door, Gaia recognized her immediately. It was less than five years since she'd last seen her, but it felt a lifetime.

"Yes? Are you after Tony?" She peered past them. "Are you delivering the fertilizer?"

Gaia shook her head. "No, we were looking for you. Ros, I'm Gaia. Gaia Christie. From Goshawk Gardens."

"Holy cow, young Gaia. How did you find me?" Ros's face flushed. "Is it Dave? Has something happened to him?"

"No, well yes, but he's OK. He's not why we're here. He

doesn't know where you are. We've been looking for you for ages."

"Why? That part of my life is long gone, and good riddance."

"I know and we're not here to upset you. I just need to talk to you about something really important. Oh, and this is my friend, Seamus Kelly. "

"Hullo, Ros." Seamus offered his hand, but Ros ignored it.

"I'm sorry you had those dreadful burns, Gaia," Ros said. "They don't look too obvious though. I suppose you've had a lot of plastic surgery."

Gaia nodded. "Yes, but when I was sixteen I went back to Goshawk Gardens, two-and-a-half years ago now."

"That's brave. I didn't think there was anything left. Did you and your brother rebuild the house?"

"No. I live in the barn where we used to dance. Bron's not here. He went overseas years ago."

"So you were all alone? That's terrible."

"Mary and Eddie have been good friends, and now I have Seamus."

"Well, you'd better come in then. Tony's gone into Bunbury to stock up."

At first Ros was guarded, but by the time they'd drunk two cups of tea and eaten some of the pastries Gaia had brought, she had loosened up. Gaia had decided she may as well tell her everything; at least everything she could remember. Which when it came to the night of the fire was nothing. "What can you remember?" she asked Ros. "Please tell me. It's worse having a blank than knowing even the grimmest truth."

Ros sighed. "I've tried to wipe it out of my head, but I still sometimes think about it, especially if there's a house fire on the TV news. Your parents had been over for dinner. When they left, Dave followed them back to your place." Ros looked at Gaia. "Are you sure you want to hear this? It's probably best left in the past."

"I need to know." Gaia's fingernails dug into her palms.

"I saw the flames about half an hour after your parents left. I called emergency services and by the time I got there—I had to run because Dave had taken our truck—the whole house was alight and you and Bron and Dave were on the grass and Bron was trying to wake you up. Then Mary and Eddie came and Eddie had the hose on the house and the fire trucks and police and ambulance were there, and you and Bron and Dave were taken away in the ambulance." She looked past Gaia, out the window.

"Mum and Dad?" Gaia croaked. "Did you see them?"

"They couldn't get to them until they put the fire out. It was an inferno. But they managed to stop it spreading, thank the Lord."

"Dave told me he'd called 000 and that he'd saved me."

"He would. You were wrapped in Bron's t-shirt and Bron had rolled you in that and in the grass to put out your nightie; it had caught alight when the two of you jumped out of his window."

"Is that what Dave told you?"

"Bron told the paramedics. There was no way he was making it up. He was in shock. Blaming himself for making you jump. Dave told them he tried to save your parents but the fire was too intense."

"Did he tell you what happened? How the fire started?"

"He gave me a different story than the bullshit story he stuck to during the police inquiry. How he saw the flames from the farm and sped to the rescue. What he told me was that he and Margot and Joe were in their kitchen chatting, and he was about to leave and the fire burst through the door from the wash-house. He reckoned it must have started in the basement and come up the steps from there, into the wash-house."

"Did you believe him?"

Ros shrugged. "I wasn't there so I don't know. But what I do know is that they weren't having a nice friendly chat."

"What do you mean?"

"Dave and Joe had a fight at our place. They'd both had too much to drink and Joe lost it and hit Dave and then they were full into it. Margot dragged Joe off Dave and pushed Joe out the door and I think she drove them home. Then Dave went after them."

"What were they fighting about?"

Ros was silent.

"Tell me."

"Bloody idiots. Just drunk, that's all."

"I don't remember Dad losing his temper much. Hardly ever. And he didn't get drunk either. I know he'd have a few beers but I never saw him drunk."

"Lucky you." She screwed her eyes shut and rubbed her forehead. "Sorry. Joe was a good bloke. It was Dave who used to overdo it sometimes. I think your dad had just had a guts full of him."

"But there must have been something that started them off. Please tell me."

"Dave had been getting too friendly with Margot and Joe didn't like it."

Vomit surged into Gaia's mouth and she stumbled to the kitchen sink and out it all came. Seamus was behind her, stroking her back, as she wretched and wretched and wretched until there was nothing but bile.

A while later, sitting on the verandah of Ros's house, wine glasses already half empty, Ros told them more. "After Margot and Joe left, I made Dave tell me what had really been going on between him and Margot. I could have killed him, both of them probably. Margot, my so-called friend, having an affair in front of my nose." She took a long slurp of wine. "Then Dave had the gall to tell me that he and Margot were going to run away together."

Gaia emptied her glass and Ros leaned over and filled it up again, then sloshed more wine into her own. "But when I thought about it later, I figured Dave was bullshitting about them running away together. Why would she? She had a great life with Joe, and she would never have left you and Bron. She was nuts about you kids and obsessed with training you to be ballet stars."

"How could she have let Dave anywhere near her?" Gaia shuddered. "He's so creepy and slimy."

"Is that what you thought?" Ros asked, her eyebrows arched high. "I thought he was a hunk. That's why I married him."

"I was 14. I didn't even think about him. It's now that he's creepy. And a drunk. My mother was so...so elegant. How could she? Dad loved her so much."

"I don't know. These things happen. Perhaps she'd got a bit bored stuck in the sticks after her exciting New York life, and Dave could be a charming bastard. Joe was so much more of a gentleman, and Margot didn't have to make any sort of effort to keep him besotted by her. That can get boring sometimes. Crazy really."

Seamus took Gaia's hand. "Just because Mason told Ros all that stuff doesn't mean it was true," he said. "He wanted to believe it, or he wanted to hurt Ros."

"Why would Dad think they were having an affair then?"

Seamus shook his head. "I don't know. But perhaps as far as Margot was concerned it was just a flirtation. They were all quite young back then. And it was the seventies. It seems everyone had affairs."

"She wasn't young. She was 47 when she died."

"But from everything you've told me, she would never have left you and your brother," Seamus said. "So Mason was definitely bullshitting about that. You know what he's like."

"Apparently a hunk back then." Gaia threw Ros a glance. "I know he was your husband...is still your husband, but I can't pretend I can ever understand how Mum could have let him anywhere near her."

"Don't apologize. I hate the bastard too," Ros said, crashing her glass down so hard the wine spilled red across the table.

~

A DUSTY UTE DROVE UP AS ROS WAS WIPING THE TABLE. "Here's Tony," she said, her face softening into a smile.

Walking up the steps to the verandah, he tipped his hat towards Gaia and Seamus. "G'day," he said.

Two hours later Gaia and Seamus were still there. Tony had invited them to stop for a barbecue. It gave them a chance to tell Ros about the proposed sale of the Mason farm for a resort, and Gaia's fears that it would destroy the wilderness, and her own life there.

"Please stop him," she begged. "If you refuse to sign, the sale can't go ahead."

"I'd bloody like to stop him. How dare he think he can just sign away my half. The capital for that land came from me in the first place, not him. It was from a legacy my mother left me when she died. Dave was skint, pretty much. Stupid me thought he loved me and we were going to have this lovely life, so I didn't think twice about putting it in our joint names."

Gaia's heart-beat thundered against her chest. "Would you?" she croaked. "Would you refuse to sign?"

"Well, I might. But I'd need to think it through." Ros looked at Tony. "We'd need to talk about it. We have a big mortgage on this property and if we got a good payout from selling the old farm, we might even be able to pay this one off. Piss Dave off as well, if I got half the loot."

"But you wouldn't want a horrible resort there, destroying all the bush and wild life," Gaia said, her heart galloping now.

"Surely there could be strict conditions on the sale?" Tony said. "Make sure the resort is done well, and doesn't destroy the environment."

"No, no, any resort will change it forever. Please don't sign, Ros. Please?" Gaia was standing up, her hands in front of her like a prayer.

"Hey, calm down. If we can find a way that doesn't stuff it up for you, we will. You don't deserve any more shit happening."

"What about looking into selling to another farmer?" Tony said. "Turning down the resort offer, but getting Dave to put it on the market as a farm?" He looked at Ros. "You probably wouldn't get as much that way, but at least you'd know you'd saved the environment. And Gaia's sanctuary." He smiled at Gaia and her heart slowed a little.

"There might be an even better option," Seamus said. "Gaia's lawyer is looking into whether the university might make an offer so they could use it for a field station. Would you be willing to refuse to sign off on the resort offer while we look into that?"

Tony's arm went around Ros's shoulders and he pulled her into him. "Hey, that sounds perfect," he said. Ros butted her head into his, her face soft again.

Gaia reached for Seamus's hand.

"Christ, now I'll need to face up to Dave." Ros shuddered. "I can always start by telling him he can forget his bloody resort."

"Why don't you go straight to the developers and tell them?" Tony said. "Prove who you are and say you'll never sign. Then if the university doesn't come through with an offer, tell Dave you want to sell it as a farm or small holding, or even a bush hideaway for some rich dude. Put conditions on the sale."

Ros nodded. "I will. That's better. I won't even listen if the resort lot want to tell me how much they're willing to pay. Bugger them all."

∾

THE DREAMS CAME THAT NIGHT WITH A VENGEANCE. GAIA wasn't even clear if she was dreaming, or awake and having flashbacks. Her mother on fire, her clothes alight, her screams, her father throwing himself over her mother, his hair flaming.

She seemed to wake, half wake, saturated in sweat, pushing off her blanket, another voice in her head. Dave's voice shouting. She forced her eyes wide open, sat up, heard her own voice screaming "Bron, Bron, wake up Bron, wake up…"

CHAPTER 31

Gaia frowned at her pointe shoes, more gray than pink. The last time she'd tried to dance on them the shank and box had felt stiff and unyielding. They were dead. She would have to break in the last pair left from her mother's stash. Somehow she'd made every pair last two months, mainly by hardly ever dancing on them.

She sat on her bed and pulled her feet together, matching their soles. They seemed to throb and warm and she felt her mother's strong hand massaging them. Was that her voice in her head? Was that how she sounded? "You have high arches, just like me," she was saying.

The shoes were the last part of her mother, almost gone. Gaia drifted back to those first lonely months when the only living creatures who cared whether she existed were Mary and Eddie, and Rita Roo and Gos. Dear Gos and his mirrored friend dancing along the barre; the barre where she and Bron had sweated together, dreaming of perfection and acclamation.

She slid off the bed and pulled the chair from her tiny desk to the full-length mirror stuck to the outside of the wardrobe door. The woman looking back at her with her steady gaze and her dancer's poise blurred, and in her place, her right hand resting on the high back of a chair, stood a girl in blue denim shorts and a gray singlet, her expression young, afraid, haunted. The girl's body began to move, her bare feet tentative — pliés, battements tendus, battement glissés, ronds de jambes, fondus, frappés, petits battements, developpés— her eyes were changing, glowing, her lips were softening, curving — ronds de jambes en l'air, grands battements. The woman in the mirror pursed her lips and a kiss of warm air brushed across Gaia's cheek and disappeared out the open window.

WEDNESDAY MORNING WAS HER MORNING OFF, AND CHECK-book in her backpack she took the bus to the dance-wear shop. Dr. Belfer was right; she should take better care of her feet and have her pointe shoes professionally fitted. She could almost hear her mother's much sterner voice, telling her to suck it up and use some of the money sitting in her bank account for new pointe shoes whenever she needed them.

The knowledgeable ballet shoe fitter asked her to put on her mother's pointe shoes, the new pair Gaia had broken in only last night, and watched her while she rose on her points. "They are well-fitting," she said, "but I think we can do even better." An hour later, Gaia left the shop with a shoe so much more comfortable and sleeker looking than the shoes she had become so used to, that she allowed a tiny trickle of hope to warm her. Might one day she be able to dance as a career, perhaps even in a small dance company?

Floating down the road she came upon a taxi stand, and before she had time to think sensibly, jumped in and showed the driver the address of the ballet school, written in Dr. Belfer's surprisingly undoctor-like legible hand. As the taxi moved into the traffic, she crossed her fingers. Hopefully the cash she had in her wallet would be sufficient to pay for such an extravagance.

Walking in the main entrance of the ballet school, she stepped around a bunch of identical girls in leotards and hesitated by a reception desk.

"Good morning," the woman behind the desk said. "Can I help?"

"Um, yes, I wondered if you had any information on ballet classes; casual ones?"

"Of course. For you?"

Gaia nodded and pulled her hair across her scars. The woman glanced down and then up again, her face flushed. "Are you a beginner? We have classes for adults. They're very popular."

"I'm… no I'm not a beginner but I haven't been in formal training for a while. I'd passed my RAD exams, Advanced One when I… I had to take a break."

"And since then you haven't danced? How old are you now?"

"Eighteen. I live miles from any ballet school usually and I've been trying to keep up my practice at home for the past two years. But I'm in Perth for a while now and thought perhaps I could take some classes while I'm here." This is crazy. There's no way…

"You know, I think Julia Morris is between classes right now. She's one of our senior dance teachers. Let me see if she's got some time to talk to you and work out where you will fit. Hang on."

And before Gaia could stop her she'd disappeared through a door behind her.

~

GAIA DISCOVERED A BUS STOP RIGHT OUTSIDE THE BALLET school with a bus that took her almost to the Children's Home.

It must be a sign, she thought, hugging the fancy shopping bag from the dance-wear shop. Julia Morris had been wonderful. She'd spent ages with her, and somehow, although she hadn't intended to, Gaia had told her she was Margot Robert's daughter. "Let's start you in my two-hour adult advanced class," Julia said. "I have one tomorrow evening. There are all levels of dancers in it; some are en pointe, some are pre-pointe. Most of them, like you, did years of ballet as a child and now want to get back into it, this time for fun and exercise. The evening classes mostly cater for young women who work during the day. Our morning classes tend to attract young mums escaping their kids for a couple of hours. I should be able to get a feel for where you're at during your first class, and we'll go from there."

"It might be too advanced for me," Gaia said. "My technique is probably terrible after teaching myself all this time."

"Given you were intensively trained by Margot Roberts for eleven years, I suspect you will have had good technique ground into your bones," Julia said.

That evening Gaia had to put on her new pointe shoes and dance for the kids. They were almost as excited as she was about her class on Thursday night. They had her dancing the Black Swan by the end of the year, preferably in the Sydney Opera House. Hannah laughed when she told them she'd probably not even be allowed to go en pointe, she was so far behind in her training. "You'll never convince our kids," she said, "so enjoy it. You'll always be their white swan and what could be more important than that?"

GAIA EMERGED FROM THE DANCE STUDIO, HER JEANS AND sweater pulled on over her wringing-wet tights and leotard. She felt as if she'd just walked out of the lake at Goshawk Gardens on a steamy hot day.

Seamus jumped up from the seat near the door to the lobby entrance and Gaia peered over the heads of a cluster of dancers and raised her fingers in a little wave. He closed the gap between them and grabbed her hands, his eyes scanning her face. "Hey you," he said.

"Hey back," she said softly. "You didn't need to pick me up. I could have got the bus."

"And miss this? Was it wonderful?"

"I was terrible, but it was wonderful too. Julia is an amazing teacher and she thinks that with masses of practice I'll catch up."

"Catch up with who? The others in the class?"

"No, with myself. Julia said that my basic technique was so good she wouldn't have to force me to unlearn bad habits. She thinks I have potential." Gaia squeezed her eyes tight shut for a second. "She said that if I worked really hard I could make it. Perhaps even get good enough to become a professional ballet dancer."

"Jaysis, that's fierce!" He gathered her in his arms and swung her around, just missing two women also leaving the ballet studio. They giggled and waved at Gaia. "See you next week," one of them sang out.

~

GAIA'S DAYS BECAME SO PACKED SHE FELL ASLEEP WITHIN minutes of sliding between her sheets. It was a new sensation for her. Perhaps when she'd been a kid she'd been able to sleep that easily, but even then she'd be reading by torchlight after the lamps were turned off. Since the fire it seemed as if she'd never slept more than six broken hours a night. Not without one of the pills the nurses had made her take, and once out of hospital, never. Sometimes after doing one of her hour-long workouts in the barn, digging all day in her gardens, swimming for an hour in the lake or snorkeling over the reef, she would be so weary and achy she was sure she'd sleep before she even got to turning on her side and getting herself into the most comfortable position. But her thoughts would start and the more exhausted she was the harder they'd circle.

No longer. Her days here all began at six am. That was no different from her routine back home. Then came her stretches and barre exercises, joined by Jarrah and random other kids—no dancing on the beach, she missed that—then breakfast, followed by three hours in the gardens of either the Children's Home or the school, who had given her some part-time work. Not much different from home either. But what was different, so wonderfully different, was that on four days each week, by 1pm she was in the dance school studio, either in a group class, or in the practice studio. Then back at the Children's Home by 3.30pm and dance lessons and rehearsals for whichever kids showed up. A full rehearsal on Sundays, compulsory for all members of the Flying Gos Dance Company. And most buzzy of all, Monday and Thursday evenings, 6.30 pm until 8pm, she had private lessons with Julia. Sometimes, when he wasn't at the hospital, Seamus would pick her up after her class and they would have a late, light, dinner at some small, cheap restaurant, or back at his apartment.

She knew her savings were steadily decreasing but she didn't care. Her mother smiled down on her with every dollar spent. The practice studio time cost nothing, her casual group classes were heavily discounted now she purchased them in blocks of twenty, and Julia had insisted on charging her only 50 percent of her usual private teaching fee. "In honor of your mother," she said. Her pointe shoes were the biggest cost. If she could make one pair last two weeks she felt rich. But her bed and food at the Children's Home were free, and on top of that her gardening brought in enough to cover her dance classes, with some to spare.

But at the back of her mind always lurked the worry over

Goshawk Gardens. A group of university lecturers from the Department of Biology had submitted a proposal that the Mason block of land be purchased by the university to be used as a field station for researchers and students. Attached was a proposal from James Ludlow and Gaia, outlining their plan to set up the 'Margot Robert's Sanctuary Trust' to collect public contributions to supplement the university purchase and support holiday camps for disadvantaged children. Gaia's dream was a camp where the kids could learn about the wilderness and the reef as well as become involved in creative activities including dance, photography and art. She would rather it had been named the 'Joe Christie Sanctuary Trust', for her dad, but James convinced her that Margot's name would be a money magnet. In addition, Gaia proposed that her land would be available to the field station and that she would covenant it so that it would remain in her ownership but would be protected in perpetuity from commercial development. If their application even got through to the next stage, they would then be called for interviews and a final decision wouldn't be made until October. A long time for the resort company to increase their offer to the Masons. Dave, still an inpatient in the rehabilitation center for alcoholics, was apparently well enough now to sign off on a deal with the resort company, but Ros, bless her, was still holding back, waiting to see if the university would make an acceptable offer. But she wouldn't wait forever.

CHAPTER 32

*G*aia plaited Maisie's curls with flowing red, green and yellow weedy extensions, not helped by the girl's constant wriggling. "Maisie, keep your head still," she said. "If you don't, you'll look like a stag-horn coral instead of a seadragon."

She still had her own seadragon costume to slither into, although at least her hair and makeup were done. Freeing Maisie, she grinned as she watched her dance off through the excited mob of kids, twirling and humming as if she didn't have a nerve in her body. Catching a glimpse of Jarrah in his costume, her heart squeezed; she could almost see him shaking from here. He was dancing the part of the boy who warned the seadragons that the developers were coming to destroy their coral reef; the boy who hatched the plan to frighten them off by disguising the benign reef creatures as poisonous coral snakes, stonefish and box jellyfish. And of course he was the front legs of Whelan the Whaleshark in the finale.

Hannah appeared, her peaceful face masked by tension. "God, Gaia, whose mad idea was this?" she said. "The auditorium is full to the rafters; kids even sitting in the aisles. What if it's a total disaster?"

"It won't be. Everyone loves kids, whatever happens. The little darlings could all freeze mid-twirl and they would still see them as prima donnas. Think of that beautiful new swimming pool the school will get."

"You're a cool one. Here's me thinking you would be a nervous wreck."

Gaia held out her trembling hands. "Ha, I'm perfectly calm. As you can see. Well, I will be if I can squeeze myself into that bizarre seadragon costume without strangling myself on its wire collar."

"That wouldn't impress your ballet friends. There's a bunch of them right in the front row."

"Really? How do you know? You've never met them."

"Trust me, they're easy to spot. And they've all got tutus on."

"Stop kidding. You're just trying to freak me out. Now help me get into this damn straight jacket."

THE CLAPPING WENT ON AND ON, THE AUDIENCE STANDING AND shouting "Bravo, bravo" as if they were the Royal Ballet and not a motley group of kids who a few months ago had never danced a step. Gaia stood taller on her toes and tried to spot Julia across the screaming, jumping, excited kids in front of her. They'd done their bows and curtseys as they'd been taught but all that had gone to hell now. She looked down as Jarrah grabbed her hand. "Come on, Gaia. You're getting a monster bunch of flowers!"

As they reached the front of the stage the lights burst on in the auditorium, and Gaia saw Julia and two of the students in her class she'd become friendly with clapping and smiling and calling out as she curtsied and took the bouquet from Maisie, her weedy extensions straggling down her back. Her entire insides bubbling and zinging like a spa pool, Gaia tried to stop the tears from streaming out of her eyes and down her sweating face, but she didn't have a show in hell. Jarrah was buzzing by her side and there it was, a moment of perfect happiness.

Escaping ten minutes later from the backstage excitement, she went out front to find Julia and thank her for coming. When she'd been hugged and congratulated, Julia introduced her to her husband, Andrew—a surprise as it had never occurred to Gaia that Julia might have a husband or a life outside ballet. "That's nice of you to come," she said. "I suppose Julia is always carting you along to ballets."

"It's a shared interest," he said, smiling at Julia and taking her hand. He turned back to Gaia. "I enjoyed it immensely, especially the Irish whaleshark."

Gaia laughed. "Yes, I fear the rest was overshadowed by Whelan. So much for prancing about on pointes!"

"Well, your en pointe impressed me too. I'd like to chat with you sometime about your dancing. What your plans are for your future."

"Oh golly, that's why I sort of recognized you. You're with the West Australia Ballet. Gosh, Julia never mentioned you." Her fingers landed on the place where they always landed. She'd camouflaged her scar with a red-spotted yellow stripe— it was probably dripping down her burning face now.

Julia grinned at her. "Nope, we try and keep our personal lives away from ballet for the sake of our boys. They find it tedious in the extreme. They prefer surfing."

"You have children?"

"Two. They're Garths like Andrew. Morris is my professional name. And Andrew's the Artistic Director of the Ballet, so he's worth chatting to some time."

Andrew Garth. Grief. "Thank goodness I didn't know you were in the audience," Gaia said, her face even hotter as he grinned at her.

"Excuse me for interrupting," said a woman who'd been

hovering behind her, "but I'm with the *Women's Weekly*, and I'd love to talk to you both about the performance. We're doing an article for our magazine. The school asked us to come." She beamed at them. "It would be wonderful to talk to you, Gaia, and have a few words about it from you, Mr Garth. I've met you before when we've done articles about the Ballet. Jackie Howieson's my name."

"Jackie, of course," Mr Garth said. "You've published some excellent articles about our Ballet Company. We're always grateful for the exposure. But I suspect your readers will love a story about *The Dance of the Seadragons* much more."

"You could be right. Our photographer's gone backstage. He's confident he's shot some wonderful photos during the performance." She turned to Gaia. "This article could be fantastic for your charity. We'll be adding a special bank account number readers can use to give donations for the swimming pool fund. I was wondering about also giving donors the option of donating to a fund to save seadragons, or to research them. What do you think?"

"Thank you is what I think," Gaia said.

GAIA DIDN'T HAVE TO WAIT LONG FOR HER CHAT WITH MR Garth. After her next private ballet lesson, Julia told her that Andrew was here hoping Gaia would be able to spare some time to talk to him at the end of her lesson. "He'll give you a ride home afterwards so you don't have to catch the bus," she said. "You can talk in my office. I'll leave you to it. I have to get back to the boys and bribe them to do their homework."

Gaia's pulse had migrated to the base of her throat when she entered the room. Mr Garth stood up from his seat on the small couch and Gaia wiped her sweaty palm on her leotard and shook his warm, dry hand. "Gaia, please sit down," he said, as formal as a stranger. "I loved what you did with your dance performance, especially the way you integrated the children's strengths. You have a real talent, and not just as a dancer, but as a choreographer. As a teacher of dance too, clearly."

Gaia's head was spinning.

"I'm wanting to expand our company's reach to include more contemporary ballet; it's becoming increasingly popular in Europe especially. Australia has some catching up to do. And dance should be inclusive, for everyone, and that's why your dance was so wonderful. That's my vision for our company, to make it a treasure and a resource for the whole community, not only the classical ballet lovers."

Gaia clasped her hands together, his passion filling her and singing along with her own. The lump of joy in her throat almost blocked his next words, but they hovered in the air between them until they'd sunk in.

"So I wanted to float an idea past you. I'd be delighted if you'd audition for a paid internship with the West Australian Ballet. If the selection committee thought you'd be the best candidate, it would enable you to continue with your dance training along with our dancers, and also work with our choreographers if you're interested. After the first year we would re-assess, and look at further options—we might decide you need a further internship year, or perhaps by then you'll be ready to audition for the Corps de Ballet. Fingers crossed we will have developed a stronger contemporary ballet stream by then and you could audition for that."

"I don't know what to say," Gaia said, her voice wobbling. "Thank you."

"I think you'd stand an excellent chance. You can take as much time as you need to work out what's best for you. We don't audition on a set date, but rather when we find a dancer we think will be a good fit for our company. I would suggest any time between now and next February. Apart from mid-

December to mid-January of course when we'll all be at the beach."

"Thank you," Gaia said again. "I can't think straight. It's all too crazy. But what about my scars?"

"Julia tells me you're thinking of having further plastic surgery on them? If so, we can delay your start."

"Truly?"

Mr Garth laughed. "Truly. Even if you decide not to have any surgery, our audition offer stands. Makeup can cover the scars on your face, and costumes can cover all sorts of imperfections. It's your dancing and your passion and values that matter, and even if you don't make the professional grade we require to join the Company as a full-time dancer, you have much more to give to dance than simply dancing."

IT WAS ALMOST TOO MUCH. THE UNIVERSITY HAD SET A DATE for their interviews next Monday, and as soon as she could after that she was on that bus to home. Perhaps after a week or two floating over the reef, she'd be able to think sensibly about what to do. So she phoned Dr. Belfer and asked him if he could delay his surgery until February next year so she at least had the summer to ground herself, and make sure the sea-dragons were still there. Keep the developers off the beach if they managed to get the Masons to sign their bloody contract.

"Of course," Mr Belfer said. "What about Boston? I sent Dr. Matthews the details of your case and she thinks your scars, and a breast reconstruction, would have an excellent chance of a successful outcome. It's a long-term study and there's no pressure to decide. Take the summer and we'll talk again in late January. How does that sound?"

"A relief. That's how it sounds. Amazing too. Thank you so much. It's a bit overwhelming. I've also been asked to audition for a training internship for the West Australia Ballet."

"Well, that's phenomenal. Congratulations! Does that affect your decision to have further plastic surgery?"

"I guess so, although Mr Garth, the Artistic Director, thought my scars wouldn't be the end of the world. I think he was thinking I might get into teaching or choreography. But he did say if I did need to take time to get my scars fixed, I could start later next year. I'd be awfully old by then though."

"You do have a lot to consider. Still, better to have too many choices than none. Take your time and have a well-deserved summer at that lovely beach of yours."

CHAPTER 33

Gaia had never set foot in a university before. She followed Professor Wright and James as they found a crooked path through the crowds of noisy students, her head turning from one side to the other and back again. The buzz of it all, their freedom to sit about on the grass in their jeans and shorts and T-shirts, their backpacks dumped carelessly beside them, their confidence, their laughs and hoots and intense discussions about art, politics, science, sex? The dance tonight? She had no idea, but how she wanted to be like that. Normal. Happy. Nothing in the world to worry about except learning and living day-to-day and being with others the same age, the same stage, with their futures mapped out or not but it didn't matter because they were all in it together. At first glance they all looked beautiful. Tanned and healthy with long shining untidy hair. No perfect buns, no dancer make-up. But then she noticed they weren't all slim and shiny; there were overweight girls, white skinny boys, some with pimples, one boy with half his face covered in a red birthmark, a girl on crutches, another girl on her own, her head in a book. But they all belonged, no one cared how they looked. She could go and plonk herself down in a group, her scarred face and limbs in the sun for all to see and no one would even notice. Not if she were a student, not if she belonged here. Is that what she wanted? Not ballet, but to go to a university and become part of her own generation? Train to be a marine biologist, like she told Jarrah he could do one day?

James's hand was on her back guiding her through a door, along a gloomy corridor that smelt of old books and into a large room with a long table. Gaia nodded and smiled as each of the four interviewers was introduced; three men and one woman. None of them wore suits and ties, the only suit and tie ensemble was on James. Professor this and Doctor that looked a bit tidier than the students outside on the grass, but not much. Gaia's churning stomach churned a bit more slowly. She'd been expecting a court and a jury; not wigs of course but the same feel as wigs.

"Here, grab a sandwich," one of the men said, shoving a tray of sandwiches and fruit cake across the table to where they were now seated. "Cheese and onion, or fish paste. The cake is more edible." And there's a pot of tea over there,"—he nodded to a side table—"and boiling water if you can stomach instant coffee."

Professor Wright shoved his chair back and wandered over to the table."Gaia, James, tea or coffee?"

Gaia shook her head. "No thanks, this water is fine." She poured herself a glass, hoping her hand wouldn't shake, and gulped down half of it.

"OK. Let's get going," said the professor who'd been intro-duced as the chairman. "We've all read your application and discussed it before you arrived. It seems pretty clear. But if you want to clarify anything in the application, any developments since you submitted it, we can talk about those first and then each of you can speak to it, add anything else that might make it even more attractive. But we agree that it's an excellent proposal and could be an exciting venture for the university to fund. The main reason for this interview is to get to know the main players and see what you will offer to it to make it a success long-term, and to raise it above the other applications. As always our problem is deciding which of several excellent projects we can fund."

Gaia listened as Professor Wright and James put their case eloquently and answered a number of questions. How could she say anything that would be different? She'd made some notes but all her points had been covered.

"Thank you. Now Gaia, would you like to tell us what this means to you? After all, you're the one who lives there and knows this area intimately. We are particularly interested in the public trust fund you and Mr Ludlow are proposing to set up that will include your placing a covenant on your own land. We understand you intend to name it the 'Margot Robert's Sanctuary Trust' after your late mother?"

Gaia nodded. "We think that her name will help attract donations."

"I'm sure that would be the case. Was she very involved in conservation?"

"She loved it there, but it was my father and his father who really understood how important it was to protect wilderness places and the reef. There's a pair of weedy seadragons there; they come every spring and dance and mate and lay their beautiful pink eggs—the male is the one who incubates the eggs. They only exist in South and Western Australia, and around our beach is their most northern boundary. There are no seadragons, none at all, not weedy or leafy seadragons anywhere else in the world. They are the most beautiful creatures and people take them for their aquariums and they almost always die. They're at risk from anything that destroys algae-covered reefs and seagrass and seaweed habitats, including agricultural fertilizer run-off. That's why we've never used fertilizer in our gardens. Any pollution from development puts their survival in danger. They're like a litmus test for a healthy reef and seabed. I was there a few weeks ago when surveyors came from the developer's company and they found the male and took him out of the sea to take home to their kids and if we hadn't been there and managed to put him back quickly he would have died and that would have been the end of seadragons on that reef."

Gaia stopped and took a deep breath.

"So if the university had a field station there, what do you see as their role in protecting the seadragons and the reef more generally?" asked the woman.

"They could do research on it and how to protect it. sea-dragons need total protection if we want them to still be around in 50 years. Perhaps researchers could find ways to bring more seadragons into that area of the reef. They could find out more about their lifestyle and behaviors. And they could teach the students and the school kids if we have holiday camps there how to protect them and the reef and all its creatures."

"But wouldn't that disturb you on your land?"

"Yes, but if they were there to protect it I would welcome them. It's not my reef, I know that. I can't protect an entire species on my own, just try and protect the pair we have there. That's why I want to start holiday camps for disadvantaged kids so they can experience the reef for themselves and fall in love with it so they'll always want to protect it. Kids like that are usually stuck in cities and they don't even have parents to take them to the beach, so how can they know how amazing it is?"

The woman pulled a magazine out from under the pile of paper in front of her. "We all read this article in the *Women's Weekly* before you came in. Are these the children you were thinking about? Children like these?" She held up the page with the vibrant photo of all the kids in their costumes, Jarrah and Maisie center-front.

"Yes, exactly like them. But lots more from other institu-tions and kids who do have families but are poor, and kids who have some physical disability like Jarrah"—she leaned over and pointed to his glowing face—"and intellectual disabilities too. We could have camps where they learn all sorts of things that truly matter, not just about the wilderness and snorkeling on the reef but dancing and art and writing. It will change their lives, I am sure of it."

"Would you take responsibility for that side of it?" the woman asked. "It would be a full-time job I would think and how could it be funded, including your own salary?"

Gaia looked down. She swallowed. She looked up again. "I haven't thought all that through, but I know we could do it. I could plan it all and the fund we want to set up could bring in money to get the kids here and pay for their food and everything. I thought the students at the field station would be able to help and teach them about the bush and reef too. We could use the field station boat and that sort of thing. I bet lots of those university students out there"—she pointed to the window—"would love to come and be camp leaders in their university holidays. Then the kids would learn about going to university one day; the possibility of it for them. It would have to be a joint thing between the university field station and me."

The chairman had the *Women's Weekly* in front of him now. "Well Gaia, I have no doubt that you would achieve all you set out to do. This performance you staged was clearly extraordinary."

"Thank you. It was a team effort. Jarrah and Seamus— he's an Irish man who helps at the Home a bit— and Hannah, she's Seamus's cousin and she runs the Home, they choreographed the final whaleshark Irish jig which was the best part. It got a standing ovation."

The woman pulled out a tissue and blew her nose. The man next to her patted her on the back and then smiled at Gaia. "Why don't you put it on again, perhaps have two or three performances? With the ticket profits going into your trust fund? If you do please let us know as we definitely want to see it."

"Yes, lots of people have asked us that. The *Women's Weekly* has already had some donations for seadragon research as a result of their article. The school might put the dance on again next year. We all need a holiday before then though. I only stayed here this long so I could come to this interview and because I needed to do whatever I could to stop those developers from destroying everything. When will you make your decision? I'm scared that if it takes too long the Masons, the owners, will get such a good offer from the developers that they'll take it."

"We'll have a decision for you on Friday. We understand the urgency." The chairman stood up. "Thank you all for coming in sharing your passion. These written applications force the applicants to be so precise and unemotional, and it makes an enormous difference to see how they really feel about their research, or their project." He smiled at Gaia and she felt his warmth expanding her chest. "And you get an A+ with distinction for that. I can't promise a positive outcome as we have to rank all our applications, but this one is outstanding and you have a very good chance."

Sleeping for more than an hour at a stretch on Thursday night was impossible. The developers had increased their offer to Dave by another $50,000 two days ago. Even Ros might be tempted if the University's offer was less. That's if they even agreed to fund it. At seven, she dragged herself out of bed, tired and fractious, and joined the noisy kids at breakfast.

"It's today, it's today," Maisie called out before she'd even sat down. Jarrah was practically bouncing with excitement, still managing to stuff cereal and toast in his mouth without pause.

"Shush, Maisie," Gaia said. "We may not get it, I've told you that. There are heaps of amazing projects and not enough money to fund them all. Let's wait and see before we celebrate."

"Yes, Maisie," said Jarrah, his eyes sparkling. "I told you it was bad luck to get ahead of ourselves."

Gaia hid her grin, feeling slightly less glum. If they missed out they would find another way. Get donations, put on the dance show again. James wouldn't let this all fizzle out. If they could convince Ros and Dave not to sell to the developers they could apply to the university again in their next round, and by then they would have set up their official trust fund and already begun to get donations.

The day bore on, and Gaia planted some runner beans, some tomatoes and a whole garden of lettuces. She thought about going into the ballet school and letting off steam in the practice room, but what if she missed the call? She picked up the phone multiple times, her finger poised to dial James's number, but stopped herself. Of course he'd call her the second he heard. She phoned Ros and told her how the interview went, and asked her to cross her fingers.

"They're already crossed," Ros said. "Have been all week."

"Have you got through to Dave yet?"

"I thought I'd wait and see what happened first. He's totally unreliable anyway. He could say one thing then change his mind the next day."

The call came just after 4 pm. Maisie reached the phone first although Gaia wasn't far behind. By the time she'd grabbed the receiver off Maisie, Hannah and Jarrah and any other kids in range were crowded into the hallway where the phone was. Hannah was shushing them.

"Gaia," came the voice. Not James, but the chairman's

distinctive English accent. A Yorkshireman, Professor Wright had told them.

"Peter Lonsdale here. I have great news for you..." Gaia's head stopped thinking and she shook it and forced it to take it in. "...everything you asked for."

"Sorry," she said, her voice sounding as if it was coming from the light bulb dangling from the ceiling. "Did you say we got the grant?"

"Yes, I did, fully funded. Everything you asked for. Congratulations."

"Really?"

"No, I was just having you on. They turned it down flat. Said it was a terrible idea, getting an incredible piece of bush and reef for a field station and a pair of seadragons thrown in for good measure."

"Oh. Don't tease. Did we or didn't we?"

"You did. All of it. The lot. Now I must phone your good friend James Ludlow, and then I suggest you go and have a few well-deserved beers."

STANDING AT THE KITCHEN BENCH IN SEAMUS'S FLAT, WAITING for the kettle to boil, Gaia could have floated away from pure happiness. A perfect night. Dinner at a seafood restaurant on the waterfront with Hannah and Seamus, Jarrah and Maisie, James and his wife, and their university champion, Professor Wright—now called Don. Then back here with Seamus for a private celebratory drink. Too much wine, and thus the boiling kettle and a nice cup of tea. Seamus had put on a tape of waltzes and she swayed as she waited. She felt him warm behind her and smiled as his arms circled her waist.

"Hey, a watched kettle never boils. So turn it off and come and dance with me."

"What about tea first and then we'll dance," Gaia said, a smile in her voice.

Seamus turned her around and looked into her eyes. "Please dance with me."

Gaia's throat tightened as she shuffled, still in Seamus's arms, into the small living room lit only by two candles on a side table. 'Lara's Theme' from Dr. Zhivago was playing, and they moved as one, Seamus leading her around the room as if he'd ballroom danced before. Gaia closed her eyes and breathed him in, the music and her memories of Julie Christie and Omar Sharif waltzing in the movie she had seen so long ago filling her senses. Then their lips were touching and their kiss deepening, and she could feel Seamus's body along the length of hers as they swayed, still in time to the waltz but no longer moving around the room.

Seamus's hands cupped her face as the waltz came to an end. His look turned her inside out. "I want to love you, Gaia. Can I?"

Gaia nodded and her breath caught as Seamus's hands touched her. Her breast reached towards his fingers through her shirt and she fumbled at her shirt buttons.

"Let me," Seamus said, and he unfastened the top button, then the next and the next, his fingers fumbling too.

"I can't," Gaia whispered.

"Why not, Macushla? We'll go only as slow and as far as you want, I promise."

"My chest, my scars, oh, Seamus, they're so ugly."

"You are beautiful, all of you, every scar on your body, beautiful to me."

"You don't know. You haven't seen them."

"I've seen you. I see you. That's all that matters to me. Gaia, trust me. Please."

Gaia raised her eyes and forced herself to look into his face. "I do trust you, but you won't be able to help how you feel when you see them."

"I know you have bad scars, Gaia. I guessed you'd lost your breast. It doesn't change how I feel about you. If you feel the same, and want for us what I want, sooner or later you need to trust me about this."

"I know," Gaia whispered. Seamus's face swam in her tears.

He touched the next button. "Can I?" he said.

Gaia nodded.

The last button unfastened, he gently lifted her shirt off her shoulders and she felt it sliding down the back of her legs, even through her skirt. She would happily take it and her pants off before her ugly, cover-all, padded bra. Now his hands were behind her back undoing her bra, his touch sending currents zinging down to her fingers. She felt the bra straps slither down her arms and heard a tiny plop as her bra hit the carpet. She stood there, exposed. The candlelight danced over Seamus's face as he held her eyes, and as it flickered over her face she breathed her thanks for its soft light. Then his lips were on her skin, on her missing breast, on her real breast and back again to her flat, welted chest. They were in his bedroom and she was lying on his bed, she was pushing her chest into his lips, her missing breast humming as urgently as her actual breast, as if it had come home. As if his loving had returned it to her.

"Seamus, I need to go home," Gaia said, as they were eating breakfast on the teensy balcony off Seamus's small bedroom the morning after. Seamus stretched his back before relaxing into his chair. He smiled at her.

"I know you do. What bliss, you'll have the whole summer to swim and snorkel and garden and dance. Poor me will be stuck here pushing beds about until Christmas."

"You could leave. See the rest of Australia," Gaia said.

"That's what I'd intended to do when I first arrived in Perth. I had no plan to meet a mermaid and end up here for a year." Seamus leaned over and kissed the tip of her nose.

The little tingle of pleasure she always felt when he did that trickled through her. Became more as her body remembered last night. No, she had to tell him, tell him now before it got any more serious. Why? What was she thinking? Why did she want to ruin it all when she'd been so happy last night? What was wrong with her? It was so nice, so good to feel normal. Her breast was tingling now, both her breasts. It was a gift. Seamus is a gift. How can I possibly tell him this morning when he's so happy? I have to. It's not fair on him not to. She took a deep breath.

"Seamus."

"That's meself."

"I loved last night. You made me so happy."

"Me too."

"But I'm not ready for anything serious. I'm only beginning and I have so much I want to do."

"Hey, it doesn't have to be serious. We're too young to be serious. We can be girlfriend and boyfriend, that's all. If it becomes more I'll be happy. But if it doesn't, well I'll be sad, but let's not get too ahead of ourselves as our wise Jarrah would say."

"I'm not. Getting ahead of myself. I'm trying to catch up on myself and I've thought and thought about it, before last night even happened, and I need to do it alone. No boyfriend. Not for a while."

Seamus was looking at her as if …she didn't know what he was seeing. Someone he'd given himself to who threw him back in his face? "I'm so sorry, Seamus. I shouldn't have let last night happen, but I wanted it so much and it meant everything, and I'm not sorry, in fact it was the most wonderful thing. But it doesn't change what I'm saying."

"That you want rid of me? Is that it? Is that what you're saying?"

"No, don't think that. I care about you so much. I always will and perhaps one day if you still want it, we might become, you know, an item."

"An item? Is that an Australian expression?"

Gaia shrugged. "I don't know. It's a stupid term. I'm sorry I said it."

"Well, get your things and I'll drop you off at the Home. You might be able to catch the bus to Jurien Bay today if you hurry."

"Stop it." Gaia saw his eyes filling even as he pushed her away, as she deserved. She turned her head away, her tears falling, falling. Snatching up the paper serviette Seamus had so elegantly put on their breakfast table, she jabbed at her eyes, blew her nose. Seamus, standing now, his back to her, was looking down at the noisy street below. She tried again. "Seamus, I'm so sorry. I know I've upset you. But you need to see the rest of Australia, not sit here in this city for months. You've told me, in a few months you need to go back to Ireland and see your mother. If we were together how could you do that?"

Seamus turned around. "You're right. I'd never be able to get you to leave your gardens and your beach and your sea-dragons. I know that. I feckin' know that. I'd never ask you to leave them if you didn't want to. I simply thought we could have a nice relationship for a while, like normal young adults do."

"And I'm not normal. You don't need to tell me that. But I have to find out if my being not normal is how I want to be. I don't expect you to understand because you're so different."

Seamus sighed and plonked back down in his chair. "Don't say that about you not being normal. I never meant that. I've never thought that. In most ways, you're the most normal person I've ever known. If normal means living in an idyllic place in step with what's important. It's me who is searching, not you."

"Perhaps we're both searching. We're—like you say—we're not very old yet. Isn't that what we're meant to do at this age? Find who we are? And I'll be at Goshawk Gardens and you'll be everywhere else. I don't think a long-distance relationship would work anyway."

"If it mattered enough we'd find a way."

Gaia dropped her head into her hands, her eyes stinging.

"Macushla, it's OK. I'll get over it. Give me a week and I'm back on the road Jack."

Gaia smiled through her tears and dropped her hands. Looked at his dear Irish face.

"An' doncha come back, no more, no more, no more, no more…" Seamus sort of sang.

"Please do. Come back I mean." Gaia said.

CHAPTER 34

*S*tanding at the edge of the ocean, Gaia waited, still, no words in her head, only the turquoise of the water, the deep blue of the sky, the hot white sand under her feet, the sun on her skin, the salt in the air filling her lungs and nourishing her soul, the wind from the wings of the Australasian gannet as it swooped and then dove like an arrow, wings folded, head sun-kissed, emerging with a fish flapping in its bill, the white-bellied sea eagle soaring higher still, his eye on the gannet, the pied oyster catchers, the red-capped plovers, the beach stone curlews probing their long bills deep into the wet sand, pulling up ghost shrimps and marine worms, the ruddy turnstones, the lesser sand plovers, the red-necked stint using their short bills to peck up tiny gastropod mollusks, the sentinel crab hiding below the sand surface alert for the safety of the juveniles exploring the sand surface, the tiny sanderlings with their twinkling feet, the banded dotterels running like the wind, dragging their wings, distracting predators from their newly hatched babies tumbling like tumbleweed across the sand.

She breathed in the cool of the water as it lapped her feet, her thighs, her stomach, her chest. She looked down through the crystal water to the rippling white sand and wondered if she could breathe under there without a snorkel. Then she spat in her mask and swilled it in the soft water before pressing it onto her face. With her snorkel in place, she sank to the white sand then rose to the surface, blowing her snorkel clear. Her feet free from confining flippers, she gently scissored her legs and glided out, out, over the sand with the tiny fish darting hither and thither, over the sea stars and starfish and crabs and slowly moving shells, over the seagrass and seaweeds, over the flat corals with their more colorful fish, between the brain coral, around the staghorn coral with its luminescent blue tips, over a bed of deep red-brown kelp—the Spangled Emperor, the Spotted Boxfish still here—and, the throb of her heart vibrating through her body, hovered once more above the familiar, long strands of waving seaweed. And there he was, waiting for her, dark red, yellow, purple, one large eye looking at her, the other swiveling the other way, looking for trouble.

"Hi there," Gaia whispered in her head. "I'm home again and I'm going to keep you safe, I promise."

THE DAYS PASSED BY SLOWLY AND WERE GONE IN A FLASH. GAIA almost forgot what she was waiting for as she hummed in her garden, sang in her shower, danced on her beach. The young farmer student still in the Mason house occasionally came by, a fish for her tea and sometimes a rabbit freshly skinned. He bore no threat, made no advances, simply smiled and sometimes stopped for a cup of tea before sauntering off. Mary and Eddie seemed themselves again, marking time, hoping that Dave Mason would never come back, that he and Ros would sell to the university. Gaia went daily to her letterbox, her heart lifting when a letter from Jarrah was there and sometimes a postcard from Seamus. He was already at a cattle station way inland from Broome, about to join a mustering gang. *Pushing around beasts instead of people,* he wrote. *Good job I've got a patient horse.* One day a postcard came from Ros with a short message—*still working on him, not giving up.* Then a letter from James. *The developers have withdrawn their offer to the Masons. They've decided it's too risky, thanks to the flurry of letters and articles in the newspaper after the Women's Weekly article came out, demanding that better protections are put in place to protect the seadragons and the reef. So either the Masons don't sell or they sell to the university. Suzanne Henderson has left Morton and McMillan. She told me she no longer has the stomach for it. She's selling suburban houses in Perth instead. The Sanctuary Trust papers are coming along. There are a few hoops to jump through but we'll get there.*

THERE WAS A STRANGE CAR PARKED ON THE TRACK BY THE barn one hot late October afternoon when Gaia returned from a swim in the lake. She stopped, her mouth dry, her heart thudding in her chest. The developers. They've changed their minds and made the Masons an offer they couldn't refuse. It was always too good to be true. Nothing is ever that easy. Shit, shit, shit. I need to get hold of James. Why don't I have a phone? We have to stop them, we have to. She tiptoed towards the barn. Where were they? Down on the beach, checking out their prize? The barn door was open. She always shut it to keep out stray birds that were always a nightmare to shoo out again. She tiptoed inside, not breathing. A tall man was silhouetted against the big windows at the end of the barn, his back to her. He hadn't heard her come in. Not Mason, who? Too tall for Seamus. Someone else from the developers? Her eyes were adapting to the dim light and she could see he was dressed in long shorts, a light shirt, boots, an outback hat in his hand. His hair was dark, not long, not short, thick, neat.

Gaia cleared her throat, her whole body tensed, on guard.

He turned, didn't speak. He grabbed his hat in both hands and twisted it.

"Who are you? What are you doing in here?" she asked, not moving.

"Gaia, I'm sorry. I'm sorry." His voice broke and Gaia's feet glued her to the old planks on the barn floor. His voice... it couldn't be...was it really him, here, alive? No, it was someone else, some stranger... "Gaia, it's me. Bron. Please let me try and explain, please."

He was moving towards her, his eyes on her face, his hat in his hands, his voice familiar and different, the words he was saying making no sense, making every sense, and now he was standing almost within arm's reach and she put out her hand, shaking, her whole body shaking as if she had a fever, and she touched his arm, hard with muscle, and she felt his trembling or was it hers, and she looked up, up into his face, into his brown eyes so like her father's, and she felt it coming, the strange light-headedness, her body crumbling, dissolving, everything dimming, going black, and she tried to put out her hands as she crashed to the floor but they were jelly like her legs. She opened her eyes and he was leaning over her. She was crumpled on the floor, his arm was under her head and she shook her head to get rid of the fuzziness and felt his fingers on her cheek, and she tried to say his name but her mouth was too dry. She concentrated on his voice, trying to make sense of what he was saying. She was dreaming, it was a horrible dream...

"Gaia, you fainted. Don't try and move. I'll get you some water" and his arm was gone from under her head and she saw his body standing up and leaving and she heard someone screaming out, and it was her and she was pushing herself up, sitting up, not wanting this to be a dream, not wanting him to leave her again and she was sobbing, her heart screaming, and he was squatting down beside her holding a glass to her lips and she took it and drank and drank still hiccuping with tears, and now she watched his mouth moving and the sounds coming out and they got clearer and became words and her fingers were on his wet face and on his lips feeling them saying her name.

~

THERE WERE LONG SHADOWS AND THEY WERE OUTSIDE SITTING at the table with only water because the time had vanished and they'd found themselves out here, Gaia still in her swimsuit that felt a bit damp, probably from her tears. She hugged the blanket tighter around her but she was still shivering as if it was cold even though she could feel the low sun warm on her face. She couldn't stop looking at Bron, his face the face she remembered and that she thought she'd almost forgotten, almost lost forever, his beautiful face that she saw now was their father's face and not their mother's. He had tried to tell her why he'd done what he'd done but he kept choking up and she couldn't listen because she thought he'd died because if he'd been alive why hadn't he come home or written her a letter?

"I know, I know," he said, again and again. "I don't know why. Because I'm a coward and I'm to blame for the fire and your burns and not looking after you or coming to stay with you when you were in hospital and instead running away and telling myself you're better off without me and you're the strong one and you'll be all right. And the longer I stayed away and didn't write the harder it got and the more lies I told myself."

And the night got dark and perhaps they made some toast and drank some tea and couldn't talk without Gaia shouting and screaming and hitting his chest. It was midnight when she lay on her bed and heard Bron's voice still broken with anguish saying he'd sleep in the car and after some sleep they could try to talk.

She must have slept because she didn't remember anything and not even any dreams when she woke up with the light hitting her face and she dropped her hand down and Rita Roo was there with her soft ears. Her head was pounding as if she'd smashed it on the ground yesterday when she'd fainted, but she knew she hadn't and that it was the ache from all the tears she'd cried and all the tears that were still bursting her head. She got up and stumbled outside to the toilet and discovered that she had dry clothes on, her shorts and her T-shirt, and not her swimsuit, but she couldn't remember putting them on. All she could remember was Bron, his head in his hands, his shoulders shaking as she screamed and pounded her hands on his body and he stood and let her.

CHAPTER 35

*I*t took two more days before Gaia was calm enough to listen to Bron's excuses. Not that he was calm enough to tell a coherent story as he broke again and again, beating himself with incriminations that seemed to diminish him even more than the angry, hurt words of blame she threw at him. It was the beach and the ocean and the snorkel they desperately agreed to try that finally soothed them enough to at last talk. Gaia was almost afraid to lead Bron over to the seadragon's weedy habitat, scared that the unsettling vibes they might send out would chase him away and her world would shatter again. But the seadragon was there, and when his partner floated out for the first time this summer and they began to circle each other, her healing began.

Out of the water, sitting on the beach wrapped in towels—Rita Roo and her joey grazing at a safe distance, twenty meters away under a Casuarina—she asked Bron to tell her about his life over the past four lost years and why he finally came back. "I'm sort of OK now," she said. "I'm ready to listen."

"I didn't intend to stay away. I got a job on a container ship heading for America and I was going to work for that one trip and be back in Perth in two months. I needed to get away, and I knew you would be in hospital in Melbourne for at least that long. I knew I needed to see you first but the truth is I was too ashamed and too messed up to face up to what I'd done to you. And then this job came up and they were leaving in four days. I told myself I mightn't get another chance. I wanted to go back to Goshawk Gardens first and see what was left. So I told myself I didn't have time to go to Melbourne." Bron reached over and gently touched the scar on Gaia's cheek. "And I thought, told myself, that seeing me might upset you even more, given what I'd done."

"Bron, the fire wasn't your fault. I couldn't remember anything about that night for a long time, but a few months ago I had some terrible nightmares and then I started having flashbacks to that night. There is so much we have to catch up on, but the worst thing is that Dave Mason was going to sell his farm to some developers for a horrible resort, and then I tracked down Ros Mason—she had left Dave after the fire— and she is still a joint owner of the farm. She's trying to get Dave to sell to the university for a field station instead. It's a long saga. I'll tell you more about it later."

Rita Roo had appeared next to Gaia and she stroked the fur on her back and then scratched the little joey's head as he peered out from his mother's pouch. "Ros told me about Dave and Mum. She said they were a having an affair"—Gaia shud-dered—"but Ros seems sure it didn't last long and that Mum had told Dave it was over. Dad and Dave got into a fight over it that night when they were at the Masons for dinner and Dave followed Mum and Dad home." Gaia stopped petting the joey and turned towards Bron. "Bron, they woke me up with their yelling and I went to see what was going on. I saw Dad push Dave and the lamp fell over and Mum's clothes caught alight and then the curtains. Dad threw himself over Mum and I rushed in and Dad screamed to me to wake you up and get out. Dave was getting water and throwing it over them, it was terrible."

Bron's head was in his hands and Gaia's arm crept around his shaking shoulders. "Bron, the fire had nothing to do with you or me. It wasn't your fault. You saved me."

After a while Bron looked up, his eyes haunted. "Do you believe that? That Mum wasn't going to leave Dad and us and go away with Mason?"

Gaia nodded. "You know she was dedicated to us. Think how hard she worked to train us to dance. And I know she never stopped loving Dad. If she had an affair with that creep, it was, I don't know, just because she was a bit bored with being at Goshawk Gardens and away from people like her."

Bron was crying, no sound, only tears rolling down his cheeks. The Bron Gaia remembered never cried.

"Hey," she said, catching a tear as it trickled from his chin. "Remember that time not long before the fire when we went to Jurien Bay for dinner and afterwards went to the movies and saw that special showing of 'Jailhouse Rock'? You already had the LP and we loved rock 'n rolling to it when Mum wasn't watching."

Bron grinned, a bit shakily, but it stopped his tears. "And when we got back home, I stuck the record on when we were all there. I'll never forget that, Dad throwing Mum around, through his legs, rolling her over his back. They were phenomenal..." Bron was almost laughing now and Gaia finished the story.

"Then you and I started dancing and we all ended up in fits of giggles on top of each other on the floor."

"When did Dad ever learn how to do that? Do you think they danced in secret when we were at the beach?"

"Of course they did. It was their special thing. That movie would have been released when they were courting. I bet Dad learned it then so he could dance with Mum in those New York nightclubs and not always be on the outside watching

her. And she always loved it because she was dancing with
him."

"OK, you've convinced me," Bron said. "Mum would
never have left us. God, Gaia, thank you for remembering. It's
horrible to think of them dying in that fire, but it's a massive
relief to know it wasn't my stupid cigarette butts. Not that it's
about that really. I know that. Nothing excuses me for
deserting you. Nothing."

Gaia sighed. "No. But you're home now, and you're alive
and you're the only family I have so I'm going to have to
forgive you." She rolled her eyes then managed a grin. "So
now you have to tell me what you've been doing all these years
and what made you come home?"

"Well, long story short, the container ship docked in New
York for ten days before it was going to return to Australia. I
loved New York. Even though I was feeling so terrible about
leaving you."

"You were born there. Perhaps that's why. Perhaps it felt
like home," Gaia said.

Bron shrugged. "Anyway, I managed to get a cheap ticket
to the American Ballet Theatre. Gaia, it was amazing. And I
was able to get money out from my bank account, the one
Mum set up for me there when I was a baby. She'd been
putting money in it for years. There'll be money in the
account she set up there for you as well, I bet."

"Because she always believed that one day we'd dance in
New York," Gaia said.

Bron nodded. "I started looking around, sussing out the
dance schools and dance companies in New York. Goodness
knows what I was thinking. I honestly intended to come back
to Australia when the container ship left. But the night before I
was due back on board I got totally plastered with some guys I
had met in a bar there. They dragged me back to their apartment and let me sleep it off. By the time I was sober, the
container ship had left."

Gaia stared at him.

"I know, it's a weak excuse. I had a fair bit of therapy later and managed to admit to myself that I probably got drunk almost on purpose...at least without thinking straight."

"Right. And no chance of getting on any other container ships or getting a flight back, given you had all that money in your account?"

"You can't give me more grief than I've given myself ever since. I was a coward, plain and simple."

"A letter, a postcard?"

"Too ashamed. Always telling myself I'd write and never quite being ready to tell you the truth. And after a while it seemed too late. I didn't even know where you were, if you were still in some hospital in Melbourne or in Perth. I couldn't even remember the address for the lawyer in Perth. Not even his name. Pitiful, I know,"

"So, what next?"

"I auditioned for an amazing dance company that was into this new style of contemporary ballet. I got in. They didn't give a toss about the burn scars on my leg. That's where I've been ever since."

"Grief. Not classical ballet. What about Mum's dream of your dancing for the American Ballet Theatre?"

"I did audition for their corp de ballet but didn't stand a chance. But you know, I didn't care, because I already loved the contemporary ballet idea way more. Gaia, it's so much more creative. Every dancer is sort of a soloist, and the other dancers are so much fun. It's like dancing for joy, not like dancing for perfection."

"Gosh, I wish you'd seen our performance. *The Dance of the Seadragons*. I taught all these kids at a Children's home in Perth to dance and we put on this show. It was hardly contemporary ballet, but it was joyous. And the Artistic Director of the West Australian Ballet asked me to audition for an internship in their company and said he thought I'd be great in their new contemporary ballet programme."

"I know," Bron said, grinning at her. "I mean about the performance. That's what finally made me realize I needed to come back and hope you'd forgive me. A friend of mine in the company is from Perth, and her mother sent her the *Woman's Weekly* with the article about the show and young Jarrah and you. The photo of you all, you dressed up as a seadragon. Ainsley knew I came from near Perth, although I'd never told her anything about you or what happened…too ashamed… and she thought my name was Oscar Cooper…but she knew I'd be interested in the article. Aussies in New York stick together."

"What do you mean, Oscar Cooper? Did you change your name even? Is that how much you wanted never to be found?"

"It was my stage name. It wasn't official. Half the company had stage names. Who wants to be a dancer called John Brown?"

"Oberon Christie is the perfect bloody name for a dancer. That's why Mum called you that."

"That's why I didn't want it. I didn't want to risk anyone finding out I was her son. At least I kept the same initials."

"What's wrong with being her son? Her ballet name wasn't even Christie, so how would anyone know you were her son unless you told them?"

"Bloody hell, Gaia, I wanted to make my own life my own way. Mum was gone. Because of me." Bron gazed past her, his eyes blurred. "I didn't have to make her dreams come true any more."

"So what did this friend of yours think when you told her that was your sister in the article? Or did you lie about that too?"

"No, I didn't. She got it all out of me."

"She was the one who got you to come home?" Gaia's fingernails cut into her palms.

"No, she wasn't. She was horrified by how I'd treated you, but as soon as I read the article and saw those photos of you and everything you had achieved all by yourself, I wanted to see you again. It was all that mattered. It broke something, the wall I'd put up. I got a meeting with the company CEO that afternoon and told him the whole thing and got an extended leave from the company. Next day I went to a travel agent and got them to book me the cheapest flights back as soon as possible."

Gaia pulled herself up off the sand and walked down to the edge of the water. Her body was empty, no stomach, no liver, no lungs, no heart, no mind. Just tears falling over her numb face, falling from empty. She didn't turn her empty head to Bron as he stood next to her. She saw his hand take hers but she didn't feel it.

"Gaia, I'm so so sorry. Please can you give me a chance?"

ANOTHER NIGHT, ANOTHER DAY, ANOTHER NIGHT, ANOTHER DAY. But each hour a little less empty, a little less painful, a little less numbing than the hour before.

"Gaia, do you want me to leave?" Bron said, as they sat, not communicating, picking at slices of toast. Gaia wasn't sure how long ago it had been, five days, a week since he'd shown up? He slept at Mary and Eddie's place but he was always around, following her about, digging in the garden, making tea, making rice, putting plates of food in front of her. She stared at him now, his words penetrating her empty head.

"Would you like me to go?" Bron's voice was so quiet she could barely hear him.

"Go where?" she said.

"Away from here. You can't forgive me and I don't blame you. I've stuffed up your life again by coming back. I'll go back to the States. Or if you're not sure I'll go to Perth or somewhere and wait so if you want me to come back I will."

"No. I don't want you to go away again. How can you think that? After leaving me for all these years. But you go if that's what you want."

Gaia looked down at her hand as Bron covered it with his. She watched—it seemed she wasn't in her body but somewhere above it like Gos flying—and she felt the plops of warm as her eyes filled and spilt over again.

AFTER THAT, SHE BEGAN TO FEEL AGAIN, HER BODY FILLING UP and her mind clearing away the fog. Sometimes she still almost hated him, but more and more she liked him being around. Sometimes she went to Mary and Eddie's for a meal and listened as they talked with Bron about this and that, and for a while she'd feel almost happy. Mary didn't say much about Gaia's awkwardness around Bron, but what she didn't say Gaia knew anyway and it helped her want to be a family with Bron again. She told him about finding Mason on the concrete and Mary and Eddie getting him to hospital and being harassed by the police. But she kept Jarrah out of it. That would still be a secret when she was six feet under.

It was easier telling Bron about the Children's Home and Jarrah and Hannah, and even Seamus. When she got to the part about Dr. Belfer and the possibility of her being in the Boston research study and getting her scars fixed, Bron grabbed her and swung her around.

"It's not that exciting. I haven't even decided if I want to do it yet. In fact I'm thinking I'll just get Dr. Belfer to do the basic plastic surgery in Perth. The Boston study will take months and I'll have to have massive skin grafts and all for what? My garden doesn't care. Even if I get the internship with the West Australia Ballet, Mr Garth said my scars could be disguised or covered up."

"But you'd be in Boston! The train from New York to Boston is less than five hours. I can come and see you heaps. We have four days off after every six days of performances. And there might be times when you are between treatments and can come to New York. I know we were there when we were kids but I bet you hardly remember that. Gaia, you'll love it."

"You'd do that? Come and see me every time you had your days off?"

"Yes. Please think about it Gaia. I promise this time I won't abandon you."

"Oh. Well, I'll think about it some more. Although I'm not sure I can leave here. It was hard enough being in Perth so long. Boston is so much further away."

"It'll be worth it in the end. Then if you wanted to audition for the White Swan, the only thing you'd be judged on is your talent, not your scars."

"Very funny. I think I'll stick to being a seadragon."

"Come on, by the time you go to Boston Mason will have succumbed to his greed and sold to the university. Then you wouldn't have to worry. Hey, you might decide to stay in New York. I bet they'd love you in our company. We'd be dancing together, just like Mum wanted."

"She's probably turning in her grave. Contemporary nonsense. I can hear her." Gaia sighed. "OK, I'll give it some thought. The Boston surgery at least. Now shut-up about it and let's go for a swim."

THAT EVENING BRON WENT OUT TO THE CAR AND BROUGHT back a fat brown envelope. "I've got something special for you." He slid out a pile of paper and placed it between them.

"These are mostly from the New York Library. They have archives and programs and photos and all sorts relating to the American Ballet Theatre. I searched them for the dates Mum was there and photocopied and took photos of everything I could find."

Gaia's gaze was riveted to the photo on the top of the pile. Their mother in glowing color as Giselle, taken from a 1954 program. "Oh I can't believe all this." She looked at image after image, program after program until she turned over a photocopied page and saw a grainy black and white photo surrounded by blurry words. "Oh Bron, this is you as a little boy with Mum and Dad. What was that doing in the archives?" She tried to make out the words. "It's an article written about Mum when she retired from the Ballet, just before they left for Australia." She swallowed. "I'd lost Dad's face. I've tried and tried to get him back but I couldn't, not really. But now I'll never have to forget again." She touched the photo gently. "I sort of remembered Mum's face, but only in all her makeup as Giselle or the White Swan. I suppose we saw all those portraits of her in the house so often that they're glued into our memory. But not like this, with her hair down and her own face." Gaia picked up another programme, this one of Margot as the Firebird. "No wonder Dad was besotted as soon as he saw her."

"She looks like you. Or you look like her. More and more," Bron said, taking the photo from her.

"Do you think?" Gaia took another look at the photo of Margot as Giselle. "I don't think so. She's very beautiful."

"She is. You are. But the one that really shows her likeness to you is that one of her with Dad and me."

"It's strange seeing her as a normal person. I suppose that's how she was when she was our mum. I could hardly remember her like that any more. In my mind, mostly I see her with her hair scraped back in a bun, her eyes lined in black, and her red smile always perfect."

Bron looked around the barn."She never looked like that here." He walked over to the barre and stood there, tall and straight and handsome like their dad. He gazed into the mirror.

He's seeing her, Gaia thought. With her hair in a ponytail, and her face bare of makeup, and those scruffy leggings she liked. She went over to the barre and stood next to him. "How many thousands of hours did we spend here with Mum straightening our backs and stretching our legs higher and higher?"

"It doesn't bear thinking about," Bron said, his eyes holding hers in their reflections.

"If she hadn't you would never have got into that dance company you love so much, and I'd never have been able to teach Jarrah and all the kids how to dance," Gaia said.

"I know. We owe her."

"We owe them both. They did love us. And we had lots of fun times." Gaia dropped her hands from the barre and went back to the photos. "Thank you for showing me these. They've brought back all sorts of memories about Mum and Dad and us. Just happy here at Goshawk Gardens being a family."

"They're for you to keep. I've got copies back in New York." Bron was by her side and then he was hugging her tight. "Love you, little sis," he mumbled.

CHAPTER 36

$\mathscr{B}$ron's car was an on-its-last-legs cheap rental he'd got in Jurien Bay, and even though it was as cheap as chips he said he couldn't afford to rent it forever. So he decided to drive it into Jurien Bay and return it and see if he could find an old bomb from the used car dealers he could get for a song. He went on Saturday so that if he couldn't find wheels he could afford, he could get a ride back home with Eddie after the market day. He wanted Gaia to come, but she still wasn't ready to go anywhere there were people and cars and noise. She waved him goodbye at the gate and checked the letterbox before wandering back to the barn. It was a stunning day and she couldn't wait to swim with the seadragons. There were two letters in the box, one from James Ludlow and the other from Ros. She ripped open Ros's first. Her eyes scanned it looking for the important bits.

"Heads up on Dave. He's been discharged from the Rehab Center and seems much better. Off the booze at least for now, and seems determined to go back to the farm to make a new start. He went to court on his Drunk and Disorderly charge and got off with a fine. He's still digging his toes in about not selling to the university. Says they can can stick their money up their prissy arses. Charming as always. So I told him the very least he

could do to thank you for saving his precious life when he splattered himself on the concrete would be to support what you want. I laid it on. Told him he owed it to Margot and Joe to look out for you. He told me to pass on to you that if you wanted him to even think about selling to the university you would have to get down on your knees and apologize to him first.

I can't even imagine what I ever saw in him. But if he does go back there take a deep breath and tell him it's nice to have him home and blah blah and take him some scones or something. If you can get him in a good mood you might be able to ask him to think about selling to the university so you wouldn't lose the only home you have left after the fire and losing your parents, sob sob. It stinks, I know, but if you can butter him up so he wants to help you, won't that be worth it? He was always a sucker for a pretty girl, and you do look awfully like Margot."

The letter from James gave her the same information about Mason but with less color. She should write to him and tell him Bron was back. She should have done it days ago but she'd been too upset. She'd even missed writing her weekly letter to Jarrah, and his letter that came last Wednesday was worried. She sighed. Why couldn't she be given a holiday from all this? Bugger it all. She'd go for her swim with the sea-dragons and tonight she'd write to Jarrah and James. Ros could wait. If Mason showed up she'd write to her. Perhaps she and her nice husband could come for a visit and work on Dave. Get the bastard to sell.

∼

BRON RETURNED IN HIS NEW BOMB, A DINGED AND SCRATCHED yellow 1962 Datsun Y with so much rust in the floor that sitting in the front passenger's seat you could see the ground going by between your feet. "I'll teach you to drive it," he said, as he patted the bonnet. "You can have it when I go back to the States next year. Unless you come with me."

"I can drive already. Don't you remember? Dad taught me when I was ten."

"And you've kept it up, have you? Got your license?"

"The last time I drove was the same day as I first had a go. It doesn't look that hard."

But any thought of learning to drive vanished when Mary showed up at the barn on Monday afternoon. Gaia knew, just from Mary's tense face.

"Him back. Out shootin' roos," she said. "You stay outta him way."

"Mason? Is he drinking again?" Bron asked.

"Dunno. Seem all right. Still mean though. Said he had some news for Gaia." She shook her head. "He bad smell."

"It's OK Mary. I won't go near him without Bron," Gaia said, sitting down quickly and wiping her clammy hands on her shorts.

Mary looked at Bron. "She tell you what happen? You look out for her. Me 'n Eddie takin' off tomorrow an' might not come back for a bit now you here. See our mob. Be back for Jarrah when him get here."

Gaia stuck her hands between her knees and gripped them tight. "I'll look after Jarrah if you're not back in time. His summer holidays don't start until 20th December. Weeks away yet."

"Does Mason know you're leaving?" Bron asked.

"Yeah. He don' care." Mary pulled Gaia into a sudden hug. "Be careful, Gaia. P'raps Mister Dave know?"

Gaia shook her head. "He's full of bullshit. He'll be mad because the developers withdrew their offer and Ros is pissed off with him because he won't sell to the university, stupid idiot. Blames me, that's all."

"You stay away, girl. Keep Jarrah away if him come early. Mister Dave funny in head."

～

"WHAT WAS THAT ABOUT? MARY WAS SCARED. YOU WERE BOTH scared. What haven't you told me?" Bron asked as soon as they got back to the barn and put the kettle on.

Gaia shrugged, her heart pounding. "What I said. Mason's mad with me because he thinks I've influenced Ros."

"Gaia, stop it. You can't bluff your way through this. What's he done to you to make you so frightened? Has he hurt you?"

"No. I'm not scared. Not really. He just turns my stomach."

"Mary seems terrified and I bet not much scares her. If you don't tell me I'm going right back there to ask her."

Gaia grabbed his arm. "No, please don't do that. Poor Mary, she's got enough to deal with."

"So you'll tell me? The truth. Nothing left out."

"Yes, you'd know about that."

"Christ, Gaia. Give it up."

Gaia sighed. "Will you promise not to do anything silly? Go rushing off to confront Mason?"

"No, I won't promise a bloody thing except that I'll listen to you. Of course I won't do anything without telling you. Is that good enough?"

"I want to talk to Mason calmly about his options for selling his land. If he really is sober he might be fine. I suppose he might listen to you more than me. He hates me."

"Why?"

"He doesn't need a reason. But he thinks I stuffed up his nice deal with the developers."

"And got him to hospital before he died. Surely he's a bit grateful to you for that?"

"He's a creep."

"For christ's sake, Gaia, stop all the shit. What did Mary mean about Dave knowing? Knowing what?" He handed Gaia a mug of tea. "Drink this and then tell me. No half-truths this time."

"I don't need to tell you. I taped it all. You can hear it for yourself in all its creepy detail. I was recording my piano practice when Mason barged in and the tape recorder kept recording. It was still recording when... when it was over."

"When what was over? What, Gaia?"

Gaia sat straighter. "We made up the story about Dave falling from his deck and knocking himself out. He tried to rape me. He didn't though. Jarrah hit him on the head with a spade and knocked him out. Mason doesn't know I taped it. He probably doesn't remember anything about it. I can use it to force him to sell to the university. Blackmail the bastard. Tell him I'll take it to the police if he doesn't sell. I'll wipe the end bit of the tape so he doesn't know Jarrah was even there."

Bron was white beneath his tan. "Gaia, if you have a tape recording you should take it straight to the police. Mason needs to be put away for a long time."

She shook her head. "No, not the police. It'll go to court and they might find out about Jarrah. I can't risk it. It would destroy Jarrah's life. I'd never get to Boston or even be able to get my scars fixed in Perth, and Mary and Eddie will get dragged in too and you know how the cops will treat them. They might throw Jarrah in jail. There are hundreds of Aboriginal kids in jail. Some of them are beaten so badly, they die. Or they want to die." A sob gulped out of her.

"Gaia, get a grip. Jarrah is safe in Perth."

"That's why I can never tell. I should never have told you. Bron, promise me you won't tell anyone." Bron jerked and pulled his arm away and she stared at the white half-moon shapes of her fingernails imprinted into his tanned skin.

"Where's the tape? I want to hear it."

"Do what you want. It's in the bottom drawer below the kitchen bench. Under the tea-towels. The tape deck's in the cupboard. I'm going for a swim."

"What about Mason? What if he sees you?"

"What if he does? It's my beach and I'm not going to stay locked in the barn for the rest of my life, am I."

"Let me listen to the tape and then we'll go for a swim together."

"No. I want to go alone. I may as well get used to it. You'll be off back to America soon."

❧

WHEN GAIA GOT BACK TO THE BARN, NAUSEA BURNING IN HER gut as she tried to prepare herself for Bron's reaction, he was sitting at the outside table, Rita Roo nowhere in sight, the tape deck silent by his side. Before she could utter a word, he was beside her, his arms around her, enclosing her. Shutting her eyes, she let herself focus on the sensation of his strong hand as it stroked her back, up and down, up and down. After a long while, her stomach calmed, she pulled away a little and they stood silently, looking into each other's eyes. Gaia felt loved, her heart almost whole again.

"Let's walk, if you're not too tired," Bron said, and she nodded. Their feet found their own way to the lake with its deep calm presence, its web of life so timeless—algae, water weeds, tiny mollusks and tinier shrimps, eels, fish, ducks, pelicans, budgerigars, fringing reeds, bush, and sky-touching white-barked eucalyptus. And high above a goshawk gliding and swooping and dancing with his mate.

Coming to Gaia's favorite sandy beach they sat with their bare feet in the soft amber water and talked, and listened.

"Gaia, you can't let Mason get away with this," Bron began. "We could talk it through with James Ludlow. Even if it's not something he could take on, he'd know a lawyer who could. If you went to the police now and explained what actually happened, and how you were too frightened to tell the truth back then, let them hear the tape, they could still get Mason, and probably put him away and perhaps even take his land off him. Get it all put in Ros's name. And you and Jarrah would feel better," Bron said. "Free."

"I wish. But this is Australia, not cloud-cuckoo land. I would not feel better. They could get me for fake evidence or something. The cops drove me into the station and I had to sign my statement. Actually, when one of them drove me back he got quite chatty and said that they knew Mason; they'd had him drunk and disorderly in their cells overnight a few times. "

"All the more reason you could own up now."

"And say goodbye to going to Boston any time soon, or having a shot at getting into the West Australia Ballet? Why should I ruin my life for him? And it would all come out about Mason and Mum, and you know how newspapers love that sort of stuff."

"Shit. I suppose you're right. The bastard will get away with it."

"He hates me. He must remember trying to rape me, or at least some of it, even if he can't remember what he was doing just before Jarrah hit him. Likely he remembers being repulsed by my chest scars. I wouldn't put it past him to clamp his grubby toes in just to hack me off. Refuse to sell to the university even now it's the only way he can get his loot."

"He's dangerous, Gaia. You realize you can't live here alone when he's here?"

"So tomorrow I'm going to bloody well confront him and accuse him of trying to rape me and tell him I have a tape recording as well, and that you've heard it, and if he doesn't agree to sell to the university, I'll go to the police."

"And if he still refuses, *will* you go to the police?"

"He won't refuse. He won't want to risk going to jail."

"I think we should talk it through with James first. Perhaps get him to approach Mason."

" Stop arguing with everything I say. Do you want to help me or not?"

294 | JENNI OGDEN

~

Mason's house was silent and the oily patch where he
parked his ute was vacant. They pushed open the door and
found his greasy dishes and a mug with coffee dregs, not yet
skinned over, still on the table. No whisky bottles. Perhaps he
really had sobered up. Gaia clenched her fists and scowled as
the adrenalin drained out of her pumped-up body.

"It's only 2pm. We'll come back later. He's probably out
mending fences or something," Bron said.

"That'll be a first," Gaia said. "More likely shooting roos.
Christ, if he touches a hair of Rita Roo's head I'll definitely
kill him."

Bron pulled her out of the house and back to the barn.
"How about we get our wetsuits on and go for a snorkel? The
tide must be high by now."

"I'm not in the mood. I can't bear thinking that it might all
be lost."

"All will not be lost. Come on, grab your wetsuit and let's
go. It will calm us down."

Bron was right, of course. Gaia almost forgot Mason as
they floated over the reef, diving down to peer at busy yellow
and blue fish fossicking under coral outcrops, admiring the
rainbow splendor of giant clams before they closed their wavy
shells, following a sinuous octopus gamboling from coral to
coral, arms coiling and dancing, its color changing instanta-
neously from blue to yellow to white to match its changing
background, then shooting in front of them, its arms flung
back like a soundless vent of steam from a rocket launching
into space, and their seadragon pair, the male in full view, the
shy female peeking out from the weeds.

By four-thirty they were ready again, Gaia failing in her
efforts not to get too pumped this time. What if Mason didn't
come back today? Perhaps he'd gone into Jurien Bay on a
drinking spree? When they got to the gate and his ute was still

missing, the air drained out of her, but then the spluttering of a vehicle had them jumping off the track as Mason drove straight at them. He swerved at the last minute, his face staring out at them, brakes grinding as he slammed to a stop. Her pulse pounding in her head, Gaia walked towards him. She grabbed Bron's arm as Mason jumped down from the ute and turned, his hat shading his eyes. She tried to blank out the memory of his face, slack and lifeless, the last time she'd seen him.

They stood there and watched him as he ignored them. There was an animal in the back of the ute; a dog. A dead dog. Mason lifted a rifle out of the back and stood it against the cab. Then he hauled the dog out and it hit the dusty drive, its ginger body and sharp head matted and streaked with blood from the gaping hole between its eyes.

"It's a dingo," Gaia whispered.

Mason turned. "Very good. I suppose you want to protect them and let them rip all my stock to bits."

"You've hardly got any stock left. What harm was it doing?"

"Living. Breeding. What are you doin' back? Thought you'd deserted to the big smoke?"

"We want to talk to you. I guess you remember Bron. It's only been four years."

Bron nodded in Mason's direction. Gaia shivered as his tension glowered across the gap between him and Mason, pushing her heart rate even higher.

Mason stared at Bron. Smirked. "The dancer back from the dead. Where have you been hiding? Leaving your kid sister to deal with everything by herself."

"You're right," Bron said. "But I'm back now. We want to talk to you about our property, and how we're going to protect it."

"You're on *my* property right now mate, and I reckon you've lost any say about your parent's block," Mason said. He squinted at Gaia. "What do you want to talk about? I suppose Ros has been givin' you an earful. Did she tell you I expected an apology from you?"

"For what? If I hadn't found you unconscious on the concrete you'd probably be dead."

"I know that's the story you've been telling, but we know better, don't we."

"I simply want to have a civil discussion. The university has made you a generous offer and the resort crowd has pulled out. You won't get another chance like this. If you don't sell, Ros could demand you pay her half the value, and where are you going to get that?"

"I'll soon pay her off. I'm staying here and getting my gardens good again now I've got rid of those two good-for-nothin' black mates of yours. Always going walkabout. I hope they never show their ugly mugs here again."

The blood pulsing in her head, Gaia stepped closer to him, shaking off Bron's hand as he grabbed her arm. "I will go to the police and tell them you tried to rape me unless you agree to sell to the university. I've got so much evidence you'll be in jail for the rest of your pitiful little life."

Mason took a step forward and Bron pushed past Gaia. Mason held his hands up, palms facing Bron. "Calm down mate. Stay out of it. This is between me and Gaia."

"It's all right, Bron," Gaia said, refusing to let any sign of a tremble show in her voice. She stuck her shaking hands in the back pockets of her shorts, images of Mason on his back flashing in her head, his pants down, his wrists and ankles trussed like a turkey. She moved closer to Mason and pinned his eyes to hers. "I have a tape recording of the whole thing. When you barged in on me I was recording my piano practice and the tape kept running right through your assault. You're welcome to listen to it if you don't believe me, but it might make you feel very sick. The original of the tape is with my lawyer. James Ludlow. You might recognize his name. He's the man who put in a joint application with me to the university, proposing they buy your land for a field station. So our wilderness will be protected. It's not been easy to hold him back from taking the tape to the police."

"You little slut. As if I'd touch your pockmarked body with a barge pole. Who did you have to help you, eh? Who nearly killed me?"

"You were so drunk I was able to shove you off me and you crashed your head on the bed. I bloody well should have hit you."

"No one will believe a slut like you. Just like your mother, pretending you're so pure but panting for it."

Gaia sprung at him but Bron was faster. His arm shot out and Mason's head snapped backwards, his hat falling to the ground. Stumbling, he found his feet and snatched up the rifle leaning on the side of the ute. "Back off, or I'll shoot the sneer off your pretty face." Gaia froze as Mason's head jutted towards Bron, his eyes slits in the face she saw in her nightmares. He lifted his rifle and pointed it at Bron. Gaia tried to pull him back but she might as well have tried to move a mountain.

"Put the gun down," Bron said, the chill in his tone freezing Gaia's feet to the ground. "You have one more chance to talk this through and be able to walk away from here with a lot of money you don't deserve." He reached his arm out towards the gun and moved one step closer. Gaia's ears exploded and she was in the dirt, her body shielding Bron as he jerked under her hands.

CHAPTER 37

*W*here's the blood coming from, too much, no, I'll stop it. "Bron, Bron, can you hear me?"

"Fuck. I thought I'd emptied both barrels when I shot the dingo. Didn't mean to shoot him." Mason's voice over the thundering in her head.

"Get an ambulance, drive to the nearest house and phone one. Hurry, he's going to die," Gaia screamed.

"It's his own stupid fault. He shouldn't have come at me like that. It's not my fault."

Where's it all coming from, I can't see, too much blood, is it in his thigh? "Bron, say something..." a voice screaming "Get me some towels and get an ambulance." Pulling off her shirt balling it up pressing it to his thigh grabbing the towel shoved at her. Press it down turning bright red more blood on her hands, keep pressing, hard, harder, stretching her body so her face was over his white face is he breathing please let him be breathing you can have everything the beach everything I don't care please Bron be breathing you can't leave me again. The sound of the ute roaring dust spurting out over them sticking to the red everywhere, Bron's body, her body, her ear to his mouth a tiny breath on her ear is it real another breath oh Bron you're alive, keep breathing you're going to be all right the ambulance will be here soon I just have to stop you bleeding you can't have much left. Press harder, harder, his body jerking. He's having a fit, what do I do, no he's stopped. "Bron, Bron," her voice calling crying yelling at him to breathe to say something. Another jerk, a sound, a groan, Bron was that you? Please make a noise. Take one hand away what if he starts bleeding again have to press harder with one hand take the other hand off grab Bron's hand squeeze it hard. "Bron squeeze my hand squeeze it, say something."

A faint squeeze on her hand yes there it was again her, face back over his face, his eyelids flickering opening closing. "Bron, Bron" —her voice yelling at him to make a noise, watching his eyes his mouth seeing the groan hearing it come out, his eyes opening her arms about to fall off with pressing, looking back at his thigh, the blood slowing, has it stopped oh please let it stop. Bron's eyes shut, his complexion clammy. Why? Why? He might be going into shock. Is he bleeding somewhere else I can't see, inside somewhere? "Bron, open your eyes, talk to me. Stay awake Bron, it's going to be all right, the ambulance is coming."

"Gaia?"

"Oh Bron, Bron it's me. I'm here."

"Wha... Shit, there's something on my leg. Can you get it off? Shit, shit, get it off. It must be broken."

"Sorry, sorry, it's me pressing to stop the blood. Mason shot your leg, I don't think it's broken I'm sorry. Lie still and I'll take the pressure off a bit and see if the bleeding's stopped." Gaia took the pressure off the bloody rags, a little bit, a little bit more, her aching hands crying in relief and the bloody towel and t-shirt stopping her from seeing if the blood was still coming but it didn't seem to be any more. She couldn't keep pressing forever her arms were falling off and what if Mason didn't get an ambulance? Her eyes glued to the bloody rags, she undid the buckle on the belt of her jeans and ripped it off, her breath stopped in her throat, and slid it, pushed it, dragged it below Bron's sticky red jeans, under his thigh, pushing it as high up as she could. What if it was his femoral artery? It could start bleeding again and never stop. Her fingers fumbled as she got the two ends of the belt above his thigh, around his jeans above the bloody rags. Pushed the end of the belt through the buckle and pulled it tight, tighter. "Sorry sorry Bron I have to get it tight" as he yelped. She needed to get Bron to a hospital, to the Anderson's house it was closest on the main road not far off where it turned onto their road, they'll have a phone why didn't she have a phone why didn't Mason or Mary have a phone she'd get one as soon as Bron was safe. He was saying something and she put her head close to his…

"Wha' happen?"

"Mason shot you. I think the bullet went in your thigh. You've bled so much but I think it's stopped now. I've got my belt around it tight but you mustn't move while I get your car."

"Where Mason?"

"He's gone in his ute. I told him to call an ambulance and he drove off so he might. But I can't risk it."

"Hurt you?" Bron croaked, his face contorting.

"No, I'm OK. I'm going to get your car and get you into it and drive to the Anderson's house and call an ambulance from there. It's not far."

She looked at Bron's face. It was pale, but not sweaty. "Are you holding up? Talk to me."

"Hurts like buggery. Leg broken. Water." He was shivering his lips shivering his teeth making little clicks inside his mouth.

"Don't move. I'll be as quick as I can." Gaia stood up and ran into the house, grabbing a cup from the cupboard and splashing it full of water. Drank a mouth full, her sticky dry mouth desperate for it, filled it again. Upstairs to the bedroom, grab blanket back down, grab water, back to Bron.

"Here, try and sip this, little sips or you might be sick." She lifted the back of his head and held the cup to his white trembling lips. He sucked it in, water dripped down his chin, sucked in more. She took it away. "That's enough."

"More, more please."

She gave him some more, his face was looking better, it must be all right let him have some more. He closed his eyes, a creep of color in his face. Gaia grabbed the big blanket thrown on the concrete beside her, folded it in half, covered him up, tucked it gently into his sides hiding the bloody mess of his thigh from the flies, keeping him warm with so much less blood in him to warm him from inside. "Bron, lie as still as you can, don't move your leg, don't go to sleep. I'll be back as quick as I can."

"Where, where going?"

"To get your car."

"Can't drive. You can't drive."

"Bullshit. I've been driving since I was ten. Don't move. Stay awake, think about every fish we saw today, say their names in your head." Gaia jumped as she felt something bumping her side. Jerking her head around she saw Rita Roo, her long eyelashes almost brushing her face. "Oh Rita Roo, thank god you're here. Stay with Bron. Don't let him move or go to sleep." She grabbed the roo's head in her bloody hands and kissed her long nose. Her joey was hidden in her pouch and behind them the dingo's body was already covered in blowflies.

HEART POUNDING AND EVERY BREATH HURTING AS IT PUSHED out of her open mouth, Gaia ran along the track to the car. Bent low with the pain in her side she stumbled to the barn, pulled open the kitchen drawer. Codeine, left over from when she needed it in hospital, that will have to do, drink bottle, fill it, torch. Looked around, head screaming with trying to think about what she needed, more blankets, pillows. Arms full, back to the car thank god always unlocked, key always in it, ready to go, stuff everything in front passenger seat, pull the driver's seat forward, too far, back again, adjust mirror, key in, turn key, engine coughs, foot on clutch, gear lever left and up into first gear, engine splutters, car jerks, stops, foot on clutch, key turned, car roars, foot slowly slowly off clutch, right foot slowly slowly press accelerator down a little, a little more, shit handbrake off, car jerks forward, keep it going. Jerks again foot right off clutch soft on accelerator better now almost dark shit where are the lights, hand off steering wheel twisting the stick thing lights blare on track scary in front, something running across track, keep going keep going. Black dark outside two green eyes on side of road, jerking and bumping down the track turn coming up slow down foot on brake not too much still in first gear, shit can't risk changing gear nearly there the dingo's body caught in the headlights, need to turn car so can get Bron in the back and facing the right way to the main road. Mouth dry, hands clammy with thinking about main road, can't back car without stopping and changing gear, drive onto paddock on side of track thank god no fence, bumping round in wide circle back to track facing the other way ready. Slam on brake, turn key half way, don't want engine to stop, headlights still on, please let Bron still be alive. Grab torch and drink bottle, need the codeine. Dark shape on ground not moving please please let him be alive. Kneeling down shining the torch, Bron blinks, shakes his head, thank you thank you, Rita Roo shuffles her body still close on Bron's other side, Gaia's heart slows a little. "Bron, try and swallow these. They're codeine. They'll help with the pain." She shook two, no three out of the bottle, undid the screw top on the drink bottle, held his head up and pushed a tablet to the back of his tongue. Bron spluttered, choked, she caught the pill, gave him some water, tried again. He swallowed and swallowed again. "Have some more water," and this time it went down. More water, pill, more water, pill. Three should help, hope they're not too old to work.

"Bron, I'm going to make a bed in the back of the Datsun and then get you into it."

Bron's eyes closing and opening as he jerked, agony on his face. "Hang in there, big brother," she said, and went back to the car and made him a bed in the cramped back seat. Back again, taking the blanket from his body, shining the torch on the bloody rags. They looked the same. He wasn't shivering now. She felt his hands, she pushed her hand into the back of his trainer on the foot of his shot leg and it didn't feel cold, she pressed her fingers around his ankle and thought she felt a weak pulse.

"Bron, I'm going to lay this blanket next to you and try and get you onto it so I can pull you to the car."

"I can walk to car."

"No, you can't. You might start bleeding again." But he helped her a bit, his hands pushing himself up off the ground enough to shuffle across, onto the blanket, as she held his shot leg. Pulling him the two meters to the open door of the car almost had her on her knees, he was tall and slim, but muscle was heavy, but she did it and stood behind him, grabbed him under his armpits, hitched her bum up onto the back seat and shuffled backwards along the seat, pulling him with her.

"Stop, Gaia, I can get myself in. Can you go outside and lift my leg in?"

"Sorry, yes." She opened the door behind her and almost fell out backwards. Around the other side, holding his poor leg steady as he breathed hard and lifted himself up and along onto the bed she'd made. She stuffed pillows along each side of him and more each side of his leg. Covering him with a blanket, she handed him the drink bottle and the torch.

Nearly tripping over Rita Roo, she patted her head. "Thank you," she whispered. "Go home to the barn and think positive thoughts."

The car coughed as she turned the key its next turn and this time she got the clutch and accelerator almost right and the Datsun drove itself cautiously along the rutted farm track towards the gate that closed the property off from the road. Gaia prayed there would be no traffic, at least on the country road, so she could get used to driving before the main road. She pushed in the clutch and pulled the gear lever down and let out the clutch and pressed on the accelerator. The Datsun purred into second gear. She saw the gate ahead, open but not completely, not enough for her to get through without bumping it — Mason must have driven through it and left it like that. She slowed down, saw her dad's hands on the wheel, his feet on the pedals, and put the car into first and came to a stop, the engine idling like a champion.

"Shit Gaia, I thought you couldn't drive?"

"Dad taught me, I told you. I'm like Gos, I never forget."

"How to fly, you mean? You never forget how to fly."

Out of the car, push the gate wide open, back in the car, onto the country road, no traffic and Gaia eased the gear lever up to third and back down again, her dad cheering her on. The turn onto the main road was easy too, no headlights coming either way. The car was purring along now, the sealed road so smooth. Gaia sped up.

"Hey, slow down a bit," Bron said from the back.

Back out of fourth, stay in third, eye on the speedometer. Bron sounded stronger, should she drive all the way to Jurien Bay Hospital? It would be quicker than stopping at Andersons and getting the ambulance. A row of headlights were coming towards her, the first cars she'd seen. Eyes straight ahead, shit how did she dip her lights? She twisted the knob on the stick thing and the road in front went ink black as the cars sped past, one, two, three of them, their horns blasting her, the stupid driver. She fiddled the knob and breathed out as the road lit up again. She turned the knob the other way and the lights dipped. "Phew."

"How much further to the Andersons?"

"Not far. Hang in there." Headlights shone in her mirror and she slowed down as a car sped past her, horn blaring, tail lights disappearing into the distance.

Lights up in front to the left, off the road. The Anderson farmhouse. Clutch, dogleg down into two, clutch out, car slowing, turn into drive. The gate was open and the lights on in the house were the warmest lights Gaia had seen in her life.

THE AMBULANCE ARRIVED FIFTEEN MINUTES AFTER GAIA HAD stumbled through the Anderson's door and screamed for the phone. She'd had two mugs of hot sweet tea and Bron had been allowed more water,

"He might need surgery," said Mr Anderson. "Better not give him anything."

Gaia sat on a kitchen chair by the open back door of the Datsun, keeping Bron talking while they waited, the Andersons hovering, their faces gradually looking less tense as the adrenalin that had surged through their door and infected them dissipated.

They were shooed aside when the ambulance arrived, and stood silent as Bron was examined while he lay in the Datsun.

"What happened?" one of the paramedics asked them.

"He was shot in the thigh with a 2-bore rifle," Gaia said.

"By you?"

"No, by Dave Mason, the man who lives in the farm next to our gardens, about twelve kilometers from here. We don't have a phone so I drove him here."

"Right. A hunting accident, was it?"

"No. Mason just shot him because he didn't like what we were saying." Gaia thought she could see the whites of the paramedic's eyes as he rolled them skywards. "Will he be OK? Will his leg be...?"

"Where's the man who shot him?"

"He drove off in his ute. I'd asked him to get an ambulance but he didn't."

"Have you called the police?"

"No. I was waiting for you. Will he be OK? Will his leg be…?"

"We'll call the police. This Mason needs to be found fast. Did he take his rifle?"

"I don't know, I think so. I don't remember seeing it after he left."

"What's his full name?"

"David Mason. The police at Jurien Bay know him. But I don't think he'll go on a shooting spree or anything."

"Let's hope not. I'll alert them." He disappeared into the cab of the ambulance

Another paramedic was there now. "You're his sister? "

Gaia nodded.

"You've done a good job. We'll need to get him into hospital and his leg X-rayed. The bullet is probably still in his leg, and I think it might have caught his femur; chipped or fractured it. We'll splint the leg and then get him in the ambulance. You'd better come too, so you can fill in some of the details. Was it you who stopped the bleeding? Obviously he lost quite a lot; just minor vessels luckily."

"She saved me," Bron's voice said from the car.

Gaia was shaking so violently she had to lie down before she fainted. Then she felt the soft warmth of a blanket being wrapped around her. "You've had a shock. That's why you feel faint. Let's get you into the ambulance. You can have a nice lie-down on one of the beds and keep your brother company while we get you both into the Jurien Bay hospital."

~

GAIA WALKED ALONG THE HOSPITAL CORRIDORS BEHIND THE paramedics as they pushed Bron on a stretcher, a nurse rolling a stand with an IV fluid bag hanging from it. Bron was drowsy, occasionally mumbling something unintelligible, his pain masked by whatever painkillers they'd injected into him. Gaia was feeling woozy herself, but forced herself to stay upright. The smell of hospitals made her sick, brought back so many memories she had fought for years not to remember. She was told to wait when they got to the X-Ray Unit, and she sat in the waiting room and pretended to read a magazine. At last a nurse appeared and told her Bron was stable enough to be taken to Perth Hospital by ambulance. "You could go home and get some sleep and drive to Perth tomorrow," she said. "He might have had his surgery by then."

"Oh no, please can I go with him in the ambulance? He's all I have."

"I'll ask them," the nurse said, giving her a strange look. "They prefer not to have the family in the ambulance, but your brother is stable so it might be OK. I just thought you might prefer to drive to Perth in your own car so you're independent and can get back home again."

"No. I'm not a very confident driver yet. I'd have to get the bus tomorrow and I've nowhere in Jurien Bay to stay tonight."

"Just a sec. I'll see if I can convince them." She disappeared and was back a few minutes later. "You can go through into the unit. They'll be going from the back bay. Try not to worry. I'm sure your brother will be fine in a few weeks."

Gaia must have fallen asleep on the hard form in the corner of the ambulance, and when they pulled up at the ambulance bay at Perth Hospital she had to force her legs to move as once again she followed Bron's stretcher along disinfectant-smelling corridors. Another waiting room, hours and hours it seemed as Bron was being operated on. She thought about phoning Hannah, but the clock in the waiting room told her it was six in the morning. At last she was allowed to see him in the recovery room. "Five minutes, that's all," the nurse said. "Then you need to go home and get some rest. Come back later this afternoon. He'll be a box of birds by then."

"Hey Bron," she said, taking his hand, and he opened his eyes. His leg was encased in plaster from his ankle to his groin, and held aloft in a sling.

"Gaia? What are you still doing here?"

"Making sure," that's all.

Bron's mouth struggled to make a grin. "Can you pass me some water? My mouth's as dry as the Nullabor."

She picked up the baby's cup with a straw sticking out of it and he grabbed it and sucked and sucked.

"Shouldn't you drink that more slowly?" Gaia said.

"Nah. The more the better."

"Does it hurt?" She touched his cast with a finger.

Bron grimaced. "No. Not yet, anyway. When the painkillers wear off it might."

"I'm sorry Bron. It was my stupid idea to confront Mason. And now…"

"I know. We were both stupid. Have they got Mason?"

Gaia shrugged. "I don't know. I suppose they will."

"You've learned how to drive at least."

Gaia blinked. She looked around and found the chair and sat down hard.

"You're done in. It must be the middle of the night. Perhaps the nurses can find somewhere you can have a sleep," Bron said, his gentle tone bringing more tears she didn't want him to see.

"It's seven tomorrow morning. We've been in here all night," she managed.

"No way. Crikey, what have they been doing? I can't have much leg left." He squeezed shut his eyes and then seemed to have to force them open again. "I guess my dancing days are over."

She phoned Hannah and ten minutes later she picked

Gaia up at the front of the hospital. When she slid into the passenger seat and Hannah leaned over to give her a hug, she felt a touch on her hair.

"Gaia, Gaia. don't be sad. You're home with us now."

She turned around and took his hand that was now on her cheek and kissed it. "Jarrah, Jarrah, I've missed you so much."

THE POLICE MOUNTED A WEST AUSTRALIA-WIDE SEARCH FOR Mason. His mugshot—a photo Ros had found in a box somewhere—was in the newspapers and on the TV, and his description was repeated on the radio stations every few hours. **Armed. Treat as Dangerous. Do Not Approach. Telephone 000**.

Gaia didn't care; she was too concerned about Bron, his leg full of metal rods and plates and marooned in bed, still encased in a plaster cast from his groin to his foot. He'd been five hours in surgery; the bullet had been slowed down by the femur but had splintered it into multiple shards in the process. It sounded horrific to Gaia, but according to the orthopedic surgeon, Bron could look forward to a reasonable recovery. It could be three months to get to a point where he could walk reasonably well, and probably six months until he was fully recovered.

"What's fully recovered? Does that mean he'll be able to dance again?" Gaia asked. The orthopedic registrar's mouth went from a straight line to an inverted moon. "Impossible to say, I'm afraid. He might be able to dance at some level, but it's hard to believe he'll get back to the professional standard he was at before."

"Does he know?"

"Not from me. Let's give him time to recover first. He needs to keep his mood up. He's got a lot of intensive, difficult rehabilitation to get through."

Gaia nodded. "I know what that's like. It's so unfair. I wish he'd never come back to Australia."

"I'm sorry. I know you went through a lot of rehabilitation for your burn scars. I hope you don't mind, but Dr. Belfer told us. He wanted to make sure we looked after you too. He told us you might be having some world-class plastic surgery in Boston next year?"

"I'd better talk to him. I've changed my mind."

Three weeks later Bron's cast was removed and he was discharged from hospital and installed in a downstairs room at a rehabilitation center where the physical therapists could torture him daily. Gaia made sure she attended as many of his sessions as possible, and was soon able to take over from the therapist, her ballet training and the memory of her mother's methods the perfect grounding for the unforgiving exercises— exhausting for them both. Once she'd proven her worth as his torturer, her plan was to take Bron home to Goshawk Gardens and continue his physical therapy there."

"Until we go to Boston," Bron said.

"Haven't I told you?" Gaia said, her eyebrows arched high.

"Told me what?"

"I'm not going to Boston. I've told Dr. Belfer."

"Not because of me, I hope. I'll be OK to come with you by next February, even if I'm not fit enough to be back with the company. I'll be able to stay with you all the time in Boston."

"Nope. Not going. I've seen the light."

"What light?"

"That one at the end of the tunnel." Gaia curled her fingers into a cylinder and squinted through it with one eye, her other eye closed.

"Gaia, stop it. This is not funny. Are you going to get Dr. Belfer to do your scar surgery here? That'll be great."

Gaia shook her head.

"But why? Not just so you can keep torturing me. I'll go to a physiotherapist in Perth if I still need to."

"You're a little bit of the reason, but not the deep-down reason. The thing is, I've realized that my scars don't matter any more. I don't even think about them. I could cut all my hair off because I don't need it to hide behind any more." She grabbed a fistful of hair and pretended to cut it with her scissored fingers.

"Don't you dare." Bron pulled her hand away from her hair and it swung free. "It's great that you don't mind about your scars any more, but that doesn't mean you shouldn't fix them. What about your worries about them stopping you getting into a ballet company?"

"Mr Garth still wants me to audition for that internship. But I'm not even sure I want to be in a ballet company any more. What about Goshawk Gardens? When the police finally find Mason, we'll know better if Ros can sell to the university without his agreement. The Court might take the land off him. I'll be able to stay there and get involved in all the plans and make sure the university keeps their buildings well away from the beach."

"You can still do that. Nothing major is going to happen until way into next year I shouldn't think."

Gaia got up from her chair. "Bron, I've made up my mind. No more plastic surgery. I'll keep up my dancing at home and get better until I'm good enough to teach classes at the kids' camps we're going to have at Goshawk Gardens."

CHAPTER 38

November, 1981

With Bron tied to his bed in hospital, Gaia had managed a three-day break to Goshawk Gardens. She checked out the barn, gave Rita Roo a hug, glared at Gos and swam with her seadragons, both still there. No bright pink eggs under the male's tail yet. She was glad; she wanted to share that joy with Bron and Jarrah. The Andersons had brought back the Datsun Y, and she thought about driving it around one of Mason's paddocks but decided that could wait. But best of all Mary and Eddie were back. Even way up north in the Kimberleys they'd heard about the hunt for Mason.

"Him gone," Mary said, looking more relaxed than Gaia had seen her since the day she and Eddie had driven Mason to the the hospital.

"How do you know?"

Mary shrugged. Then she thumped her chest. "Inside, init. Him gone."

Back in Perth and ten days into Bron's boot camp, as he called it, Gaia had a day off from helping with his torture sessions. It was good to get her hands in the soil again in the Children's Home gardens. Pulling out another weed, her thoughts wandered. Would Mason ever be found? Was he dead? Is that what Mary felt?

"Hey there, Macushla."

She looked up, a smile splitting her face.

"Seamus." She was up and in his arms. Pulling back, she looked at him. "What are you doing here?"

"Came to say goodbye. I would have come sooner, but I was on a horse, and didn't get Hannah's letter until ten days ago. It's taken that long to get back."

"It's so good to see you. You look wonderful."

Seamus looked at her, his eyes soft. "You look happy, Macushla. I thought you might be sad. That monster Mason shooting your brother. It could have been you."

"Yes. But it wasn't and Bron is doing OK. I'm taking him back to Goshawk Gardens in a week or two. He can do his rehab exercises just as well there."

"That's why you're happy. And it's all OK between you and Bron?"

"Yes. It took a while to forgive him, but he was so upset. We both were."

"I'm glad it's worked out. Gaia, I'm off in a few days, back to Ireland to see me mam. I'm thinking of looking for a course I can take, perhaps even university, where I can train to become a social worker. I want to work with kids like Jarrah."

"That's exactly right. You can teach them to dance."

Seamus did a little jig. "The céilí though, none of that prissy ballet."

Two police arrived at the Children's Home on a hot late November day, one day before Gaia's nineteenth birthday. She was packing, getting ready to take Bron home to Goshawk Gardens two days after her party tomorrow. She wasn't allowed to know anything about it, other than it was beginning at lunch time, and ending in the wee small hours. The giggles and shushings from Jarrah and Maisie whenever she strayed into the kitchen made her wish she'd never told them that she even had a birthday. Then she'd remember that this was a goodbye party as well, a chance for her to say thank you, and to make final precious memories of the friends she had here and the wonderful things they had shared.

So the police came as a surprise. Of course, she knew at once. It could only be Mason. They'd found him at last. Otherwise they wouldn't have sent an Inspector to tell her. Her pulse going like an Irish jig, she took them into the small room next to Hannah's office."Have you got him?" she asked, her voice sounding, to her ears, surprisingly calm.

"Not exactly," said Inspector Bragg. "He's been found though. No doubt it's him."

"What do you mean?" She held her breath, wanting him to say it, that he was dead.

"They were mustering on Wyloo Station, 320 kilometers northeast of Exmouth; you get there along the Nanutarra-Muniina Road. It's a big bugger, over 3000 square kilometers. They use small planes to look for cattle in the most remote areas. The pilot spotted a ute they hadn't seen lying about before. It's not a good spot to park a ute so they found a place to land and hiked back to it."

Gaia forced herself to keep quiet, let them grind their way through their laborious details.

"It had been there a fair while, almost rusted out. It was a fluke they even saw it from the air, it was half hidden by a tree. Anyway, they decided to have a bit of a look-see around the area and if they couldn't find anything, come back another time and do a proper search. They were already thinking about Mason of course. We'd sent out letters to all the stations with his details, asking them to keep an eye out."

"I know, you've been very thorough, but did they find

him?" Gaia said, no longer able to keep the impatience out of her voice.

"They were just about to give up when their dog started barking. Did you know they take their dogs in those little planes?"

"No. Whatever. So the dog found him?" Gaia asked, almost hissed.

The sergeant looked surprised.

Bloody hell, does he really think I'm so dumb?

"They found a skull, a few bones, not much else. Picked clean by dingoes and vultures. Died of thirst probably, or perhaps the dingoes got him first. They found his rifle a few meters from his skull. Poor bastard."

"How do you know it was him?"

"The ute still had its license plate, and we already had Mason's dental records. We were prepared, you see, just in case we found him dead."

Gaia closed her eyes, her insides jelly.

"I'll go and see if I can rustle up a nice cup of tea," said the young constable, the first words he'd uttered since his initial greeting.

"Yes, please, thank you," said Gaia. She looked at the Inspector. "Does that mean his wife is now the sole owner of their land?"

"That's not for me to say. Your lawyer will be able to help you with that. But if the two of them owned it jointly, I would say so." He grinned at her and she decided perhaps he wasn't so bad. "It'll take a while for the case to be closed; it's been quite an operation. But it will be a relief for your brother. You too. Now you won't have to go through a court case to prove he shot your brother. Cheaper for all of us."

Gaia's hands covered her face. It was over. At last it was over and their reef would be saved.

∽

IN THE EARLY MORNING BEFORE THEY CAUGHT THE BUS TO
Jurien Bay, Hannah drove Gaia and Bron to the crematorium
to collect their parents' ashes. Home at the barn they tucked
the two copper boxes in a corner, under Margot's barre. On
the sixteenth of January, on a still, beautiful evening on the
night before the fifth anniversary of their parents' deaths, they
rested the two caskets on the worn table outside the barn and
opened them for the first time. Carefully, they spooned all the
ashes from Margot's casket into Joe's, and with their hands,
gently mixed them together.

Next morning at dawn, they carried the casket to the
beach, Bron now walking unaided with barely a limp, and
Jarrah, Mary and Eddie, Rita Roo and Joey Jandamarra
following a little way behind. Looking up, Gaia smiled at Gos
flying above, his eyes on the treat he knew Jarrah had
concealed in his hand. Putting on their masks and snorkels,
together sister and brother walked into the soft sea. Floating
out over the reef flats, the precious casket held safe in their
joined hands, they hovered above the weeds where the seadragons mated. They lay still for a while, watching the male
with his newly-laid bright pink eggs held safely under his tail,
his mate circling him, waiting for a last waltz before she disappeared into the unknown blue. And there, as the seadragons
danced, they dove down and opened the box and watched
their parents' ashes, lit by the sun's rays, shimmer to the
surface and vanish into the circle of life.

EPILOGUE

*G*oshawk Gardens, January, 2003

The man stood still, his boots, socks stuffed roughly inside, discarded by the side of the track. He closed his eyes as yesterday's stored heat in the parched red land he'd been away from for too long warmed the soles of his feet. The old barn stood as it always had, silent in the new dawn light, harder to see now through the wilderness around it. He listened and smiled—the wind sighing in the tops of the tall gum trees, the rustles of the tiny feet of lizards and insects in the dry leaves around his bare feet, the whistles and screeches and melodious calls of the birds he had not heard for so long but were as familiar as his own voice. He placed his right foot carefully on the narrow side track that branched off through the bush, his left leg with its stubby toes, free of the boot with its sole as thick as a python, following with ease. His mind and his heart and his soul were eleven years old again as he wandered along the meandering track, making no sound as he stepped tenderly through the leaves left brittle since falling last September.

And now he could hear the lull and swish of waves licking a shore, whispering, soaring, dancing. He stopped and narrowed his dark eyes, sending his sight through the bush and out the far side. The blue sea was glinting through the trees and he breathed in a great gulp of air. In it he could taste salt and smell seaweed and coral and fish and rock oysters and dolphins and crabs and sharks and whales. Not the whale sharks he had travelled the world to study, but he felt their spirit here. He tasted the sea air again and it took him out over a reef, the many reefs he'd swum over, weeping as their seas grew too warm, their corals turned white and then slimy, their fishes turned hungry and vanished, the seas around them turned barren, driving the whale sharks away. But this reef was different— he could smell it, taste it, hear it in the joyfulness of its waves as they lapped the white sand. The clear waters of this reef were warmer too, but below them their corals were flourishing, adapting, free of pollutants, of the greed of men with their fishing rods and dragnets and mass tourism and collecting of pretty shells for their children. Over this reef with its warmer seas would one day swim large numbers of turtles, Greens and Hawkesbills and Loggerheads. Turtles who'd swum these oceans for more than a million years, through more changes than a human can comprehend, their slow ways helping them adapt as their habitat changed. In this special part of their world, as the sea grew warmer, they'd find new beaches where they could bury their eggs in cooler sand, where their nests would be protected from humans, leaving their hatchling sons and daughters to find their own way out to sea so they could return one day to the beach where they were born.

And here—yes, he could sense it now, see it in his heart— here the seadragons still danced. Here, protected by this Sanctuary enclosing this beach with its bush and its reef with its pristine corals, its healthy sea grass beds, the kelp where mysid shrimp, plankton, larval fish and tiny crustaceans flourished, here the seadragons could adapt to the slowly warming waters.

The man swallowed the urge to dance, right there on the

track, but continued on his path until he came to the Casuarina tree shading the white sand, its branches loaded with
messy nests and birds squawking and chattering as he sat
down, his eleven-year-old self sitting with him. And as the first
notes floated towards him, he saw her. His breath catching in
his chest, he watched, enchanted, as she twirled and leapt and
spun and glided back and forth across the sand where the low
tide had left it hard and damp. She hovered and stopped, her
bare right leg long and straight, its foot arched above her tippy
toes, her back and left leg a curved new moon, balanced like a
bowl in the blue, her left foot pointed and as high as her head.
One arm was a swan's neck reaching for the sky, the other a
swan's wing. But most beautiful of all was her face, eyes closed,
worshipping the sun.

He watched until the music died and the dancer walked, as
light as a winged gum seed, towards him, her body shining in
her sleek blue swimsuit. And as he rose and left the shade of
the tree, she smiled, and his heart leapt with a love so
profound that he knew that at last he'd come home.

AUTHOR'S NOTES

Seadragons

Seadragons are in the same family as seahorses (*Syngnathidae*) but are very much rarer. There are about 47 species of seahorses and they are found in temperate to tropical waters world-wide, but seadragons are exclusive to Australia (although many large public aquariums in the US and other countries have them in their display tanks).

Both the Weedy seadragon (*Phyllopteryx taeniolatus*), also called the Common seadragon, and the Leafy seadragon (*Phycodurus eques*), also called Glauert's seadragon, are found only in the temperate waters of Tasmania, South Australia and the south-west coast of Western Australia. Although seadragons are not currently considered 'officially' endangered, pollution, the illegal pet and alternative medicine trades, and warming seas with climate change is likely to change this. The weedy seadragons Gaia discovered on the southern (subtropical) end of the Coral Coast were at the very northern limit of their current range, and thus quite a rare find. They are dramatically colored and spotted in red, blue-purple and yellow with paddle-like appendages (see the seadragon photo on the cover of this book), individual seadragons varying in shade and depth of color with the males darker and narrower than females. Weedy seadragons grow to a length of 45 cm (18 in), have long pipe-like snouts with a small terminal mouth and feed on small crustaceans including mysid shrimp. As they do not have a prehensile tail to anchor them to hard-to-see plants like the seahorse, their only way to avoid predation is by camouflage as they swim slowly in the seagrass and seaweeds of reefs. Following their courtship dance in spring and early summer, a spectacle that can last many days, they mate, and then the female transfers up to 250 eggs to a spongy patch on the underside of the male's tail. (The male seahorse also incubates the eggs but within a fully enclosed pouch.) The eggs are fertilized by the spermatozoon penetrating the dermal cells of the male's tail and entering the eggs. Incubation time is 70 days and while a few of the babies mature within a year, most do not breed until fully mature in their second year.

The smaller leafy seadragon which grows to a length of 20 to 24 cm (8.0 to 9.5 in) is even more flamboyant, with numerous rippling frill-like protrusions that camouflage it from predators. This species can change color to blend in with the environment. The leafy seadragon was adopted as South Australia's marine emblem in 2001.

A third seadragon, the Ruby seadragon (*Phyllopteryx dewysea*) was discovered in much deeper Australian waters in 2015. It looks similar to the weedy seadragon but is redder in color. (More recently the orange and yellow spiny seadragon (*Solegnathus spinosissimus*) was discovered in the cold deep waters of New Zealand and South Australia. This is not a true seadragon but halfway between a pipefish and a seadragon; it has a long colorful body like a seadragon but has no weedy/leafy appendages and has a prehensile tail.) In our oceans there are still thousands of new species to discover, but untold numbers have already become extinct—another reason for protecting our marine environment.

I recommend watching these two entrancing YouTube

videos featuring weedy seadragons and see whether an aquarium near you has a seadragon tank. In recent years a small number of aquariums have successfully managed to breed the weedy seadragon, although it is very difficult.

1. Life - Weedy seadragons dance into the night - BBC One David Attenborough

2. The Weedy Sea Dragon | Oceans | BBC Earth (Environmentalist Philippe Cousteau Jnr and marine biologist Tooni Mahto)

How to access my books and me!

To quickly access retailer links in all countries to all my books (and Audiobooks) go to my dedicated Book page on Books2Read.   (https://books2read.com/ap/RWJlYa/Jenni-Ogden)

To receive notifications of my future novels please follow me on BookBub: (htpps://www.bookbub.com/authors/jenni-ogden)

And do follow, like, or friend me on Goodreads: (https://goodreads.com/JenniOgden)

Facebook: (https://facebook.com/JenniOgdenbooks)

X(Twitter): (https://twitter.com/jenni_ogden)

Instagram (https://www.instagram.com/ogden.jenni/)

READING GROUP QUESTIONS
AND TOPICS

1. What do you see as the main themes of the novel? What is the over-arching theme? How many members in your book club agree about this?

2. Do you think the cover and title of the novel work? Why or why not?

3. Have you ever snorkeled over a coral reef? If so, what are your most powerful memories of that experience? How did it change the way you felt about the marine environment?

4. Whether you are a "city" or "country" person, or somewhere in-between, do you sometimes find solace, alone, in a "wild" place? Do you think that this need is an intrinsic aspect of human nature, or is it learned—for example from good wilderness experiences in childhood.

5. Wild places and wildlife—particularly seadragons—and the wonder and joy these bring to Gaia, play a pivotal role in her healing. She identifies with the seadragons—their reclusive nature, their dancing, their need for her protection. Have you

ever had a strong emotional connection with an animal—perhaps a pet? What do you think of the notion that lonely people are more likely to build such deep bonds (even if one way!) with animals? (You may have spotted some similarities in theme if you have read *A Drop in the Ocean* where sea turtles were so central to Anna's transformation.)

6. At the beginning of Part II there is a quote from polar explorer, Robert Swan. He writes *"The greatest threat to our planet is the belief that someone else will save it."* What could you contribute to saving our planet?

7. How much do you know about the history of Australia's Aboriginal peoples and especially the terrible ways they were treated by the colonizers. Still today Aboriginal people are discriminated against and fall into the lowest socioeconomic group in Australia. In your own country are there any parallels?

8. This novel barely touches the surface of the divide between White Australians and Aboriginal people, and Jarrah was probably unusually 'fortunate' to have Irish woman, Hannah, as his main 'caregiver' in the Children's Home. The reality in the late 1970s/80s for most indigenous children like Jarrah, forced to live in a white-dominated world, would have been overtly and harshly racist. If Gaia had not herself been scarred and isolated, do you think such a deep friendship between two young people, one white, one Aboriginal, seven years apart in age, could have flourished?

9. Leading on from that, in your own world, what are the ingredients that are key to your most mutually nurturing friendships?

10. Mary and Eddie, and Seamus, become important parts of both Gaia and Jarrah's lives. What is it about these three people that draw Gaia and Jarrah to them?

11. If Bron had been your brother, could you have forgiven him?

12. As the book developed, how did you think the story might end? With Gaia succeeding, against all odds, to become a professional ballet dancer? Or did you think she might find a different way to find fulfilment and happiness?

13. Have you ever had to give up a passion because you weren't good enough to make the grade, or because of some other unfair factor outside of your control (such as the fierce competition to reach the top of many arts and sports?) How did you move on from that?

14. Did the ending and the Epilogue work for you? If you could rewrite the ending, what would it be?

15. Gaia was 39 and Jarrah 32 at the time of the Epilogue. Where do you hope this story might take Gaia and Jarrah over the next 5 years?

ACKNOWLEDGMENTS

The writing of every novel is a journey, both on the page and in one's real-life experiences. John and my adventures on Western Australia's Coral Coast were especially valuable for this book.

Thank you to Josie Ogden-Schroeder and Belize Schroeder whose passion for ballet inspired me to write about a dancer. All the dancing mistakes are mine!

Thank you to Debi Alper of Jericho Writers, UK, for her wise critique of the manuscript, suggesting a re-think of the ending, and pointing out the obvious about one of my characters. (That character quickly left the story...)

To my friends, mentors, and early readers of all cultural self-identities, thank you for your ideas and informed and helpful comments that have made this story stronger. When we take the time to appreciate and value the unique cultural identities of others, we gain a deeper understanding of the shared values and characteristics that unite us all.

For the stunning photograph of a Weedy seadragon on the book cover, thank you to photographer Neil Richardson and The Examiner Newspaper, Launceston, Tasmania/ACM.

And as always, thank you to John, husband and travel companion, for his passion and knowledge about ecology and conservation, and hats off to our children, grandchildren and friends, most of whom still patiently put up with or energetically engage in endless discussions about books—mine and others — and the desperate state of our world.

NEWSLETTER SIGN-UP

Go to 'Jenni's Off-Grid Newsletter' (www.jenniogden.-com) to subscribe to my occasional e-newsletter about living life on an off-grid island, book reviews of books I love, and a little writerly news.

If you enjoyed *Dancing with Dragons*, please do review it on Goodreads and also on your favorite online bookstores (a few sentences—or even just a rating—is all it needs although in-depth reviews are always a treat.)

Then read on for brief descriptions of my other novels, especially my award-winning, best-selling novel *A Drop in the Ocean* (my novel most similar to *Dancing with Dragons*) which also floats on a coral sea (but with a 'middle-aged' protagonist and turtles rather than sea-dragons as the heroes).

OTHER NOVELS

A Drop in the Ocean —about the book

Anna Fergusson runs a lab researching Huntington's disease at a prestigious Boston university. When her long-standing grant is pulled unexpectedly, Anna finally faces the truth: she's 49, virtually friendless, single, and worse, her research has been sub-par for years. With no jobs readily available, Anna takes a leap and agrees to spend a year monitoring a remote campsite on Turtle Island on Australia's Great Barrier Reef. What could be better for an introvert with shattered self-esteem than a quiet year in paradise? As she settles in, Anna opens her heart for the first time in decades—to new challenges, to new friendships, even to a new love with Tom, the charming, younger turtle tagger she sometimes assists. But opening one's heart leaves one vulnerable, and Anna comes to realize that love is as fragile as happiness, and that both are a choice.

The Moon is Missing—about the book

Georgia Grayson has perfected the art of being two people: a neurosurgeon on track to becoming the first female Director of Neurosurgery at a large London hospital, and a wife and mother. Home is her haven where, with husband Adam's support, she copes with her occasional anxiety attacks. That is until her daughter, 15-year-old Lara, demands to know more about Danny, her mysterious biological father from New Orleans who died before she was born. "Who was he? Why did he die? WHO AM I?" Trouble is, Georgia can't tell her. As escalating panic attacks prevent her from operating, and therapy fails to bring back the memories she has repressed, fractures rip through her once happy family. Georgia sees only one way forward; to return to New Orleans where Danny first sang his way into her heart, and then to the rugged island where he fell to his death. Somehow she must uncover the truth Lara deserves, whatever the cost.

Call My Name—about the book

Her mother dead from a drug overdose, thirteen-year-old Olivia is rescued by Cathie Tulloch, her mother's friend throughout the years they were held captive in Japanese prison camps in Sumatra in WWII. Welcomed into the Tulloch's remote family home in the Australian tropics, introverted Olivia is claimed by dramatic, generous, controlling Cassandra Tulloch as her sister and best friend. Moving to the UK at 18, Olivia finds her independence, and partner Ben. But in 1970, after five years away, she is homesick, and ready to fulfill her long-held dream: to make a family of her own. Back in Brisbane she and Ben share a hippie lifestyle with Cassandra and husband, Sebastian, while earth-mother Cassandra effortlessly produces beautiful babies. But for Olivia, becoming a mother is hard. Even harder is discovering the truth about her own mother. And when the unimaginable happens, destroying the friendship with Cassandra that has been her bedrock for so long—and Olivia tells herself that she doesn't deserve a family, nor a place to call home.

ABOUT THE AUTHOR

Jenni Ogden and her husband live off-grid on spectacular Great Barrier Island, 100 kms off the coast of New Zealand. They often spend time in Australia, preferably near a coral reef. Her debut novel published in 2016, *A Drop in the Ocean*, won multiple awards and has sold over 85,000 copies. *The Moon is Missing* followed in 2020 and *Call My Name* in 2022. Jenni, who holds a PhD in Clinical Neuropsychology and was awarded the *Distinguished Career Award* by the International Neuropsychological Society in 2015, is also well-known for her books featuring her patients' moving stories: *Fractured Minds: A Case-Study Approach to Clinical Neuropsychology*, and *Trouble In Mind: Stories from a Neuropsychologist's Casebook*.

Made in the USA
Coppell, TX
02 October 2024

38019661R00204